When Four

Believe in yourself
& follow your dreams,

ARyroll.

When Foundations Crumble

First novel in the Foundations series

by

ANNMARIE WYNCOLL

Felidae Books

FELIDAE BOOKS LIMITED

Paperback Edition 2017

ISBN 978-0-9956424-0-9

Cover design: Rachel Lawston

Editing: Esther Newton

Felidae Logo: Lisa Moldau

For Mum and Dad,

Who never stopped believing

and

For Mark,

Without whom, I'd be lost

Acknowledgements

Writing is often considered a solitary activity but nothing could be further from the truth. Without the help and support of a great team of people, this book simply would not exist.

Firstly, to my amazing beta readers who helped shape '*When Foundations Crumble*' into the novel you're reading today. Rachel, Harriet, Sarah P, Sarah H, Tracey, Tracy B and my Mum. You all gave your time willingly and provided constructive feedback – without all of you, this book would be half what it is today.

A special thank you also goes to Rachel who has shared my enthusiasm and kept me motivated throughout. She hasn't (to my knowledge) switched off during one of my 'author' moments, and that means a lot.

Thank you to Elaine and Kate, my UK writing buddies. We've shared our journeys for a long time now and your constant presence in my life has helped me get to the end. We're all nearly there now and wow – who'd have thought it?

I've been blessed to work with Esther Newton who has been a truly inspirational editor. Not only has she pointed me in the right direction, she's removed the glutton of 'that's' for which I'm sure you, as the reader, are eternally grateful.

Thank you to Rachel Lawston for my beautiful cover design. I had no idea what I wanted and with very little to work on, she has turned my vision into something special. So, thank you.

I also want to thank Lisa Moldau who designed the logo for Felidae Books. Again, I had no idea what I wanted but somehow, she made me the perfect logo.

Phew! I feel like I'm at the Oscars...

I need to thank my family. My parents, who have always supported me no matter what, my in-laws who have generously funded my work, my sister for simply being my sister and my own family, my two beautiful boys and my husband, Mark. Without them, literally, none of this would be possible.

And finally, thank you to all of you who are reading my book. It means more to an independent author than you can possibly know to have readers taking a chance on them. So, thank you, from the bottom of my heart.

AnnMarie x

Resurrection Book Two in the *Foundations* series is the conclusion of Cal's story and is due out later this year.

To keep up to date with all my news and info,
please sign up to my newsletter at
www.annmariewyncoll.com.

Prologue

The fern was dead. Its once green leaves, now a yellowed brown, draped forlornly over the pot.

"Plant's dead," Cal observed. He watched as Matt turned towards the window where the sorry specimen was residing.

"I deal in minds, Cal. Plants are not really my thing." His therapist shrugged.

"Maybe it needs water," Cal suggested.

"Perhaps," Matt agreed, "but you and I both know you're not here to discuss the foliage in my office." Matt's gaze collided with Cal's as he turned back from the window and Cal read understanding in the other man's light blue eyes. Cal didn't believe he deserved to be understood so, shifting his focus, he looked around.

The box shaped room was like any other office: clean, tidy, functional; not entirely what he had been expecting. "I thought it would be more…touchy feely," he observed as he turned his attention back to Matt.

Matt laughed. "I'm not into couches and candles. This, I am afraid, is it."

Cal looked at the therapist again, wondering how old he was. He looked to be a similar age to Cal's twenty-seven years, yet Matt's face was definitely less worn. Had the other man always wanted to do this, Cal wondered? Sort out people's heads?

"Have you ever been to a therapist before?" Matt asked and Cal shook his head.

"Ah, okay…"

There was a moment's silence and, feeling restless, Cal stood and walked to the window.

1

"I don't know what to do," he said. Deliberately he kept his back to the room. The window was uninspiring, the view concrete and clinical. Like the office.

"Shouldn't this be more... comforting?" Cal asked as he turned around and faced Matt once more. "I thought there would be soothing pictures, lovely views, happy thoughts everywhere..." he tailed off and again Matt laughed.

"I think you've probably watched one too many movies," the therapist replied, "and you don't need to do anything. I'm here to listen and support you without judgement or prejudice."

Cal snorted. "Tami told you what happened, right? How can you not judge or have prejudice?" He walked back to the centre of the room where Matt remained seated and resumed his position in the opposing armchair. For the first time since he'd entered Matt's office, Cal looked the other man directly in the eye without flinching. This time he saw empathy reflected back at him and he had to force himself not to close his eyes. Cal's instinct was to block out any good, any sign of caring and the fact that Matt was offering both made him feel uncomfortable.

"Yes, Tami gave me some background," Matt replied as he dropped his eyes to the pad resting on his lap as if in reference, "but that doesn't mean I judge. Or have prejudice." He held up his hand when Cal went to speak again. "I'm a professional, Cal. It's my job to help you and the only way I can do that is to listen to you and hear *your* story. The little I know is not enough, only you can tell me that. And then, when I've heard your story, I still have no right to judge you or any other person who walks through my door. Everything between us remains entirely confidential and I will always be completely professional. There will never be one word of censure, regardless of what you tell me. You have my word."

Cal continued to regard Matt whose eyes had once again turned back towards him. This time their blue depths revealed honesty and truth, his therapist's face soft beneath the almost harsh military cut blond hair. Immediately Cal relaxed. He knew instinctively that he could trust this man, professional or not.

"Okay," Cal said after a moment, "I believe you."

Across from him, Matt nodded. "I wouldn't be able to do my job if I judged. It's not the way it works. Wherever this goes, however it plays out, you, Cal, are my only concern."

"Okay," he said again. The silence in the room weighed heavy as Cal once again looked around. Grey. The walls were grey. Whoever had decorated this office needed sacking.

"Where would you like to start?" Matt asked into the silence and Cal shrugged.

"Do you understand why you're here?" Matt spoke again.

Cal nodded and at the same time he ran his fingers through his unruly fair-coloured locks. He needed a haircut.

"Can you tell me why you're here?" the therapist asked.

Cal looked up from his inspection of the mismatched teal green carpet. The decorator definitely needed sacking. "Because I did a terrible thing," he replied simply.

Matt nodded.

"I have a referral here from your GP," Matt said as he shuffled through some papers. "It would appear that Tami isn't the only one who believes I can help."

Cal shrugged. "I've been having a few difficulties."

"Go on."

"I made some bad choices and I did a terrible thing. I owe it to a couple of people to get straight."

"What about owing it to yourself?" Matt asked, his forehead creasing a little.

Cal shook his head. "Nah. I don't owe myself anything. I don't deserve anything."

Matt jotted something on the notepad.

"Do you want to be here?" Matt asked after he had concluded his writing.

"To be honest, I don't get how you can help. I'm broken. Nothing you can say will change that."

On the opposite armchair, Matt crossed his legs. "You'd be surprised how many times I hear that," he said, "but the reality is, no

3

one is broken, it's just that sometimes we have to look really deeply inside of ourselves to heal."

"That all sounds like mumbo jumbo," Cal commented.

"Mumbo jumbo or not, it works," Matt affirmed.

Cal shrugged. "If you say so."

Matt regarded him for a moment. "It works, but you have to try."

"I'm here," he said in frustration, "now all you have to do is fix me."

"I'm not going to fix you, Cal. *You* are going to fix you."

Cal stood again and jammed his hands into his pockets. "I've never heard so much crap in all my life. If I could fix me then I would've done it by now."

"Sit down," Matt said, his voice calm.

Cal eyeballed him for a moment.

"Please, Cal," the therapist said.

Oddly, he sat.

"Just try it, okay? One session and if you don't think it's going to work then you get to leave."

Cal grumbled under his breath.

"What did you say?" Matt asked.

Cal raised his eyes to the other man. "I said alright."

Matt made another note on his pad. "This might be tough," he warned as he looked back up, "so you need to be prepared."

"If I can live through what I did," he countered, "then I'm damn sure I can answer a few questions."

The therapist watched him for a moment. "It doesn't always work like that. Usually we have to find a place to start. An event. A person. A moment. A job. That kind of thing."

"You don't just ask questions and tell me what to do?" As Cal contemplated him, Matt smiled.

"No," he replied. "Part of my job is to ask questions, but my focus is on getting you to open up so you can discover the answers for yourself. It's of no benefit to you if I just tell you what you should do. That's not how it works."

"So I have to talk?" Cal queried suddenly feeling tense.

Matt nodded.

"I'm not big on talking."

"Not many people are. Not when it really comes down to it and we're stripping away the layers. All I ask is that you give it a try. Nothing that you say to me will ever leave this room. You have my word." Matt shifted a little in his armchair as he uncrossed his legs.

"I know," Cal said, "I get that it's all confidential and stuff, but the things that you're going to need me to talk about...I don't think I can go there."

Matt nodded. "I understand, but just take your time, Cal. We're in no rush here. We take as much time as you need. Okay?"

Cal remained silent as he considered for a moment. "I don't think my last job is a great place to start."

"Why's that?" the therapist asked as he leaned forward and rested his elbows on his knees, hands clasped together as if in prayer.

"It's too painful," Cal began as subconsciously he mirrored the other man's position and dropped his head to once again regard the carpet. "I don't think that going there right now is going to help me at all. If I'm going to do this I need to start with the easy stuff." As the words left his mouth Cal wished he could call them back. There was no such thing as easy in the story he had to tell.

Matt shifted again and leaned back a little causing the leather of his armchair to creak. It was about the only piece of furniture in the room that seemed at one with its purpose. "We can begin wherever you like," he said, "but you need to know that we'll have to visit some painful places too. If you really want to heal."

Cal didn't think he would ever be ready to visit some of those places. He couldn't think about them let alone voice them. Agitated, he stood. "This is crap," he said as he paced again to the doomed fern. "Talking, talking, talking... how the hell is that going to make things better? Mend me in here?" He turned and thumped his fist to his chest in illustration.

As before, Matt remained seated. Part of Cal wished the other man would stand too so that he could go toe to toe with him. They were both of a similar height with slim build and if they stood opposite each other Cal could gesticulate, make Matt understand his frustration.

5

That was, however, impossible to do with a man who stayed calmly in his chair.

"Have you ever had anyone to confide in?" Matt asked softly after a moment of pause. "A father figure? Best friend?"

Cal clenched and un-clenched his fists as he felt his heart stop; that wound might be ageing, but it was still too raw. Anxiously he paced to the other side of the office and stopped next to the large bookcase, which covered the entire length of one wall. This was metal, bog standard and lacking in any beauty.

"Cal?"

"No," he replied carefully. This was one of those places, the painful ones, the ones he didn't think he would ever be ready to go to. He continued to regard the shelf unit and as he did so, he reached out and fingered the spine of one of the books. A thesaurus. What, he wondered absently, if he picked it up and leafed through to the word 'father', would the book suggest as a substitute?

"I've never had anyone," he confirmed before dropping his hand from the spine and walking slowly back to the armchair.

He could feel Matt watching him but he refused to raise his eyes. He didn't want to see pity or worse, to know that Matt had seen through him. If the other man saw through Cal's lie then they would have to talk about Zach, and Cal was in no way ready to go there. After a while Matt began to scribble something in his notepad and so Cal chanced lifting his head. Matt continued to write.

"Is that where we start then?" Cal asked after a moment. "My lack of confidante?"

The therapist raised his head and looked directly at him. "We can start there if you like, although I'm thinking it might be useful to start a little earlier in time than that. I have a feeling a lot of your difficulties surround your past and it might be easier to link them if I can get an understanding of the events that have brought you here. Does that make sense?"

"I suppose so." He shrugged once more. "What do you want me to say? Failed marriage, failed life, failed career, failed man…?"

Matt smiled gently and not for the first time Cal wondered at how he remained so calm. Cal had not been the easiest client so far.

"Is there anything that in your mind links all of those things?" Matt asked. "Not that I am agreeing with you of course – far from it. I don't believe you to be a failure at all. However, if that's how you see yourself, then that's where we have to start. So," he paused for a moment, "anything that links all of those things, Cal?"

Cal leaned back in his chair in the same manner as Matt had done a few moments before. His chair also creaked and he smiled a little. The colour scheme and furnishings were crap, but at least the leather chairs had co-ordinated creaks. "One thing that links everything in my life?" he repeated and Matt nodded.

"Well, then that's easy," he said as he calmly clasped his hands behind his head, feeling comfortable for the first time since he'd walked across the threshold. "One thing that links everything – or should I say – one person."

He exhaled slowly as he closed his eyes and pictured her as he last remembered her. Running for her life, eyes wild, fear pushing her on and then nothing – a crumpled heap on the ground.

She had been Cal's world and now he only had himself to blame for the fact that she was no longer in it.

One thing that linked everything? Easy.

"Lexi," he said aloud. "Lexi links it all."

Chapter One

Cal

October 2012

She walked past the building site every single day. And every single day the guys whistled at her. When they did she looked up, smiled and then continued serenely on her way. No one knew her name; she was an enigma. A gorgeous blonde enigma with bright blue eyes that could pierce your soul. An enigma that several of his co-workers wanted to get to know better. But not him. Not Cal Strudwick. He didn't deny that she was beautiful, nor that she walked with an alluring air of fragility, but he never wanted to objectify a woman again. That was why he never whistled. Let them whistle. Let them lust after her. The tilt of her head, the clothing she wore told Cal she was way out of his league and he was fine with that. Let her be out of his league because as far as he was concerned, that was precisely where she needed to stay.

***

"Cal?" He looked across as Zach, site foreman and best friend, called out to him.

"Boss?" He was in the middle of finishing the outer skin of the third floor. He seriously hoped this didn't mean moving on. His rhythm and line was near perfect.

"Chute's broken. Something's blocked it at the bottom. Need you to go down and sort it."

"K." He waved to his boss and sighed as he removed his bricklaying gloves. He loved bricklaying – it was the best part of his job. He got to see buildings grow and take shape, become something other than a vision in his mind. Clearing out the rubbish chute was not a job that he relished.

Swinging underneath the scaffolding, Cal shimmied down the metal steps until he reached the tarmac below. A couple of female students walked past and, as he landed, they whistled under their breath. He smiled. They could objectify him, just not the other way around. The pair paused for a second and looked him up and down as if waiting for him to speak. When he didn't, they shrugged and continued on their way. Cal watched for a moment as their Jean-clad bottoms swayed from side to side and then he walked around to the large skip located at the base of the scaffolding.

"Boss?" he called up as he shaded his eyes with his arm. Zach's head appeared over the top of the scaffolding. "Just going to check it out now. Can you make sure no one chucks anything down?"

Zach nodded and then disappeared. A few moments later he heard the older man commanding the other men to stay clear of the rubbish chute and when Cal was satisfied that nothing else was coming down, he reached into the skip and began to move the giant plastic pipe. The tube ran down from the top of the scaffolding where they were working and ended in the skip below. Its purpose was to allow for the safe transportation of rubbish, however, as Cal moved it, he noticed a large sheet of metal stuck at right angles. Covering his hands with his gloves he carefully dislodged the metal and then quickly stood back, allowing any waste that had backed up to fall into the skip. As he watched, the remainder of the waste fell easily. Job done. Cal turned back in the direction that he had come, unsurprised to hear his workmates whistling once more. They were currently doing some renovations on a rural university campus and numerous women walked past the building site daily. Smiling to himself Cal rounded the corner and grabbed the rail that would lead him back up the scaffolding. Before he could take the first step, however, a soft voice spoke to him from behind. Startled, he whirled around.

"How come you never whistle?"

It was her. The enigma. The woman they all wanted to get to know. And she was talking to him. He swallowed and hastily wiped his dirty

9

palms down his work-worn Jeans.

"Er…" he was lost for words. Her eyes, deep ocean blue, regarded him and he was mesmerised; locked into a helpless tussle. He blinked as she tilted her head to one side, waiting. Up close he could see that she was tall, only a few inches shorter than his six feet. Long legs dressed in casual blue trousers led to a light blue shirt, the colour of which emphasised her eyes. Small breasts pressed against the folder that she carried across her chest and when Cal breathed in, he smelled citrus. She fiddled aimlessly with a strand of her long, blonde hair and he followed the movement as her fingers twirled one way and then the other.

"I'm just not like that," Cal replied eventually, all the time aware of her watching him – closely.

"Like what?" she asked and he mentally kicked himself. Good question. Like what?

"Some women don't like it and I've a job to do. I can't afford to jeopardise my career with a complaint." Cal's answer was, at least, partly true.

She continued to peruse him, her perfectly formed lips pursed in question. "And that's the only reason?"

Cal nodded.

The woman shrugged easily. "Okay."

They stood for a moment, each watching the other as an awkward silence descended and then, remembering that he was in full view of his workmates, Cal backed away towards the scaffold opening, his heavy duty work-boots scraping along the rough tarmac.

"Well, it was good to meet you," he said as he created a necessary distance. He barely knew this woman, yet his body was beginning to respond in a way it hadn't done for a long time. In his head though, he knew he wasn't ready to meet someone like her. He had to get back to work. "Good luck with your course." Cal gestured to the university building behind them as he all but stumbled over the iron scaffold fixings.

"Thanks. I'm Lexi by the way," she said quietly, her eyes still watching him. For a moment, he allowed their gazes to meet, hers boring deeply into his until he felt as if the very soul of him had been laid bare. This was not good.

"Cal," he replied as he turned away from her once more and began to ascend the ladder. He needed to get away.

"Short for Calvin?" she asked and he paused a moment, hands stretched above his head.

"No," he half twisted his torso so that he could see her out of the corner of his eye. "It's just Cal."

She smiled, her mouth half open, her teeth white, lips luscious. "Cal," she repeated, "it was nice to meet you too."

With a last smile she took a couple of steps back and then walked determinedly away in the direction of the main campus. Cal remained where he was, rooted to the spot, trying to calm his racing heart. He blinked, eyes continuing to follow her as she became little more than a speck on the horizon. Lexi. She was even more beautiful close up and Cal knew that his dreams tonight and for a long while to come, would be occupied by those eyes. Jesus. He was in big trouble.

Predictably, the men had seen everything. He clambered back onto the scaffolding amidst catcalls and whistles. He ignored them all. It didn't matter what they said or thought. Cal had no intention of telling them anything. Besides, there was nothing to tell.

"So, when are you taking her out then, Cal?" Zach asked with a wink. It was harder to ignore Zach, but Cal tried his best, picking up his gloves and tools and carrying on with the outer skin. Working swiftly, he laid the next brick, all the while aware of Zach leaning against the scaffold post, watching him.

"I was getting worried about you," Zach observed and this time Cal directed his attention to his friend.

"How so?"

"You never talk about women – girlfriends, partners," Zach waved his hand, "I was worried you might have become a loner."

Cal shook his head and returned to the task in hand. "Nope. I just don't want a woman in my life right now."

"Even her?" Zach thumbed towards the ground where Lexi had stood only moments before.

"Especially not her."

"Hmmm…" Cal could hear curiosity in the other man's tone. "You know her then?"

"Nope." Cal collected the next brick and began to prepare the surface for laying it.

"Then why are you so sure you don't want her in your life?"

He turned, brick in hand and shifted onto his knees so that he could look fully at Zach. "I told you, I don't want anyone in my life right now."

Across from him, Zach hunkered down so they were on the same level. "Some of the lads…" Zach began as he glanced quickly behind him, "…they think you bat for the other team."

Cal laughed. "You and I both know that's not true," he responded with a smile.

"I know," his friend countered, "but it ain't my place to tell them what I know."

Cal dipped his head. "Thanks, although right now, there's nothing to tell."

Zach lowered his voice. "I was talking about the past."

Cal nodded. "I know."

"So, you really okay?" Zach asked.

"Yeah. I'm happy just working and getting my head straight. I don't need a woman messing up my brain."

To Cal's surprise, Zach laughed. "Women," he said. "They sure do have a way of doing that."

Cal smiled with him. "Yeah, that they do." He shifted back around so he could lay the brick he was still holding. Zach remained where he was.

"You know I appreciate everything you did for me?" Cal asked as he concentrated on preparing for the next brick.

"I do."

"I wouldn't have made it without you," Cal said.

Zach clapped him on the back. "Yeah, you would. I just gave you a bit of a shove. Now stop getting all sentimental on me."

Cal smiled. "Okay, boss." He worked in silence for a moment.

"I can't imagine doing anything else now," he said as he placed the next brick.

"Keeps you in shape," Zach commented as he patted his own, still toned stomach. Cal turned to look at his friend noting the flecks of grey in Zach's formerly black hair. Zach was the closest thing to a father Cal had and their bond was what saved him daily and kept him moving forwards. "Inside here," Zach continued, "is a belly just waiting to get out and as soon as I down tools, I know it'll be right there."

Cal laughed. "Too right. I need that physicality. You know?" As soon as the words left his mouth, he regretted them. Why had he brought that up? He held his breath as he waited for the older man to respond. He knew Zach would understand why Cal needed physical work – he was the only one who would.

"There's no shame in it, Cal," Zach responded after a pause, "I've told you that before. It's who you are."

Cal shrugged. "I don't like who I am. Who I was."

"I know that and believe me, I understand," the older man responded. "Right now though, you're doing good and this job, it's giving you what you need. Don't worry about the rest. One way or another it'll take care of itself."

Carefully Cal selected the next brick and began mixing the cement with his trowel. He could feel his palms beginning to sweat inside the leather gloves as memories fought their way to the surface. Focus. He'd worked so hard to move on from his past. He needed to get back into the present.

"Well," Zach pushed himself up from his haunches and started to move off, "I'll leave you to it."

"Thanks." Cal focused on his work, methodically laying one brick on top of the other. It was much like putting one foot in front of the other and that's all he could do, every day. Keep putting one foot in front of the other.

"Oh, Cal?"

He looked up as Zach called to him.

"Boss?"

13

"What *is* her name?"

Cal swallowed. He'd nearly done it. The physical work of laying the bricks coupled with his chat with Zach had almost erased her from his mind, but not anymore. There she was, right back in the front, that hair, those gorgeous eyes, tattooed on his brain. Damn.

With an air of nonchalance he laid the next brick, delaying the moment when he would have to say her name and make her real again. Finally though, he could delay no more and so he looked up, surprised to see Zach's features softening as he continued to watch Cal's every move.

"Lexi," he said quietly, her name rolling off his tongue and heading straight to his groin. "Her name. It's Lexi."

* * *

For the next two days, Cal did nothing but focus on his work. Whenever the guys whistled, he avoided looking down. He didn't want to see her again. As he had predicted she'd played far too vivid a part in his dreams; he had to wipe her firmly from his mind.

Friday, the traditional end of the working week, was generally celebrated in the local pub after work and Cal usually attended. It was the only time he allowed himself to relax.

"You ready, Cal?" Zach called to him as the rest of the workers set about cleaning and storing their tools.

"Sure, just a sec." Gathering up his own tools he clipped them to his belt and then followed Zach and the others down the scaffolding to the ground below.

"I'll meet you there," he called as he walked off in the direction of his car. "Just going to put these safe." Even though they were on a university site that was monitored by twenty-four hour security, Cal never trusted leaving his tools behind. They were the key to his livelihood and were not cheap to replace.

"Sure," Zach fell into step behind the other men and Cal struck out in the opposite direction alone, heading for the rough piece of land where the workers were permitted to park. The university was unusual being situated in substantial grounds. Formerly a nobleman's residence it had been converted into a school in the late 1900s. Over time the school had evolved to the prestigious campus it now was. Several buildings had been added through the years – one of which Zach's team were currently constructing – yet it still retained its rural feel. Even though the nearest town was a short drive away it didn't seem to affect the popularity of the university and, as Zach had drilled into all of them, it was one of the top five in the country, which meant that their craftsmanship had to be close to perfection. Cal had come from the city before he'd met Zach and was used to noise and imposing skylines, yet he found himself enjoying his time here. The calm solitude was a far cry from his past but he almost felt that it was healing him. Almost.

In less than five minutes he'd reached his car. It was an old model Ford that Cal had lovingly brought back to life. Unlocking the boot, he placed his tools and his belt safely inside and then, after freshening himself up with a couple of sterile wipes, he slammed the boot closed. Just as he'd finished a crunch on the gravel distracted him and, turning to the source of the sound, he froze. It was Lexi. Shit.

Taking a deep breath he walked towards her, noting that her eyes were already fixed to him, watching his every move.

"What are you doing out here?" he asked when he was close enough. "This isn't part of the university."

She shrugged causing her long blonde hair to slowly lift and then fall back to her shoulders. "I've been asking myself the same question." Her voice was quiet and, Cal thought, a little unsure.

He nodded. "Well, it's probably not a good idea for you to be here." He glanced around. The light was dimming as twilight descended and there was no artificial illumination in the makeshift car park.

She nodded slightly and then paused a moment, still regarding him. "I have a problem," she said and Cal looked at her in confusion.

"Okay…" he replied carefully.

In the half-light he watched as she dipped her head and for the first time, he noticed her vulnerability. Somewhere, deep inside his chest, something began to stir. Crap. She lifted her head once more and he blew out a sigh of relief. The vulnerability, thankfully, had gone.

"The thing is," she began, "I've met someone I like but I suck at knowing what to say. I don't even know if he likes me – it's just a feeling."

Cal frowned at the boldness of her words – they seemed at odds with the fragile woman he'd thought her to be. It wasn't what he'd expected her to say to him. He, who was in reality, a complete stranger. Outwardly calm, his brain began to work overtime. After what they'd experienced a couple of days ago, he was certain she was referring to him and, even though she'd not revealed as much, he had to stop her from going any further with that thought. No good could ever come of anything between the two of them. Cal took a moment as he considered what to say.

"I'm not sure what that has to do with me," he said eventually.

"Well," Lexi smiled. "I want to know if he likes me and that's where I thought you might be able to help."

"I'm not sure how," he hedged. Cal had never been good with words and, confronted by someone as beautiful as Lexi, he stood no chance.

"It's someone you know," she said. She took a step closer as if to share a confidence. Citrus floated to him on the breeze and his groin hardened. Cal could hear his heart beating as blood surged around his brain.

"Someone you work with," she clarified and, for a moment, Cal was taken aback, unsure if he'd heard correctly.

"Someone I work with?" he choked out and as he watched, she nodded.

"Tall guy, dark hair, deep brown eyes. He watches me every day. I don't know if I'm just imagining it, but I figured now you and I know each other," her smile was almost shy, "I could ask you to help."

Cal frowned. Wait a minute. Tall guy, dark hair, deep brown eyes. Mace? Surely she couldn't be falling for someone like Mace?

"Mace," Cal said aloud. His throat had suddenly constricted and an unwelcome feeling of something very close to jealousy stabbed at his gut. But then her liking Mace was a good thing, right? It meant he was off the hook. "I think you mean, Mace."

"Odd name," she said as she continued to watch him, "but I kind of like it."

Cal shrugged. "I'm not sure if it's his real name."

Lexi moved slightly, shifting her weight from one foot to the other. "That's okay. I just wanted to know if I was imagining things. I don't suppose you could ask him? If he likes me?"

Cal swallowed whilst he considered how to respond. This really was the last thing he'd been expecting. A light breeze blew across the car park causing Lexi to pull her jacket more tightly closed. Automatically his eyes followed her movements, noting the sweet swell of breasts beneath the material. Again his groin responded and angrily he stepped to one side, frustrated at himself and his reaction to her. He didn't want anything to do with her, and, it would appear, the feelings were mutual. It sucked that his body didn't seem able to comprehend that.

"I can go one better than that," he replied carefully as he began to walk towards the exit of the car park, "I can introduce you to him."

Lexi fell into step beside him. "Oh, okay..."

Cal picked up the hesitation in her tone. "What's the matter? Isn't that what you wanted?"

Lexi stopped walking and looked up at him. "Yes, I guess so."

Again that vulnerability and Cal closed his eyes, cursing himself for being drawn to her. "You don't sound so sure."

Beside him he felt her shrug. "This made more sense in my head," she said. "I don't know you, what the hell am I doing here?"

The question seemed rhetorical and so Cal didn't answer. Inside, his brain was still processing her attraction to Mace. How the hell could she like someone like him? She was far too good for him.

"I'm not an axe murderer – in case you were wondering," he said. They'd walked in silence for a few paces. "All the lads are at the pub and since that's where I'm going, I figured it was as good a time as any for you to meet him. Mace."

She nodded.

"I don't usually do this," she said after a moment, and Cal remained silent. He didn't want to know what she did or didn't usually do. "I just thought, since we spoke..."

"It's fine," he glanced down at her but didn't interrupt his stride.

"Actually, I kind of admire you, for going after what you want." It wasn't the only reason he admired her, but he pushed those thoughts to one side. "I'm all for the modern woman."

Beside him, she laughed. "I would hardly call myself modern."

"You just approached a virtual stranger in a darkened car park and asked to be introduced to a bloke you don't even know. That's either very modern or very stupid." He smiled across at her. "I'm giving you the benefit of the doubt and going for modern."

"Crap," she replied, "it really did sound better in my head." She slapped her forehead.

"If you don't want to meet him right now I can just pass your number on," Cal offered. Again he wondered at the contradictions in her. One minute she was bold as and the next she appeared fragile as hell.

She shook her head. "No, thanks. It's okay. I trust you."

Cal stopped a moment and turned to face her.

"You know how naïve that is? Trusting someone you barely know."

She snapped her head up to him and when she spoke, her tone was defensive. "Are you saying I'm naive?"

He shook his head, wondering at the fight in her tone. "This," he gestured between the two of them, "is not the smartest thing for a beautiful young woman to be doing – and you know that," he added, "on some level. But you still did it anyway. Maybe you just don't realise the level of danger you could've put yourself in. So, yeah, I'm saying you're naïve."

He felt her bristle and realised he'd hit a nerve but what she'd done here wasn't smart.

"It's fine," he said when it became clear she wasn't going to respond, "forget I mentioned it. But for future reference – what you did tonight…not a good plan."

He turned to continue walking but Lexi remained where she was. "Are you coming or not?" he asked. The fading light was interspersed with manufactured illumination and she was standing beneath one of those lamps now. The effect silhouetted her body and Cal stifled a groan. She was too much. Too beautiful. Too much of a contradiction.

Too much out of his league. If she stayed where she was then as far as he was concerned, that would be the best possible result.

"I'm a good judge of people," she said almost to herself. Shaking his head he waited as she slowly caught him up.

"How old are you?" he asked as they resumed their pace.

The question clearly threw her. "Pardon?"

"I asked how old you were."

She looked sideways at him from underneath her lashes. "Nineteen. Why?"

"Do you still live with your parents?" They had reached the narrow cut through which led to a small road. The pub was at the end of the road. Cal paused and stepped aside to allow Lexi to precede him through the gap.

"What the hell has that got to do with you?" she asked. She had her back to him as she walked through the cutting ahead, yet Cal had a feeling that if he'd been able to see her eyes, they would've been angry. He must have really touched a nerve. "At least I know better than to tell a stranger where I live," she finished. Her tone gave little away.

As they exited the cut through, Cal held up his hands. "Personally, I don't care where you live," he said as he came to stand beside her, "but I'd put money on you still being with your parents. I think this," he gestured towards the campus they'd left behind, "is a whole new world and you're trying to find your way."

She regarded him for a moment and then, almost reluctantly, nodded.

"That's cool," Cal responded, "but not everyone has family – some people don't know what it's like to be protected. I've learned the hard way – you don't need to learn that way. That's all."

She scuffed her foot in the gravel where they stood. "Okay, but just because I live with my parents, doesn't mean you can judge me. I know about life. I know how things work."

Cal ran his fingers through his hair. "You're missing the point. Look…" he gestured towards a bench situated beside the road, "…let's sit."

They walked as one towards the seat, settling themselves in unison.

"You've got to be careful," he began as he rubbed his hands up and down his thighs. "There are people out there in the big world who aren't nice. They don't know how to treat women right..." he swallowed. Shit. Memories stirred that were best left buried. He swallowed again, "... and you need to be careful who you trust." Like him. "Just because you see someone every day, doesn't mean you know anything about them. That's all I'm saying."

"So you're saying Mace isn't a good guy?" Her innocence radiated out as she looked at him and again he wondered at her contradictions. One minute she was feisty, fearless almost and the next, painfully innocent. It had been a hell of a long time since he'd met a woman this unspoilt. She seemed out of touch with reality yet knew what she wanted. To Cal it didn't add up.

"No," he replied slowly, "I'm not saying that, but Mace has had a lot of girlfriends. He likes to play the field. I don't want you to end up being one of his number."

"And you're so different?" she asked sarcastically.

Cal closed his eyes and swallowed. Yes, he was different, but he was pretty sure she didn't want to know how.

"Who's the one judging now?" he asked as he fought with cursed memories. "We're not all the same. You don't need to settle for someone who'll just use you." Bile rose at his hypocrisy and he swallowed again.

"Maybe I want to have fun," she replied.

He took a deep breath. "Then have it with uni guys. Guys that come from your world. Not this world." Cal indicated his scruffy Jeans and scuffed boots. "You're young, you have the world ahead of you. Don't let your view be jaded."

She snorted. "Jaded? You sound like my dad. I don't need to be lectured."

Cal shook his head. She was, it seemed, intent on a path of self-destruction. "Suit yourself," he responded off-hand, "I'm not much older than you, but I've lived a very different life and I know bad stuff happens. I'm just trying to help."

"Yeah?" suddenly she stood and pointed her finger at him, "then why don't you just introduce me to this Mace guy? That's all I want from you." Her anger flared from nowhere and Cal knew his instinct to stay away from her had been right. In that moment she reminded him of a young kid playing grown up, a woman out of her depth trying to fit in, definitely not someone he needed in his life. She was far too innocent, far too naive – but then at least he cared. Mace on the other hand...

He took another deep breath as he watched her. After a moment she dropped her finger and a look of embarrassment crossed her face. She knew she'd over-reacted. He knew she'd over-reacted and now Cal wondered how the hell he'd got into this. "Let me ask you something," he said slowly. Reluctantly she sat back down beside him. "How many men have told you you're attractive?"

As she'd sat her head had dropped between her knees and the light cough she gave was muffled. "What?" Her voice was small.

"I mean," he clarified, "you know that you're attractive?"

She looked sideways at him and he dipped his head to her level so their eyes could connect – a move which he instantly regretted. Cal was certain he could see unshed tears and his stomach contracted. He hated that he was this attracted to her which...he ploughed on with his earlier thought. "If a guy finds you attractive," he continued, "it means they read your signals – even ones you don't know you're giving off. For example," he coughed to clear his throat, "you have a habit of looking directly into my eyes, almost as if you can see right through me. That's a signal." Their eyes were still connected, unwavering, and Cal felt his groin stir into life.

"I do that with everyone," she commented.

"Which is my point." He shook his head to free himself of their connection. "To you, that's what you do, it's who you are. But to me – or to anyone who's attracted to you – it's a signal that you like them. More than like them. And that's the kind of thing that can get you into trouble. Some men will read your signals and act on them."

She watched him for a moment, her forehead creased. "I'm confused," she said at length, "why are we having this conversation?"

Cal rubbed his hands over his face. He'd been wondering the exact same thing. "Because you want to meet Mace and because you're doing that by spending time with a virtual stranger. You're beautifully innocent and naive and I don't want to see you getting hurt. You need to be more aware of the effect you have on men and not put yourself into situations like this. Look," he blew out a breath, "let's just go to the pub and forget I ever said anything. Okay?"

She frowned but nonetheless followed his lead and stood. "You still sound like my dad," she said and he smiled.

"Yeah well, I've been around a bit. Come on." He held out his arm and she linked hers into it. Her fingertips brushed against his palm and he felt a tingling begin at the base of his spine. His reaction to her was not good. Not good at all. But at least he was sure now that she had no interest in him. He only wished she'd set her sights higher than Mace.

A few minutes later they reached the dimly lit porch that led into the rustic country pub. Situated at the end of the lane that ran parallel to the university, the building stood on a small plot of land and incorporated a wrap around beer garden with small parking area. The pub itself oozed olde-worlde charm having a whitewashed exterior and traditional thatched roof. Several small leaded windows allowed the warm light from inside to coat the few wooden benches dotted out front and sounds of merriment could be heard from within. Cal preceded Lexi into the low-roofed interior, taking care not to catch his head on the traditional oak beams. Quickly he scanned the bar, locating the men who were already occupying a couple of the tables adjacent to the large, log fire. Mace was ordering the drinks. Leading Lexi up to the bar he nudged Mace who turned around, eyes wide when he saw who was with him. Cal completed the introductions.

"I'm not gonna hang around though," he finished, declining Mace's offer to buy him a drink. "I've got stuff to do." He hadn't, but he knew he couldn't spend the evening watching Mace fawn over Lexi. Even though he'd resolved to have nothing to do with her, it didn't mean he would find the spectacle easy to view.

"Are you sure?" Lexi looked up at him, eyes wide, and for a second he thought he saw uncertainty cross her face. He blinked, but when he opened his eyes, it was no longer there. Inwardly, he smiled. He'd introduced her to Mace, that was – as she'd so succinctly put it – all she wanted from him. Besides, Zach was there. Zach wouldn't let anything happen to her.

"Yes. Have fun." He slapped Mace on the shoulder. "Take care of her," he warned.

Mace laughed. "I will."

Every atom in Cal's being told him to stay, told him to look out for her, to protect her, but he ignored it and began to make his way to the exit. He wasn't the man for her and he had no right to act as if he was. Pulling on the ornate, round iron door handle he took a step outside and was about to take another, when he felt a light touch on his arm. Looking down he caught Lexi's gaze.

"Cal?" she whispered and he nodded. "When you said about the effect I have on men," her voice grew ever more quiet and he strained to hear, "were you talking about you?"

He watched as a blush crept up her cheeks enhancing her beauty and reminding him of just how innocent she was. This was innocent, Lexi. Contradictory, Lexi. Far too innocent for him. Yet, somehow, he was helpless.

Silently, he nodded, completely unable to force words past the lump that had formed in his throat. He could've lied but he didn't.

After a moment Lexi echoed his nod and then fixed her eyes back onto his once more. "Stay," she whispered imploringly, her deep blue gaze boring right into his soul. "Please."

He sighed, watching her for a moment, seeing himself through her eyes. He couldn't stay, yet…eventually he nodded. He had to. He had no choice. He'd never had a choice. He already knew that he would never be able to leave her, and the worst part? The part that now filled him with utter dread?

Not leaving her…he wasn't just talking about tonight.

Chapter Two

Lexi

Rough denim tingled beneath her palm as she gently pressed her fingers into Cal's arm. She felt him stiffen slightly and then he turned, dropping his gaze down to connect with hers. For a split second she had questioned her actions, but the moment he turned back, all misgivings fled. This felt totally right and she knew it was what she had to do, whether or not it made sense.

"Stay," she whispered, unsure if he would hear her or not. "Please."

His green eyes widened and then he glanced down at her hand resting on his forearm. Lexi swallowed as she waited for him to say something. The dim light from the porch bounced off the bridge of his nose and settled on his lips. They were pursed and Lexi noted a small dimple on his chin, barely hiding beneath a light dusting of stubble. He smelled of hard work and outdoors, an oddly attractive scent that teased her nostrils. She was attracted to Cal, she belatedly acknowledged, something she'd never expected to be. Maybe it was the way his messy blond hair flopped endearingly over his forehead, or maybe it was his stance, tall and proud which emphasised his lithe physique. Her instincts told her she could trust him and that he would keep her safe. The moment held, suspended in time and then Cal raised his eyes to hers once more and slowly nodded. Lexi blew out the breath she didn't realise she'd been holding.

"Thank you," she whispered and then, turning back into the pub, she walked towards an empty table situated a short distance from where Cal's work colleagues were seated. Colleagues that included Mace.

As she settled herself in one of the wooden carver chairs she looked across to where Mace remained standing, reading the question on his face, but when she simply shook her head, he shrugged and moved back towards the rest of the men who were becoming increasingly boisterous. Opposite her, Cal sat down on a matching chair and rested his forearms on the table. Lexi watched as the aged denim of his shirt stretched across his muscles.

Cal spoke first. "I'm confused. I thought you wanted to meet Mace? Why did you ask me to stay?"

Fair questions, but Lexi wasn't sure if she could own the truth. Even with her sheltered upbringing she knew that to trust someone you barely knew was crazy and to admit her attraction to him – that would just be too uncomfortable.

"I guess…" she started hesitantly, "…I enjoyed talking to you."

She heard Cal shift in the seat opposite and so she raised her eyes up to his, momentarily halting her study of the worn oak table. "That sounds lame."

Across from her, he shrugged. "A little, but it's cool." He smiled and she noted that his teeth were white and even. "Was Mace not what you were expecting after all?" he asked.

Lexi smiled back a little sheepishly. "I actually don't know. I didn't give him chance."

Cal laughed. "Cruel."

She widened her eyes. "Really? What if I've offended him?" Lexi glanced hastily in the direction of the other man. So consumed had she been by her need for Cal to stay that she'd barely considered Mace's feelings.

"Relax," Cal reached forward and rested his hand on her forearm, "I was teasing. Mace is cool. He's a 'win some, lose some' kind of guy."

"I don't know whether to be thankful or offended," she commented as Cal's words registered. Again, he laughed.

"You don't need to be anything. All I'm saying is you don't need to worry about Mace. He'll be fine."

Lexi nodded and blew out another breath. "Okay, thanks." Absently she fiddled with the cheap, cardboard beer mat on the table – a requisite in any respectable pub. Watching her, Cal rose to his feet.

"Would you like a drink?"

Lexi tilted her head to look up at him and as their eyes connected once more she felt her cheeks begin to heat. "Sure, thank you."

"What would you like?" he prompted.

"Er…white wine spritzer, please. Thank you."

Cal nodded and moved away towards the bar. She watched as he went, noting the small wave he directed towards his colleagues. Given a moment alone, Lexi closed her eyes and took a deep breath as she tried to assimilate what had happened this evening.

The idea to talk to Cal about Mace had hit her a couple of days ago, when she'd seen Cal on the ground. He'd seemed pleasant and even though they'd not exchanged more than a dozen words, she'd had a feeling about him. Approaching him had suddenly made more sense than anything else in a very long time. Until, that was, she'd actually done it. Now she was stuck between embarrassed and foolish which was why his comment about naivety had struck a chord. Her sheltered upbringing had, she realised, ill-equipped her for real life and real men but without any form of guidance, she was going to have to brave this out. Right now she was following her gut. It was the only compass she had.

Dropping her head into the cradle of her hands she rubbed her eyes and then, after a moment, lifted herself back up. Rounding her shoulders she sat up straighter in the chair as she looked across to the bar where Cal now stood. In keeping with the rest of the interior the bar was old although the area behind it had been modernised. From what she could see the optics hanging on the back wall contained a large variety of spirits and there were several beer pumps attached to the bar itself. Although popular with the uni crowd, this was the first time Lexi had been inside. She usually stuck to the small student bar on campus. Cal was leaning against the heavy oak, one foot resting on the brass rail that ran its entire length. He was conversing easily with the barmaid as their drinks were poured and for a split second, Lexi experienced a stab of jealousy. Rigorously she shook her head in an attempt to send the negative emotion away. Being here with Cal had not been on her agenda for the evening. Jealousy – however fleeting – had no place here.

A few moments later Cal returned and carefully placed her drink on the mat nearest to her. "Thank you." She caught his eye and smiled.

Settling himself back into the seat opposite, he returned her smile. "You're welcome."

Lexi picked up her glass and gratefully took a sip of the cool liquid. Cal did the same and she noticed that he'd only ordered himself a half pint. She gestured towards his glass with hers. "Are you not one for pints then?"

Cal replaced his glass on the table. "I figured I'd probably need to keep my wits about me tonight."

"Ah…" she tilted her head to one side. "Because…?"

He laughed and leaned over the table a little so their heads were closer together. "It depends how you look at it. I could be worried that I might need to protect myself from Mace, or I could say that I want to drive home afterwards…" he smiled, "…or I could say that I don't trust myself when I'm around you."

His tone had lowered as he'd spoken the final words and Lexi felt a shiver run the entire length of her spine. Damn, she was attracted to him. Maybe she should give alcohol a miss too.

Nervously she coughed and then eased away from him a little. Space, she figured, was good. "So, you really meant it?" she asked, "about being attracted to me?" Her naïve self berated her for being so forward but she was emboldened by the atmosphere and her attraction to him. The words fell out before she could consciously consider them.

Cal nodded. "Yes, I did."

His reply was sincere and Lexi was grateful. Had he tried to joke about it, or build it up into some great romantic speech, it would have had less of an impact. As it was, her heart began to beat just a little bit faster and in the gloom of the pub lighting, she allowed herself to look at him, really look at him. His green eyes twinkled back at her and his lips lifted in a half-smile, almost as if he knew she was studying him.

"So, what was it about Mace?" Cal spoke after a moment and she blinked as she tried to replace her mental image of Cal, with that of Mace.

27

"He was always the first to whistle. And the loudest," she added. "And he used to smile at me. He just seemed like a really nice guy. I thought we had a connection..."

"Yes, you mentioned that earlier," Cal commented, "but not anymore?"

Lexi shook her head. "I don't know whether we do or not. But when you left me with him, it just didn't feel right. Does that make sense?"

He shrugged. "Yeah, I guess so. And you do say you're a good judge," he winked and she smiled.

"Perhaps not," she allowed and Cal grinned.

"You're here, with me. I'd say you're a pretty good judge." His smile was almost wolfish and she felt herself responding to him as the last of her nerves evaporated. The awkwardness of only moments ago had vanished and out of relief and instinct she threw the beer mat across the table at him.

"Got tickets on yourself, huh?" she asked and he laughed.

"You picked me over Mace, so yeah, I'm feeling pretty good."

"I didn't pick you over Mace," she countered, "I just didn't want to spend the evening with him and you're the only other person in here I know."

"Ouch," Cal mimed a dagger to his chest and Lexi laughed. It felt good to know their sense of humour meshed.

"So, tell me about Lexi," Cal said after a pause.

Taking a sip of her drink she allowed the cool liquid to balm her throat before she spoke again. "Not much to tell. I live with my parents – as you know – and this is my second year of uni."

"Brothers? Sisters?" he asked and she took a deep breath before slowly shaking her head.

"No, I'm an only child."

"Me too," Cal responded.

Lexi felt the stirrings of anxiety and her palms began to sweat. This was not a subject she wanted to pursue and she wondered how she could steer their conversation to safer ground.

"What about your parents? Friends? When you were growing up," he continued, oblivious to her discomfort.

Lexi picked at an invisible spot of dirt on the table, unable to meet his gaze. "Sure, I had friends. My dad, he's a solicitor, so he works long hours. Mum stayed at home with me, but I don't think she found it all that easy to be around other people. We spent a lot of time on our own, just the two of us."

"That sounds sad," Cal responded. Lexi kept her gaze lowered. He had no idea how sad.

"Not really," she replied carefully, "my mum and I are incredibly close." She kept her answer short in the hope he would realise this was not an area she was comfortable talking about.

She felt him regard her but she refused to raise her eyes.

After a short pause he spoke again. "What are you studying?" he asked and this time she did look at him. He'd obviously realised something was off and she was glad he'd chosen to move on, not question her further.

"Business and accountancy. My goal," she laughed a little self-consciously, "is to have my own financial services business. One day. Like my dad."

She watched as Cal's face creased into a frown. "I thought you said he was a solicitor."

Lexi laughed, relieved they were now on safer ground. "Yes, sorry. I meant that I want to own my own business – like my dad. The practice – it's his."

Cal let out a low whistle. "Sounds like high level stuff. You never wanted to follow in his footsteps?"

She shook her head. "I've seen how tough some cases can be and the affect it has on my dad. I wouldn't want that kind of pressure in my career."

"I can understand that," Cal agreed, "but owning your own company isn't exactly going to be easy street."

Lexi nodded. "I know, but I figure when the time comes, I'll be confident enough to be able to balance my life properly. Oh, I don't know," she waved her hands, "it's all just pipe dreams at the moment."

"Maybe, but it's good to have a goal."

"What's your goal?" she asked as she picked up her glass once more.

He smiled. "Time to reverse the questions?"

She nodded and raised her glass to him. "Had to be done."

He grinned. He seemed to be completely at ease with himself, something that Lexi greatly admired. "I'm training to be an architect," he replied, "working my way through a day release course at college right now, and then working for Zach too."

"Sounds like you have it planned out," she responded. It felt good to know he had a long term plan, although right now, she refused to analyse why.

"I didn't have the same kind of opportunities as you growing up, so I've just been really lucky that Zach was able to take me on."

"I'm sure it's more than luck," she observed. "They must like you if they let you do day release."

"Yeah, I guess."

She regarded him for a moment. "For someone who was telling me exactly what I should and shouldn't be doing you seem pretty low on self esteem." Maybe he wasn't as comfortable with himself as she'd first thought.

Cal looked directly at her and she felt the full depth of his gaze. "I never had anyone telling me I was any good growing up. Even though I've proved myself – that stuff kind of sticks."

Lexi shook her head and tilted it to one side. "I picked you as someone completely sure of themselves. I never figured you'd have childhood hang-ups too."

He smiled. "Don't be fooled. I've been around, I've seen a lot and I know that I want to be the best person I can be. That doesn't mean I've got it licked right now."

She leaned forwards. "I can tell you're a good person, Cal. We may have only just met, but I knew that I trusted you. That counts for a lot where I come from."

Cal smiled as he shook his head. "We've already established that your judgement of people is off. And just because you *think* you can trust me, doesn't make me the kind of person you should have in your life. Whoa…" Cal sat back and ran his hands through his hair, "…how the hell did I get to that? I never talk about this stuff."

For some reason, she felt oddly flattered that he'd let his guard down. "What stuff?" she asked.

He braced his hands on the table and began to study the backs of his fingers. "My past."

Lexi swallowed. She didn't really know what to say. "If you want to talk…" she began.

Cal raised his eyes. "I don't talk about it for a reason," he responded. His tone was emotionless.

She nodded. "Okay." The atmosphere between them shifted and Lexi had no idea how to get back to where they'd been. She drained her glass.

"I'd rather talk about you," Cal said into the silence. He spoke quietly but the warmth had re-entered his voice. "Have you always lived around here?"

Lexi looked at him in disbelief and then burst out laughing. He'd got them back to that place where they'd been before it had gone weird – she needn't have worried. "Isn't that just one tiny step away from 'do you come here often?'"

Cal had the grace to look sheepish as he joined in with her laughter. "Yeah, I guess it was a bit lame but I want to get to know you and it was the first thing that came out."

She laughed again. "Fair enough." At least for her this was easy ground too. "I've been here most of my life," she began, "Dad's business took us to the Midlands for a couple of years, but Mum got homesick so we came back. Ledgeworth is where I call home."

"That's about half an hour from here?"

Lexi nodded. "Yes. I get the bus to and from, but the connections can be a pain." Even though the university was situated just outside of the main southern English city of Brufton, the buses seemed to run rural timetables. Frequent they were not.

Cal nodded, "I can imagine. Why don't you live closer or get a flat share?"

"To be honest, I never thought about it. It just seemed easier to stay at home and commute. But, I don't know… maybe I should think about it."

"Might be worth it."

"I guess," she voiced her thoughts aloud, "if I did live closer, then I'd be able to make more friends, get involved more. That could be good."

Cal placed his empty glass on the table. "I'm sure it would, and then maybe you could find that uni guy we talked about earlier." He winked and she resisted the urge to throw another beer mat at him. Just.

"I thought we were getting to know each other?" she asked instead and he smiled.

"Yeah, but I still don't want you to think I'm something I'm not."

"What do I think you are?" she asked, curious.

He tilted his head and soft highlights bounced off his unkempt mane. "I'd guess..." he paused and played with his empty glass for a moment, "...actually, I have no idea what you think of me. I just want you to be aware..."

Lexi held up her hand for him to stop. She didn't know what she thought of him either and she was far from knowing what he was going to be to her, but she was attracted to him and he was attracted to her. That was a good starting point.

She took a deep breath and leaned back a little. "My one and only boyfriend was a childhood friend. It was a tame relationship and I don't want that again. I want to experience what life has to offer. Have fun. That's all."

Opposite her, Cal sighed and reached across the table to loop his hands into hers. His thumbs began to massage the sensitive pads of her palms and she shivered. His digits felt rough against her tender skin. This was what she wanted. She didn't want tame childhood friends; she wanted someone who excited her. Someone who could help her discover who she really was.

"Lexi," Cal began, his thumbs continuing their sensual massage. "I'm not going to lie. I like you. I'm attracted to you and I think we could have some fun. But I have to warn you – my kind of fun will be very different to your 'friend' or any college dude you might hook up with. I need to be straight with you because I don't want to hurt you."

32

She lifted her head from where she'd been contemplating their joined hands. "Sounds like you're trying to put me off." Her voice was small as her confidence – boosted only by her gut – ebbed and flowed.

He shook his head. "Nothing could be further from the truth, believe me. But when you said you wanted to be with Mace, I didn't know what to think. He's a player and if that's the kind of fun you're looking for, that won't happen with me. I work hard and I play hard but I'm a one-woman man. If you want to see where this is going, then you have to accept I won't tolerate any other man in your life. I don't know if you're ready for that, Lexi."

His words were hard, tough and to the point but somewhere deep inside she felt a stirring as her arousal began to make its presence known. She was inexperienced; she'd only ever had one boyfriend; she was younger than Cal and she'd not lived the kind of life he alluded to yet what he'd just said and the way he'd said it was damn hot. If she hadn't registered it before, she knew for certain now. She was attracted to him, falling for him and it didn't occur to her to care.

Clearing her throat she made sure her eyes looked deep into his. "I understand, Cal. And I'm ready for that." She watched as something flared in his green depths and then he grabbed her hands harder. Closing his eyes Cal swallowed, as if he was battling some inner war. Lexi watched, waiting, comforted that his grip on her hands remained sure. Finally he re-opened his eyes and focused his intense gaze directly to hers. Tingles ran from the top of her head and down her body, coming to rest at her very core.

"Let's do this, Lexi," he said slowly. His voice was low, the sound oddly erotic. Her arousal immediately responded.

"Let's have some fun," he finished and Lexi nodded, mute.

There was no way she could have formed any words, even if she'd wanted to.

Chapter Three

Cal

Cal glanced at his reflection in the mirror as he passed it on the way to the door. He looked fine, same as usual, but something stopped him and he paused awhile, trying to picture his face as Lexi would see him. At twenty-four, he was five years older than her and he examined his features closely. Did he look too old for her? He had lines around his eyes where hers were smooth and the years of working outdoors had given his skin a rough glow. Pulling his chin from one side to the other he continued with his perusal. He looked like he had lived, that was for sure, and maybe the story of his life thus far had not preserved his looks as he would have liked, but he looked okay.

After one more final glance he stepped back and ran his fingers through his hair deciding it was pointless trying to second-guess Lexi. They'd been dating for a couple of weeks and he felt their connection was growing ever stronger. He knew he needed to accept that she liked him and quit worrying.

"Seven years bad luck if you break it."

Cal turned as his lodger, Keith, entered the foyer from the lounge. After Cal had begun working for Zach he'd been able to secure a mortgage on the tiny property but the payments had left him little to live on. Cal had decided to place an ad for a lodger and Keith had applied. They'd been living together in relative harmony, ever since. A typical bachelors' pad, the flat was sparsely decorated but functional, with each of the two bedrooms opening from the central living area off the small entrance foyer. There was only one bathroom, which was in need of a re-paint, and a small alcove off the lounge that contained a basic kitchen. The walls were all covered in a dull shade of brown and most of the furniture and curtains were mismatched, but it was home, somewhere Cal felt safe and secure. Situated in a central location on the first floor of a block of ten similar flats, it served its purpose for both Cal and Keith.

"Yeah, very droll. I was making sure I hadn't cut myself shaving." Beside him, Keith guffawed. "Likely story. We both know that the closest shave you ever have is trying to fool Zach on the morning after the night before."

Cal threw his friend a look. "I was just wondering what a nineteen-year-old girl could possibly see in me. I'm five years older than her for God's sake."

"Just enjoy it, don't question it," Keith returned. "I know I would."

"And that's the difference between you and me," Cal replied. "I like this girl. I don't want her to think I'm someone I'm not."

Keith sighed. "If I hear you say that one more time then I swear I'm going to personally give you a lobotomy. You told me you warned her."

"In a manner of speaking. I told her I'm a one-woman man."

"Right. So surely she gets that you can be kind of possessive?"

Cal shrugged. "I don't know. But I don't want to be. I want to be normal around her, do the things normal guys do."

Keith laughed. "Dude, you'll never be normal."

During a drunken evening Cal had told Keith a little of his past – not much – but enough for the other man to understand why Cal sometimes behaved the way he did. Only Zach knew it all.

"That's not what I meant," he countered. "My childhood was so screwed up and I don't want that to be the thing that comes between us."

Keith whistled. "You really like this girl, don't you?"

Cal nodded. "Yeah, I do. And I don't know if I should tell her what happened to me in the hope she'll understand, or if I should just leave it alone. Move on and live for the here and now."

"If you want my advice," Keith suggested, "then just go with the flow. Let life take its course. You've moved on, you've come good. Let that be what she sees. The rest of it can stay right where it belongs."

Cal looked at Keith in surprise. Rarely was his friend sober, let alone giving out sage advice, but it made perfect sense. Lexi didn't need to know the ugliness he'd left behind. He was a different person now and that was all that mattered.

"Okay, thanks," he said as he pulled his shirt down one final time. So what if there was five years' age difference between them? So what if she was naïve? He liked her enough to take care of her, and the fact that his nineteenth year had been so vastly different to hers, had no place in his life right now. He was a twenty-four-year-old man, no longer that confused and scared teenager.

Even though he'd determined to put his youth behind him, Cal couldn't suppress the memories as he descended the stairs from the flat to the car park. He couldn't help thinking back to when he'd been nineteen years old. His life had been so different to Lexi's and whilst he always sent those memories and demons away, tonight they refused to be banished. Opening the car door he settled inside and then briefly closed his eyes. At nineteen years old he'd been an entirely different man to the one everyone knew now. He breathed deeply, once, twice, three times and then, as the visuals became stronger, he let them in. Maybe, he figured, he needed to remember them in order to finally free himself.

* * *

May – Five years earlier

He found himself inside an exclusive establishment; one where the customer could order anything provided he had enough money to pay. Although still a teenager in years, he had grown into a strong man and he knew exactly what he wanted and needed.

He approached the bar and ordered a whisky straight, downing it in one. He'd been here before, many times and he scoured the floor area looking for Aria. She was the best.

He saw her, lounging against one of the upright poles at the edge of the floor and he approached her with a jaunty stride. He didn't speak – they rarely spoke; it wasn't needed. He nodded and the two of them headed away from the floor and into an area at the back where the private rooms were located. Aria selected a key and then he followed her to number nineteen. Ironic really, tonight was his nineteenth birthday.

They entered the room and Aria immediately began undressing, understanding what was required of her. As he always did, he admired her small, lithe frame and as she turned to show him her back, he felt the stirrings of arousal at the sight of the string of healing welts that he'd inflicted the last time he had visited.

She lay on the rickety couch, face down, her back now showing, almost proudly, the welts. They were still shiny and slick and reverently he caressed her, pausing now and again to brush his lips across one particularly deep wound.

Money changed hands and then he removed his top and selected an implement from the rack. He didn't want to hurt her too much tonight, she was still recovering so he selected a fairly lightweight paddle and began gently rubbing it over her back. Aria moaned. She always did, she was so damn responsive.

The first hit was gentle, it was designed to be.

"Ten?" he asked.

Aria nodded.

Slowly the pace built; Aria remained mute but writhed around under his ministrations. She loved this; he knew she did. Each and every blow she took in her stride as he walked around her prone body, viewing her from this side and that. He'd been careful to avoid the still healing wounds and her back was now becoming a criss-cross of heated warmth.

"Eight," he counted as he lowered the paddle once more, knowing in his heart how wrong this was. He knew that this behaviour, this part of his life made him no better a man than his father – but he tuned that out. Aria loved this – he needed this and so he re-adjusted his focus, bringing himself back into the present.

"Nine." She lay perfectly still, eyes closed and he took a moment to admire her beauty, long dark hair billowing over pale, alabaster skin. She was perfect, in every way.

As he reached the climax, the tenth hit, he felt his body respond. His erection hardened and threatened to burst from his jeans. He delivered the final strike, "Ten," and as he did so, he lost it. Exploded. Inside his *jeans, inside his head. He shuddered as he dropped his chin to his chest and his hand slackened by his side, the paddle slipping un-noticed out of his grip. He closed his eyes and took a few calming breaths. He felt damn good.*

Happy nineteenth birthday.

* * *

Ledgeworth, where Lexi lived, was one of the more upmarket suburbs of Brufton. From his flat it was a twenty-minute drive and Cal took advantage of that, using the time to calm himself after the onslaught of memories. Part of him wished he hadn't embraced them, that he'd fought them down in the same way he'd always done, but part of him knew that he'd been right to face them. Although Cal was no innocent, he'd never felt a connection to any woman the way that he did with Lexi and he'd been serious about not wanting to hurt her. The problem was she didn't realise that he was capable of far worse than simply wounding her emotionally.

No, he counselled himself. That part of his life was over. That had ended the day he'd met Zach. The other man had seen something in Cal and had taught him to believe he could make something of himself. And he could. He knew that he could. He just hoped his feelings for Lexi were enough to keep him on the right track. He felt good now, strong, but if his life should come crashing down around his ears again he wasn't sure he could guarantee how he would react. And now that Lexi was involved, it scared the shit out of him.

She was waiting for him on the porch as she always did. He wondered if she would ever feel able to introduce him to her parents but then, their relationship was still new. She waved as he pulled up to the kerb and his breath hitched in the same way it did every time he saw her. Tonight they were going bowling and so she'd dressed in simple Jeans and jumper, but even still, she was damn sexy and he struggled to control his arousal as he got out of the car. Embracing her lightly, he opened the passenger door for her.

"Bowling?" she asked as he walked around and got back behind the wheel. Cal nodded.

"Yep. That okay with you?"

"Sure," she smiled across at him in the gloom of the car's interior. "I haven't been bowling since I was a kid, so this may be your fastest victory ever."

"What makes you think I'm any good at it?" he asked as he indicated and pulled the car away from the kerb.

Lexi laughed. He loved to hear her laugh. A light, beautiful, musical crescendo. "Men always are," she replied. "It's like one of those unwritten rules, or whatever. Men can always mow lawns, trim hedges and ten-pin bowl better than women."

Cal chuckled. He loved her innocence and simplistic view of life. "I'd say that's a tad sexist," he commented, "there are many women who burned their bras just to prevent talk like that."

She laughed again. "Yeah, true. Okay, well I take it back. I'm going to whip your ass and make all those bra-less women proud."

He looked across at her and smiled. "That," he said, "sounds like fighting talk."

She waggled her finger at him. "You better believe it."

Cal stopped at a red light and glanced across at Lexi, noting how the yellow hue of the streetlights played across her face. "How was your day?" he asked after a moment and she shrugged.

"Usual. I saw an advert for a flat share though. Thought I might check it out."

"Sounds good," Cal nodded. "What's it like?"

Lexi shrugged. "One room, communal facilities. Looks okay from the pictures."

"You seriously thinking about it?"

"I don't know, maybe. I like the idea of having a bit more independence now."

Cal nodded. "I can understand that." Privately he couldn't believe she'd managed to live with her parents for as long as she had, but then he'd never had the option so he could hardly draw a comparison. "What did your parents say?" he asked as he took the right turn that led onto the leisure complex where the bowling alley was situated.

"I haven't mentioned it yet. I want to think about it before I talk to them. Be certain it's what I want."

Cal nodded as he took a moment to locate a parking space. Pulling in he applied the handbrake, turned off the engine and then looked across at her. Lexi returned his smile.

"You could also learn to drive," he said with a wink, "that would give you independence."

"I will…" she said, "but since I have my own personal driver…"

He laughed. "Yeah, so what you're saying is that I'm taking over where your dad left off?"

She nodded and smiled widely at him. "Pretty much. Problem?"

He laughed again. "No."

Leaning forward she dropped a kiss on his cheek and then moved to open her door. "I will learn," she said as she grabbed her bag from beneath her feet, "I just never needed to, what with Dad driving me around."

Cal followed her lead and alighted from the car. He knew that Lexi's dad had always taken her wherever she wanted to go – another stark contrast to his life – but for the first time he pondered her father's motivation. Why did the man drive her around and not encourage her independence? Was it for her safety or did he just want to keep her close to him – his little girl? If it was the latter then Cal was very much afraid that his own presence in Lexi's life might not be welcomed by her dad.

They joined each other at the rear of the car and Cal slipped his hand out to grasp hers. Even that slight touch sent tingles through his entire body and he reminded himself to breathe.

"When did you move out?" Lexi asked and, for a second, Cal froze.

Up until now he'd safely managed to avoid giving much detail about his childhood, however, Lexi asking about his past in the same evening he'd forced himself to relive soul destroying memories caught him off guard and he struggled to force leaded legs towards the building ahead. His heart threatened to beat out of his chest and he swallowed in an effort to regain some calm. Cal understood that if he and Lexi stayed together for a long time then he would have to tell her some of it, one day, but that was definitely not going to be today.

"I was younger than you," he responded finally, careful to control his voice.

"Did you house share?" she asked, clearly oblivious to his discomfort.

"Kind of," he said. Well, he'd stayed in a hostel.

"Did it work out okay?"

Cal flexed his fingers within the comfort of her hand. "It was fine," he replied, "and you'll be fine too." Adding a little pressure he squeezed her fingers in reassurance. He also hoped it would divert her from the current conversation.

"I guess. It's just strange to think of moving out on my own."

They'd reached the glazed entrance door and so Cal grasped the handle and pulled the door open, gesturing for Lexi to precede him inside, a move that effectively prevented him from having to make any further comment. As soon as the door closed behind them the noise hit and they were both instantly distracted. Several bowling alleys and a dodgy music system combined to make an odd kind of melodious thud that although loud, was strangely comforting. It felt like a different world; neon lights shone from every beam, arcade games lined the perimeter of the large converted warehouse building and in the middle, the bowling lanes were mostly occupied. Cal paused a moment to watch the large balls rolling along the polished wood towards the target pins before gently pulling Lexi in the direction of the kiosk situated to their right.

"Any chance of a game?" he asked as the woman behind the desk gave him her attention.

She looked down at her computer screen. "Just the two of you?" she asked and Cal nodded. "I can do lane ten in about half an hour if that's any good? You can get a drink in the bar while you wait and I'll let you know if it's ready any earlier."

Cal looked at Lexi who nodded and so he signed them up. After paying the fee they walked in the direction of the bar and, finding a cosy booth, he settled her in.

"White wine spritzer?" he asked, and she nodded. This was their fourth official date and he'd yet to have her order anything else. One day he determined that he would expand her palette. "Be right back."

The bar was furnished in bright reds and cool creams. With a nod to the old American diner – or, at least a British interpretation of one – the floor space was filled with cream plastic booths and red leather seating. The bar was also cream having a large, silver jukebox at one end and the same, red leather lining along its front. Everywhere he looked Cal could see American road and place names, most of them lit up in neon and he smiled. Given this was a former warehouse, the brightness was effective in disguising its origins but he did wonder if it was all just a little too cliché.

Waiting at the bar to place his order, Cal turned back and took the opportunity to admire Lexi from afar. She was beautiful, he already knew that, but there was something else. She had an almost ethereal quality, an air of the untouched that reached deep into his soul. Perhaps it was simply because she was the polar opposite of him, because her life thus far could not have been more different to his. He didn't really know. All he did know was that his feelings for her, his connection to her was becoming stronger and stronger with each date. He had no idea if the way he was feeling was reciprocated, but Cal knew that he was falling for her. Given the length of time they'd known each other the depth of his feelings felt wrong yet it was the truth, and oddly it didn't scare him. There was something so right about Lexi, something so right about the way he felt when he was around her and something so right about the way she made him feel, like he was really someone, like a real man. It was what he'd been searching for all of these years and now that he'd found it, the feeling was heady and freeing. It felt fast, too fast and yet utterly honest. The memories he'd allowed headspace to earlier, began to bang at his brain, but this time he quashed them down. Facing up to them was one thing, but letting them ruin something this precious, this wonderful and this true was another thing completely.

Lexi Donaghue was his destiny. Of that he had absolutely no doubt.

* * *

The bowling game ended and, as Lexi had predicted, Cal won. Convincingly. At one point he'd tried to throw the game but even that had backfired. Lexi's skill had gone downhill in sympathy and there'd been little that Cal could do to avoid the inevitable.

"Are you sure you didn't cheat?" she asked with a wink as they drove out of the leisure complex and joined the main road back to Ledgeworth.

Cal glanced at her in the gloom. "Are you serious? How the hell does anyone cheat at ten-pin bowling? You either hit the pins or you don't. You, sadly, didn't hit them."

She laughed. "Yeah, I kind of noticed. That was fun though. I haven't laughed that much in a long time."

"Oh?" Cal asked.

"You sound surprised," she said and he nodded.

"I am, a little."

"Why?"

Cal shrugged. "You've got a family. I figured you'd laugh a lot. Be happy."

He felt Lexi turn to face him. "You know what, Cal. That's just about the most judgemental thing I've ever heard anyone say."

"What?" he asked in confusion. He could hear censure in her tone and was at a loss to understand why. To him family equalled happiness. She had people who cared. "You have people who love you, who're there for you," he responded, still unsure how the conversation had turned so fast.

"Do I though, Cal? How can you possibly know that? We've seen each other, what – four times? That hardly qualifies you to make such a sweeping judgement." He could hear her tone changing. She sounded almost angry.

Cal shook his head in confusion. Spotting a parking place on the left, he pulled over. The rest area was deserted, yet the road adjacent flowed freely with traffic travelling to and from Ledgeworth and beyond.

"Have I offended you?" he asked as he parked the car and killed the engine. "I feel like something got a bit weird just then."

Lexi took off her seatbelt and shifted to the right so that she was looking straight at him. Even in the gloom he could feel the pierce of

43

her deep blue eyes. He'd been right, she was angry, yet he didn't have the first clue why.

"Damn straight you offended me. I would never have picked you as someone who judged."

"Whoa...hang on," Cal held up his right palm as he continued to shake his head. "All I said was that I was surprised you didn't get to laugh more. How the hell is that judgemental?"

"Because," he watched as she dropped her gaze and picked at the knee of her Jeans, "you took one look at my life, and assumed. You assumed that because I have a family and because we have a nice house and because I'm not poor...you assumed I was happy. That's pretty damn judgemental."

Cal hadn't seen this side to Lexi before and even though he hated being the one who'd ignited it, he couldn't help feeling aroused. Her face and eyes were animated as she continued to press home her point and his groin began to respond. Hating that her anger did this to him and registering that his feelings of arousal were completely inappropriate, he willed his body to behave.

"All my life, people have judged me: the only daughter of a solicitor, a mum at home who couldn't do enough for me. Everyone I've ever met has told me how I should feel and how grateful I should be. But you know what? Sometimes, my life sucks. Just the same as yours does. Just the same as every single other person's life sucks. You think that because I have material things, I'm happy? Because my parents are still married, I'm happy? Because I don't have to drive myself anywhere, I'm happy?"

"Lexi – I..."

She held up her hand and he closed his mouth. Obviously he'd hit a nerve.

"For years I've had to live up to a certain expectation, behave a certain way, dress a certain way. I'm a clone, Cal. I'm the person *they* wanted me to be. The person *they* brought me up to be but the truth is, that's fucked up. Seriously fucked up."

He watched as a single tear plopped down and landed on the gear lever between them. The arousal that had begun to recede returned and his heart melted. Anger and vulnerability had always been a potent mix for him.

"And for you – of all people – to subscribe to that," she continued, "well, that's even more fucked up. So, yeah, things have got weird and right now, I don't know how I feel. I don't even know if I want to be in this damn car with you."

She began to look frantically around. Rapidly Cal placed his hand on her arm and applied enough pressure to stop her fidgeting. Something had definitely shifted between them; she'd opened up to him, albeit in anger, and Cal knew enough to understand that this was about so much more than the few words he'd spoken.

"There's nowhere to go, Lexi," he said softly. "Please, calm down." He reached into the glove compartment and withdrew a tissue. Handing it to her he watched as she blew her nose and dabbed at her eyes.

"I'm sorry," he said simply once she'd finished, "I never meant to hurt or judge you." He waited a moment but she remained silent. Frantically he searched for the right words – emotional conversations weren't something in which he was greatly experienced.

"I forget sometimes how little time we've known each other," Cal offered as an attempt at explanation. "I didn't think before I spoke. To me, family means happiness and I just assumed you had that, mainly because I didn't." He had no idea if he was saying the right words but he was speaking from the heart – it was the only pen he had.

Carefully he reached across and placed his finger under her chin, lifting her head and turning it slightly so that he could connect their eyes. The un-shed tears in hers tore at his heart. "I get that this is about so much more than what I just said," he spoke softly, "but I regret being the one to trigger this. I never, ever want to see you hurt and I will personally take down and fight anyone who tries to get to you. You're the most beautiful, honest and sincere person I know, Lexi, and I'm falling for you. Hard." Cal swallowed as he continued, careful to keep their gazes connected. "This, between us, feels so damn good, I don't want it to end here."

Her eyes stayed with his for a moment longer and then she

45

dropped them down, focusing on the crumpled tissue in her hand. "You weren't to know," she said after a moment. "It's a touchy subject. I over-reacted."

"No – no, you didn't." He grasped her hand in his and began to massage her palm with his thumb. "Don't be ashamed of your feelings or emotions. They're yours and you have every right to let them out." Lexi didn't respond and so he continued his silent massage. "I'm sorry," he finished gently, "for making assumptions." Cal wanted to offer to listen, he wanted to offer his support, he wanted to tell her that she was safe with him and that he would make her happy, but he revealed none of those thoughts. He could tell from her reaction she had a past to share yet he knew the time wasn't right.

Lexi's head remained bowed and so patiently Cal waited, sensing she would talk when she was ready. After a few more moments she slowly lifted her eyes and at last allowed him to see deep into her gaze once more. "It's okay," she said finally, "I understand. I know you didn't mean to upset me. You had no way of knowing."

Cal momentarily closed his own eyes thankful she had belief in him. *He* knew he'd never meant to hurt her, but knowing she got that, blew him away.

"I never want to upset you," he said into the emotional silence. A lump formed at the back of his throat and awkwardly he swallowed over it. Cal could feel the beginnings of tears forming and, as nervous feelings travelled from his stomach to his heart, he had a moment of pure clarity, a moment when everything suddenly made perfect sense. He'd fallen in love. Cal Strudwick had fallen in love. In that moment, as he'd witnessed Lexi's reaction and vulnerability and considered his part in its cause, he had fallen helplessly in love. The power of his feelings scared him, yet they also liberated him. Giving himself over to another finally meant that he was no longer alone. Cal had no idea if she felt the same way, yet, in his loved up mind, it didn't matter. The all-encompassing love he now recognised he had for Lexi, was powerful enough for the both of them. Of that he would make damn sure.

Tentatively he shifted his hand to the back of her neck and gently drew her head forward, watching her eyes the whole time as he slowly closed the distance between them. When their lips were mere inches apart he closed his eyes and allowed himself to just feel. Their lips met a moment later and then he was lost, kissing her as though his life depended on it. She felt so good, tasted so good and he begged to deepen the kiss, darting his tongue inside as she opened to him. He let out a sigh and grabbed her head more firmly, pulling her ever closer as their tongues duelled and fought.

She met him kiss for kiss and, emboldened, he allowed his hand to rake down her back, shifting her across the centre console and closer to him, needing to feel more of her. Lexi responded by mirroring his actions and he groaned again as his fingers reached the bottom of her sweater. Lifting it up he pushed his hand inside where he met her warm, soft skin. This was the closest they had yet been and his erection pushed ever harder against the zip of his Jeans. He knew they couldn't take this much further here, but he didn't want to stop. She felt and tasted so damn good. Slowly he moved his hand around to the front and pushed ever upwards until he reached the cup of her bra. Inside his mouth he swallowed her moan and then, as he rubbed his thumb across the thin material that covered her nipple, she wrenched her mouth from him and threw her head back. Cal shifted in his seat as his arousal hardened ever more. He was on fire and he knew he needed to pull back before he got to the point where he couldn't.

Taking a long, deep breath in he gradually removed his hand from inside her jumper, sliding it up to the side of her face where he cradled her cheek. She leant into his palm and opened her eyes. Even in the dim light the road afforded, he could see that she was dazed, her eyes wide. She was as affected as he was. Tenderly he ran his thumb across her lips before briefly closing his eyes. When he opened them, she was watching him.

Closing the space between them he placed a final kiss on her lips. "If you'll have me," he whispered as his breathing began to calm, "what just happened is only the beginning."

She reached her right hand up and ran it gently through his hair; Cal felt his body tingle from head to toe. "I'll have you," she whispered in reply, "but don't ever judge my life again."

Cal smiled. That was easy. He'd been a fool. He'd made a mistake and had almost paid the price. Now, realising he was in love with her, he knew he would never do anything to jeopardise what they had. For as long as he lived.

Chapter Four

Lexi

Lexi lay awake for a long time after Cal dropped her home. She kept replaying the scene around and around in her head; at times she felt ashamed for the way she'd reacted and at others, she was proud of herself for finally voicing feelings that were deep down in her soul. Cal had apologised and she knew her reaction to his simple comment had been over the top, yet still it played on her mind – definitely not helped by their heated kiss, the effects of which still lingered down below in her most secret of places.

After a restless night she awoke early and padded into the kitchen. Her parents were still in bed and so she took her morning cup of tea into the breakfast room, settling herself in the little nook of the bay window that overlooked the garden. Lexi had been born in this house and grown up here. It was her home and she loved it. Just beyond her eyeline stood the tree that her father had crafted into an adventure house when she was five. From her perch, high up in that tree, she'd been able to see the countryside for miles around and watch the path of the river as it meandered through the fields. It was an idyllic place to live and Lexi had missed it terribly when, at the age of twelve, her parents had rented it out and they'd relocated to the Midlands.

"Penny for them?"

Lexi turned as her mother entered the room.

"Just looking out at the garden. I don't think I'll ever tire of this view," she replied.

Her mother came and sat on the bench beside her, cradling her own steaming cup. "Is everything alright, Lexi?"

Lexi nodded. "Of course. Why?"

Bren Donaghue shrugged. "We've not seen much of you recently. I just wanted to check in."

"I'm good, Mum. I promise. The course is really getting heavy now so I have to spend a lot of time in the library. I'm loving it, but it's way more intense than I figured it would be."

Bren laughed. "That's the trouble with being bright. You naturally assume everything is going to be easy so it comes as a shock when you have to work at things."

Lexi smiled. "True. But it'll be so worth it. Can you imagine? Me with my own business one day, just like Dad?"

"I know. And it will happen, love. I know it will. Although you're going to have to put in some work by the sound of it."

"Yeah, I know." She reached to the side and hugged into her mum.

"You were home late last night," Bren observed and Lexi lifted away slightly.

"I was in before curfew."

Her mother held up her hand. "I know, I know. I was just worried about you. I didn't know where you were."

Lexi sat back and resumed looking out of the window. "I had my phone, you could've called me."

Bren nodded. "I know, but I didn't want to ruin your night. Whatever you were doing."

"I was bowling, Mum. I told you, remember?"

"Well, yes," Bren took a sip of her tea, "but I've never known it take that long to have a game."

Suddenly, something inside of Lexi began to unfurl. She wasn't sure if it was anger or frustration, but her mother's line of questioning was starting to rankle.

"We had to wait for a lane," she replied, careful to keep her voice neutral.

"We?"

Lexi took a deep breath. "Cal and I. He's someone I've been seeing a bit." She waited. This was the first time she'd mentioned Cal's name to either of her parents.

"Cal? That's the first I've heard of him. I'm not sure you should've been going out with someone I've not met. What does he do? How do you know him? When were you going to tell us?"

Lexi held up her hand to stop the tirade. "Mum. Seriously? I'm nearly twenty years old. Do I really have to run all of my boyfriends past you? Of course I was going to tell you." The anger, frustration, whatever it was, was taking hold and her tone reflected that. She was an adult and her parents' continual lack of recognition of that fact, clearly demonstrated by their attempts to remain in control of her life, was something she no longer welcomed.

"Alexa. That's no way to speak to your mother."

Lexi sighed as her dad entered the room. Great.

"It's fine," Bren said, her tone clipped. "Lexi's right. It's none of our business."

"I disagree." Colin Donaghue advanced towards the bench where Lexi remained. "She's still living under our roof which means our rules apply."

At almost twenty years old? Anger radiated from her core. This was not the first time Lexi had been party to a similar conversation with her parents, only every other time she'd capitulated. Now though, she didn't want to. She was an adult. She had her own life and was responsible for her own decisions. Of course she wanted to include her parents in that, but they no longer got to dictate to her. She felt almost ashamed of her life as she thought of Cal and how independent he was. He would never consider asking anyone else's approval and if he were here now, she knew he would run for the hills. She loved her parents dearly, they were the most important people in the world to her, but she also knew it was time. Time to make that move. Time to make that separation. Time to stand on her own two feet and become the woman she'd allowed Cal to glimpse, not the young girl she felt like right now. It was time for her to grow up.

"I'm moving out." She stood up and walked a few steps away from the window. "It's time."

"What? You can't. Where are you going to go? Wait. Don't tell me. You're going to shack up with this Cal character?"

Lexi whipped her gaze to her mother astounded at the tone she was using and even more so by her assumption. After chewing Cal out last night for making a judgement about her life, Lexi's own mother was now doing exactly the same thing. The anger was boiling and so she clenched her fists at her side.

"Do you really think so little of me?" she asked, still unable to assimilate that her mother had uttered those words. "For your information, I'm moving into a flat share. A *female* flat share. A room came up yesterday. I hadn't decided, but now I have. I don't want to be cruel, but I can't do this anymore. I'm not your little girl any longer, I'm a grown woman and it's about time I stood on my own two feet. Did you hear that, Mum? My *own* two feet. Not yours or Dad's, or Cal's. My *own*."

Bren's hand flew to her mouth in shock and Lexi wasn't surprised. She'd always been more than willing to go along with her parents' plans for her in the past, even though sometimes she'd been screaming inside. She'd done that out of respect for them but today, the comment her mum had made tipped her over the edge. Today, the situation and Lexi's relationship with her parents had changed. For good. She felt both terrified and empowered.

"How dare you, Lexi?" her dad spoke and she could hear the wavering in his tone, an indication he was holding on to his temper. Just. She knew she'd pushed it this time, gone too far but she couldn't call her words back and nor did she want to. This had been a long time coming.

"Dad, please." She turned to face him. "Try to understand. This isn't about you or Mum, it's about me and what I need to do for myself."

"And this Cal person by the sound of it," he muttered and sadly, she shook her head.

"I can't believe both of you think this is something to do with Cal. You haven't even met him and yet you're judging him and not only that, you don't believe I'm strong enough to make my own decisions. You brought me up to be the best person I can be and that's what I want to do. I want to make you proud. I want to show you that everything you've done for me has been worth it. Every sacrifice. But I can't do that if I don't have any freedom to be myself and find out

52

who I am – who I really am – and that has nothing to do with Cal."

"You say that now," Bren commented, "but how do we know he won't be shacking up with you as soon as our backs are turned?"

Shocked, Lexi stood motionless. Her voice broke when finally she spoke. "How can you possibly think so little of me?" she asked. "What have I ever done to make you think that I have no respect for myself or for you?" Her head was all over the place. Never had she anticipated this kind of reaction. She hadn't planned to make this decision today, but her hand had been forced yet even so, she'd honestly believed her parents would trust her, understand her decision and support her. Not fill her head with bitter, hurtful and judgemental comments.

Squaring her shoulders, she turned to face her father. "Dad?" she asked. "Do you feel the same? Do you think that if I leave here I will somehow let you down?"

Colin looked up and his blue eyes, identical to hers, glistened with un-shed tears. "I don't know what to believe, Lexi," he said finally. "I never thought I would hear you speak to either of us the way you just have. I'm disappointed in you. Really disappointed." The older man, who always stood tall and proud, slumped his shoulders as if in defeat.

"But," Lexi defended whilst simultaneously hating the pain she was causing, "it's only natural for me to want to move out eventually."

"Moving out isn't the issue," Bren replied, "that, I understand. What I don't understand is why you did it behind our backs. Why you didn't tell us you were thinking about it. Why you kept this Cal a secret. That's what I don't understand."

"There are reasons for all of those," Lexi countered, "most of which are to do with timing, but, if you believed in me, trusted in me, none of those things should matter."

Her father winced and then crossed the room. She watched as he reached Bren and then looped his arm over her shoulders. Bren's bobbed dark hair contrasted with Colin's short sandy cut as they cuddled into each other's side. "We do believe in you," Colin said quietly, "but trust – that's something else entirely."

Lexi shook her head bemused as a sharp stab of hurt twisted

through her gut. How could her parents not trust her?

"What?" she vocalised. "How in the world can you not trust me? What have I ever done to make you doubt me?" The words rolled off her tongue as she tried to understand what the hell was happening.

"Oh, Lexi," this time it was her mum who spoke, the words slow and measured. "You know perfectly well what you did."

Suddenly, as if in slow motion, it all clicked into place. What she had done? Really? They really still blamed her? Lexi shook her head. "Mum, that was seven years ago. I thought we'd moved on."

"We have," her father commented, "but we can't forget. You acted selfishly that day, Lexi. You put yourself before others. If you hadn't, then Bobby would still be here."

Silently Lexi closed her eyes and inhaled deeply. Bobby. This was about Bobby. Her parents' comments were grossly unfair, yet this was the stance they'd always taken. At the time of the accident her parents had blamed her and no matter how many times Lexi had told them what happened, they'd never changed their view. Her hope that time would heal their hurt and absolve her from their blame was pointless. It would appear they blamed her every bit as much now as they'd blamed her then. Yet, there was a blessing, she remembered. At least they didn't know about the ultimate lie; the lie that she hadn't told but had innocently corroborated. If they ever discovered the real truth then Lexi feared there would be no going back for any of them. The truth should have been told seven years ago yet she'd been unable to form the words. Instead she'd hidden it deep inside in a place she never visited and had moved on with her life in the only way an innocent twelve-year-old child could. She'd blocked it out.

Her father was right of course. If the accident hadn't happened then her handsome, brave, strong brother would still be here now but he wasn't, and that was not Lexi's fault. Regardless of what her parents chose to believe.

Taking a final deep breath she placed her cup on the breakfast table and then slowly and carefully, walked out of the room. She loved this house, but she was done here. Today, after what had just happened, it no longer felt like her home.

Grabbing her phone she tapped out a quick text to Cal. It was Saturday and although they'd made no plans to meet, she hoped he would be there. She really needed him right now.

'Can you come and pick me up? I need to talk to you. L xx'

Whilst she waited for his reply she sank onto the softness of her bed and lay back, studying the ever-familiar ceiling. When she was ten she'd been fascinated by astrology and her parents had indulged her, painting her ceiling blue and recreating an entire galaxy. Countless nights she'd fallen asleep studying the glowing orbs, taking safety and comfort in her belief that the universe was never ending. By the time she was fourteen and they'd returned from the Midlands, her fascination had gone and so the ceiling was re-painted. She remembered her parents' frustration at how long it took to cover the blue. They'd got angry but she'd just accepted it. Things for everyone were still too raw.

A sharp beeping jolted her out of her reverie and immediately she dived for her phone. Please let him say he could come.

'Sure. On my way. C xx'

Lexi blew out a sigh of relief. She had no idea what she was going to say to Cal, but she knew she would have to tell him a hell of a lot more about her life. Telling him, she understood, was a risk – they barely knew each other – but at the same time, she felt the connection that he'd mentioned. Instinctively, Lexi knew she could trust him.

A soft knock sounded at the door and she sat back up on the bed. A few seconds later Bren walked in, closing the door behind her. Lexi watched as her mother came around the bed and then sat quietly down on the other side.

"So, you're really going then?"

Lexi nodded.

"But have you thought it through? What are you going to do for money? How will you afford to live?"

In reality, she had no clue. "I don't know," she admitted. "Maybe I can get a grant, loads of students have one."

Beside her, Bren sighed. "Does it have to be like this, Alexa?"

She turned to face her mother. "I think perhaps it has to be. Otherwise I would probably never leave."

"You don't have to leave now. It was just a stupid argument. We all said things we shouldn't have done. For my part, I'm sorry."

Lexi shook her head sadly. "Those things that you said, Mum – about Bobby – they were wrong. You know that. We went over it so many times and even the police said that no one was to blame."

She felt her mother stiffen beside her.

"I know that you don't like to talk about Bobby," Lexi continued. "But maybe that's been part of the problem. Maybe we should all have talked about him more – perhaps then you would've been able to move on and…" she paused, "…been proud of me."

Bren lifted her head and a moment of pain stabbed at Lexi's heart as she looked at a face so similar to her brother's. The likeness was uncanny and there were still occasions, like now, when it caught her off guard. She swallowed and took a deep breath.

"Perhaps you're right," her mother said quietly. "Perhaps we didn't handle things in the best way, but nothing prepares you for losing a child. Nothing. Dad and I, we did the best we could."

"Mum, I know that. I really do. And I'm sorry for what I said too. But don't you see? This is always going to be there, coming between us. We've been through so much as a family and we've kept it to ourselves, behind closed doors. None of us reached out for help and now I think that we should've done. We internalised everything and in our own ways, we've all been stuck in the past. I can't live like that anymore, Mum. So I have to go."

Bren reached a hand across the duvet and grabbed one of Lexi's. "When did you get to be so grown up?" she asked, her smile sad as she regarded her daughter.

Lexi shook her head. "I actually don't know, but today, it just all seemed to make sense. You and Dad, you need to have your time now, your life, and you need to deal with the past in a way that works for you. I have to deal with it too and now that I've made my decision, everything seems so much clearer. I hope you understand," she added.

Slowly her mother let out a sigh and then grasped Lexi's hand more tightly. "I do understand," she said quietly. "I knew this day would come, I just hadn't expected it to happen like this."

"I know." Lexi leaned forwards and embraced her mother, closing the ocean of duvet between them. "I didn't plan it either, but you have to know that regardless of what's happened today, I love you and Dad. You've been the most amazing parents and maybe time apart will heal us all."

Bren hugged into her and Lexi took a moment to enjoy the familiar, homely smell. She would miss her parents, especially her mum, but the time had come. The two women embraced for a few more moments and then her mother pulled away.

"You're our only daughter, Lexi. You'll always be our little girl. Go out and do what you have to do and enjoy your life. Learn what you have to and take your own direction. We'll support you no matter what." Bren brushed away a tear with the back of her hand. "This will always be your home. Be safe – that's all we ask. Oh, and…" she eased herself away from the bed and began to walk towards the bedroom door, "Dad and I will sort out a loan for you, for money. You can pay us back whenever. We love you, Alexa, and that's never going to change."

Opening and then closing the door softly, her mother exited the room leaving Lexi alone on the bed, staring at the white panel of wood where a moment ago Bren had stood. Her scent lingered, but her mother had gone and a wave of sadness engulfed Lexi as she realised that today, something fundamental had changed. Her relationship with her parents was never going to be the same again – they still blamed her and yet they still loved her. It was beyond complex. The change in her circumstances felt daunting yet exciting. Finally, at the age of nineteen years and eleven months, Lexi Donaghue had allowed herself to become a woman. Now she had to learn to face the world on her own and hope that in doing so, she would somehow survive.

* * *

Cal turned off the engine and Lexi watched as he unbuckled his seatbelt, shifting sideways to face her. After picking her up they'd driven a short distance to the country park. Lexi had not yet uttered one word and now, Cal was waiting for her to speak.

"So, what happened?" he asked gently and she took a moment, gazing out of the windscreen at the trees and woodland beyond.

"I had an argument with my parents," she began, "and it got out of hand."

"Okay," he reached across and gently placed his left hand on her thigh. "Do you want to talk about it or do you just want to sit here awhile?"

Surprised, she turned to face him. "I never picked you for the sensitive type, tuned into emotions. I figured you'd just expect me to spill. Especially as I dragged you all the way over here."

Cal smiled revealing his even, white teeth. "You have a lot to learn about me, Lexi. I can do sensitive and I know how close you are with your parents. If you want to talk, I'm here, but I get it if you don't. Sometimes, when things get rough, we just need space."

Lexi nodded. Space. Space sounded good.

"And you didn't drag me all the way over here," he continued, "it only took me half an hour and I was planning to call you anyway; you just got in first." She felt him move his hand soothingly, up and down her thigh. "So quit worrying about me and what I think and let's just deal with what happened at home. Okay?"

She smiled at him. "How come you're so wise?"

Cal laughed. "You're the first person to ever call me wise. If Keith, that's my lodger, could hear you saying that, he'd be in total disagreement."

"Why?" Lexi asked fascinated.

"Let's just say that I don't always make the smartest choices. But anyway, this is about you and what you need. We can talk about me anytime."

"Okay." She liked the sound of that – anytime. It meant Cal was considering they had a future. "I think I want to talk – if that's okay?" she asked.

"Sure." Cal fiddled with the seat controls and reclined his chair a little. Following suit, Lexi did the same. It felt good to relax.

"So, anyway," she began, "I'm moving out."

"What?" Cal coughed as he sat back upright. "You could have warned me you were about to say something huge."

Lexi giggled. "Sorry."

"Wow," he said when he'd caught his breath, "that must have been some argument."

"It was and it wasn't. We all said things we shouldn't have done, but the bottom line is, I know the time's right. I have to do this."

"Okay…" she could hear the shock in Cal's tone. "So where are you going? What are your plans?"

"Remember that flat share?" she asked. "The room's still available so I asked if they could hold it for a week. I wasn't sure about making the move but I must've sensed I'd be needing it – and now I do."

"And you're okay with that?" Cal asked. "It'll be a hell of a change."

Lexi nodded. "I know and yes, I'm okay with that. More than okay. I finally realised something today. Living at home with my parents, I was always their daughter. They always had a part in my thoughts and my decisions and that's not wrong, but I have to find out who I am without anyone else influencing me. Does that make sense?"

Cal nodded. "Absolutely. I still can't believe you're actually moving out though. Wow."

"I know. Crazy, huh?"

"No, not crazy," Cal replied, "brave."

"I don't feel very brave," she commented, "I actually feel a bit like I'm copping out."

"How come?"

"The argument," she paused, "it was about something really personal. To us. Our family. Something we should all have faced up to a long time ago and instead of dealing with it, I feel like I'm running away."

"From what you've said, it sounds like you're just doing what's best for everyone." Cal increased the pressure on her thigh a little. "Try not to be too hard on yourself. How did your parents take it?"

Lexi shrugged. "Yeah, okay I guess. It didn't happen how I planned, but it was fine. They're going to loan me some money, just to get started. But I was thinking, d'you reckon I could get a job anywhere?"

Cal nodded, "I don't see why not. Loads of uni students have part-time gigs. I'll keep an ear out."

"Thanks."

For a moment they sat in silence.

"Do you want to know what the argument was about?" she asked eventually.

"Sure, but only if you feel comfortable to tell me."

"Yeah," she looked down at her hands which she'd crossed in her lap, "am I wrong in thinking we have something here?"

She caught his gaze and read the confusion in his eyes.

"I mean I feel like I can tell you this stuff, but I've never told anyone before. It's like there's a connection or something. Christ, I sound lame." She shook her head and looked out of the side window.

"It's not lame, Lexi."

She turned back around to face him.

"We do have something," Cal continued, "I feel it too, and to be honest, it scares the shit out of me."

Lexi's pulse picked up at his words and she laughed a little awkwardly. "I thought you were supposed to be the grown up here?"

He shook his head. "Nope. Not when it comes to stuff like this." With his spare hand he patted his chest in the region of his heart. "When this gets involved, I'm as lost as you."

She regarded him, eyes wide. "When your heart is involved?" she whispered and he nodded.

"You get to me, in here," he indicated his heart again, "and that's what scares the shit out of me."

Lexi could barely hear for the sound of her own heart beating out of her chest. Her palms began to sweat and she took a deep breath. His words, his honesty, they spoke to her on an elemental level and if she hadn't realised she was lost before, she knew without doubt that she was now.

"So, we really do have something?" Her voice remained low as she allowed her eyes to lock with his. "It isn't just in my imagination?"

"No," he confirmed, his voice barely audible. "It's not in your imagination."

She closed her eyes and allowed the beauty of the moment to permeate. It was quick, too quick, but it was right. This. Him. Cal. This was all part of her new journey.

Opening her eyes she looked at him once more. "What are we doing?" she asked and then watched as he shook his head.

"I don't know," he replied, "I really don't. But one thing I do know. I don't want it to stop."

As if by unspoken agreement they both leaned forward and connected their lips, tentatively at first, but it wasn't long before passion built and they deepened the kiss. Lexi pulled herself towards him and ran her hands around his collar, pulling his head closer, his lips deeper. He groaned and she swallowed it, loving this feeling, this heady sensation of passion and knowing that she was the one who incited it in him. He was such a strong man, yet right here, right now, she had him in the palm of her hand and the power was overwhelming.

Running her lips across his teeth she darted her tongue inside, sweeping around and kissing him with everything she had. Hands caressed as they both fought to get closer, fingers tugging at hair, palms massaging thighs and when they finally pulled apart, Lexi was breathless, her hair a dishevelled mess.

"Fuck," Cal said as he dropped his head back onto the headrest. She did the same and then rolled her head to the right so she could look at him. Down below her arousal beat in time with her heart and she fidgeted a little on the seat.

"Yeah, you could say that," she agreed.

Cal turned his head so he was looking at her too. "I have to be honest – I'm not sure how much more time I can spend with you without wanting to…" he broke off, "…take things further. Have you ever…?"

She smiled at him, admiring his honesty. "I'm not a virgin, Cal, if that's what you're asking."

He nodded. "Okay." She watched as his face creased into a frown. "Actually no, that's not okay. I wish I could've been your first."

She let out a sigh. "That's so old fashioned, but I kind of like it. That you care about things like that."

"Of course I care," Cal replied. "I thought we already established that."

"Yeah, yeah, we did," Lexi waved her hand. "I guess I never thought that stuff really bothered guys anymore."

"Well, it bothers me. But, that doesn't change anything. I'm just warning you that I won't be able to indulge in this kind of steamy session for too much longer, without wanting a hell of a lot more."

Lexi smiled. Their steamy sessions had been affecting her too, and, now that they both agreed what they had was special, she couldn't wait to take things further. She was attracted to Cal on every level and after what had just happened with her parents, a physical distraction was just what she needed; in more ways than one he was a man after her own heart.

"Cal," she started and then waited for his eyes to meet hers, "I wouldn't have it any other way."

Chapter Five
Cal

Cal was feeling hornier than he had any right to; especially as he was sat in his car in the middle of a country park in broad daylight. The problem was, Lexi had just moved their relationship onto a whole new level and whilst his brain was struggling to assimilate, his groin was having no problem keeping pace.

"Hold up," he said after a moment. "You're saying that you're ready to…"

"Have sex?" Lexi finished. Her words were confident but her eyes were shy. She was such a contradiction.

"Are you sure?" he asked.

He watched as she slowly nodded.

"I wasn't trying to pressure you," he added hastily, "I just wanted you to know how I felt. So we could adjust things, you know?"

She smiled across at him. "I don't feel pressured. I'm with you. It feels right."

Cal sighed and turned his head away, staring out of the windscreen. When she'd texted him earlier, this was the last conversation he'd expected to have. As it was, her reaction to his need excited him. He drew in a breath.

"Are you okay?" she asked. Her voice was quiet and he twisted back towards her with a gentle smile.

"More than okay," he said as he grasped her hand. "I didn't expect to have this conversation today, that's all," he clarified.

Her smile mirrored his. "Neither did I."

Cal nodded. "You're so beautiful," he said as he reached his free hand up and caressed the side of her cheek. She nuzzled into his palm and his heart melted just a little bit more.

They sat in silence for a moment.

"I didn't love him," she said after a pause, "not really."

Cal used his hand to tilt her head back up.

"It doesn't matter," he said, "you're here with me now. That's all I care about."

She smiled. "I wish it'd been you too." Her voice was low and her cheeks flamed a little beneath his palm.

"I didn't really expect you not to have a past," he said.

"We grew up together," Lexi continued. "He was Bobby's friend..."

"You don't have to explain," Cal cut in, "wait...who's Bobby?"

Abruptly Lexi moved her head away from his palm and straightened up in the seat. Instinctively Cal sensed she was beginning to shut down, yet he had no idea why. He'd not pressured her; all he'd done was ask who Bobby was. He shook his head and leaned back in his seat too. They may not have known each other for long but he understood enough about women to know he needed to wait. The ball was in her court. In front of him a lone walker crossed the grass field, his boots kicking through the fallen autumn leaves. A small dog bounded ahead with a brightly coloured ball in its mouth, heavy breath visible in the cool October morning. Cal watched the man and dog in silence as the atmosphere in the car became heavy. He wanted to break it but he didn't know what to say. Eventually, when he could wait no longer, he took a deep breath and dropped his head to the side. Lexi was staring absently out of the windscreen in the same manner he'd been only seconds before.

"Are you okay?" he asked finally.

For a moment she remained motionless and then slowly she shook her head. Her eyes shifted to meet his and in them he saw the beginning of tears.

"Hey," he said, "it's okay."

As Cal watched she dashed at her eyes with the heels of her hands. "Yeah, sorry," she said after a moment, "it just gets me every time."

"D'you want to talk about it?" he asked.

She tilted her head towards him. "Bobby," she said the word slowly and reverently. "Bobby was my brother. And the reason why my parents and I argued today."

Cal regarded her in confusion. "I didn't realise you had a brother?" he asked. She'd only ever talked about her parents.

Lexi shook her head, eyes full, and finally the unchecked tears fell from her beautiful blue gaze. "I don't," she said quietly, "Bobby was killed seven years ago. He was fourteen."

"Shit." Cal swiped a hand through his hair. "Christ, Lexi. That's rough. I don't know what to say."

Beside him he felt her shrug. "Not much to say really. He was the most amazing, wonderful, strong brother anyone could ever have wished for. But he's gone. And we all have to live with that. Every day."

"Bloody hell."

The one advantage to the almost nomadic life Cal had led thus far was that he didn't get too attached to anyone enough to really miss them – regardless of the circumstances in which they left his life. He could barely imagine the pain of losing a sibling and a child. Crap. He was so ill equipped to deal with this kind of stuff.

"What happened?" he asked, hoping she would open up and talk to him. He was out of his depth, but he knew more than anything he wanted to support her and be there for her.

Lexi took a deep breath and then settled back into her own seat, looking out of the side window for a moment. "We were just kids," she started, "having fun, messing about." She turned once more towards him and he could see the pain written on her face. "We were out one day in the summer. It was really warm, stifling hot and a few of us were having a water fight – a few of the kids from our street. Mitch, that's my ex, he was really going for it and he and Bobby were a formidable team. The rest of us didn't stand a chance." She smiled wistfully and Cal took the opportunity to reach out and hold her hand. Slowly he stroked her fingers. "They went round the back of our house and got the hosepipe out; our bottles and buckets were no match for them then. I ran away and cowered against the wall of our front garden, but Bobby was after me and before I knew it, I was saturated."

Lexi stopped and Cal could feel the pain as her hand clenched within his. He sensed it was still raw regardless of the passage of time.

"I," she swallowed again, "I twisted around and managed to catch him off guard and before he realised, I had the hosepipe out of his hands. I aimed it straight at his body, but he must've crouched down because it hit him square in the face. It knocked him off balance and he stepped back." Her breath faltered and Cal knew she was almost there. Almost at the point where pain knew no bounds and life changed forever. "There was a kerb," her voice was low, barely audible, "he tripped down it and into the road. There was a car…" She closed her eyes and he watched the pain grip her beautiful, tender features. "It was too late. They couldn't save him." She opened her eyes and looked directly at him and Cal felt his heart being ripped from his chest. "I blamed myself," she said, "I knew I was the one who killed him, but the police and the counsellors, they were really kind. They reassured me, told me that it was an accident and no one could be responsible. It was just one of those really cruel twists of fate."

"I was twelve years old, Cal. I lost my brother, my best friend and I just shut down. So did my parents. We moved away. Dad got a transfer to a place in the Midlands, but it didn't work out. I guess we thought if we didn't see Bobby in our house every day, we'd cope but it just made it harder for all of us so, two years later, we came back." Lexi sniffed and then wiped at her eyes once more. "I got back in touch with Mitch and he helped me. We went to counselling together – he was still dealing with it too. Gradually I found peace and I began to understand that I wasn't to blame and then Mitch and I started to see each other as more than friends. I think it was just comfort to begin with and then it developed. Physical release helped us both and so we took that; it got us from one day to the next."

Wordlessly Cal shook his head. She'd been through so much, and he thought he'd had it rough? No wonder she'd reacted the way she had last night when she'd thought he was judging her life.

"Anyway," she looked up at him and pasted on a smile, "in the end that's the only thing Mitch and I had in common. We were together for all the wrong reasons and so we just agreed to let it go. We got each other through and we'll always have a special connection, but that's all it ever was."

"Christ, Lexi," finally he found his voice, "I'm so sorry."

She dropped her head back on the seat and closed her eyes for a second. "It was tough," she said when she opened them, "but the thing about Bobby, he loved life. He embraced it and he would've wanted me to do everything he could no longer do. That's why university and my own business. They were Bobby's goals, not mine, but I knew I had to do those things for him. That I owed him."

Cal shook his head. "Are you sure? I mean, I don't know anything about this kind of stuff, but wouldn't he just want you to live your own life?"

"Of course," she looked directly at him, "but this *is* my life now. He's a massive part of that and I need to live for the both of us."

Privately, Cal disagreed. Living for someone else or even living part of your life for someone else, never worked – at least not in his experience. You had to be true to yourself otherwise you had nothing. But then what did he know? He'd never experienced a close family bond and he sure as hell never had a brother. Wisely, he let that part drop.

"So how come you and your parents were arguing about it?" he asked instead.

She sighed. "They still blame me. They say it was my fault. That I was being selfish because I didn't want to lose the water fight. As if," she snorted and what was left of Cal's battered heart went out to her. "They refused counselling, any kind of help, choosing to deal with it themselves. . ." she paused, ". . .they've never had their beliefs challenged. Even when the coroner ruled it was an accident, it made no difference."

"And you continued to live with them?" Cal was aghast. He'd been at the hands of parents who'd let him down. He'd done the only smart thing he could think to do which was leave. He couldn't believe that until today, Lexi had never considered moving out.

"I felt like I couldn't leave them. As much as they resented me for what they believed I'd done, so they loved me for being their only child. To them I was Lexi and Bobby all rolled into one and I couldn't hurt them any more. Besides, this is the first time I've really had anywhere feasible to go."

"What about Mitch?" Cal asked. If Cal had been in her life when she'd lost her brother then he was damned sure he wouldn't have left her to take the blame.

"He tried to talk to my parents," she replied sadly. "He told them he was there and it wasn't my fault, that it was just a game but my parents," she sighed, "once they get an idea then it's usually pretty stuck."

"And so you've dealt with your guilt and their guilt for what...the last seven years?"

Lexi nodded.

"Shit." It was the only thing he could think of to say.

"Yeah, shit," she echoed and for the first time since she'd begun to tell her story, he raised a smile.

"I bet they don't like your mouth either, huh?" he asked, relieved to see Lexi muster a smile too.

"No. But then I'm usually on my best behaviour when I'm at home," she stopped. "When I *was* at home."

Cal shook his head and let out a deep, cleansing breath. "You're the most amazing person I know," he said.

"Why? I'm nothing special."

He shifted sideways in his seat turning his legs to the left so he could face her full on. "You're the most special person I've ever met," he said, impaling her eyes with his. "Crap, you've dealt with more in your nineteen years than most people do in a lifetime and yet, here you are, this beautiful, amazing woman. Don't ever sell yourself short, Lexi. I don't ever want to hear you talk about yourself like that."

With a half-smile she nodded. "Okay, boss."

He laughed.

"There are so many people who go through appalling pain though," she continued. "The people I met at counselling, some of them had lost everything. How they coped and carried on with their lives I'll never know."

"But you were a kid, Lexi. You were twelve years old. You could've given up and screwed up your life. You could've lived off drink and drugs and called the streets your home, but you didn't. You faced life

68

head on, even when it was bloody painful and you took on everyone else's grief and responsibilities. If I wasn't jealous that he got to be your first, I would take my hat off to Mitch and thank him for giving you the respite he did."

Lexi tilted her head to one side. "You have nothing to be jealous of."

"No, I know," Cal waved his hand dismissively. He'd said it earlier: she was here with him now and that was all that mattered. "I'm just glad he was there for you."

Lexi nodded. "I think…" she began hesitantly, "…I think I need you to hold me."

Cal smiled across at her. He'd been itching to reach for her, hold her, comfort her, but he'd been scared of her shutting down. Now that he knew she needed his comfort he shifted across the space between them and engulfed her in his arms. Citrus floated to him and he breathed her scent deeply. Resting his head on her shoulder he allowed them both to take the comfort they needed.

"Thank you for telling me," he whispered, "I know that must've been tough."

She squeezed him hard and then leaned back a little. Citrus retreated and immediately Cal felt bereft.

"I needed you to know," she said simply. "If we're going to have a future, then I needed you to know."

He removed one hand from around her waist and lifted it to her cheek. Her face was so soft; he could caress it for hours.

"We are going to have a future," he replied softly. "You can be damn sure of that."

Their gazes connected and silent messages passed between them. He watched as the sorrow that had filled her eyes only moments before, gradually began to dissipate. Slowly her cheeks reddened and he could sense the desire between them building. Without hesitation he leaned forwards and gently placed a kiss on her lips. He felt her hands shift to his hair and he angled his head to allow her easier access. Beneath his lips hers opened and he deepened their kiss, taking the sweet taste that she was offering. Teeth meshed as all of their emotions poured into the physical act and Cal shifted closer, allowing the moment to hold. Their breath became heavier, their moans louder and suddenly Cal pulled away. Lexi looked at him in confusion.

Taking a steadying breath he gestured with his hand to the fogged up windscreen. "We're in way too public a place for this," he explained. "Much as I don't want to stop, we have to."

Lexi nodded. "You're right," she said as she ran her hands through her hair and then rubbed at her eyes, "but I don't want to stop either."

Cal waited a beat. "Are you sure?" he asked.

She dragged her palms away from her eyes and looked directly at him. "I'm sure," she replied.

Cal closed his eyes and let out a breath before slowly opening them again. Her beautiful blue eyes had remained unmoved, focused on his face. He lifted his and, as their gazes collided, it hit him. He realised, in that moment, he would never be able to deny her anything – least of all something he wanted just as much, if not more.

"Keith's out," he said as he reached forwards and gently caressed her neck with his fingertips. "We can go to my flat."

* * *

He didn't bother to give her the guided tour. Entering the flat he grabbed her hand and took her straight to his bedroom, kicking the door closed with his foot. On the journey here his desire had built and so, he sensed, had hers. The looks, the heaviness of her breathing, they were all dead giveaways and by the time they reached the sanctity of his room, he was done for. He had to have her – have all of her – now.

They met at the foot of his bed and he mashed his mouth onto hers, feeling her wrap her arms around him in response. Never in his life had a woman tasted so good, so right and he knew that whatever this damned connection was it was strong. Moving carefully he broke away from her and then slipped his arms underneath her jacket, drawing it down until it dropped to the floor. The T-shirt she wore beneath was thin and he could see the outline of her breasts, even in the dim light of his room. She was so beautiful it was breathtaking – he could scarcely believe she was here with him.

As he looked at her he felt her tug at his shirt freeing it from his

Jeans and he clenched his jaw, reminding himself to take it easy, slowly. Her palms smoothed up his chest following the crumple of his tee as she raised it up and over his head. Obligingly he lifted his arms and then dropped them to his sides, loving how she was looking at him, drinking her fill. He kept in shape and his work on the site definitely helped, but never had he been devoured in quite the way he was being devoured now.

In an act of mimicry he did the same thing to her, carefully lifting her T-shirt off and over her head, leaving her standing in her lacy bra. He almost forgot to breathe.

"Christ," he said as he looked at her and she smiled.

"I could say the same thing."

As one they reached for each other, their mouths meeting once more as they tumbled together onto his bed. The softness of the duvet wrapped around them and Cal took his time as he deepened the kiss, gently moving his hands over her body as he explored the softness of her skin.

His breathing hitched as she began to writhe beneath him and emboldened he reached down and unbuckled her trousers. In a matter of moments she had shimmied out of them and he followed suit, eager to get as close to her as he possibly could.

Their desire built and their breathing deepened. Slick skin slid against slick skin as they both took everything they needed. He was more turned on than he'd ever been before and even though he would've liked to spend longer here enjoying her, he knew he was going to have to get inside of her soon.

As if sensing his need Lexi sat up and rid herself of the remainder of her clothing. Cal watched helplessly as her bare breasts bounced into his line of vision. Unable to resist he reached forward and caressed one of the globes, feeling the rigid peak of her nipple and he fastened his gaze to her face, watching as she dropped her head back and closed her eyes. For a few moments he enjoyed the sensation and then, knowing he was close, he removed the rest of his clothing, drawing her down beside him as they finally fitted their naked bodies together.

Their kisses and caresses intensified as they fought to get closer still and eventually Cal could wait no longer. He reached over to his drawer and removed a condom, taking a second to sort out his protection before positioning himself above her, watching her eyes dilate as she waited for him.

For a moment he paused as he fought down his darker side, the side that told him to be who he had been – to make love to her without mercy. He hated that it was still there, but he knew he was in control of it now. With a deep breath he closed his eyes and filled his head with images of her, his beautiful, fragile, brave Lexi and then, as he exhaled he pushed himself forwards, opening his eyes finally as he guided himself into her very core, gently, carefully. The waiting heat and softness swallowed him up and he stiffened, holding on, slowing things down, knowing he needed to take his time.

Beneath him Lexi squirmed and he began to rock into her, mirroring her every move as they joined together as one. He could feel the sweat dripping from his forehead, but he kept his eyes open, steadfastly refusing to close them and miss a second of this time. Their eyes connected and she focused her gaze right through him in the way that only she could. He increased the pace allowing their passion to build until the only sound in the room was their soft, muted groans. As he neared his release Cal pushed into her one final time, deeper and ever deeper until he was buried to the hilt. He felt her begin to convulse around him and at last he let himself go, emptying his very life force deep inside this incredible woman. As the sensations overtook him he collapsed on top of her, pulsing into her as they both took it all and, with a final groan, he tipped over the edge. In his ear he heard her soft cry.

Cal was totally spent. He'd given her everything and she'd taken it all. As he lay slumped on top of her and allowed his breathing to return to normal he closed his eyes. There was nothing in his head except for her. His every sense was heightened to her, her citrus scent surrounded him and, right before he allowed himself to drift into a wondrous and peaceful place, he formed one final thought.

He was home.

After twenty-four long years, Cal Strudwick had finally found his way home.

Chapter Six

Matt had so far remained silent and Cal was glad. Recalling the events of the past three years was one of the hardest things he'd ever had to do. If Matt had continually interrupted, he was certain he wouldn't have got this far.

"Do you want to take a break?" Matt asked and Cal shook his head.

"Okay. So I'm starting to get the picture that your relationship was full on from the day you first met?"

"Yeah, you could say that," Cal nodded. "I knew, the moment I saw her and then the more time we spent together...it was just so perfect."

They were still seated in the matching armchairs and, across from him, Matt smiled.

"Right, and not long after you met, Lexi moved out of her parents' house?"

Cal nodded. "It was about three weeks after we met I think. She got a flat share and we never looked back. We could spend as much time together as we wanted and as I was working on site, I saw her every spare minute. It was real love."

"I can tell. So, is it fair to say that the first few months were good?"

"They were better than good. We just fit. The guys on the site used to tease me, tell me I'd gone soft, but they didn't know what it was like. The intensity, it was out of this world. I would've laid my life down for her. In all truth, I still would."

"You're still in love with her?" Although Matt phrased it as a question, it may as well have been a statement.

Cal nodded. "Yes. Yes I am."

Matt smiled gently. "That's tough. But we'll get you through this. Okay?"

"Sure." It wasn't as if he had many other options right now.

"It does get better. I promise."

Cal nodded. If he had a pound for every time someone had told him that after the divorce, he'd be living it up on a Caribbean island. Well, maybe not. But he'd heard that same comment, time and time again and as yet, nothing had changed. It still hurt so damn much.

"Does it ever though? Really?" he asked and Matt nodded. "But this pain, she's there, with me, inside here every day," he thumped his chest.

"I know and I wish there was a quick fix, but there really isn't, Cal. Sadly this is one of those things you have to allow to heal on its own."

Cal shook his head. "What if I don't want it to heal? What if I feel that I deserve this pain? This life?"

"Which is exactly why you're here, so we can break it all down and take apart those feelings, work out what's reasonable and what isn't. Between us we're going to get you to a place where you value yourself again, regardless of what's happened."

"I still don't get how you can't judge someone," he commented and Matt shrugged.

"We've been over that and it won't make any difference to talk about it again. I'm here to help you. Whatever has happened in the past we can't change, but what we can do is make your future positive. And happier. That's what we need to focus on."

"I guess," Cal mirrored his therapist's shrug. "So you got lucky getting me to work on then?" His voice held a trace of sarcasm and he knew Matt would detect it.

"I want to help you, Cal. That's the end of the story, but I can't do that if you won't help yourself. The things we're going to be talking about will be tough, really tough, but you're going to have to hang in there. It's not about me fixing you, it's about you fixing you. I'm just here to facilitate. Does that make sense?"

Since Cal had opened up a little to Matt about the start of his

74

relationship with Lexi, he could kind of understand what the other man was saying. He nodded.

"Great. So now, I want to focus on what happened after those first few months. Perhaps try to pinpoint where things started to go wrong?"

Cal sat up straighter. "That's easy, I can tell you exactly where things went wrong..."

Matt held up his hand. "Perhaps, but I'd really like to take it step by step if that's okay. There may be parts of your recollection that really add to the bigger picture and allow us to work out how to move forwards. I wouldn't be doing my job if I just skipped to the big events and didn't look at the whole situation."

Again Cal nodded amazed at how calm Matt still was. He couldn't imagine listening to one person's life story let alone the thousands that Matt must've heard.

"What do you want to know?" he asked.

"Well," Matt jotted a few things down in his notebook, "was there anything that happened early on in your relationship? Maybe after those first few months?"

Cal swallowed. He knew they would get here, but he still didn't know if he could do it. Talk about it. He swallowed again.

"There is something," he said slowly, "and even though it happened before we got married, I know now it was kind of the beginning of the end." He closed his eyes, the images, sounds and smells still so vivid in his mind. "I don't know if I can do it," he said as he opened his eyes again, relieved to find he was still in the quiet solitude of Matt's office. He dealt with the memories every single day and at times he felt as if he was actually back there. Sometimes it was so real it terrified him.

"Are you okay to try?" Matt asked. His tone as ever was soothing and understanding.

Cal reached to the table beside him and picked up the glass of water. Taking a sip he placed it carefully back onto its coaster. "How much time do we have?" he asked and watched as Matt glanced at his watch.

"You're my last client for the day so there's no rush. Now we've started I think it's important to make as much progress as possible – if that's okay?"

"Yeah, that would be good," Cal nodded. "I don't know if I'll be able to start all over again."

"Sometimes a break in the sessions is not a positive thing," Matt confirmed. "It's tough to talk about anything this deep and emotional for any length of time, but when the session is going well, it's beneficial to get as much out of it as we can. So, if you're okay to continue, we can keep going."

"Yeah, I'm okay." He wasn't but then that was why he was here – so he would be okay again. And now Cal finally understood the only way he was going to achieve that was by facing up to his demons. He couldn't hide them in the closet any longer.

"Start whenever you're ready," Matt encouraged and so Cal took another sip of water. This was going to be hell, but then again he was already in hell. Now it was time to start the journey back.

With a deep breath he replaced the glass and, folding his hands across his arms, he closed his eyes, hugging himself for strength and comfort.

"It was my twenty-fifth birthday," he began, drawing out each word, "and I had bought myself a motorbike."

Chapter Seven

Lexi

May 2013

There were definitely two lines.

Lexi dropped the plastic stick and paced the small room she occupied in the flat share. Two lines. How the hell could there be two lines?

Reaching into the waste bin she picked up the packet and checked the instructions again. One line – not pregnant, two lines – definitely pregnant. Shit. She sat on the side of the bed and dropped her head into her hands. This couldn't be happening. How could it have happened? They'd been so careful. There was no way she was ready for a baby, she still had so much to accomplish. She had another year before graduation and then she needed to get out there and work, gain experience. Never in hers, or Bobby's plans, was there a baby. Christ. And what would Cal say? She had no idea if he wanted kids or not. They'd never discussed it. Shit, shit, shit.

Standing up she went back to the small adjoining bathroom and picked up the stick from the floor. Still two lines. Hold on – what if the test was wrong? That happened sometimes. Diving into the cabinet she retrieved the two remaining tests and quickly dipped those. Best of three. Seemed to work in most other areas of life.

Her watch ticked agonisingly slowly as she monitored the second hand on its journey, counting in her head. She wasn't going to look at the tests until the correct time. There was no way she wanted to know until the last possible minute. Eventually it crawled round to the time required and, with a deep breath, she carefully picked up the two most recent sticks. Two lines. On both. Fuck.

Dropping all three sticks into the bin she went back into the main bedroom and picked up her bag. Sifting through it she unearthed her diary and began to page back. So, last month – nothing. Rapidly she paged back another month – still nothing. One more month – crap. Her last period had been three months ago. How the hell had she not noticed?

Lexi shook her head. The answer to that was actually simple. She'd been so consumed with Cal and with her university course, she barely took any notice of the time going by. It was only today she'd realised she'd not had a period for a while, but she'd never considered it had been a whole three months ago. She couldn't comprehend it. According to those damn test sticks, Lexi was at least three months pregnant.

Feeling a sudden wave of nausea she flopped down onto the bed and put her hands over her eyes. No, no, no – there was no way this was happening. Mentally she did some calculations. If she were three months, give or take, then the baby would be due in December, right around her birthday. Her twenty-first birthday. And she would have a baby. This was so not in her schedule.

A knock at the door brought her to a sitting position and taking a deep breath she walked across to open it. She could have pretended she wasn't there, but she knew who would be on the other side and Lexi really needed to talk to them.

"Hey," she said with a brightness she was far from feeling.

Mel walked into the room and collapsed on Lexi's bed, right where she'd been sat herself just moments ago. "Oh my goodness, did you see that hottie in class today?" Her best friend imitated a swoon and then lay right down. "Of course you didn't. You don't need hotties, you have Cal. And I'm not jealous – of course."

Lexi smiled in spite of her turmoil. Mel had always had a soft spot for Cal.

"No," Lexi sat on the desk chair adjacent to the bed, "I didn't see the hottie. Who was he?"

From the depths of the bed, Mel growled. "That's what I'm trying to find out. He was just…"

"Yeah, yeah. I get the picture. You're incorrigible, Mel, you know that?"

Mel sat up and winked. "That's what uni is all about, my friend."

Mel, one of her fellow lodgers, had an unquenchable zest for life, which was what had initially brought the two women together. Lexi had been drawn to the other girl's opposing personality and somehow, their different characters complemented each other. It hadn't taken long for them to become close friends.

The ample flat they shared was a modern and luxurious new-build with three bedrooms, each having their own en-suite. Built specifically for the student market the flat was within walking distance of the university campus – once the two floors to the car park had been descended. Inside, in addition to the bedrooms, it contained a communal lounge and well-equipped kitchen. It had been tastefully decorated in neutral colours and the furnishings were minimalist in style. The girls had added their own touch with colourful throws and cushions along with bold mug trees and ornaments in the kitchen to break up the endless stainless steel. Their third lodger was Faye who had bought into the flat initially with Mel. After a few months they'd decided to advertise for a female to share and, thanks to the generous allowance from her parents, Lexi had been able to take the room. Faye worked shifts as part of her nursing degree, which meant Lexi and Mel spent most of the time there on their own which was fine by Lexi. Since moving in she'd not looked back. She'd settled in well and was enjoying the independence and freedom that came from living on her own.

"Not for me it's not," Lexi defended. Immediately she was reminded of her recent discovery that, caught up in Mel's enthusiasm, she'd momentarily forgotten. What was uni going to be about for her now?

"I need to talk to you," Lexi said. "I was going to come and find you."

Mel leaned forward and put her hands on her thighs. "Well, here I am. Saved you the trip."

She smiled. "Yeah, thanks."

"Are you okay?" Mel asked as she leaned closer towards Lexi. "You look really pale. Like you've seen a ghost."

Briefly Lexi closed her eyes and rubbed at them with her hands. This was so hard, but she had to tell someone and she knew she could trust Mel – both to keep her secret and to give her advice.

"Are you ready for this?" she asked as she took her hands away and allowed her friend's face to come into focus. Mel's brown eyes regarded her and Lexi read the concern within.

"I'm pregnant," Lexi blurted out, "at least three months."

As Lexi watched, the colour drained from Mel's face. "Crap, Lexi. Are you absolutely sure?"

She nodded. "Three tests, every single one positive. And I've not had a period for three months. Pretty conclusive."

"Crap," Mel repeated. "Does Cal know?"

Lexi shook her head. "No, I've only just found out. I don't know what the hell to do. Mel, I'm so scared." She dropped her head down and shook it.

"It's okay," Mel soothed as she reached forward to clasp Lexi's hands. "We can sort this out, work out what to do. Maybe see the nurse?"

Lexi nodded. Mel's small hands around hers were warm and soothing and she began to feel a little calmer.

"But you're going to tell Cal though?"

"Yeah, I guess, but I have no idea how he feels about kids. We've never talked about it. Whenever I try to ask him about his childhood and his friends, he just clams up. It's like there's a part of him that I'm never going to get access to. What if that part includes kids?" She could feel the panic rising again so she gripped Mel's hands harder.

"Hey, hey, hey…" Mel soothed "…you're getting way ahead of yourself. No one knows how they're going to react, not until they actually get pregnant."

"How do you know?" she asked. "Have you ever been pregnant?" Lexi knew her voice was barbed, but she couldn't help it. This was a major crisis.

"Of course not," Mel seemed unperturbed by her tone, "but my brother's girlfriend got pregnant at our age. Everyone thought he would freak out, me included, but he didn't. Cool as you like. Now they're happily married with number three on the way. You just never know – that's all I'm saying," Mel finished.

"I guess," Lexi allowed, after all, what her friend said did make sense. "But does Cal really strike you as the paternal type?"

Mel dropped her head to one side. "No, not right now, but neither did my brother. I think you should give Cal a chance to tell you what he thinks, without pre-judging. Remember how mad you get when people judge you?"

True. This is why she'd needed to talk to Mel, someone to give her a healthy dose of common sense.

"Anyway, how do *you* feel about it?" Mel asked.

Lexi shook her head. "I really don't know. My head is kind of scrambled right now. Terrified? But then at the same time I can't help thinking how amazing it is. I have this person, growing inside of me. That's surreal."

"Yeah," Mel agreed, "it sure is. I'd be terrified too though, if it were me."

"I mean, I don't know the first thing about babies," Lexi continued. "All I know is my life would never be the same again and the path I promised I'd follow – that would be gone."

"It would. Everything would change," Mel agreed, "but Lexi, that path you talk about. That's not your path, is it?"

Lexi had told Mel about Bobby and how she was doing what she believed he'd want her to do. Mel had listened to Lexi's reasoning but had been of the opinion that she should be her own person and had often voiced her thoughts to that effect. Compared to Lexi, Mel had it sorted. She knew exactly who she was and it was that very independence that had brought them together. Lexi admired that in Mel. Even though she was a good head shorter than Lexi and petite in build, her personality and zest for life more than made up for what she lacked in size. Mel was also unfailingly honest which, after the lies of Lexi's youth, was something she embraced. Except now, when her best friend was lecturing her about the path she'd chosen to take.

"That's beside the point," she vocalised, "it's the path I've chosen and I made that vow to myself. This," she gestured to her belly, "means I'll never follow that path. You've no idea how much guilt would be attached to that."

"Of course there'll be guilt," Mel agreed, "but that doesn't mean you shouldn't do what's right for you."

Automatically, Lexi argued. "I won't feel any guilt if I do what Bobby was going to do, then I'll know that I've finally atoned for what happened."

"Lexi, stop. Seriously. You told me yourself you weren't responsible – it was an accident. A 'cruel twist of fate', I think you said. Do you honestly think your brother would want you to compromise your life for him?"

"What life?" Lexi stood up and began to pace again. "What life do I have now?" She felt her face crumple and once more, dashed at tears. "Before today I had a plan, a destination. Now I have nothing."

Mel stood too and walking towards her, reached out and engulfed her. Gratefully Lexi sank into her friend's embrace.

"You have to get some advice," Mel soothed, "find out your options. And you have to talk to Cal."

Lexi pulled away and grabbed a tissue from the cabinet. "I know, but I'm so terrified I'll never see him again. What if he walks away, Mel? What then?"

Mel sighed and, taking another tissue, she gently dabbed at Lexi's eyes. "If he walks away he doesn't deserve you. He'd be a fool. And I honestly don't think Cal's a fool, Lexi. He totally adores you. Anyone can see that."

"Yes, exactly," Lexi retorted. "He adores *me*, not me plus one."

Again, Mel shook her head. "That 'plus one' is his baby. Yours and his. It's a beautiful, wonderful symbol of your love. What could be more perfect?"

"But the first thing you said when I told you was 'crap'. Now you're making it sound like this is the best thing to ever happen."

"I said 'crap' because I was shocked," Mel replied, "and in no way am I suggesting this is a great plan – far from it. But it's kind of done now. The horse has bolted. So unless you're considering an abortion, we have to try to be positive."

Lexi sniffed. "How did she cope?" she asked.

"Who?" asked Mel.

"Your brother's girlfriend."

"Ah…it was tough I think. I was quite a bit younger so I don't remember all that much about it, but they were at uni together. They got a flat and then just tried to make it work. Seth – that's my brother – got a job and when the baby was born, Deana studied from home."

"What was she studying?" For some reason, that seemed important.

"Law, I believe. When Abby was born she switched to teaching. Now she teaches law rather than practises it."

"So she still made a go of her life?"

"Yes, she did. And as I said, they have number three on the way. So they got through it and even though the path changed, they still did okay. All I'm saying is it can work. It doesn't have to be the end of the world."

"Maybe not, but it feels like it all the same," Lexi commented.

Mel draped an arm around her shoulders and guided her back to the bed. They sat down, side by side. "I'm sure it does," her friend said softly, "but you have to talk to Cal, only then can you really know what you're facing. There are so many options for young mothers and working mothers now. The two of you are amazing together. There's no reason why this can't work out. Honestly."

"You really think so?" Lexi turned her tear stained face up towards Mel.

"Yes," Mel hugged her tightly. "Look, it won't be ideal and it'll be a long, tough road, but if you're willing to follow a different path, *your* life path, then you'll be okay. I know you will."

Lexi sniffed and blew her nose, loudly. "Thanks, Mel. I'd be lost without you."

Mel hugged her in tight one more time. "I'm not going anywhere," she said.

With a small smile, Lexi dropped her head onto her friend's shoulder and closed her eyes, blocking out everything but the blissful darkness as she allowed herself to let go and totally relax. Could she change her path? Would she and Cal cope?

There was only one way to find out.

* * *

He arrived promptly at seven pm. They were going out for dinner to celebrate his twenty-fifth birthday and Cal had booked a taxi. Lexi was currently learning to drive but had yet to pass her test and now she was mentally kicking herself for not getting around to it sooner. Once Cal clocked her not drinking he would start to ask questions. She'd still not decided how the hell she was going to answer them.

"Ready?" Cal asked as she answered the front door to his knock.

She nodded. "Let me just grab my jacket." Turning away she walked over to her room and the desk where she'd left her coat. Even though it was May, the evenings were still chilly and she didn't want to get cold. Especially not now.

Cal whistled as she returned to the doorway. "You look – amazing," he said and she smiled in return. Over the past couple of hours she'd been schooling herself on how to get through the evening without telling him and still appear normal. As long as she didn't open her mouth, she figured it was actually not too difficult.

They exited the flat and after securing the door she followed Cal down the grey concrete stairs that led to the car park.

"Did you have a good day?" he asked as they began to take the second flight down.

"Yeah, good," she said automatically. "What about you, birthday boy? Did they make a fuss of you at work?"

"Nah," Cal stopped on the step in front of her and waited for her to join him. "They grumbled something about buying me a pint next time we're in the pub, but other than that, it was a normal day."

"That's sad," Lexi said and Cal just shrugged.

"To be honest, it's not. I'm so used to my birthday being just another day that if someone does make a fuss, it feels plain wrong."

"Aw, shucks," Lexi said, "better not give you my present then." She'd deliberately left his gift in her room for Cal to open on their return from dinner.

Cal laughed.

"You know," she said softly, "if you ever want to talk about your childhood, I'm here for you." She felt Cal stiffen beside her and then he continued down the stairs. Inwardly she berated herself. She should've known better than to mention his past again, but now that she had her own news, it was even more important to understand what had happened to him and why he was so closed up when it came to his childhood.

Taking the last couple of steps together, she caught up to him and gently placed her hand on his arm. He stopped and turned to her. "Sorry," she said, "I know you don't like to think about it."

He touched her hand with his and then reached it up to caress her cheek. "It's okay, it's not you. I wish I could talk about it and one day, I hope I will. I just don't want to do that today."

Lexi leaned her cheek into his caress. "I understand," she whispered. And she did. Yet maybe they didn't have as much time as he thought because unless she had an abortion, this baby wasn't going anywhere. Cal's demons could potentially be on his doorstep way sooner than he imagined.

They continued on their way in silence and then, when they got to the part-glazed metal door that led out to the car park, Cal stopped.

"Wait here," he instructed, "I've got a surprise for you." His eyes were shining and Lexi couldn't help but smile.

"It's your birthday. Shouldn't I be the one surprising you?"

Cal laughed. "You can do that later. This though, is for both of us now. So, close your eyes and don't open them until I tell you to. Okay?"

"Okay." Lexi positioned herself adjacent to the doorframe and closed her eyes. She felt Cal leave, heard his footsteps departing and then a few moments later she heard laboured steps approaching accompanied by an odd kind of swishing sound. It was torture, but she kept her eyes firmly shut. Finally, Cal called to her.

"You can open your eyes now."

With relief she opened them and after waiting a moment to adjust to the light, she moved away from the door and out into the fresh air. Immediately she focused on Cal and the object he was supporting. The moment she recognised it her heart began to thump with increasing speed and her mouth instantly dried. Nausea hit. *This*

85

was his surprise? With a large gulp she attempted to swallow down her terror.

"What do you think?" Cal asked excitedly. Momentarily she saw a glimpse of Cal the boy but she was paralysed. Too scared to appreciate the minute insight.

"It's not what I expected," she said carefully. Her heart was racing and she could feel her palms starting to sweat. This was not good. Although he couldn't possibly have known, Cal had just presented her with the worst surprise imaginable. Tremors ran the entire length of her body.

"It's beautiful." It was all she could manage.

"Isn't she?" The excitement was still shining from his eyes as he began to run a hand caressingly over the bright red metalwork.

She?

Slowly, Lexi made her way towards where Cal stood adjacent to the shiny new motorbike; his pride was blatant. This – it – she – was his surprise? Lexi swallowed. This was her worst nightmare, yet, for him and for the boy he'd once been, she knew she had to focus and get a grip – fast.

"I didn't know you rode," she said finally. Her voice was scratchy as she forced it over a throat lacking in moisture. The pulse in her neck began to resonate in her brain. "I mean do you have a licence?" Somehow she held it together.

"Sure do," Cal said, totally oblivious to her discomfort. Lexi had never told him how she felt about motorbikes and she couldn't let on now. Even a blind man could see how much this meant to him.

"Great," she said as she did a slow circuit of the bike. It was a good-looking machine, granted, but that still didn't take away the panic that was building inside of her. "So this was your treat to yourself? What about the taxi?" He'd told her they were getting a taxi tonight. She clung to the hope that he was simply showing her the bike and not expecting her to ride on it.

"Yes, this was my treat and I cancelled the taxi. This is a way better mode of transport." Cal was immersed in running his hands all over the bodywork and the leather seat. Watching him she noted the pillion bench at the rear and went cold from head to toe. Did he really expect her to...?

"So, shall we go for a spin?" he asked. Lexi almost stopped breathing. He did expect her to.

"I'm not sure." Especially now, she added to herself. "I've never been on one before. They kind of scare me." Scare was nowhere near close to what they did to her.

Cal reached over and pulled her close to his side. "It's okay, I'll go slow. I promise." She could feel the buzz radiating from him and she knew she was going to have to do this. Because it was his birthday and because she loved him.

Taking a deep breath she swallowed. "What do I have to do?" she asked.

"Nothing really. I got you a helmet, look." He leaned over towards the handlebars and unclipped a lime green helmet from a small hook. Her favourite colour. "Try it on."

She looked at it dubiously, scarcely able to believe that she was going to be getting on a motorbike which was to her, the machine of the devil. Her palms were now sweating profusely and yet still Cal remained oblivious.

"And then, when you get on," he continued, "I'll help you. You just have to hold on to me and lean into the corners. That's pretty much all there is to it."

Lexi couldn't form any words and so she just nodded. Cal handed her the helmet and with shaking hands she took hold of it, slipping it awkwardly over her head. It felt enclosed, stifling, uncomfortable.

"Great. It fits," Cal said as he reached under her chin and began to adjust the straps. Inside the helmet she concentrated on breathing, in and out, in and out. She could do this – she had to do this. Instinctively her hand went to her belly and her fear doubled. She was carrying a baby inside of her, Cal's baby, and he didn't know. She had to tell him. Had to tell him that she was scared, that she couldn't do this. Not only because of her own fear but because she had another life to protect. Lexi opened her mouth to speak, but no words came out. She swallowed over the dry lump in her throat and tried again. Cal was adjusting some dials on the dashboard and shrugging into his own helmet.

"Isn't this great?" he asked, the sound muffled inside her padded chamber.

She nodded. Tell him, tell him, a voice inside her head chanted. "Cal?" she forced the word out through lips lacking in moisture.

"Uh huh?"

"There's something I need to tell you..."

He stopped fiddling and looked across at her. "Okay."

"It's just that..."

"Yes?" his eyes shone into hers, happiness and excitement radiating from them. Christ. She couldn't do it. She couldn't burst his bubble. He was so animated, never had she seen him more so and a part of her knew this connected to his past somehow. That even if he wasn't ready to tell her, this was a part of him he wanted her to know. A part he felt ready to share. She couldn't tell him her fears – or about the baby. Not now. She loved him with all of her heart and she had to let him have this moment, whatever it cost her.

Still he looked at her, his eyes glowing as he waited for her to answer. Quickly she swallowed one more time. "It's just that... I have no idea how to get on." He beamed as he reached forwards and gave her a massive hug.

"I'll help you," he said as he pulled away and unable to say any more, she let him. She relaxed her body as he positioned her to the side of the bike and encouraged her to lift one leg and secure it to the peg whilst using the opposing pressure to swing her other leg up and over. She said nothing as he helped settle her, making sure she was in exactly the right place as he too swung himself on board. She remained mute as he reached behind and grabbed her hands, pulling her arms forward and securing them around his middle. And she made no sound as he started the engine and the sickening rumble began from beneath her. Gritting her teeth she closed her eyes and focused on the leather of his jacket, the scent of Cal and the love she had for him; the very same love that was forcing her to face her biggest fear.

Perhaps she should have told him the truth in the first place, it would've been so much easier now, but she had no way of knowing he'd buy a motorbike. She'd never told anyone the truth – even her parents didn't know. The only other person who knew what really happened that day was Mitch. Lexi regretted the lie they'd told, but she'd had no choice. They'd lied because they were in shock. They'd lied because they were kids and they had no idea how to even begin to process what they'd seen. And they'd lied because it wasn't just about her and Mitch; they were protecting someone else.

A car, Mitch had said. Bobby had been hit by a car. But he hadn't. In her infantile mind she'd watched as a lone motorbike, out of control, ploughed into her brother. She'd seen a man dressed in leather stopping, watching and then riding away like a bat out of hell.

Lexi gripped tightly onto Cal as the images returned thick and fast. She was helpless to stop them; the motorbike had become an unwelcome trigger. Inside her tortured mind she saw Bobby trip and fall. She watched him laugh as he tried to get up, looked at his handsome face as he saw the bike approaching and witnessed the fear in his eyes when he scrambled unsuccessfully to get out of the way – and then she saw nothing. Blackness. Until the man alighted from his bike, briefly lifted his visor and then remounted and gunned the engine. A few seconds later her mother had appeared, fear making Bren's strides rapid as she raced to help her only son. Lexi hadn't moved. She'd been transfixed. The body of her handsome brother lay crumpled in the road but she hadn't moved. Nor had Mitch. During the ensuing chaos they'd both remained in precisely the same places they'd stood when the bike had hit. It was a car, Mitch had said and his had eyes implored her to agree. A car. A hit and run. Numbly she'd nodded. She'd had no other choice. Her world as she knew it had ended yet her defining memories of the tragedy were not of Bobby in the few moments before, but of Mitch and his cool grey eyes as they'd begged her to keep his secret. She'd been twelve years old. She'd just watched her brother take his last few breaths. She'd been traumatised. Nodding at Mitch had been her only option, her brain too full to compute anything else and so she'd agreed with him by omission and no one had ever asked her again. And Mitch's secret?

The rider of the bike had been his older brother, Ellis. The troublemaker. The jailbird. The black sheep. Ellis had been fresh out of jail and Mitch had done what he'd thought was right to protect his family, but in doing so, he'd devastated hers. It didn't matter that Ellis drove drunk into a tree a couple of months later and ended his troubled existence. Nothing that happened after Bobby's devastating death could ever atone for it. She gripped Cal even tighter as she remembered how grateful she'd been to leave their home for those two years. Even though she'd covered for Mitch, she'd never wanted to see him again and yet, when her family returned home, he'd been the only person able to comfort her. There'd been no love lost between Mitch and Ellis yet Mitch had wanted to protect his parents and, after seeing what losing Bobby had done to her own parents, Lexi understood that. Oddly she and Mitch had found physical solace in each other, but deep down Lexi had never forgiven him. The secret that she kept still burned in the depths of her heart and no matter what happened in her future, she knew that she would never truly recover from the events of that day. Not in this lifetime.

Now, years later, she found herself pretending again, this time for a different man, but this time for a man she loved. All she could hope was that her love was strong enough to get her through this nightmare and protect not only herself, but also the tiny life that was just beginning to grow inside of her.

Chapter Eight

Cal

Sunlight glinted off the polished chrome as he carefully took yet another corner. Behind him he felt Lexi begin to relax, the tension in her arms releasing as they wound their way through the beautiful countryside. When the night was like this, the air warm and still, Cal could think of nothing better than the freedom he felt right now. He turned his head a little to the side.

"You okay?" he shouted. He felt Lexi nod.

It meant so much to him that she was sharing this day, this experience with him. He'd been caught off guard earlier when she'd mentioned his childhood and he knew one day he would tell her. This though, this was part of him and to know she was able to see that part of him made his heart swell. Never could he remember being happier than he was right now.

Ahead he saw a pull-in and, making a decision, he indicated to the left and then slowly steered the bike over. Stopping, he turned off the engine and kicked down the stand, easing himself off the bike. His legs groaned reminding him it had been several years since he'd ridden properly. Releasing his helmet he secured it on the clasp at the front and then, reaching underneath Lexi's chin, he did the same to hers. For a moment she remained on the bike and he watched her, searching her eyes, looking for clues as to how she felt, whether she had the same sense of abandonment that he had. When she remained speechless he lifted his hand and gently caressed her cheek, moving a tendril of hair away and back behind her ear.

"You okay?" he asked again, only this time his words were softer.

Lexi nodded. "Yeah, I think so."

"Good." She was so beautiful it made his heart stop. Sitting there astride his bike, her hair mussed by the helmet and the sun low in the sky behind her, she was a picture of perfection and not for the first time he wondered how he'd gotten so lucky.

"I love you," he said reverently.

"I love you too," she said simply and he smiled. They'd been together six months but to him it felt like a lifetime. She was his other half, the person that made him whole and even though their relationship was still new, for him there would never be anyone else. With his left hand he touched the pocket of his leather coat, relieved to feel the box shape still inside. Was now the right time?

"Can you help me off?" she asked and Cal jolted back to reality.

"Yes, sorry," he said as he encircled her waist with his hands and lifted her bodily from the bike. Placing her gently on the ground he watched as she stretched her legs and rotated her neck.

"Helmet gets a bit heavy after a while," she commented.

"Yeah. The physical side of biking does take a bit of getting used to," he agreed. "We'll probably both be a bit sore in the morning."

Lexi smiled. "Well, my legs haven't done anything like that in a while."

Cal smiled a wolfish grin and she reached forwards, swatting him. "Cal," she admonished and he laughed.

"Sorry." He wasn't.

She gave him a sideways look and he resisted the urge to crush her to him and show her what she did to him. If they hadn't been on the side of a busy road in full public view he knew he wouldn't have been able to hold himself back.

"What did you think?" he asked instead. It mattered to him that she got this. Got what this meant to him; the freedom, the buzz, the joy.

"It was…good."

He picked up on her slight hesitation and frowned. "Sure?"

"Yes." She walked away from the bike and towards the small fence that separated them from the fields beyond. "It wasn't something I ever wanted to do, but it was okay. Honestly."

Cal walked over to join her and leaned against the fence beside her, both of them looking out over the golden landscape. "You don't sound convinced though? Didn't you get the buzz? The freedom?"

She turned to him and shrugged and for the first time he noticed the residual fear in her eyes. Crap. Had she really been that scared?

"Lexi, are you okay?" He hated that he might have put her through something she really didn't want to do. Cal waited as she continued to look straight ahead and then eventually, she turned to the side to face him. His heart constricted as he saw the raw pain in her eyes.

"Lexi? What? What is it? Oh my God, what have I done?"

She shook her head and then, after taking a deep breath, she began to speak.

"It was a motorbike," she said. He heard the tell-tale tremor in her voice and a feeling of complete dread swept over him as, with devastating certainty, he put the pieces together.

"It was a motorbike that killed Bobby," she said slowly and Cal's world stood still as he realised what he'd just done, what unimaginable hell he must have put her through. And she'd done it. For him.

"Christ, Lexi. I'm so sorry." Rapidly he pulled her into his arms and held her tight. "You should've said something, if I'd known..."

"It's fine," she said, her voice muted as she snuggled deeper into his shoulder, "I wanted you to have your time. I guessed this really meant something to you."

Using his hands he gently moved her a little bit away so he could look directly into her eyes. "Yes, this does mean something to me but hell, Lexi, nothing is ever going to mean as much to me as you do. If I had any idea I'd never have suggested you ride with me. I'm so sorry." He shook his head. "I'm such a fool."

Lexi lifted her hand and placed a finger gently across his lips. "Shh...You're not a fool. How could you have known? And it was actually okay. Honestly." Quickly she replaced her finger with her lips and he took the brief contact, revelling in it.

"It was a shock," she continued, "that was all. But I can't live my whole life dictated to by one tragic event. That's not right for anyone."

"But Christ, Lexi." He ran his hands agitatedly through his hair. "I never should've assumed you'd be okay with it."

Again she placed her finger on his lips. "It's okay. Honestly. I got that buzz and freedom. I can see why it means so much to you."

Cal shook his head, barely able to comprehend what she'd just done for him. "I don't deserve you," he said.

Lexi smiled and for a moment they regarded each other. Cal watched her face closely and finally he saw her features relax.

"I realised something," she said quietly, "when we were on the bike."

"What?" he asked. She reached forwards and clasped both his hands with hers.

"What happened to Bobby is something I'll never truly get over, but that has nothing to do with us." She paused for a second. "I realised I have to let some of that go."

Cal squeezed her hands in response.

"I can't live my life for someone else," she continued, "it isn't fair to me, you or Bobby. I need to find my own path and follow that…" Abruptly she stopped and released his hands then turned sideways towards the fence and the field beyond. He sensed she'd been about to say something else but, when nothing was forthcoming, he closed the couple of steps between them.

"Lexi?" he asked as he settled at the fence beside her once more. "What is it?"

Cal knew instinctively she was holding something back. The way she'd just disconnected from him, shut him out – there was something more than what had happened to Bobby.

Gently he draped an arm across her shoulders. "That's not everything is it?" he asked softly and she shook her head. "Then tell me, tell me what it is. You're my life, Lexi. You mean everything to me. Please?"

Cal could sense her reticence, but he had no idea what else to say. She remained still, staring out at the field beyond and, with a sigh, he followed her gaze.

In the distance a horse jogged to its mate and he watched as they nuzzled each other in recognition. On the ground lay a foal, its spindly legs struggling to hold as it raised itself unsteadily to its feet.

Both parents watched on and then, when it finally righted itself, they nuzzled it too. The picture of a perfect family. A moment ago Cal had been thinking about freedom, the kind he got from riding his bike, but watching the beauty of nature unfold before him, he realised there was another kind of freedom. One that didn't involve being on your own. One that involved being with the person you loved with the entirety of your being.

Eagerly Cal turned to face Lexi, wanting to tell her how much he loved her, wanting to reiterate what she was to him and how perfect their life could be. Simultaneously he dropped his hand to his pocket and closed his fist around the heart-shaped velvet box. Now was the time – he had no need to wait.

As if she sensed the shift in him, Lexi also turned and fixed her gaze right through him in the disarming way that only she could. Pulling his hand out of his pocket he spun the box around in his fist, making sure that when he presented it to her, the heart faced the right way.

"Lexi," he began as he kept his fist firmly closed. He didn't want to spoil one single element of the surprise. "Lexi, will you…"

"I'm pregnant," she blurted out.

Cal felt himself go hot and cold and rapidly he shoved the box back into his pocket. Never had there been a more effective way to ruin a marriage proposal. He blinked, watching her as she waited for him to react – but he had no idea what to say.

"I…" he said and then closed his mouth. I what? Pregnant? Kids? What the…?

"I… shit…" he tried again. "Are you sure?"

Lexi nodded and he nodded back, puppet like.

"You're sure. Okay. Crap. Wow. Okay." He was making no sense, but his brain was just too scrambled. He'd been about to propose, to ask her to spend the rest of her life with him and then bam. This. Right out of left field.

"How do you feel?" he asked finally as he searched in vain for the appropriate response.

Lexi shook her head. "I don't know. I only found out today. I haven't got my head around it. What about you?" There was little emotion in her words and Cal knew he was going to have to be careful what he said. For the first time in ten years he cursed his lack of a father figure. Emotionally he was totally ill equipped.

He swallowed. "I'm okay, I think. I mean, I want kids – eventually. So, yeah, it's a bit earlier than I would've liked, but…"

Lexi nodded. "But you think we can do this?"

He could hear hope in her voice and he swallowed again. "I guess so, I mean, there's a lot to sort out but I guess we could. You want to keep it?" He hated asking but knew he had to – they needed to be on the same page.

She shrugged. "I don't know what to do. You?"

He took a step back and then dragged his hand across his brow. This day was not turning out the way he'd planned. At all.

"Crap, Lexi," he said. "Me? A father? Shit." Again, he rubbed at his forehead. "I've not had a father in my life for ten years. I wouldn't have the first clue. What if I suck at it? What if I'm like my own father?" He was rambling and revealing things he'd previously kept close to his chest, yet this was the crux of the issue for him. His mind went back to his nineteenth birthday and then further back still. Could he do this? He shook his head. Being a father was genetic – wasn't it?

"My dad," he clarified, "was no father. What if I'm the same, Lexi? What if I can't give our child the love it deserves? I don't want my child to go through what I did. I don't know if I can trust myself not to be like him."

Lexi closed the gap between them and held out her arms. Slowly, he walked into them.

"Cal, you really think I have this so together? I'm scared out of my wits." Her familiar citrus scent floated to him on the early spring breeze. He held on tight needing her comfort, warmth and strength.

"We'll be okay," he said with more conviction than he felt, "we'll be okay."

He buried his head in the golden locks of her hair and took a deep breath. Would they be okay? He sure as hell hoped so.

When Cal awoke his head was pounding and the first thing he noticed was the stark whiteness of the room. Blinking, he turned his head to the side.

"Ah, great. You're awake." He focused his vision on the man stood beside his bed.

"What the…?" He tried to sit up, only to find the pounding in his head intensify.

"Try to relax," the man spoke again, "everything is fine. Do you know where you are?"

Cal looked around the room again. Panic began to bubble inside. It looked like a hospital room but…crap. He sat up again and this time he was successful. His head pounded, but he ignored it. He was in hospital?

"You're in hospital," the man confirmed. "You've had an accident, but you're totally fine. I'm Doctor Geller and I've been looking after you. Can you tell me, do you remember anything?"

Did he?

"Lexi," he said aloud, "where's Lexi?" Agitatedly he began to pull at the covers as he tried to get out of bed. Lexi. Where was she? He had to find her.

"Relax," the doctor said again as he pressed a hand gently onto Cal's shoulder. "She's doing well. I promise."

"Doing well?" he croaked. "What the hell does that mean? What in the hell happened?" His earlier sensation of panic had now reached his heart and was clawing its way inside, squeezing harder at every beat.

"You came off your bike," Doctor Geller replied, "we're not entirely sure what happened, but the good news is that you and your girlfriend are both going to be fine."

"Where is she? I need to see her." Again he tried to get out of the bed, but once more the doctor stopped him.

"She's in good hands, I promise. You can see her soon, but she really is okay. Now, let me have a proper look at you."

With a gentle nudge the doctor settled Cal back down and then began to press all over, examining him. As each question was posed Cal responded, but his mind was elsewhere. What had happened? He tried to remember. They'd been standing by the fence talking and then – damn... what else? With his left hand he slapped his forehead. He remembered the bike and taking her out, he remembered stopping and then talking. He remembered about Bobby and the accident and ... crap. The rest was blank.

"What's happening?" he asked urgently. "What's wrong with me? Why can't I remember?"

Doctor Geller took a small torch out of his pocket and shone the light into Cal's eyes. "You have a mild concussion and a few cuts and bruises. As far as I can tell there's no reason why your memory won't return. Sometimes the shock can wipe things out but usually, it comes back."

"I need to know," Cal said as he reached up and pulled at the doctor's sleeve. "I have to remember, Doctor. We were on the bike, we stopped, we talked and then...damn, nothing."

He watched as the doctor scribbled a few notes on his chart, carefully extracting his arm from Cal's grasp. "Do you remember what you talked about?" he asked and Cal nodded.

"Yes, some of it. But I can't help thinking that there's something missing. Something big. Dammit." His voice raised in frustration. "I have to see her," he reiterated. "I don't understand what happened. And now I can't remember a bloody thing..." He slammed his fist into the covers in frustration.

Doctor Geller walked back to the head of the bed. "Lexi is with her own doctors right now, but I promise a nurse will come and get you as soon as they've finished. You have some nasty bruising to your thighs so you might find it painful to walk for a few days. We'll bring a wheelchair for you, especially as you're still a little concussed."

Cal waved his hand in dismissal. "Can you at least tell me what's wrong with her? What happened to her?" he persisted. He didn't care about himself – only Lexi.

The doctor shook his head. "I'm sorry, I don't have all of the information. All I know is that she's okay, but you'll have to speak to her doctors if you want to know anything else."

"And they're still with her?" Cal confirmed. Doctor Geller nodded. "I guess I'll have to wait then," he said as he slowly released a breath.

The doctor nodded again.

"And you have no idea what happened, Doctor?"

"Not really. You'll need to speak to the police soon."

"Why?" Cal asked as he felt panic grip at his throat. "Why are the police involved?"

"It's normal procedure. Please, try to rest and not worry. Lexi's in good hands. You're both doing well. I promise."

With a deep sigh Cal flopped back onto the pillows. Rest? It didn't look like he had much choice.

Doctor Geller left the room and closed the door quietly behind him leaving Cal alone. He followed the swirling pattern of the ceiling with his gaze as he tried to force his memory to work. The horses. He remembered the horses, but he knew there was something else. What was it? After minutes of fruitless searching he let out a loud growl of frustration. Bottom line was, he couldn't remember.

Resignedly he shook his head and then pressed the heels of his hands against his eyes. They must've got back on the bike otherwise there wouldn't have been an accident, yet there was no way he could piece any of it together. There was a complete blank between the horses, the fence and the hospital room.

Cal banged his fists into the bed again and let another cry of frustration go. Never in his life had he felt so weak and helpless. Never had he felt less of a man than he did right this moment. He'd promised to protect Lexi. He'd told her that she could trust him and what the hell had happened? She was in a hospital, because of a motorbike, in exactly the same way as Bobby had been. Christ. How was he ever going to get past this with her? How was she ever going to forgive him? What the hell did this mean for them now? He had no answers. He had no memory and no answers. As far as Cal was concerned, he was royally fucked.

Turning over he curled up into a ball, ignoring the screams that came from his thighs and lower limbs. Making himself as small as he possibly could he hugged into himself, trying to find comfort as he fought a memory he couldn't reach and a devastation from which he saw no way out. Six years ago he had celebrated his nineteenth birthday in a way that defined who he was then. Today he was celebrating his twenty-fifth birthday in a way that was supposed to define who he could be now. Yet, as he lay there, Cal could find no discernible difference between the two.

As the tears began to fall he curled up ever smaller, wishing he were invisible like he'd once wished to be as a small boy. Whoever said life could change for someone like him? He was cursed and he'd ruined his one chance of a different life. With Lexi.

He shook his head for what felt like the hundredth time. Aside from all of that he wished to hell he could remember what else it was they'd talked about. He had to remember, he just had to. Because somewhere, deep down inside, he knew it had been damned important.

Chapter Nine

Lexi

She felt empty; there was no other word for it. Looking at sterile surroundings and unknown faces, she felt lost, like a little girl again.

She was going to be okay – physically. The doctors had taken great care to explain that all of her injuries were superficial – except for one. No one seemed to know what had happened in the accident and Lexi couldn't remember. She knew she and Cal had been returning to her flat and in her mind she could hear the screeching of brakes, but after that there was nothing. Not until she'd woken up here in the hospital with a searing pain tearing her stomach in half. The door to her room swished open and she focused hollow eyes towards the sound.

"Lexi, oh my goodness. Are you okay?"

She braced herself against her mother's hug and looked beyond Bren's shoulder to where her father stood. His eyes were red and she could tell he'd been crying.

"I'm fine," she whispered as her mother continued to embrace her, "more shocked than anything. They say it's all superficial." Well, not quite all.

"What happened? What were you doing on a bike?" Bren relinquished her hold and sat on the side of the bed, grasping both of Lexi's hands. Her father remained static; his identical blue eyes a reflection of hers, watched on.

"It was Cal's birthday," Lexi answered her mother, "and the bike was a present to himself. I don't really know what happened. To be honest, I don't remember much."

"Oh, my poor baby…" again Bren reached forwards and Lexi allowed herself to be comforted. "But you're going to be okay?"

"Yes, Mum. I'm going to be fine." Physically.

Internally she marvelled at the calmness in her voice, how she was able to deliver the information without inflection. Controlled to the nth degree.

"Is Cal okay?"

It was the first time her father had spoken and Lexi snapped her gaze to his. Odd those were his first words.

"Yes. I haven't seen him but they told me he's okay too. Superficial."

"Good." Colin's response was monotone and Lexi frowned at him. "I'm glad you haven't seen him."

"Why?" Lexi asked, and this time her mother turned to face her father too.

"Because it means he hasn't had chance to persuade you it wasn't his fault and that he's not responsible for you lying here." As they watched, his normally pale face began to redden beneath his crop of sandy hair. When he next spoke, his words were tinged with anger. "I want to see that..." he trailed off and coughed. "I want to see him first," he started again, "and I want a bloody good explanation as to what the hell happened. No one puts my daughter through something like this."

"You're angry with him?" Lexi asked, shocked. "I didn't have to get on that bike," she defended, "I'm old enough to make my own decisions."

"He was the driver. He's the cause of you being here," Colin stated as though it were an undisputed fact.

"We don't know what happened," Lexi responded. Having been through every emotion possible in the last few hours, she didn't need her father assuming the facts were cut and dried, nor did she need there to be a stand-off between the two men she loved most in the world. "Until we speak to the police," she finished.

"It doesn't matter what happened," Colin continued. "If he hadn't bought that bike then you wouldn't be here." He was still angry. Her words had fallen on deaf ears.

"Dad, please, I'm fine. Let's just wait until we talk to the police," Lexi implored. She was in pain, exhausted and had just suffered a devastating tragedy. Her dad really needed to back off.

"I agree," said Bren who had so far remained silent.

"Thank you," Lexi breathed as she allowed her eyes to close momentarily.

"No, Lexi," Bren continued quietly, "I agree with your father."

Lexi snapped her eyes back open. "Both of you blame Cal?" she asked incredulously. "What happened to innocent until proven guilty? Dad, you're a solicitor. You of all people should allow both sides of a story to be told."

"We're not talking about work here, Lexi. We're talking about my family and I'm not prepared to stand by and watch another one of my children be hurt or worse, at the mercy of a damned motorbike." The tick in Colin's jaw began to beat and Lexi stared at him in horror unable to believe the speed and sudden depth of his anger. The last time she could remember him being this mad was when she'd been twelve years old on that day of total devastation. Her shock now, at what she perceived to be his misplaced anger, delayed the processing of what he'd actually said and, when finally she realised the content of his words, Lexi could do nothing but gape at her father. He'd said a motorbike. He'd said another one of his children. Did he know about the lie? The room had fallen into deathly silence.

Lexi looked from one parent to the other. Bren remained seated on the bed and was wringing together hands that she held in her lap, her focus on the simple action. Colin was by the door in the same position he'd been since they'd entered the room. His face was still red but his eyes were clear and now they were looking directly at Lexi. She shivered as, for the first time, she understood what Cal meant when he talked about her looking straight through him. Colin was doing the same thing to her now, his gaze intense.

Licking suddenly dry lips, she opened her mouth to speak. "What did you mean, Dad?" she forced out, her voice small and unsteady.

Her father didn't pretend to misunderstand. "We know the truth, Lexi. We've always known the truth." His voice had calmed some although his gaze remained intense.

"Why? How? What?" There were so many questions and Lexi didn't know which she needed answers to. She felt her mother's hand reach across the bed towards her and instinctively she grasped it. Rather than the warmth Lexi was used to though, Bren's hand was cold and damp.

"I saw what happened from the upstairs window," Bren said quietly. "How else do you think I got there so quickly?"

Lexi shook her head in confusion. "You knew?" Her voice was small, barely audible. "All these years, you've known?"

Bren nodded. "Yes."

"Then why didn't you say something? Why didn't you challenge the story Mitch told?" Lexi's head was spinning. Her parents had been lying to her all this time. Somehow the fact that she'd been lying to them too, didn't seem relevant right now.

"My boy was dying in front of my eyes," Bren choked out a sob, "all I cared about was Bobby. I didn't give a damn what happened."

Again, Lexi shook her head. "But later, when the police were interviewing me, why didn't you say something then?" This whole situation, the hospital bed, her parents' revelations, it all felt surreal.

Colin stepped away from the doorway and moved towards the bed. "Bobby had just died, Lexi. None of us were thinking straight. Mitch had already given his statement; it seemed easier to let it go. We knew the police would never find the rider."

Abruptly, Lexi pulled her hands away from her mother. "But you were adults," she said incredulously, "I was a twelve-year-old child. I was scared out of my life but *you* knew better. Both of you." Suddenly she felt an overwhelming sense of anger. "You lied to the police too, yet you let me carry that lie alone, that responsibility. How could you?"

"It didn't matter," Colin said. "Nothing we told the police would bring Bobby back. So what if it was a motorbike? Bobby was dead. Nothing else mattered."

Lexi looked up at her mother, eyes pleading. "Tell me," she said, "tell me why you did this? Why you made me carry that burden of guilt? What kind of parent would do that to their child?" She turned to her father, "And you, you're a man of the law. Did that somehow make you above it?"

Tears dropped down from Bren's eyes and landed on the bed; Lexi

104

couldn't find it in her heart to care. Not now. Colin spoke first.

"We should talk about this some other time. This isn't the right place."

Lexi almost laughed. "You brought this up, Dad. There's no way we're leaving it here. Dammit, you made me believe I killed him." Eight years of buried emotion bubbled to the surface; the anger and resentment she'd felt at losing her precious brother now had a focus. And that focus was her parents. It was the cruellest twist. "Yet you both knew what happened. Who the hell are you?"

She was having a nightmare, she must be. For this to be reality was just too hard to bear. Her parents had known the truth all along, hell, they'd even seen the accident and yet they'd still allowed her to take the blame. And they'd allowed her to live with the weight of a lie.

"We knew who he was," Bren said quietly, "and so we knew why Mitch lied."

"And you chose to protect Mitch?" Lexi could scarcely form the words. "You saw what happened, you *knew* who killed Bobby, yet you chose to protect Mitch rather than your own daughter? You told me I was to blame..." she shook her head, "...and you let me lie."

"It wasn't like that," Colin interjected. "Bobby had just died..."

"I know," Lexi held up her hand in anger, "I was there!"

Colin swallowed and then cleared his throat. "Mitch was Bobby's best friend. He was a last link to Bobby. We didn't want him to hurt any more than he already was so we chose to protect him. We knew he wouldn't get any support from his parents, they weren't like us."

"Like you?" Lexi spluttered. "D'you have any idea what you've done? You put a stranger before your daughter. How the hell am I supposed to deal with that?" Tears ran unchecked down her cheeks.

"No, Lexi," Bren implored, "that's not how it was. We love you. We've always loved you, we just didn't want Mitch to suffer either."

"But it was okay for me to be responsible and carry the guilt and blame?"

"We tried to support you," Colin offered, "you had counselling and anything else you needed."

Lexi brushed at her eyes and, as if clearing them of tears gave

105

clarity, suddenly broke into a sickening laugh.

"Oh, yes," she said bitterly, "I had counselling and a mother at home all the time, but neither of you *ever* gave me what I really wanted. Not emotionally."

She paused and watched as confusion clouded both of their faces. They had no idea what she meant and for the first time, with ever increasing lucidity, she realised they didn't get it. In her parents' minds they'd done the best they could in the circumstances and it was clear to Lexi that neither of them understood the emotional damage they'd done to her along the way. Oddly, she didn't doubt they loved her, but she now understood that neither her mother nor her father had been emotionally equipped to deal with Bobby's death and the inevitable fallout. Did she blame them? Yes. But her over-riding emotion was one of sadness.

"All I needed," she said sadly, "was my parents."

"We were there for you," Bren said, but Lexi shook her head.

"Physically, yes. But not in the way that really mattered. You blamed me, both of you, for being the one who made Bobby fall in the road and neither of you let that go. That was all I ever needed."

Simultaneously, as one unit, her parents moved towards her with outstretched arms, faces etched in pain. Lexi allowed them to embrace her but she tuned out their platitudes. It was too late for those words now. Her relationship with her parents had changed the day she'd moved out and now it had changed again. Whilst Lexi knew she should be feeling distraught, in a way she felt free. The truth was finally out there. No longer did she need to hide behind a lie or smother false guilt. There was no one left to be hurt. Not any more.

Finally the embrace ended and her parents stood up, side by side. They looked destroyed and suddenly older than their years, but Lexi had no interest in offering soothing words. She still loved her parents and she knew they loved her, but now it was time for all of them to let go of the past.

"We truly are sorry, Lexi," Bren said, "we just didn't know what else to do."

Lexi nodded and gave them a sad smile. Finally, slowly, so slowly, they realised there was nothing more to be said and turned to exit the room.

After they'd gone she leaned back in the bed and closed her eyes; she was emotionally and physically spent. Automatically her hand went to her empty womb and for a moment she considered what her parents had done. It felt strange that she wasn't hurting more, but she wasn't. It was as if, for the brief moment of time she'd known herself to be a mother, she'd become grounded and all she could feel now was sadness. Sadness that her parents had never truly connected with her in the way that mattered most and, with that sadness, came knowledge. The knowledge that should she ever nurture a baby in her womb again, she wouldn't let it down, she wouldn't fail it. Not like her parents had just failed her.

* * *

Lexi jarred awake as bile rose up in her throat. The sickening sound of metal hitting metal pounded into her brain and a recollection hit. She closed her eyes against the pain and nausea. Her memory was returning. In her mind she saw another bike, not just the one she and Cal were riding. She remembered it speeding past them on a corner and then she'd heard the squeal of brakes. She saw Cal react as the other bike spun in front of them and then remembered them skidding – a skid which had taken their bike directly into the other heap of pulsating metal. She recalled looking around and moments before blacking out she remembered seeing the other rider lying on the side of the road. The image of the man lying prone now haunted her and she closed her eyes even more firmly in an effort to stave off the memory. He looked exactly like Bobby had done on that fateful day eight years ago – small, young and helpless.

The bile rose again and, unable to prevent it from happening, she retched and grabbed for the cardboard bowl adjacent to the bed. This was too much. After her parents had left she'd thought she couldn't possibly feel any more pain, but now, as she finally remembered exactly what had happened, the pain intensified anew. They hadn't told her but instinctively she knew. The way he'd been lying; it was identical. She knew he hadn't survived. The other rider had died. Two lives had been lost that day.

She closed her eyes against the onslaught of nausea as her stomach emptied. She should have listened to her inner voice and never got on that bike – but regret was pointless now. She had to find the strength to face the next chapter of her life. When finally there was nothing left Lexi raised her head and wiped her mouth. Setting the bowl to one side she leaned back in the bed and placed her hands on her belly. Silently the sobs came and this time she allowed them in. She cried for the tiny life she'd lost. She cried for her parents and for the relationship they'd all sacrificed. She cried for Cal and for his dream that would now be tinged with nothing but tragedy and she cried for the other nameless rider who would never get to ride again. And finally she cried for herself because, at the age of only twenty, Lexi had no idea how she was going to have the future of which she'd been so certain. For only the second time in her young life, she was genuinely terrified.

Chapter Ten

Lexi

"Hey," the door opened to reveal Cal, struggling to negotiate a wheelchair through the frame.

"Hi," her smile of relief quickly turned to a frown. She'd been waiting to see him, sure, after her deep introspection, that he was the key to her future. After crying herself dry she'd realised that Cal was the only person who could heal her pain and she'd been desperate for his comfort. She had not, however, expected to see him in a wheelchair. "Are you okay?"

Cal waved his hand as he finally managed to get through the door and up to the bed. "I'm fine, but I've got some nasty bruising," she watched as he indicated his groin area, "so it's sore to walk. They'll probably give me crutches to go home, but they say it should only be a few days."

"Thank God," Lexi reached down from the bed and hugged him as best she could.

"But that's not important," Cal said. "What matters is how you are. Are you really okay?"

She nodded. "Physically, yes."

"Fuckin' hell," Cal said, "I've been so worried." He let out a long sigh and Lexi waited. Waited for him to ask about the baby. He reached up and entwined his fingers with hers and gently used his thumbs to massage her palms; like he wanted to make sure she was real.

"Do you remember what happened?" Lexi asked as Cal remained silent. She needed to tell him about the baby but he'd made no mention of it so far and it wasn't something she was ready to just come out and say.

"No." He sounded angry. "Not one single thing. I remember the horses in the field and you telling me about Bobby, but then nothing."

At least she knew why he hadn't asked about the baby.

"What did they say about it?" she asked tentatively.

"It should come back; just shock, but shit, I hate this. I hate feeling so useless. And I hate what I did to you." Cal looked up at her and she saw the beginnings of tears forming in his eyes. "I'm so sorry, Lexi," he said. "I can't believe after everything you went through with Bobby..." he closed his eyes and so did she, mirroring his, hiding the pain. He squeezed her hands and after a moment she opened her eyes again. "What a bloody fool I am. I should never have made you get on that bloody bike. I don't know what to say to make it right. You're my life, my world. I should never have forced you to do something like that."

Lexi shook her head and pressed her finger to her lips as tears began to roll down her cheeks. "Shh...please, Cal. You didn't know. You weren't to know. I didn't tell you until we stopped and by then it was too late. I don't blame you. You have to believe that."

"Why?" He pulled his hands away from hers, shards of fire spitting angrily from his eyes. "Why don't you blame me? You sure as hell should."

Lexi shook her head, watching as, agitated, he wheeled himself to the end of her bed. "It's not your place to decide who I should blame." A sudden twinge of pain caught her in the stomach and she winced. Cal appeared not to notice.

"And I don't remember a bloody thing," he continued angrily, almost as if she'd never spoken. He thumped his fist on the end of the bed and Lexi took a deep breath in, riding out the wave of pain. She couldn't, however, prevent herself from grimacing.

"Are you okay?" Cal asked, rapidly wheeling back to her side.

She nodded, waiting. This was going to be it. The moment when he saw her holding her stomach and pieced everything together.

"Where does it hurt? I mean I got lower body injuries mainly, where the bike fell on me. Is it the same for you?"

Speechless, Lexi nodded. He still didn't remember. She wished he did – anything to spare her from the pain of telling him. "Mainly lower body too," she replied, her voice barely more than a whisper as she rode the last of the pain. "All superficial."

Cal grasped her hands and she welcomed their warmth against her ice-cold palms.

"So you're really going to be okay?" he asked and she nodded once more.

"Cal?"

"Lexi?"

They both spoke at the same time.

"You go," she said and he shook his head.

"No, you. It's fine."

"Okay." She adjusted her position in the bed a little and then took a deep breath. "You still don't remember the accident?"

Cal shook his head. "No. I can't help feeling I'm missing something important. Bloody hell."

Lexi could hear the frustration in his voice.

"What the hell was it, Lexi?" he asked as he released one of her hands and used his free one to slap his forehead. "What is it I'm trying to remember?"

Lexi swallowed as she watched his face crumple into a frown. She had two very clear choices – she could either tell him and they could mourn their loss together, or, she could say nothing and see if he remembered in time. She remained motionless as she fought a war in her brain. Right now she was dealing with this alone, this devastation, this emptiness, this overwhelming sense of grief. If she told Cal what he wanted to know, then he would be dealing with it too. Together they would work their way through this and she really needed his support, but then...the other side of her brain kicked in; if he didn't know, then she could save him this grief, but more than that, they hadn't talked properly. She had no idea if he'd wanted the baby. If he hadn't, then she would still be alone with her grief.

Whatever decision she made now would almost certainly change her life.

"Cal?" She made her decision. This was about learning from her past, about realising that hiding behind untruths was never going to bring peace in her life. There was no choice, never had been; she had to tell him.

He looked up from where he'd been holding his head in his hands. "Yes?"

"D'you really want to know what it was?"

"You know?" he asked softly, "you really know?"

"I remember everything," she replied. "I didn't remember the accident until a short while ago, but now it's all clear. I know what it is you're searching for."

Cal lifted his head closer to her, eyes boring into hers, imploring her. "Then tell me, Lexi. I have to know."

"I will, but you need to be prepared."

"Prepared?" Cal asked and she nodded.

She watched as he took a deep breath. "Okay," he said.

"When we were by the fence," she began, "and we'd talked about Bobby, I told you something."

Cal inclined his head. "Go on..." he said. "Whatever it was, I can handle it."

She swallowed, unsure he would handle it, but she'd come this far. "I told you," she closed her eyes for a second and then as she opened them, pinned him with her gaze – she needed him to see the full depth of her emotions. "I told you I was pregnant."

Instantly, Cal's face lit up. "That's it. Shit, Lexi. How the hell could I forget that?" He slapped his forehead. "Crap. I remember now. You're pregnant and we were talking about how we were going to make it work – about our future..."

Slowly, Lexi shook her head and Cal stopped.

"What?" he asked and she continued to shake her head slowly, left to right, allowing the tears once more to fall. "What?" he asked again and then, eventually, she saw the penny drop, noted the precise moment he realised what had happened and witnessed the first seconds of his grief.

"You lost it," he said slowly, quietly, and she nodded.

"Crap." His eyes filled with tears and for an instant she glimpsed Cal, the boy again. Everything was raw, out there for her to see and her heart contracted and then shattered. She couldn't bear to see his pain and she couldn't bear to feel her pain.

"Cal?" she reached a shaking hand out to him and he grasped it, dropping the gentlest of kisses onto its back. For a moment their eyes connected and then she watched as the man she loved crumbled in front of her. Closing his eyes he released her hand. He remained still and then, as if he could no longer bear to be motionless, he grabbed angrily onto the wheels of his chair and steered himself towards the door.

"Cal?" she called. She'd made the right decision, she knew she had, but the fact he was leaving her now when she needed him the most, tore her apart. "Cal?"

He turned at the door, his face ravaged with pain and looked at her one last time before slowly, in the same way that she'd done only moments ago, he shook his head.

The wheelchair crashed against the doorframe as he pushed his way through and then, when the door had closed behind him and silence was all that was left, Lexi let the floodgates open.

She'd been correct, she reflected. Whatever decision she'd made would have changed her life and now she had to live with the path she'd chosen. It was the right path, there was no doubt, yet it may be a path she followed alone. It was like she was twelve years old again only now she didn't have her immaturity as a mask. Today, on Cal's twenty-fifth birthday, every last semblance of innocence she'd retained had been cruelly ripped from within.

And never before had Lexi experienced so much pain.

Chapter Eleven

Cal

It sat in the middle of the bed, its battered redness symbolic somehow. Wheeling back into his own room Cal dashed at the tears that were ever present as he manoeuvred himself to the side of the bed. Carefully he lifted the item from amongst the uniform white sheets, marvelling that it had suffered so little in what had been a life-changing event. The clasp on the box was broken, but still he was able to open the lid. Nestled inside its luxurious lining was a simple yet elegant diamond ring. A ring he'd been planning to place on Lexi's hand tonight. Instead, his stupidity had caused heartache and he didn't have the first clue how he was going to get past this – with her or, worse still, without her.

He studied the ring, turning it this way and that as he watched the light glinting from the single cut stone. It had cost him a whole month's wages, but he hadn't cared. He still didn't care. When he'd bought the ring, however, he'd had no way of knowing that, on the day he planned to propose, he would be alone, in a hospital room counting the unimaginable emotional cost.

"The true paradises are the paradises that we have lost."

Cal spun around to see Lexi standing in the doorway. He shook his head in bewilderment. She was the last person he'd been expecting.

"The true paradises are the paradises that we have lost," Lexi repeated and Cal watched as she made her way slowly into the room. "It's a quote by Marcel Proust – I went through a French phase." Her tone gave little away.

Cal nodded although he was no more the wiser. Rapidly he stuffed the ring box into his hospital gown pocket and watched as she stopped beside the bed.

"This is killing me, Cal," she said as she looked down at him. "And

114

to watch you just leave like that…" she extended her arm to indicate the room further down the hall, "…you can't just expect me to deal with this on my own." Her voice was firm, but Cal heard the wobble and he knew without asking how much this was costing her.

Carefully he lifted himself out of the wheelchair and settled on the bed, patting the area beside him. With equal care, Lexi lowered herself down.

"I didn't think you'd want to see me," he said. Turning his head he looked into her eyes noting the rings around them and the bloodshot remains from where she'd been crying. Moisture was ever present in hers as it was in his and his guilt doubled.

"It was my fault," he said, "that's why I left. I can't bear to see what I've done to you."

He felt her reach for his hand as it lay limp in his lap. She squeezed it, but he didn't respond.

"It was an accident," she said softly. "There was nothing you could've done to avoid the crash."

He shook his head. "If I hadn't wanted to show off, if I hadn't forced you to get on that bike…" he shivered, "…we would still have our baby."

Lexi shifted beside him and he turned. "It wasn't your fault," she repeated.

Cal raised his eyes up to hers and saw nothing but honesty within. "You really don't blame me?" he asked.

"No," she said softly, "I don't."

He let out a sigh and rested his head gently on top of hers.

"We're going to be okay," she said after a moment, "we'll get through this."

Above her, he shook his head. "How the hell did we end up here?" Life had been so good; it had held such promise. For a moment he allowed his thoughts to darken as he considered the part his own selfishness had played in where they were now. It was his desire, his dream to get the bike and he'd given scant regard to how Lexi would feel. Fuck. He was still the same, selfish Cal. He hadn't changed at all.

"My bloody selfishness," he said and abruptly pushed away from her. Though Lexi didn't blame him and deep down in Cal's heart he knew it was an accident, it didn't change the outcome. They'd lost their baby because he'd done exactly what he'd wanted – just as he had when he was nineteen years old. With as much strength as he could muster, Cal moved away from the bed, needing to create distance. Behind him he heard the sound of the mattress creaking as Lexi slowly lifted herself from it.

"If you want to feel sorry for yourself, Cal, then go ahead," she said. "We both lost our true paradise today but we can get through this, I know we can. The question is – do you want to?"

Cal stood rooted, understanding she was leaving and that he should stop her, but he had nothing else to say. He was the eldest, yet she was the one showing maturity and, try as he might, he couldn't bring his thoughts around to anything other than self-blame and yes, self-loathing. He heard her steps shuffle towards the door and then the quiet sound of the lock clicking as she exited. Knowing that he was barely holding himself together and hating himself for letting her walk away, Cal retreated to the bed and, when he reached it, curled once more back into a tiny ball. He needed to hide, just like he'd hidden as a child, only this time he wasn't hiding from his father, he was hiding from the woman he loved and the scars that only he could've inflicted. Cal didn't know how long he needed to hide or, if he would ever be able to face Lexi again, but one thing he did know for sure – he'd never felt brutal desolation such as he did right now.

* * *

"You're a bloody idiot."

Cal had been home for two days and had finally opened the door to Zach's intermittent, but nonetheless insistent, knocking.

"Haven't you got anything better to do?" he grumbled as he shuffled down the foyer and back towards the lounge. The taller man followed behind.

"Nope."

"Then can I suggest you get a life?" he asked.

"Well, if you'd answered the door the first time I came over, then I'd have time for a bloody life," Zach responded.

"I didn't want to see anyone," Cal replied as he settled into the dark brown, oversized armchair. An impulsive charity shop buy, the chair had fast turned into the most comfortable item of furniture he and Keith owned.

"Where's Keith?" Zach asked. "Hasn't he talked some sense into you?"

Cal ignored the second part of Zach's question. "At some conference. Left a couple of days ago after he brought me home."

"And let me guess, you've barely shifted your arse from that chair?" Zach exited the lounge and entered the small alcove kitchen. "Shit. No milk. Seriously, man?"

Cal shrugged as his friend's dark head appeared around the corner. "Not my fault these bastard bruises are killing me."

Zach shook his head and disappeared again. A few moments later he returned with two steaming mugs of black coffee.

"So," he said as he placed them down on the side table, "you bought a bike, you had an accident, you and she got hurt and now you're wallowing – that about sum it up?"

Cal scowled and Zach laughed as he settled on the green fabric sofa opposite.

"Scowl all you like, mate, but I ain't the one feeling sorry for myself."

Cal reached forward and picked up one of the mugs. Without milk it was way too hot and rapidly he replaced it. "It's not that simple," he said, "she was pregnant."

Zach sucked in a breath. "Shit."

"Yeah, shit," Cal agreed.

They lapsed into silence for a moment.

"How is she?" Zach asked.

"No idea. I figured she wouldn't want me around."

Zach had picked up his mug and taken a sip. He choked on his mouthful. "You bastard," he said.

Again Cal scowled.

"You've called her, right?"

He shook his head. "No."

"You selfish bastard," Zach said. "She lost a baby and you're sitting here wallowing?"

"She's better off without me," Cal said, "I am, as you say, a selfish bastard."

"No," Zach said as he rose from the sofa. Crossing the small distance he reached Cal's chair and towered above him. "No," he repeated, "you don't get to do that. Not again."

"What fucking good am I to her?" he asked as he raised his eyes to meet his friend's. "She deserves someone who knows how to look after her. Not me."

"Wow," Zach said as once more he shook his head. "You really are wallowing."

Cal ignored him.

"What did she say? After the accident?" Zach prompted.

He shrugged. "That she didn't blame me."

Zach burst out laughing and then slowly retraced his steps back to the sofa. "I stand by what I first said – you're a bloody idiot."

"Yeah, maybe," he allowed finally.

"Not maybe, you are," confirmed Zach. "You reckon you're selfish? Well, let me tell you what being selfish means."

Cal looked across the room to where his best friend sat.

"Selfish means looking after number one and that's not you. You care about people and the guys and me, we respect you for it. Yeah, okay, in the past you were a selfish bastard, but not anymore."

"You just called me a selfish bastard," Cal pointed out, "less than two minutes ago."

"Yeah, I know," Zach replied as he crossed one Jean clad leg over the other, "but only because of what you're doing now."

Cal leaned his head back against the chair and closed his eyes. This conversation seemed utterly pointless.

"I'm not going anywhere," Zach said from across the room and reluctantly Cal re-focused on his friend.

"Alright," he said, "you can explain how calling me a selfish bastard means I'm not a selfish bastard."

"You're not, you're one of the good ones, Cal, but not right now.

Right now you're sitting here feeling sorry for yourself whilst the woman you love is dealing with the loss of your baby. Alone. If that's not selfish then I have no bloody clue what is."

Cal stared at Zach noting the wise features that he'd grown to love. Dark brown eyes under hooded brows were earnest as they delivered their message, his lined face open and warm. Short black hair bobbed in time with his words and the work shirt and Jeans his friend wore reminded Cal of the work he was missing.

"I don't know what to say to her," he admitted. Which was partly true.

"Well, fuck me, neither do I," Zach responded, "but saying nothing's not working for you, is it?"

No. The pain at losing the baby coupled with the pain of losing Lexi was tearing him apart.

"Just call her."

Cal shook his head. "She'll think I'm a selfish bastard too."

"And she'd be right, but you love her."

Although it was a statement, Cal nodded.

"Then get off your arse and sort this out before you really do lose her."

"It's that simple?" he asked."How the hell should I know?" Zach responded, "but sitting around here in the mood you're in is only going to lead you to one place."

Cal swallowed. "I'm stronger now, you know I am. There's no way I'm going back there."

"I hope for your sake you're right."

"You're supposed to be supporting me," he argued. "Sounds like you've made up your mind I'm going back."

"No. I'm supporting you by pointing out the dangers. Don't let yourself down, Cal. You've worked too damn hard to get away from all that."

"You really think she'd have me?" he asked and Zach shrugged.

"There's only one way to find out."

* * *

He was twenty-five years old yet he felt fifty. Did he look fifty? Years of working outdoors had tanned his face and the light flecks in his hair could be mistaken for grey. What the hell did Lexi see in him?

After Zach had left, it hadn't taken long for Cal to work out the only way he was going to move on was if he was with Lexi – but he also recognised he needed to take the next step. Not only did he need to talk to Lexi, tell her what he now realised and help and support her, he also needed to let her into his life, into that place where no one else had ever gone: into his past – maybe not all of it – but enough. Enough for her to connect with him and for him to feel like their relationship was real, not something that skirted around the outside but never made it to the core. He needed her to know who he was – who he really was – and he needed to trust her to understand. Not only that, he needed to learn to trust himself again and confide in the only woman he'd ever loved. The single obstacle?

Pray that she loved him enough to remain by his side.

Chapter Twelve

Lexi

She'd been back at the flat for three days when finally he called. Part of her wanted to ignore it, treat him the way that he'd treated her, but bottom line was she loved him. Without the support of her parents', Lexi needed Cal more than ever and so, with shaking hand, she pressed the button to connect.

"Lexi?"

Her insides tightened as she heard his familiar voice. It was unchanged yet he sounded older – and hesitant.

"Yes?"

She heard him swallow. "I'm so sorry," he said, "I've been an insensitive bastard. Can we talk?"

For a moment she closed her eyes. She needed him so much, yet, with the pain of the accident, the pain of losing the baby and the destruction of her family, Lexi didn't know if she was strong enough to let him back in.

"I fought with my parents," she said, ignoring his initial question, "right before you and I talked. In the hospital."

"Jeez, Lexi. Why the hell didn't you say something?"

Silently she shook her head. "Would it have made any difference? You were intent on blaming yourself no matter what. You left me alone, Cal. I had no one."

On the other end of the line she heard him draw in a breath. "Shit. I don't know what to say."

"I asked you a question," she continued, needing to get the words out there, "before you left the hospital. I asked you whether or not you wanted to fight for us – to get through this."

"I remember." His voice was so quiet she had to strain to hear.

"And you never answered me."

"I know. I have no defence, Lexi."

She knew, even though she couldn't see him that he would be sitting hunched over, head in hands. Her pose was similar as she snuggled into the warmth of her duvet and the comfort of her bed.

"I've let you down. I know that. I guess I just figured you wouldn't want me around. I thought you'd go back home. To your parents."

Lexi laughed without humour. "No, I had no one, Cal," she repeated. "A fact you would've been aware of had you bothered to call before now."

He remained silent, a moment that stretched between them, weighted. Eventually he spoke.

"There's nothing I can say to make it right, I know that, but I love you. More than you know. Give me a chance to explain – at least let me tell you why I'm the way I am. I want to let you in. I want to tell you about my past. I want you to know the real me."

His words were heartfelt and her resolve began to melt. Even if there was nothing left to salvage, their feelings for each other were too strong, too intense to just throw away. He'd been in the accident too, he'd lost a baby too and even though she hated him for the way he'd treated her, she still loved him and ultimately he was the only other person who knew how she felt. In the end there was no decision to be made.

"You can come over," she said after a pause, "and we'll talk."

"I'll be there in half an hour." The relief in his voice was palpable.

"No promises, Cal."

Down the line she heard him let out a breath. "I know," he said slowly, his words measured, "I know."

Chapter Thirteen
Cal

Nerves sent butterflies chasing around his stomach but Cal did his best to ignore them. She sat on the plain beige sofa in her flat, knees curled beneath her, hands resting on a bright red cushion pulled protectively over her middle. His heart bled as he watched her move her hands slowly up and down, stroking her abdomen through the fullness of the cushion. Grief lay heavy on both of them but he understood that if they were going to have any kind of future, he needed to be strong and open his heart.

"I want to explain something," he began as he settled awkwardly in the matching armchair adjacent, "about why I treated you the way I did in the hospital."

She looked up at him, beautiful blue eyes empty. "Go on," she replied, "I'm listening."

"I've never really had anyone to bounce things off before," he said, "no one to challenge what I thought or believed and so I guess I just got used to doing things my way."

"I can understand that," Lexi responded, "but it's not like we've only just met. We share things, that's the way it works."

"I know," he said, "and you have no idea how many times I've wanted to share this with you but…"

Across from him she shifted to the side, half lying as she settled her head on another cushion, this one bright pink. Absently he watched her movements as he tried to formulate the words.

"In answer to your question," he began again, "of course I want to fight for us. I thought you knew that. I'm sorry I didn't say it."

Lexi nodded but made no comment.

"I realise," he ploughed on, "that if we're ever going to make it through this, we need to be together, and the only way is if I let you into my life – properly. I don't want you on the outside any more. I want you to know who I am and why I'm that way." He paused for a moment and took a breath. "If you'll let me." This was going to cost him, it was going to be one of the toughest things he'd ever done, but Cal knew he had to. There was no other way.

Lexi's eyes remained trained on his face and for the first time he allowed his up to meet them. In their depths they were still empty, but he could see a spark, a light as she weighed up what he'd just said. He waited as she processed.

"You want to tell me about your past?" she asked eventually and he nodded.

"You trusted me with Bobby and now I need to trust you. I have to let you in."

She uncurled her legs from beneath her and sat forward on the sofa, resting her elbows on her knees. "I love you," she said, her gaze downward as she apparently studied the carpet, "so I don't want to end this, but I don't know if telling me about your past is going to help right now."

For a moment he was a little taken aback. Before the accident she'd routinely asked him about his past, his parents, his life before working with Zach, but he'd always negotiated his way around it. Now, he was offering it to her on a plate and she was stalling.

"I don't understand," he said, "I thought you wanted to know about my past. You've always asked about my family, my parents..." he swallowed over the nausea that immediately rose up. "I think it's important we talk about this otherwise I don't see how we can get over what happened."

"How's it going to help me to know what the first twenty-four years of your life were like?" she asked. "Is it going to make the pain go away?"

"No, no..." Cal shook his head and then gingerly moved from the armchair to the floor beside her feet. "Of course it won't, but the way I treated you, that wasn't fair. I want to make it right."

Lexi shrugged and then turned her head to the side to face him.

124

"We were both in shock."

"Yes we were," he agreed, "but I'm not in shock now. I know this is the only way forward for me."

His insides were churning and he felt sick. The things he had to tell Lexi weren't pretty, but if the two of them had any hope of a future there was no way he could keep them from her, not anymore.

He remained on the floor beside her, caressing her calf as he waited. Her eyes flickered, blinked and then he saw the droplet of moisture escape and hit the carpet. His free hand lifted to her face and he rubbed the pad of his thumb gently across her tears. She closed her eyes and then slowly, tilted her head into his palm and dropped a tiny kiss there. After a moment, she brought her head back up and allowed their eyes to meet. He knew that the moisture in her eyes was reflected in his, but he stayed strong, unblinking, letting her know how important this was to him and to them.

"Please, Lexi," he pleaded softly, "let me try to make this right."

Finally, she nodded. "Okay, Cal," she said, her voice little more than a whisper. "You can tell me what you think I need to know."

Chapter Fourteen

Lexi

It felt surreal to be having this conversation now. A week ago she would've jumped at the chance to find out more about Cal and his past, yet now she just felt numb. She was struggling to comprehend so much and had no idea how she was going to take anything else on board. Yet – she must. Shifting a little on the sofa, she nodded.

"Go ahead."

Lexi watched as Cal awkwardly rose from the floor and then moved onto the sofa beside her. She felt his weight rock her slightly as he shuffled until their thighs touched. Reflexively she took his hand as he placed it gently on her leg, his presence beside her reassuring. With Cal she felt safe.

"It started when I was about three or four years old," he began. "My early memories are fuzzy so I can't be certain, but I just remember my dad being angry."

Lexi made no comment. It didn't take a genius to work out he'd had problems with his parents and she didn't want to break his flow. The sooner he told his story, the sooner they could start to rebuild, which was ultimately what she wanted.

"He would come home from work," Cal continued, "and his clothes would smell. Mum would hang them out on the line, trying to rid them of the stench, which, as a child, I couldn't identify. Later I worked out it was smoke and booze. Dad had a fondness for visiting the pubs after work." Lexi nodded.

"Anyway, sometimes when he got home, he'd be really angry. More so than an average day. He would shut me in the cellar and drag Mum off upstairs. I had no idea what was happening. All I remember is the dark and being scared and then hearing Mum crying and knowing I couldn't get to her. I don't know how long I was down there. Sometimes it felt like hours, others, just a matter of minutes."

Lexi dragged in a breath and grasped his hand a little tighter. This was worse than she'd imagined. "Bastard," she muttered.

"Yeah, but d'you want to know the odd thing?" Cal asked and she nodded. "It felt normal. It was like this was the way life was supposed to be. I had no idea it should be any different."

"Christ. How the hell could you think being locked in a cellar at what – five years old – was normal?" She was beyond shocked.

"Because there was only me," Cal explained. "I hadn't started school yet, I think Dad wouldn't let me go to begin with, and so I had no one to compare life with. The kids on the street," she heard him sigh, "they weren't like the kids you grew up around, Lexi. They were rough. Streetwise kids. Used to looking after themselves. In their own way, they were pretty scary too."

"So, what did you do?" she asked, barely able to believe that he'd been brought up this way in what purported to be a modern world.

Beside her, he shrugged. "Dealt with it. Lived with it. It wasn't until I made some friends at school that I realised how wrong it all was. My best friend," he paused a moment and Lexi waited, "he talked me into telling the teacher – so I did. She got the authorities involved, but it was as if someone had tipped my dad off. The day they visited he was sober, not a whiff of anything on him. He explained it away – said we played hide and seek in the cellar and they believed him. My mum supported his story and so that was it. We were left alone."

"And it carried on?" she asked, even though she knew the answer. "Yeah."

"And you didn't tell anyone else?"

She watched as he shook his head. "No point. I worked out pretty early on that my mum would stick by him no matter what, and, without any siblings, I was just one voice. Mum never told me what happened whilst I was locked away, even though I asked her. By then I was still only eight years old. Even if she had explained, I wouldn't have understood."

Lexi widened her eyes. "But he was doing what? Raping her?"

Cal nodded and she watched as shards of pain chased across his eyes. "Pretty much. I never knew the full story, but eventually I worked it out. Wasn't hard."

"Shit, Cal." She had no idea what else to say.

"Oh, there's more," he said, "way more."

"And you were completely alone?" she asked. It didn't bear thinking about a child so young being subjected to so much with no one there to help him.

"Not completely. I had my best friend. His parents weren't that great either and so we hung around a fair bit. Talked about all the things we were going to do when we finally got away. He was really switched on – knew things. He told me he was going to find a way for us to leave and live a better life. Whenever I was with him, I felt hopeful, like I could take on the world, even though at the end of each day I had to return home. But he was amazing. He gave me something to hold on to so between us, we managed to survive."

"Where is he now?" Lexi asked. She couldn't remember Cal mentioning a best friend or indeed anyone from his past.

Cal looked up and caught her gaze. "I honestly don't know," he said, "and that's the saddest part." For a second she watched as tears formed in his green orbs, but then he turned away again. "It all changed when I was around twelve years old – just starting puberty."

Lexi sucked in a breath. "Don't tell me…"

"He didn't abuse me, if that's what you're thinking. At least, not initially."

"Not initially?" Her voice was incredulous.

"No, look, shit…" he rubbed his palms across his face, "this is so bloody hard."

She placed a consoling hand on his arm. Despite the trauma of the last few days she felt hopelessly ill equipped to deal with what Cal was telling her. Did he want more comfort? Less comfort? She had no idea.

"Just take your time," she said soothingly.

Cal shifted in the sofa and leaned his head against the soft back, closing his eyes. Lexi maintained the light pressure on his arm. She needed him to know that she was here, whatever he was about to tell her.

"He explained everything to me, you know, the birds and the bees." Briefly he opened his eyes and Lexi nodded so he could see she'd heard. "He told me – graphically – what was about to happen to me and he explained that it was about power. Fuck." Cal sat forward and then winced. "How fucked up is that?"

She nodded. Seriously fucked up.

"He said that women, they liked us to be in charge. That it was important to show them who was boss and that I would understand as I got older. He made it sound so – normal."

A feeling of cold dread ran through Lexi as she rapidly put some pieces together. His father had schooled him how to behave around women? A father who had undoubtedly been raping his wife on a regular basis. Had he schooled Cal on that too? Quickly she searched her memory banks for every time they'd made love and then instantly hated herself for harnessing the thought. Yet, had it been making love for him? A sudden wave of nausea hit and rapidly she released Cal's arm as she awkwardly got up from the sofa and paced, breathing deeply, trying to control her reactions. He hadn't even finished yet, but did she want to hear the rest? What if he'd been a rapist too? What if he'd been an extension of a sick old man?

"Whoa – wait, no." Cal held his hand out palm towards her. "No way, Lexi. You can stop thinking whatever it is you're thinking. I've never raped a woman. Shit. After everything? You seriously think I'd do that?"

Eyes wide she regarded him. Did she?

"You drop this on me like it's – normal, Cal? You've got to give me a minute. Okay?"

Rapidly he shook his head. "No. No. I never said it was normal. I said he *made* it sound that way. There's one hell of a difference. Believe me."

"But he was your father. How do I know there wasn't some part of you..."

"He was my father in name only," Cal said forcefully. "I knew what

129

kind of a man he was and somehow, even though I was only a child, I understood that what he was doing was wrong. He wanted me to be like him. In his eyes he was all man – no one could better him – and he wanted me, his only son, to emulate everything he believed he was. But I never did, Lexi. You have to believe me. I never did."

Cal's face when he looked across at her was wretched and she registered the honesty with which he was opening his heart. Until tonight she'd never had cause to believe him capable of anything as abhorrent as rape – yet...

"This is too much," she said as she paced once more, "way too much. I have no idea how you think telling me something as *disgusting* as this is going to help our future?" The sickness continued to churn in her stomach and she walked into the small kitchen to grab a glass of water. She was unsurprised when Cal followed. For a moment they stood completely still, flooded by the unforgiving luminescent light that flickered and crackled and bounced off the stainless steel surroundings as they remained locked in an uncomfortable silence.

Finally, Cal spoke quietly. "Maybe I didn't explain it too well."

"You think?" The sarcastic remark was out before she could check it, but she had no energy left to care.

Cal sighed and leaned himself against the counter, running his hands through his hair before dropping his chin down to his chest. "There's no good way to tell you this stuff," he continued quietly, "which is why I've never told you before. I figured maybe it would be better left alone. I didn't want you to judge me for where I'd come from. I wanted you to see me for who I am and I was too scared to take that risk. I don't want to lose you, Lexi, but if you can't trust me enough to even hear me out, then there's nothing left."

Carefully she placed the empty glass into the sink and then mirrored Cal's actions, resting against the worktop opposite. Slowly she shook her head.

"This is all kinds of screwed up – you know that?"

"Of course I know that." He snapped his eyes up to hers and she could see his pain. "If I didn't know that, d'you really think I would've tried so hard to protect you from it? Shit, Lexi, I've only just started and already you've distanced yourself. What can I possibly gain by laying this on the line for you? Let me ask you something – have you ever, until today, considered me to be capable of something as terrible as my father?"

The very question she'd posed to herself only moments before. "No." Her answer was honest and she heard Cal's release of breath.

"Then what's changed?" he asked. "I tell you something about my father and what? I'm automatically him?"

Lexi shrugged. "No, of course not."

"Then trust me. Hear me out. I'm not my father, nor will I ever be."

She nodded and began to move away from the counter, closing the distance between them.

"It kinda hurts that you doubted me," he said softly.

"I didn't doubt you," she responded, her voice as quiet as his. "I just...it was so out of the blue. I didn't know what to think."

"Without trust, there's nothing," he said and she nodded.

"I know and I do trust you. Honestly."

He inclined his head. "Okay."

They were now mere inches apart, their toes almost touching. Lexi could feel his warm breath caressing her cheek; see the sincerity in his clear green eyes. His hair was a little longer now than when they'd first met and the dark blond strands fell in waves across his forehead. Her hands itched to brush it back, her fingers anxious to feel his skin but she remained still. Their physical attraction had never been in doubt but now wasn't the time – they still had an emotional journey to travel.

"There's more," he said, his voice quiet. The words broke through an atmosphere rapidly heating with sexual tension and his breath ruffled the top of her hair. Lexi shivered, both from the sensation of his breath and the anticipation of what may yet happen. Now, standing this close, being back in his aura again, she wondered how she could ever have doubted him – even for a second. He was no more his father than she was like her parents and she'd done wrong by Cal to have that thought – however fleeting.

"D'you want to hear it?" he spoke again.

She waited a beat and then nodded. "Okay."

Cal studied her for a moment, his eyes roving over her face and then he nodded. Interlacing their fingers he guided her back to the sofa where Lexi settled herself and then waited for him to get comfortable beside her.

"So, my father," he continued and then shook his head. "Why the hell I still call that bastard my father I'll never know."

"Doesn't matter," she commented, "just because you call him your father doesn't make him so."

She watched as slowly he nodded. "Anyway," he continued, "he started *educating* me. He told me that women needed to respect me and the only way they were going to learn to do that…" he broke off and looked sideways at her, "…well, you can imagine. On my fourteenth birthday he took me out – I had no idea where we were going – but we ended up in a basement. A club."

"A club?" she asked. "At fourteen?" Why that small fact shocked her considering everything else Cal had revealed was beyond her.

Cal nodded. "He knew the owner. Seemed they were of the same idea. So," he flicked at a speck of dirt on the sofa and Lexi watched as his throat moved. This was getting tougher for him. She could sense his increasing discomfort.

"It's okay, I'm not going anywhere, Cal. I promise," she soothed. "I can deal with it." Could she?

Cal nodded, but his focus remained straight ahead. "He took me to a back room, told me he wanted me to see first-hand what it was all about. There was a girl there. Waiting. He…" Cal swallowed and Lexi felt her heart begin to break in two. She pictured him, a confused, pubescent boy watching his father do unspeakable things to a woman. The only man he'd ever had in his life, the man who was supposed to guide him – but not like this.

"It's okay," she whispered, "you don't need to go on."

At last he turned sideways and she saw his face for the first time since he'd begun this part of the story. His eyes were empty yet still she could see the pain, the raw ache slicing through them as he tried to tell her about his childhood. She could scarcely breathe.

"I'm not going to fill in the blanks," he said, "but what you have to understand is that he made me go to that place again. And again. And again. Until I understood every single thing he did." She felt him shiver and so she reached across to grasp his thigh. Unsurprisingly it quivered beneath her touch.

"Eventually, I told my best friend. I didn't know what to do. I had hormones raging through me. My body was saying one thing and my mind was blown in the other direction. I was so confused. After I told him, we hatched a plan. He made me understand that what was happening was wrong, even though my body responded. Because it did respond, and that's something I'll always be ashamed of." He shook his head and she squeezed his thigh tighter.

"You were a kid," she whispered, "it wasn't your fault."

"No, I know. That part wasn't my fault but…" he linked his fingers with the ones she'd rested on his thigh and then ever so gently removed her hand placing it carefully beside him on the sofa. Releasing it he leaned forwards and rested his elbows on his knees, head in hand.

"He got us a motorbike. I don't know how. My best friend that is," he clarified and Lexi nodded. Now things were beginning to make sense.

"One night, when we knew everyone had gone to bed, we piled onto the motorbike. He had a sister, she was a couple of years younger than us, and he knew he couldn't leave her behind. Somehow the three of us got away on that rusty old bike."

Lexi watched his face and saw the faint traces of a smile.

"That's what the bike's all about," he confirmed. "I saw it as a symbol of freedom and ever since that day I've wanted to own one, to experience that overwhelming sense of freedom again, that release. Only now…" he closed his eyes as she watched and after a moment she mirrored him. She knew he was thinking about their accident, about their paradise lost, because so was she. "Now, it's just a killing machine." His voice had hardened and rapidly she opened her eyes. She was losing him, he was backing away from her, becoming unreachable and she didn't want that to happen. Not now. Not when he'd told her so much.

"Cal," she whispered as gently she pressed against his thigh once more. "Cal, look at me." It took a few beats, but eventually he turned and when he did, she took his face in-between her hands. "It wasn't your fault," she said slowly. "The accident. Our baby. The same way it wasn't your fault what happened to you as a child."

"You sound like Zach," he said quietly. She could hear the emotion in his voice, the tears. "If it wasn't for him," Cal continued, "I'd never have got through. He saved me. He always told me I wasn't to blame."

He looked directly at her and their gazes meshed for what felt like an eternity. Green eyes clouded with tears stared back at her and she held her ground. She had to make him understand that this wasn't going to change anything. Make him see that she and Zach were both right –what happened in his past and again now were cruel twists of fate, nothing more. After endless moments of silent communication, Cal finally dropped his gaze.

"I know I wasn't to blame," he said, "I know that in here." He reached his hand up to tap his temple. "But in here," he tapped his heart, "I'm nineteen years old again."

She looked at him confused. "What do you mean? Nineteen years old? I thought you were fifteen when you left?"

"Yes," Cal nodded, "I was. But it wasn't that simple." He shook his head once more and then pushed himself away from the sofa standing up carefully, his restricted movement an ever-present reminder of the last few days. Lexi watched as he paced away towards the window, staring out, keeping his back to her.

"We got lucky and found a hostel. They took us in. Arranged for us to get help. We even got school places, but I couldn't settle. There was something missing. Something didn't feel right and I knew it wasn't anything to do with being in a strange place. It took me six months until I finally worked out what it was." His shoulders rose and then fell as she watched him take a deep breath. "He'd awakened something in me," he continued, his back rigid as he remained standing. "That bastard had awakened something in me."

For a moment Lexi stared at his back in confusion as she struggled to follow his train of thought, then suddenly it hit her and she recoiled, bile rising up in her throat. No way. No bloody way.

"Sexual awakenings?" she asked, her voice small, waiting for an answer she knew she didn't want to hear.

Cal remained mute, but she saw him nod, bowing his head gently and then letting it remain. As she regarded him, she saw him clench his hands at his sides. "I fought it, Lexi. I really, really did…"

Her mind went blank. Her heart stopped and then re-started somewhere in the region of her throat. A shiver ran through her entire body as dread filled her very being. He'd just confirmed her worst suspicions.

"Stop." The sharpness in her tone surprised even her, but she had to make him stop. If this was heading where she thought it was then she was in no shape to hear any more. Cal remained unmoving. "Stop," she said again, this time a little more calmly. "Please." Still he remained immobile, hands clenched tightly at his thighs.

Her voice broke as she forced herself to speak. "I thought you said you'd never raped a woman." The words coming out of her mouth were alien. This whole experience was happening outside of her conscious mind. "You promised me…" she broke off on a sob and this time Cal did move. He turned slowly around, pivoting on the spot and she looked at him, trying to read his eyes, his body language, anything to make the sickness go away, anything that would stop her stomach churning and the fear from rising. He gave little away. He merely pivoted and then stopped, his hands still clenched firmly at his sides.

"I didn't lie to you, Lexi," he said quietly, "I've never lied to you and I'm not about to start lying now. But the way you're looking at me right now – like you hate me, detest me – is precisely why I've never told you this before." He stayed where he was, across the room and in the back of her mind Lexi registered thanks that he was keeping his distance.

"What are you saying?" she asked eventually, her voice cracking as she forced out the words. "If you found out you needed to deal with those feelings, what are you saying?"

Cal sighed and again closed his eyes. His face was ragged, the effect multiplied by the desolation that hugged his person; the same desolation she was feeling. He said nothing, mute once more and so she took another shaky breath – waiting. It was like a game of poker only there was no pleasure in trying to work out who would break first. It was a matter of survival. Finally, after another two shaky breaths he opened his eyes and looked up.

"I'm trying to tell you," he spoke softly, "that I've never raped a woman. I'm trying to tell you that even so, I've not always treated women the way they deserve. I'm trying to tell you…" He let out a strangled sigh and scrubbed the heels of his hands across his eyes. "I went back to clubs," he cleared his throat. "I visited the same kind of places my dad took me when I was fourteen. I…" she watched as he swallowed, his gaze never wavering from hers, "…I've paid women to let me do things to them. I…" He shook his head and she watched his eyes close once more. Inside of her she felt something die. "What I'm trying to say, Lexi…" his voice cracked but she didn't try to stop him. Not this time. This time she had to hear him out. "I'm trying to say that in a consensual environment, I *have* forced a woman. And that's something of which I'll never be proud."

The cold feeling that had started at her temple gradually made its way down to her toes. He'd paid for sex. He'd forced women and he'd paid for sex. Who the hell was he? This couldn't be happening. This wasn't Cal. Not her Cal. This was someone else. Lexi dropped her head and looked down at her palms. She had a choice, either walk away or accept it and deal. For a moment she searched her heart but she already knew what it would say. She loved Cal and being without him was not an option, which meant she needed him to answer two more questions. Two more questions so she could begin to negotiate this life and allow her heart to start beating in her chest once more.

Finally, she looked up. Cal was still standing by the window. "Is there anything else?" she asked quietly. This was the first of her two questions. Slowly, Cal shook his head.

"Then I have just one more question," she said.

Cal nodded. "Sure."

"Why, Cal?" she asked, watching him closely for any hint of a reaction. He didn't move. "Why the fuck would you do something like that?"

Chapter Fifteen

May 2015

A knock sounded on the heavy wooden door, making Cal jump.

"Sorry," Matt excused himself and went to answer it. Cal didn't bother to follow his movements. The last hour had been the most draining of his life. Living his experiences once was bad enough but now, laying it all out there one more time, was killing him. Emotionally he felt completely done.

"Sorry," Matt said again as he returned to his seat in the chair opposite. "My secretary thought we could use refreshments."

This time Cal did look up and watched as Matt poured out two coffees from the glass cafetiere. Cal had never understood cafetieres. He was an instant coffee man. Just spoon it in and add boiling water. It all tasted the same to him.

"Here." Matt handed him one of the steaming mugs and he took it. The dense bitter smell reached him first followed by the warmth of the cup, which permeated his hands. For the first time Cal realised he was cold. Bone achingly cold.

"Is it normal to feel like you've been chewed up by a ten ton lorry and spat out the other end?" Cal asked as he took a sip of the warming brew and then placed it back onto the table. This was antique and oak with a dark red leather inlay on top. It almost matched the armchairs. Almost.

"Talking therapy affects people in different ways," Matt responded, "but in my experience, reliving the past and particularly painful experiences...it takes it out of you. Yes."

Cal nodded. At least that part was normal.

"Do you feel able to go on?" Matt asked as he too took a sip of his coffee.

"I don't know. What time is it?" Not that he had anywhere to be but it just seemed important somehow.

"A little after five. I'm okay if you are."

"Sure." He turned his gaze to the window and took a deep, cleansing breath. Outside he could hear the dim noise of life carrying on yet in here, it felt like his had stopped – again.

"What happened next?" Matt asked, "once you'd told Lexi everything."

"We took some time out. It was her choice, but I got it. There was so much going on between us and we both shut down. That night. That was when it started."

"It started?" Matt queried.

"The beginning of the end," he replied, "although I didn't realise it at the time."

"She still judged you?"

Cal looked across at Matt as he considered his answer. "I don't know that she judged me, she just couldn't make sense of the person I'd been. She told me she could never see me in the same way again after what she'd learned – and that's okay. I get that. I got that. I really did."

"Even though you'd moved on with your life and changed? Even though you weren't that person anymore?"

He nodded. "Yeah. Lexi grew up in a very different place and although she had her own trauma to deal with, she was always pretty straight down the line. I don't think anyone had challenged her perceptions as much as I did that night."

Matt crossed and then un-crossed his legs. "Cal, you really need to give yourself credit for the way you're handling this, not the events that have brought you here…" Matt held up his hand as Cal began to speak, "…those we still have to address but, to be able to understand the way Lexi was feeling at the time, that takes a real emotional connection. That's what you have to give yourself credit for. You knew when you needed to back off. Many people don't."

Cal snorted. "I knew when to back off then, but that's kind of irrelevant now. Wouldn't you agree?"

Matt shook his head. "No. I don't agree."

Cal snorted again.

"Let's start by looking at what happened when you took some time out and maybe then you'll understand what I mean."

"I doubt it. There's no way you can make me any kind of hero and I won't let you."

Across from him, Matt shook his head. "No. This isn't about making anyone a hero or apportioning blame. Making one person good and another bad is pointless. We all make decisions, Cal. Some of them are not good decisions and we have to live with the consequences, which is what you're doing now. I'm not talking about the person who made that decision. I'm talking about the emotional understanding you have inside of you. The connection you had with Lexi that made you realise you needed to back off previously. How you tuned in to what she wanted from you. Not everyone has that quality."

"Then why the hell didn't I use it when I really needed to?" Cal asked angrily. He'd had no emotional connection or whatever the hell it was Matt was going on about then; back at the precise moment when his life had finally hit the fan.

"As I said, it's not that simple. Sometimes there are external factors, other triggers that make us lose sight of something that at other times might be there in plain view. That's what happened to you and listening to your story thus far, I can't say I'm surprised."

"That doesn't make it right. I can't blame my past for what happened to me. Thousands of people have a shit start in life, but they don't respond the way I did."

"I understand." Matt took a last sip of his coffee and placed it down on the table beside Cal's. "But what I need you to understand is this isn't about making it right. It doesn't matter how many therapists you talk to, how many people hear your story, how many times you apologise – you can never make it right. But, by being here today and by facing it and by learning to understand why it happened and how you can move on, prevent it from ever happening again, that's what this is all about. It's about facing up to who you are, not who you think you should be, not the person your father made you into, nor the husband you felt Lexi needed. This is about who *you* are and that's what we need to focus on. Does that make sense?"

Cal considered for a moment. "I guess."

"The thing is," Matt continued, "you've come here today and that tells me something. It tells me you recognise you need help, that you know deep down inside this person who did what you did – that's not you. And so we need to find you. We need to find the Cal you really are. And the only way we can do that is to move blame to one side. We have to look at your feelings, consider what you felt at the time and how you feel now. Address them, talk about them and piece them together until they make some kind of sense because only when it makes sense to you, will you be able to become who you really want to be."

As Matt finished speaking, Cal allowed a small smile. "You're a hell of a politician," he commented and the other man laughed.

"Yeah, kind of comes with the territory."

"I'm not sure about the blame thing though," Cal added, "I have to take blame and guilt. I'm not ducking away from that."

"No, and I'm not suggesting you do. What I'm saying is that you have to put them to one side for a moment and allow us to move past them and focus on feelings that are going to be more helpful right now. You and Lexi have made peace?"

Cal shook his head. "Not exactly. She isn't pressing charges, but we're not talking. And that bastard Jae, he's baying for blood."

"He might be a bastard to you," Matt observed, "but to Lexi he's important and so you have to try to put your feelings for him to one side too. This is about you and you alone. Does that make sense?"

Cal nodded, albeit reluctantly. He knew what Matt was talking about, but Jae was a bastard. End of.

"Yeah, I guess." If he had to forget about Jae for the sake of his career, nay, his sanity, then he would do his best. The way Cal saw it now he had two choices. One, sit here with Matt and work out how to get his life back or two, continue descending ever further into the pit where he was now and accept that his father had won. Reliving the memories as he'd just done with Matt had made him certain of one thing – he was never going to let his father win and so, with a swift intake of breath, he picked up his coffee cup and drained it. Placing it back down on the table he settled into the chair and then looked directly across at Matt. "Where do we go from here?" he asked.

"We have to go back to where we were. I think it's important. Are you okay with that?"

"Yeah." He was okay with that. In many respects, this was the easiest part of the story. "I can do that."

"So, what happened after you'd spent some time apart? How long was that?"

Cal didn't even need to think. Every single day they'd been apart was burned onto his soul. "Two weeks."

"Right. Two weeks." Matt jotted something onto his notepad. "So, what happened at the end of the two weeks?"

"At the end of the two weeks?" Cal confirmed even though he understood precisely what Matt was asking. "Lexi turned up on my doorstep. Said she needed to talk."

"Uh-huh." Matt scribbled something down again. "What did she want to talk about?"

"It was the strangest thing," Cal replied. Even now, two years later, her opening line that night still threw him. "She knocked on the door, I let her in, she stood in my hallway and looked me straight in the eyes. And then, as if nothing had happened, she calmly took my hand, led me to the sofa and then told me why she'd come."

"And why had she come?" Matt looked up from his furious scribbling.

Cal shook his head in disbelief. "Of all the things she could have said...of all the reasons she could have wanted to be there...it was none of those. She asked me to tell her about Zach. She said, 'I want you to tell me about Zach'. Just like that."

"Okay," Matt nodded. "So, what did you do?"

Cal shrugged. "I told her about Zach."

Chapter Sixteen

Cal

June 2013

He'd not expected to see her again, much less have her take him by the hand, walk him into his lounge and calmly ask him to tell her about Zach. He steadfastly ignored the tingling sensation in his fingers where their hands connected, surprised when Lexi didn't release him as they sat on the sofa side by side.

"I met him when I was nineteen," he began, aware that the mention of his age would likely cause a reaction. It did. Beside him Lexi drew in a breath.

"A hell of a lot happened when you were nineteen," she noted although there was little emotion in her voice for him to decipher.

"Yeah, it was kind of like my turning point." And it had been. Up until he'd started this journey with Lexi, he hadn't realised how much had happened to him at that age, but he was rapidly becoming aware of the symbolism of that particular milestone.

"Where did you meet him?" she asked and Cal drew his attention back to the present.

"Does it matter?" This was the only part of his story with Zach he wasn't proud of.

"Yes." She turned her head to the side to look at him and he felt himself immediately drawn into her. If it mattered to her, then he would tell her and the hell with the consequences. It wasn't as if life was all that rosy anyway.

He cleared his throat and then spoke. "It was at the club. I was there on my nineteenth birthday and so was Zach."

"Right." Lexi nodded and Cal frowned.

"Is that it? Is that all you're going to say?"

Lexi shrugged. "For now."

He watched her for a moment. "Why do you want to know about Zach anyway?" he asked.

Again she turned to face him. "You told me he saved you, that he was important to you. I figured he held the key to how you got from being *that* person," her distaste was clear as she spat out the word, "to being the person I first met. So, I want to know about Zach."

He nodded. Made sense – kind of.

"He was at the club," Cal continued, "just sitting at the bar. I went to the bar after – you know – and we got talking. He's a few years older than me and he didn't look the type. So I was curious."

"There's a type?" Lexi asked and Cal shook his head.

"Well, no. Not really. But he wasn't watching any of the girls or making any moves. He was just sat there drinking. Odd in that kind of club. No one just sits and drinks. Not alone."

"Okay."

He heard her swallow and then felt her grip tighten on his fingers. He was amazed yet relieved she was still allowing them to be connected. With their hands joined he felt like he had a chance.

"He wasn't there for the entertainment. The owner had asked him to quote for some building work so he was looking it over. Zach was waiting for the guy to show, but he was running late – the owner – that's when I came across him."

"Did he show?" Lexi asked and Cal frowned again.

"Who? The owner?"

Lexi nodded.

"Yeah. Eventually. But by then we'd had quite a chat. He asked me how old I was and what I was doing there. I told him it was my birthday and I remember him laughing. He said when he was nineteen he'd done a bar crawl with his mates and ended up on someone's sofa. That's when I began to realise I was missing something."

"What d'you mean?" she asked.

"Mates. Friends. I didn't have any. Even if I'd wanted to spend my birthday a different way, I didn't have anyone to spend it with."

"What happened to your friends? The guy and his sister."

"I left the hostel, Lexi. When I realised I was struggling with my thoughts I knew I had to leave them behind. I didn't want to take them where I was going. Neither of them deserved that and so I left. In the same way we left home, I ran away from the hostel. I haven't seen them since."

Lexi shifted a little beside him. "Where did you go?"

Cal's laugh lacked humour. "The police station. I had no idea what to do so I went up to the desk and told the guy I was homeless. They called social services and found me another place. Another hostel."

"Didn't you make any friends there? What about work? What did you do for money?"

"No. I didn't make any friends there for the same reason as I left that first hostel. I kept to myself. I figured if I was going to be that way it was better if I was a loner. I finished school and then did part time gigs. Whatever I could get."

"That's no way to live," Lexi commented and he shrugged.

"I know that now. But at the time I didn't feel like I had a choice. I got work to live. Did some hod carrying, worked with the bin collectors, knocked on doors for charities – anything that would give me a bit of money."

"How could you have no idea of your future? Did you really think you were going to carry on forever with that kind of half-life?"

Again, he shrugged. "I didn't think about it. Not until the night I met Zach. I always thought I was the smart one. Being on my own, doing as I pleased, no one to worry about or to tell me what to do. I was young, inexperienced in so many ways and so damn cocky." He smiled. "You would've hated me even more if you'd met me then."

"I don't hate you," Lexi said quietly.

Cal snapped his head towards her as he quashed down the small sliver of hope that had just crashed into his heart. "You don't?"

"No." She shook her head. "After what we've been through, I couldn't hate you."

He didn't know how to answer that and so he remained silent. He hadn't finished telling her about Zach and regardless of how they felt around each other, he figured it would be best to finish his story and tell her what she wanted to know.

"So, that night," he continued, "I started to realise how wrong I'd got it. When Zach was talking about his life and what he'd done at my age, I felt this emptiness inside of me. It was like I was this man, this person, but there was nothing other than my physical self. I tried to find something to give me the feelings he was talking about, but apart from the times I'd spent with my best friend as a kid, there was none. I knew then I couldn't live like that anymore. I didn't want to allow myself to become who *he* had been. Who my father had become."

"Talking to Zach made you realise all of this?"

Cal shook his head. "No, not straight away. He told me he needed labourers. Work was really taking off. He suggested I drop by the site the following day to interview, see if I was the kind of guy they were after. So I did and he took me on. It was my first job with regular pay. I can't tell you how good that felt. The first month he kept me really busy. So busy I was too tired to do anything other than work and sleep. I didn't go to the club that month at all. He knew what he was doing, Lexi. He was keeping me away."

"Wise man."

"Yeah," Cal smiled as he remembered. "Funny thing was, I didn't even miss it. The second month he gave me a bit more down time. Told me to relax, do whatever it was I liked doing. He knew. He knew who I was. So, first chance I got, I went back, like I was pre-programmed to go there. Everything was still the same, I mean, why wouldn't it be? It had only been a month. But as I stood there at the entrance, it all looked different – like another world. I couldn't make sense of it. I went to the bar and ordered a drink and sat alone, trying to work out what the hell was going on. Trying to understand why I wasn't in a private room by then..." he tailed off as he felt Lexi stiffen beside him. Shit. He'd got so carried away with recounting the story he'd forgotten she didn't need to hear certain things. "Sorry. Do you want me to stop? I guess hearing about the club is rough."

Lexi squeezed his hand. "No, it's okay. I didn't have to come here and I didn't have to ask. I want to know. I want to understand."

Cal considered her reply for a moment. "What is it you want to understand?" he asked. There was so much to this story, so much to his past, and most of it *he* didn't understand.

"I don't know," Lexi replied, "I just said it."

"Because there's so much to this," he said, "I don't know if I could ever make you understand it all."

She nodded. "That's okay. I just want to hear it.

He inclined his head and regarded her a moment before carrying on. Disentangling his fingers from hers he linked his hands in his lap. "I was in the club alone and had been for some time," he continued. He kept his head lowered, staring at his hands. "I was thinking I needed to decide what I was going to do – stay, or go home. It was a real battle. Part of me wanted to cling on to the familiar, but the other part of me knew it was time to let go. Just as I was about to make up my mind, Zach arrived. He'd known where to find me. He told me the first month had been about keeping me away, breaking the habit and the second month; that was about me working it out. And I did. Zach and the guys, they'd been good to me – kind of like a family and I realised that was the life I wanted for myself. It was the kind of life my father would've detested, but I'm not my father, so I let him go. I've not visited a club since. So, yeah, Zach did save me. Without him I don't know where I'd be today. He saw something in me that I wasn't ready to see myself and he encouraged me to be the best version of myself. He did what my father should've done all of those years ago. He may not be my blood father, but Zach is more of a father to me than that man will ever be."

"He sounds like an amazing person," Lexi said at length.

For Cal, there weren't enough adjectives in the English language to describe Zach. "He is," he agreed simply.

Neither of them spoke and for a few moments, silence descended. It wasn't an awkward silence but, after a short while, Cal felt the need to fill it.

"How're you doing?" he asked.

"I'm functioning," she replied, her voice completely lacking in emotion and mentally Cal kicked himself.

Good question, Cal, he admonished. She'd been injured in a motorbike accident, lost her baby, confronted memories of her dead brother and discovered her boyfriend was a former sex fiend. How the hell was she supposed to be?

"Sorry…" he said. Silence descended once more.

"What're you thinking?" he asked gently when again he could no longer bear the quiet.

Lexi shook her head. "I'm not sure."

Cal nodded. He'd dropped a hell of a lot on her. Being unsure made sense.

"You haven't been to a club since?" she questioned. Her blue eyes searched his and he couldn't remember a time when she'd been more beautiful.

Cal shook his head. "No."

Lexi nodded. "Have there been any other women?" she asked.

"Since the clubs?" he queried and again he saw her nod.

"Not really. No one serious until I met you."

"Did they know about all of this?" She was mirroring his pose, hands clenched in her lap as she studied them.

"No. It's not something I'm proud of. They weren't serious. They didn't need to know."

"You destroyed us, Cal," she said softly as she tilted her head to the left. "You went from being the man I'd fallen in love with to this person I barely know."

Cal nodded. He had no defence. "I needed you to know, Lexi," he said simply. "Nothing has changed for me but what happens now is up to you. If you want to leave, I won't stop you." They were seated so close on the sofa he could smell her familiar citrus scent. He wanted to crush her in his arms and never let her go, but he couldn't. This had to be on her terms.

"I love you, Lexi," he whispered, looking for any sign, any indication that she still wanted him. He would take whatever he could get, whatever terms she offered. He didn't want to face the future without her.

"I don't want to lose you," she responded, "but I can't forget this is a part of you."

"Was a part of me," Cal corrected, "it's not any more."

He watched her beautiful face as emotions raged. He could see his love reflected in her eyes and he knew that she was doing battle with herself. There was something between them, something that had always been there and he needed her to believe in that again. Slowly, carefully, he reached out and touched her face lightly, gliding his palm down her cheek and resting it in the crook of her neck. He knew a moment of relief when she didn't pull away.

"I don't want to fight this, Lexi," he whispered. "It's there, we both know it is. Please believe in me again. Believe in us."

His hand slid around to the nape of her neck and gently he massaged it as he pulled her head closer. She didn't resist and he took that as encouragement, using his other hand to mirror his actions. Cradled between his palms he drank his fill of her beauty, knowing she was giving him a chance. Her eyes told him the battle was over and he blew out a breath. She was letting him in. Giving him one more chance to make them something truly great.

He tugged, slowly, carefully, bringing her lips nearer still and he leaned forwards to close the last, infinitesimal distance. She didn't fight and so he sealed his lips over hers, gently at first, feeling his arousal wakening as it did every time he touched her. He closed his eyes, drinking in her scent through his nostrils, feeling her beauty with his hands and tasting her nectar with his lips. She felt so damn good, tasted so damn good and he needed her.

Within seconds he had deepened the kiss, pushed inside with his tongue, played and sparred as he shifted closer on the sofa, pushing his torso against hers. He was gentle, yet firm. He needed her to be in no doubt as to his feelings and desire and finally, she pushed back against him, anchoring him ever closer as she locked her arms around him.

Inside his mind Cal rejoiced before passion took him prisoner and he growled as he begged to get ever closer, running his hands over her body as he felt her every curve, every sensual inch of her. She was his and he was hers, it was as simple as that.

Cal burrowed his head into Lexi's neck, breathing in her unique scent, one that he would recognise anywhere. She dipped her head to the side and he took the tiny nips that she allowed before he slid his arms beneath her and standing, gradually lifted her from the sofa. With sure strides he covered the distance from the lounge to the bedroom, carrying her with him. As he entered, he kicked the door closed and he knew in that moment, with absolute certainty, he was carrying his future into that room and in doing so he was leaving his past, way, way behind.

Chapter Seventeen

Lexi

August 2013

Aside from when Bobby was killed, the last two months had been the most traumatic of Lexi's life. Coming to terms with the accident, the loss of her baby and her parents' dishonesty was tough enough, but then to find out about Cal's past – it had literally blown her away. There were days when the pressure was simply too intense and trying to complete her uni course was fast becoming a battle she was losing. She and Cal were seeing each other again, but they both knew something had shifted. It didn't mean their love was less real, it just meant they needed to refocus and forge ahead in a different way. The uni library, where she now sat, had become something of a refuge.

"How're you getting on?" Mel whispered as she leaned across the desk towards Lexi.

Lexi looked up from the book she was studying and sighed. "It's not happening. I can't seem to focus."

"Wanna get out of here?"

She nodded. "Yes. Please."

"Great."

They packed up in unison emerging into the breezy, summer afternoon.

"Coffee?" Mel asked.

"Sure. Sounds good."

By mutual consent they headed towards Student Zone, the on-campus coffee shop. Situated in what had once been the large, original drawing room, the Zone still retained many period features including a huge, inglenook fireplace. Low-level wooden tables were dotted around the room adjacent to several mismatched sofas selected purely for comfort. When the fire was lit there was nothing more relaxing than the woodsy scent mingling with the smell of freshly brewed coffee. In many respects entering the Zone felt like a step back in time, yet, the glossy black bar and high-tech steel fixtures brought it up to date both technologically and functionally. It was the hub of the student community and a place Lexi enjoyed being. The noise and the atmosphere always lifted her spirits and she liked that she could be anonymous there; her fellow students too busy with their own lives to know she was the girl who'd lost her baby.

Drinks purchased they selected a couple of sofas towards the back of the room and Lexi sat down gratefully. Like most days she was emotionally worn and she'd long since realised that no amount of physical rest could cure her. It was simply a case of sitting it out until time decided to give her a break.

"Have you heard from your parents?" Mel asked and Lexi shook her head.

"I don't know what hurts more," she responded, "what they did or the fact they've made no attempt to contact me since."

Mel frowned. "I don't understand why they wouldn't try to see you."

Lexi shrugged. "I know, and that really sucks. They're still my parents and whatever happened, we've always been a unit. Not picking up the phone to Mum, not knowing if they even care, it's killing me." She swallowed over a sudden lump. "With everything else that happened I figured giving them space was best. I thought being with Cal would be enough, but it's not. I miss them."

Her friend nodded and reached an arm around to briefly embrace her. "I know. Have you thought about going over there?"

"Only about a thousand times, but I don't know what I'd say. It still hurts they protected Mitch over me. I mean, after Bobby, did they ever love me?"

Mel tilted her head. "I'm sure they did, maybe they didn't deal with Bobby's death and you paid the price. I really think you need to talk to them."

"I thought, after I got out of hospital and felt so alone…I thought Mum would know I needed her, but she never came. Never called." Lexi felt her stomach constrict as the pain pulled at her insides. "Parents are supposed to be there when their kids need them."

"In an ideal world," Mel agreed, "but we know so many people who've been let down by their family."

Instantly Lexi thought of Cal and with a sigh she leaned forwards and lifted her mug. She'd tried to keep busy, seek support and comfort in Cal but life felt empty without her parents. "I do really miss them," she said quietly as she replaced the mug. The liquid had been warm and sweet, providing a soothing balm for her dry throat.

"I think you're going to have to make it happen," her friend suggested. "I'm not advocating what they've done, but there must be a reason they've not contacted you."

"I don't know what though," she responded. "I know it'll never be the same for us, but to shut me out like I've never existed…"

"How about I come with you?" Mel offered. "We'll go after uni today – I don't need to come in, I can wait in the car, but at least you'll have moral support."

Lexi thought for a moment. "Thanks," she said, "but it's okay, Cal's coming over later. Maybe another time."

"No worries," Mel replied, "I'll be here for you whenever and, if Cal's coming over later, I might go check out the new bar in town with Faye. She mentioned a group of them were going, let you have the place to yourselves." Her friend winked and Lexi blushed.

A sudden commotion to one side drew their attention; it appeared to concern a short, slender girl with long brunette hair who was standing at the bar.

"I gave you a tenner," she was saying, her voice carrying around the room despite her diminutive size.

Perce, the bar worker, an older gentleman who tended the bar voluntarily, shook his head. "I'm sorry, love," he responded, "this is the note you gave me and as you can see, it's only a fiver."

The girl slammed her fist on the bar. "You've switched it in the till. I know your game. I gave you a tenner, now give me the right change."

Her voice raised even more and Mel stood.

"What're you going to do?" Lexi whispered to her friend.

"I don't care who's right or wrong," Mel replied, "but I'm not having anyone talk to Perce that way." Within moments she'd made her way from where they were seated to the bar at the front.

"I need it for my 'leccy," the girl was saying, "if I don't put a fiver on the key today then I can kiss goodbye to my 'leccy for another week."

"It's okay, Perce," Lexi heard Mel say as she arrived at the bar, "I'll sort this out."

As Lexi watched, the girl turned around to Mel and snorted. "Who the hell might you be?"

Mel smiled and placed her hand gently beneath the other woman's arm. "Someone who can make sure you get your 'leccy this week. C'mon." And with that she gently, but firmly, steered the shorter girl towards their table.

"This is Lexi," Mel said as they arrived, "and I'm Mel."

The other girl glowered. "What you getting involved for?" she asked. "This is between me and him." She gestured behind her towards Perce.

"Perce is a good guy," Lexi said, "and he works for free."

"So? That just makes him a mug as well as a thief."

Mel kept her arm braced around the short brunette before unceremoniously dumping her in the armchair opposite.

"Nosy bitch," she grumbled under her breath and Lexi inhaled sharply.

"That's no way to talk to someone who's about to give you a fiver for your 'leccy," Mel admonished.

The girl looked up at her. "Straight up? Why the hell would you give me money?"

Lexi watched as Mel reached into her purse and extracted a five-pound note. "Because Perce is a good guy who doesn't deserve abuse from the likes of you."

"Regular Samaritan, aren't you?" the brunette commented sarcastically.

Mel shrugged and handed over the money. "Not particularly, but

I want to drink my coffee in peace and if a fiver will do that, so be it."

Taking the note from Mel, the girl pocketed it. "Thanks," she said, although her tone lacked sincerity. "I'm Tami."

Mel and Lexi nodded.

"You new?" Lexi asked.

"Yeah."

"You won't get far with that attitude."

"I don't need to get far," Tami shrugged, "I just need to do what I came here for."

"Maybe, but you might need some friends along the way."

Tami shook her head. "Nope."

"Suit yourself," Mel responded.

There was a moment of silence and Lexi could feel Tami's eyes on her.

"You the girl who lost the baby?"

Lexi froze. How the hell did someone like Tami know about that?

"Some bloke mentioned it at the bar," Tami said, almost as if she'd read Lexi's mind. With her hand Tami gesticulated towards Spencer, the course dork who'd been trying to date Lexi ever since day one. When she'd refused he'd made it his life's work to taunt her. It figured he'd be the one to spread gossip.

"Yeah," Lexi replied as she returned her attention to Tami and away from the grinning Spencer. Out of the corner of her eye she saw him lift a finger and draw an imaginary 'one' in the air. She shook her head. If he wanted to score points based on her tragedy, then he was even more distasteful than she'd first thought.

"Sorry," said Tami, "must suck."

"Yeah, it does."

"But you and your fella, you're okay?"

Lexi regarded Tami with curiosity. It seemed an odd question.

"Physically? Yes, we recovered from the accident."

Tami nodded. "My mum lost a baby once. I wasn't very old. She cried a lot."

"Yeah. It has that effect. I'm sorry for your mum."

The brunette shrugged. "Long time ago."

"So," Mel interrupted, "hadn't you better go get your 'leccy?"

Tami shot Mel a look, which Lexi couldn't decipher. It was almost like a challenge but for what? The two women regarded each other for a moment and then Tami reached down and collected her bag from the floor.

"Yeah," she said at length, "time I wasn't here. Thanks for the cash." She stood. "Might see you around." She slung her bag over her shoulder and walked away from their sofas and out of the bar.

"That was weird," Mel said.

"*She* was weird," Lexi countered. "The way she looked at you and then came right out and asked me about the baby. Who does that to a complete stranger?"

Mel shrugged. "Beats me, anyway, chances are we won't run into her again."

"I hope not. There was something about her that didn't sit right with me."

"Apart from being bold, brash and rude?" Mel asked and Lexi smiled.

"Yeah, apart from that."

They both laughed.

"Well, I need to go," Lexi said as she glanced at her watch. "I've got to finish the planning for my dissertation and then get ready to see Cal. You don't have to go out later you know."

"I know, but I want to," Mel responded. "You two need some time together after all that's happened – and I sure as hell don't want to listen to it."

Lexi widened her eyes and blushed. "You really hear us?" she asked, her voice lowered.

"Sometimes," Mel smiled, "but it's okay. When I get my hot man, you'll be hearing me *all* the time."

"Ugh." Lexi made a face and her friend laughed.

"Might see you at home later," Mel said as she stood. Together they walked the same path Tami had mere moments before.

"Yeah, okay. And thanks."

"What for?"

"For giving us some space and offering to help with my parents."

"That's what friends are for." Mel embraced her in a quick hug. "Have fun tonight."

Lexi smiled. "Will do." She watched Mel's departing form for a second as she thought about seeing Cal tonight. Things had changed between them but, in the last couple of weeks, she'd felt they were closer together again – not back to where they had been, but getting there. Hugging herself she walked back towards the library with a heart that felt lighter than it had in a long time. Something told her that tonight would be a good night and, if that was true, she was going to grab it with both hands and never let it go. So absorbed was she in her thoughts of Cal that she didn't notice the slender brunette watching her every move from within the shadows of the corridor's decorative foliage.

* * *

Cal's knock came right on time and, predictably, her breath hitched the second she opened the door to him. Seeing Cal still gave her ripples of anticipation and tonight was no different. He'd always had the power to make her heart skip a beat – a hold over her that he knew he had. Dressed in casual Jeans and a light sweater with his jacket slung over his arm he looked every inch the rugged outdoor worker he was. His clothes fit to perfection and outlined his torso in a way that literally made her mouth water and as for his eyes – they'd always been her weakness. His hair had grown even more over the last month and was beginning to hang in a shaggy mess – a mess that Lexi found infinitely sexy. Physically he was her true perfection.

"Hey," she said with a smile, feeling herself completely relax for the first time that day.

"Hey, yourself." He pulled the door behind him and then kicked it closed. "Are we alone?" he asked. Lexi nodded. Bracketing her with his arms he pushed her back up against the door. Lexi's heart rate increased.

"You're so fucking beautiful," he murmured as he pressed his forehead up against hers. "You have no idea."

Lexi clasped her arms around him. "You're not so bad yourself," she commented, her breathing losing its rhythm as he pulled closer. Imprinting his torso into her she felt the ridge of his erection pressing against her stomach and immediately her body responded. This. This physical attraction. This magnetic pull they had to each other. This was what made sense of the rest of the world.

Leaning her head back she connected her eyes with his, studying his depths as he studied hers.

"I will never, ever get enough of you, Lexi," he whispered, "you have no idea how much I need you right now."

Moving her arms from his waist to his head she pulled him the rest of the way and kissed him hungrily. His desire always ignited hers and when it came to making love, they were both as desperate as the other. Equally matched, two starving souls finding sustenance together.

He ran his tongue over her lips and she opened her mouth allowing him access. He tasted of mint and she lapped it up, knowing that he would've made an effort for her. He always made an effort for her. Her hands tangled in his longer hair and she grated her fingernails across his scalp, gently massaging and teasing as she went. In response he ground ever closer to her, his masculinity pushing her hard against the door as they rocked and groaned, each trying to get closer.

"Fuck," Cal pulled back abruptly. "We need to move." He began to tug on her arms, pulling her in the direction of her bedroom but she resisted. It was always in the bedroom – she didn't want to go into the bedroom today. At least, not right now.

"No," she said with a smile, "I don't want to move."

Cal looked at her quizzically and she could tell he was unsure what she meant. "You don't want to carry on?" he asked and she smiled again.

"That's not what I said. I said I didn't want to move."

Cal frowned and then she watched as the penny dropped, a lascivious smile replacing his confusion.

"You want to make love – here?" he asked, gesturing at the tiny hallway.

Lexi nodded. "Yeah. Right here." She pushed her back up against the door so he could be in no doubt of her meaning.

"Are you sure?" he asked and she nodded.

"I realised today it was time to start living again. Really living I mean. Nothing can take back what I lost – what we lost – but I don't want to feel this way anymore."

"And you think that having sex against your front door is going to help?"

Lexi laughed. "When you put it like that it sounds ridiculous, but I don't know. It's just different. Convention states we have sex in the bedroom – but why? We're young. We're not dead yet. I want to live. I'm sick and tired of this weight bearing down on me. So yeah, maybe fucking in my hallway is as good a place to start as any."

Six months ago those words would never have left her lips but, along with her sexuality, she was exploring her own mind now and that included the freedom to say whatever she wanted. She was working hard to lose the shackles of propriety – although she never stepped out of line in public. With Cal though…all bets were off. Especially when she knew precisely what those words would do to him.

"Did you just say what I think you said?" he growled as he advanced once more. The darkness of his eyes told her he'd heard her perfectly and, as she'd known he would, he took no prisoners and thrust her back against the door. Hard. Her femininity responded immediately and her heart rate rocketed off the scale.

This time he initiated the kiss, sealing his lips over hers with force, pressing her as hard as he could, embedding the imprint of his manhood into her stomach. Deep in her throat she groaned. She'd discovered over the months that she liked for him to be like this sometimes, a little on the edge. Since his confession about his past though, their loving had been much more tender, both of them afraid to go back to where they had been. Just in case.

"Shit, Lexi. Really?" He pulled away again and his eyes searched hers. She knew what he was asking. Did she really want it like this? Was she ready?

"Yes, Cal. Seriously. I need this and I trust you. I need you just as much as you need me."

"What if I hurt you?" she could see the concern marring his face and she reached across, smoothing it with her palm.

"You won't hurt me," she said softly. "I won't break and we both know you're not that person anymore. You've never given me any reason to think you are and today I want to live. And I want to trust you. With my whole being."

She watched as Cal closed his eyes and then slowly shook his head. "You have no idea, Lexi," he said as he opened them again, "no idea."

Lexi smiled. "I think I do. And I trust you not to hurt me. It's the next step, Cal, giving in to our true desires. I'm ready. Are you?"

Again she watched as he shook his head. "For fuck's sake, Lexi, what kind of question is that? Of course I'm ready. I'll do whatever you want me to – whenever. All I care about is you. You're my world, my life and my reason for getting up every day. You're beautiful, clever, funny, smart and wise beyond your years. Whatever you tell me to do, I'll do it. Wherever you want me to be, I'll be there. Always. I promise."

His words touched her soul and then flowed out through her veins, affecting her deep inside. For someone who'd been brought up the way he had, to be able to speak from his heart without filtering, was something of beauty. She admired his ability to lay his love out there for her; he knew who he was, who he had been and who he wanted to be and that never changed. He was comfortable in his own skin and he didn't care who knew it. For someone who'd spent her childhood years hiding from truths and reality, it was refreshing.

"I feel the same," she replied as she allowed her hand to gently caress his cheek. "We're never going to forget what happened or likely even get over it, but we can't live on eggshells forever, both in our lives and in the bedroom. I want to be true to myself again, Cal, and to find the magic we had. Does that make sense?"

"Yes," Cal ran his hand through his hair and then lowered it to grasp the one she still held on his cheek. "Yes, it does. Christ, I love you."

159

"I love you too," she replied with a smile, and then she turned it into a saucy wink. "Now, will you just fuck me already?"

"Anything you say," he responded his voice gruff, as once more he ground his lips into hers and secured her firmly against the door.

* * *

Their earlier coupling had been frantic and now they were lying in bed, gently caressing each other in the glorious aftermath. Despite their recent adventures, Lexi felt her body responding again as he swept his hand gently over her bare breasts. For her part she mirrored his actions, tweaking his flat nipples as he lay on his back, head turned to look at her.

"You okay?" Cal asked and she nodded.

"Uh-huh."

"Did I hurt you?"

She smiled. "I think I may have a door handle shaped bruise on my back but other than that, I'm good."

Cal's eyes widened. "Really? Let me have a look. Does it hurt?"

Lexi swatted his hand away as he began to burrow beneath the covers in an attempt to access her back. "Any excuse?" she asked as she threw him a knowing smile.

"Gotta take the breaks where you can," he replied and she laughed.

"You know, sometimes, you only have to ask." Gently she increased the pressure she was applying to his nipples, feeling him jerk beneath her as she did so.

Cal rolled over onto his side and gathered her close to him. "You," he said as he pointed a finger to her forehead, "are insatiable. Some of us are not as young as we used to be."

"No?" Her tone was cheeky. "Lucky for me there are plenty of young men at uni. I guess I'll have to try one out – see how they compare to the old man."

With a growl he pulled her ever closer. "Don't you dare. I might be older than you, but I'm sure I can keep pace with whatever you have in mind. Which begs the question – what do you have in mind?" He winked and she placed a finger over his lips.

"Wouldn't you like to know?"

Automatically he opened his mouth and she pushed her finger inside, groaning lightly as he sucked at the tender pad.

"If it's anything like your hallway idea," he murmured from around her finger, "then you can be damn sure I want to know."

"Well," lifting her left leg she glided it over his and gently ran her foot up and down his calf. His dusting of leg hair tickled which heightened the sensation and her body began to helplessly respond. "I was thinking," she said as she dipped her head to his chest and began to suck on his nipple, "there's nothing wrong with using the bedroom either."

"Hmm…I like your thinking," Cal growled as he arched his back to give her greater access. Following the line down his chest she nipped and licked, knowing without even needing to look, that he would be aroused. Removing her finger from his mouth she shifted a little and placed her left hand on top of the sheet and over him, gently squeezing the hard ridge as she caressed her fingers up and down.

"You better have something in mind if you're going to keep doing that," he growled and she looked up to see him throwing his arm over his eyes. Beneath her hand he bucked and she squeezed a little harder, loving how responsive he was to her touch. Sliding back up his body she pressed a kiss to his chest and then moved upward to his lips. Taking them prisoner with hers she allowed him one deep kiss before sliding her mouth around and down his neck, stopping once more to taste his nipple. Lower down her hand continued to massage him and she felt him buck again. Her own arousal heightened and she knew she couldn't tease either of them for much longer. Not if they wanted to enjoy this moment together.

She shimmied her left leg further up his thighs and used it to free him from the covers. Laid out on his back he was nothing less than glorious and even though she was desperate for him, Lexi allowed herself a moment to just look. Her eyes were drawn helplessly to his groin and for a second she stared, looking at its beauty but also at the light yellow bruising around his upper inner thighs. Almost gone but still faintly there. A reminder of their journey, their tragedy and their paradise lost.

Gently she pressed against one of the bruises with her hand and he lifted himself up off the bed, their eyes instantly connecting. For a moment they held each other's gaze, knowing they were both thinking and remembering and then she shifted her hand, taking his manhood in her palm once more as she raised herself up to a sitting position. Cal dropped back down on the bed and she ran her other palm up and down the entire length of his chest. His breathing hitched and she could feel the hurried rhythm of his heart – she was barely touching him, but she knew that he was close; such was the intensity of the attraction between them.

Carefully she lifted her leg once more, sliding over him so that she could sit astride him, settling herself near to his very essence. He watched her as she looked down at him and connected their eyes, but he remained mute – words were not needed. With a final push she adjusted her position and then slowly took his length inside, feeling him fill her in a way she'd come to need. Cal bucked up to meet her and she threw her head back, pushing her breasts forward into his waiting hands.

With patience she barely felt she began to move, slowly rocking forwards and backwards, allowing him to join with her and bond on the deepest level. It was silent, yet beautiful as they watched each other, eyes telling the story of their love, this coupling reaching her soul in a way their earlier activity had not. That had been about pure need but this was about love too. The elemental eternal meeting of two bodies and hearts. As old as time, unchanged through history, the physical display of feeling and intensity from one person to another.

Beneath her Cal bucked again and this time he remained raised, his face contorted as he fought for his release. Lexi responded, pushing down firmly onto him, moving faster, deeper, harder until she knew there was no way back.

Sensations began to consume her as her heart opened and she gave herself and her love to this man. Whatever the past, whatever the future, they were together in this moment, sharing their love in unison in a way that eradicated any other conscious thought. Cal pushed up one final time and as she watched him groan and find his release she tipped over the edge with him, flopping down onto his chest and curling into him as she allowed the current of their loving to overwhelm her before finally it calmed and slowed. Chests pressed together, bodies entwined they fell asleep, her heart on top of his heart, their very life forces mirroring each other as they slowly began to beat as one.

Chapter Eighteen
Cal

It was in his pocket, precisely where he'd left it and Cal reached for it now, shifting carefully from the bed so he didn't disturb Lexi. His Jeans were at his feet and he felt, rather than looked for the battered red box contained within. He'd kept it. Foolishly perhaps and God knew that during the weeks of their separation he'd intended to return it to the shop more than once. Somehow though he'd never been able to do it and thus it had remained; battered outside, yet beautifully whole inside. Symbolic of who they had been and who he still wanted them to be.

Beside him Lexi stirred and so he rapidly shifted from the bed, box in hand and padded out to the kitchen. He glanced at the bedroom doors belonging to Mel and Faye; they both stood open, beds immaculately made, indicating that neither had come home last night. For Cal, the situation couldn't have been more perfect yet still nerves chased around in his stomach as he began to question the wisdom of what he was about to do. Moving around the kitchen though, he knew he wouldn't delay. Last night had been so perfect, so real and if the last month had taught him anything, it was to grab every single opportunity and make it work. Life was too short – for some it didn't even begin and although he'd never been a philosopher, Cal was determined to learn from his recent harsh lessons. And that started right here, right now, when he asked Lexi to be his wife and secured their future together. For him, there was nothing else as important.

Walking into the hallway he removed his jacket from the coat hook and retrieved a small, buttonhole rose from the inside pocket. Replacing his coat he took the rose back to the kitchen and set it on the tray alongside the cup of freshly brewed coffee he'd just made. He'd never proposed to a woman before and Cal knew he was not the most romantic of men, but he hoped Lexi would appreciate the simplicity of his gesture. Adding the battered box to the tray he picked it up and walked slowly back towards her bedroom. It was now or never and Cal hoped and prayed that what he was about to do would dictate his future and not write his past.

* * *

Lexi sat up as he walked back into the bedroom and he saw her eyes widen as she spotted the rose. The box was tucked a little behind it and Cal knew she hadn't seen it yet.

"Mornin'." He placed the tray on the small table beside her and leaned in for a kiss. She gently responded and he allowed himself a moment to enjoy her taste.

"I made you coffee," he said, lifting the cup and placing it into her waiting hands.

"And bought me a rose," she murmured. Cal smiled; she'd still not noticed the box.

"There's something else," he said and picked it up, watching her face for any sign of a reaction. She frowned a little.

"What happened to that?" she asked. It was, he reflected, a reasonable question given the condition of the rich velvet case.

"It was in my pocket, the day of the accident." Again he watched her face for any kind of response. She remained unmoving, regarding the box, expression unreadable.

"Okay."

Cal wished she would give him something to go on. Some hint that she knew what he was about to do but still she gave none.

"So," he sat down on the bed beside her, "I was going to give you this on my birthday, but things happened and so…" he stopped, that wasn't important right now. "I feel exactly the same now as I did then – more so," he added, "and I can't think of a more perfect time than today to show you how much I love you." Carefully he opened the lid and presented the case to her, revealing the diamond ring nestled safely within. Still her expression was unreadable, but he ploughed on, needing to say the words before all courage failed him.

"Lexi, I love you. I love you with all my heart. I love everything about you. You make me who I am and you've shown me who I want to be. Lexi," he swallowed, noting she'd not taken her eyes from the silver gem that remained in his hand, "will you marry me?"

He watched as her eyes widened and then slowly, she lifted her head. She looked at him, shock, confusion and something else in her eyes. For a moment he panicked. Had he read this wrong? Was this too soon? The butterflies in his stomach began to dance and he felt a sudden wave of nausea. Say something, Lexi, he prayed. Say something.

She lifted her right hand and gently touched the ring, running the tip of her finger over the sparkling stone. "You want to marry me?" she asked and Cal breathed out a sigh of relief as he finally nailed her tone. Disbelief. She couldn't believe he was asking her to become his wife.

"Yes," he replied simply, "I want to marry you."

Lexi raised her eyes up once more and he could see the beginnings of tears starting to form. Happy tears? He desperately hoped so.

"There's nothing in this world I want more," he continued. "To be with you every single day of my life, to wake up with you, to go to bed with you, to eat with you – just everything. I want you, I need you, in every single part of my life. So yes, Lexi. I want to marry you. Please answer me. Please – say something."

He waited a beat, eyes desperately searching hers for any clue as to how she was going to respond, what she was going to say. It took a moment and then she glanced down at the ring one more time. He thought he'd lost her, he thought she was going to reject him and inside he began to brace himself, tell himself that it was okay, maybe he'd just got the timing wrong. Perhaps later, when they'd been together longer, she'd want to commit to him – she was, after all, only twenty years old. She was young. She had her whole life ahead of her. He started telling himself that he'd been foolish, misread their relationship, but it was okay. It didn't mean it was over it just meant it wasn't going to be the marriage he wanted right now and he would need to put things on hold for a while. Still he watched and waited and, when the silence stretched to unbearable proportions, he fidgeted on the bed, ready to leave her, ready to walk away and admit he'd got it wrong. He began to rise, pulling his hand away, the box still safely held within his palm He dropped his head a little as disappointment overwhelmed him, but it was okay, he kept telling himself. It was okay.

He'd just about risen to his feet when her palm connected with his forearm, the pressure gentle, her touch warm. "Wait," she said softly and he chanced one final look at her. The tears he thought he'd seen earlier were flowing freely down her cheeks and he looked at her in confusion.

"I thought…" he said and then broke off. "I thought…"

Lexi shook her head. "I know you did and I'm sorry – I wasn't expecting…"

Cal nodded. "Yeah, I know."

She kept the pressure up on his arm. "Don't go," she said and then slowly, surely, she extended her left hand towards him, spreading her fingers out as she did so. "Not before you've put it on."

It took him a moment to realise what she'd said and then suddenly it sank in. Relief flooded through his entire body and he took the ring from its safe place, sliding it quickly onto her finger, movements hurried in case she changed her mind. Their eyes connected as it settled perfectly on her hand and she smiled, a beautiful, all-encompassing smile.

"Yes," she said at last, her voice soft but firm. "Yes, Cal, I will marry you."

Leaning forwards he gathered her into his arms and held her tight – tighter than he'd ever held her before. Inside, his soul was doing flips, his heart was jumping up and down and his mind was spinning. She'd said yes. She had actually said yes. Lexi, the most wonderful girl on the planet, his true love, his soul mate, had actually said yes. They were going to get married. Fucking hell.

* * *

A pounding on the front door interrupted their whispered plans as they sat cocooned on the bed.

"The girls are out," Cal said, "are you expecting anyone?"

Lexi shook her head. "Maybe they forgot their key." She moved from the bed and Cal watched her delicious backside sway beneath her nightdress as she crossed the room and exited. They'd been sat for what felt like hours discussing their plans and yet still he could scarcely believe his luck. Back when he'd been nineteen, never had he considered getting married yet here he was, engaged to someone he knew he didn't deserve.

Raised voices reached him from the hallway and so shucking into his Jeans, he followed the source of the noise. He could hear Lexi talking and what sounded like another man, yet he couldn't be sure. Exiting the lounge and entering the small hallway he stopped short. On the threshold, front door still wide open, stood Lexi and opposite, her parents. Immediately Cal sucked in a breath. He knew what had happened in the hospital and how hurt Lexi had been by her parents. He also knew this was the first time she'd had any contact with them since and, from what he could see, the reunion wasn't going well.

"Colin, Bren," he said from behind Lexi, "why don't you come in?"

Lexi turned and pierced him with her eyes but he ignored her. Even if she didn't want to see her parents, arguing in the hallway was not a good option.

Colin and Bren looked at him, distaste to find him there, shirtless, in their daughter's flat, clearly written on their faces.

"Look," he tried again, "you all need to talk and that can't happen when you're on opposite sides of the doorway."

Bren sniffed. Cal could still feel Lexi's eyes burning into him.

"Well, I suppose we could," Colin said after a moment. "We didn't come over to argue in the corridor."

"No?" Lexi asked as she moved aside to allow her parents entrance. "What did you come over for?"

Cal preceded them into the lounge and then moved towards the kitchen. He'd not spent enough time with Lexi's parents to know if they drank coffee but he would make some anyhow. He figured Lexi would need it if no one else.

He returned to the lounge to find the three of them sitting stiffly on the sofa. If the situation hadn't been so serious, Cal might have laughed at the sight of Bren and Colin surrounded by various loudly coloured cushions. Instead, he placed the tray of coffee on the glass table and listened to Colin tell Lexi how much they loved her. Lexi remained unmoved.

"So," Bren addressed him as he sat in the opposing armchair, "you're still around then?"

Cal smiled. "Yes, very much so."

"You know it's your fault, don't you?" she asked.

He inclined his head. "My fault?"

"This breakdown in our family." Bren used her arm to encompass the three of them. "Before you came along we were close and now look at us."

Cal began to speak but Lexi held up her hand.

"Really, Mum? You're really going to sit here and blame everything on Cal? Do you know how long it's been since the accident?"

Bren mumbled beneath her breath and Colin had the grace to look shamefaced.

"Precisely," Lexi confirmed. "You have no idea how long it's been and even less idea how much I needed you. I was hurt and alone and you weren't there for me. That can't be Cal's fault. That's on you."

"If you hadn't got on that damned bike…" Colin began.

Cal let out a sigh and closed his eyes. "Why've you come here today?" he asked.

Bren fixed him with the full force of her stare. "To see our daughter. I would've thought that was obvious."

"Then why're you looking for someone to blame? Lexi's been through hell and you've not been there for her through any of it. Maybe I played a part in what happened but you sure as hell could have helped afterwards. You need to accept culpability, just like I do."

"So you agree it's your fault?" Colin asked.

"No! Of course it's not Cal's fault," Lexi interrupted. "Why don't you understand that I made my choice? I chose to get on that bike, just like you chose to support Mitch over me."

"It wasn't like that," Bren defended, "we didn't know what to do, we explained that."

"And I explained it was my decision to ride with Cal that day, no one else's. If all you've come here for is to bring up the past I'd rather you left. I've had to make peace with what happened *on my own*. I don't need you here now, not anymore."

"This is your doing," Bren aimed at him, "before you she'd never have spoken to us this way."

Cal leaned forward and clasped his hands on his knees. "With respect, I don't think you know your daughter as well as you think you do. One of the things I love about Lexi is her spirit. That's part of who she is – nothing to do with me or anyone else."

Bren watched him for a moment, her short dark bob swinging from side to side as she shook her head. "There's spirit and then there's disrespect," she said. "Lexi would never have disrespected us before."

Cal dropped his head, shaking it softly in frustration.

"If we're talking about respect," Lexi offered, "where was the respect when you accused me of leaving home to 'shack up' with Cal?"

He snapped his head back up. Lexi had never told him that part.

"That was a long time ago," Colin countered, "we were angry. Of course we respect you. You're our daughter."

"The thing is, Dad," as Cal watched, Lexi shifted to the side so that she could face her father, "those two things are not supposed to be mutually exclusive yet it would appear they are. For you."

"What's that supposed to mean?" Bren asked.

"Your reason for being here is because I'm your daughter. Not because you respect me. I figured I lost your respect when I moved out but now I'm wondering if I ever had it. You've always blamed me for Bobby and then I find out you protected Mitch…was I ever anything to you other than your daughter?" Lexi held her hands out in question and as she did so, her ring caught the light. Cal saw Bren direct her gaze to Lexi's left hand.

"What the…?" Bren took her daughter's hand and turned it over. "What the hell is that?"

"It's an engagement ring," Lexi responded. She held her chin defiantly, yet Cal could sense how much their approval would mean to her. He shook his head as the silence built. When he'd first met Lexi he'd had a chip on his shoulder the size of England. He'd been lost in his own world, believing his life was worse than hers and yet now, as he watched her parents, he realised he'd been the lucky one. He'd never wondered how his parents felt about him, yet Bren and Colin were as fucked up as anyone he'd ever met. He doubted if even they knew how they felt about Lexi. Clearly something else had died with Bobby that day.

Colin coughed. "You're engaged?" he asked. The shock in his tone was evident.

"Yes. We are."

"I only asked her today," Cal interjected in Lexi's defence, "we were going to tell you."

"Whatever happened to asking a father for his daughter's hand? Huh? Didn't they teach manners where you came from?"

Cal took the hit on the chin. He could take any amount of this if it meant deflecting it from Lexi. "Yes, sir," he responded coolly, "I have manners as good as the next man, but Lexi didn't even know if you wanted her in your life anymore. For the last few months, I'm all she's had."

"Well, I won't allow it," Colin blustered.

Cal tried not to but he couldn't help it. He burst out laughing.

"She's over eighteen, she doesn't need anyone's permission."

"Why can't you just be happy for me?" Lexi asked. Bren, Cal noted, had remained ominously silent.

"This man…" Colin began, "…this person to whom you're going to shackle yourself – he nearly got you killed. There's no way I can ever support this marriage."

Across from him Lexi stood and then paced slowly towards the armchair where Cal sat. Carefully she located herself on the arm. "You don't get to care now," she said quietly. "You weren't concerned enough for my life after the accident so I'm sorry, you don't get a say now."

Cal reached an arm around her for comfort. He could feel her shaking and knew how much this was costing. Lexi was someone who valued family and to have the carpet ripped from beneath her again was pouring salt on barely healed wounds. Still Bren remained silent.

"Look," Cal said, "we love each other and we want to be together."

"No," Colin said again, "I won't allow it."

Sadly, Lexi shook her head. "I'm sorry," she repeated, "but we're getting married, with or without your blessing."

Cal could feel the hurt pouring from her as the two people who should've had her back forever, let her down once more.

In the loaded silence, Bren cleared her throat. She'd been staring down at the carpet and now, as she raised her eyes towards Lexi, Cal could see the sheen of tears.

"I love you, Alexa," she said quietly, "and I'm sorry."

Slowly Lexi shook her head.

"We both love you," Bren continued, "and we know we've not done right by you in the past. We never got over Bobby, not really."

"And you think I did?" Lexi asked before holding out her hand. "Never mind. This is old news, and we can go over and over it but it won't change a thing. Bobby's dead and you betrayed me, like it or not."

Bren sucked in a shocked breath.

"Alexa…" Colin warned but Lexi ignored him.

"It's the truth," Lexi affirmed, "and we have two choices, either we move on and learn to become a family again or we stay bitter and angry. I'm ready to move on, I'm ready to forget but Cal is part of my future. If you want us to have any kind of relationship then you have to accept Cal too. It's your choice. The question is, do you love me enough to accept my engagement and support me on my wedding day?"

As Cal watched from across the room, Bren and Colin exchanged troubled glances.

Chapter Nineteen

Lexi

December 2013

By mutual agreement they'd decided on a small wedding. Bren and Colin had sought counselling following the altercation at Lexi's flat and the three of them were working towards becoming a family again. Whilst neither of them approved of Cal, they'd learned to respect Lexi's decision and so, on the chosen December day, almost four months since their engagement, Lexi was preparing to walk down the aisle on the arm of her father. It wasn't perfect, but it was how it should have been.

At Cal's suggestion they'd chosen the quaint church where her parents had married – an olive branch that Lexi knew meant a lot to Colin and Bren – and the reception was to be held at the adjacent hall. Mel, Lexi's only bridesmaid, along with Zach, Cal's best man, had been tasked with decorating it in accordance with their red and green theme. In keeping with this, Mel was wearing a luscious green velvet floor length gown and Lexi was adding a red velvet sash to her simple, but elegant slip-style, cap-sleeved white dress that grazed the floor and then extended out behind her in a short train. Zach and Cal were to have green and red velvet cravats respectively.

Just before 12pm, in beautiful winter sunshine, Lexi entered the church accompanied by her father. Fresh sprigs of holly, ripe with berries, adorned the entrance porch and the scent of white and red roses assailed her senses. Several floral arrangements comprising the roses and holly hung from every pew and Lexi breathed it all in as she began the short walk down the aisle. At the end stood Cal, tall and handsome and she fixed him with her gaze as he waited in front of the altar steps. His dark navy suit fitted to perfection and a warm feeling settled over her as she drank in the image of her soul mate. She smiled when their eyes connected and then swallowed as a flutter of nerves rippled from her stomach and settled somewhere in the region of her heart. Slowly she continued to traverse the aisle, looking at Cal, her gaze never wavering, yet the fluttering sensation moved with her and lodged itself at the back of her throat. She swallowed again as she experienced a moment of panic, her breath unexpectedly feeling restricted as her palms began to sweat. For some inexplicable reason Lexi suddenly felt compelled to chant, 'it's only Cal, it's only Cal', in her head even though it did nothing to alleviate her rapidly closing throat. Today had the makings of a perfect day. She was marrying the man she loved, her parents were there to support her and her best friend had her back, so why was she nervous? Why was she panicking?

When Lexi finally reached the altar, a wave of coldness ran from head to toe and as she turned to pass her small bouquet to Mel, her hands began to shake. Mel gently removed the flowers from her grasp and their eyes briefly met and as they did so, realisation hit Lexi. A rush of nausea joined the chill now roving throughout her body and, with a certainty she didn't want to acknowledge, Lexi finally understood what was happening to her. She didn't feel nervous, no; it wasn't nerves she was plagued with at all. It was another sensation. One she recognised only too well for it was the exact same sensation she'd felt when she'd watched Bobby lying on the tarmac, crumpled and dying. The feelings coursing through her as she stood next to Cal, ready to take her wedding vows, were the furthest from nerves they could possibly have been; the ice cold shiver and nausea had been the giveaway.

Lexi was experiencing a basic fight or flight response, a feeling of impending doom – yet why? It made no sense. With a determined shake of her head she pasted on a smile and looked into Cal's gorgeous eyes. This was what she wanted and she was going to enjoy every single minute of it – unwelcome feelings of panic and doom be damned.

Cal

They had done it. They'd legally been pronounced husband and wife. Against all the odds they'd survived the worst that life had to throw at them and now they had the rest of their lives to be together and make a future.

"So, Mrs Strudwick," he murmured as they danced later, her sleek, satin gown brushing up against him as he pulled her ever closer, "are you happy?"

Their friends, he had to acknowledge, had pulled it off and the building in which they now celebrated was a far cry from its usual bare existence. A village hall, it consisted simply of a large room with a small kitchen annexe and a corridor that led to the rest rooms. Decorated in utilitarian white, it was usually a cold, functional place yet tonight it felt cosy and warm. Glowing lamps had been erected in place of the bright, fluorescent strip lighting and flowers and balloons hung from every available ledge. The wooden trestle tables were covered in green and red cloths, each of these embellished with a holly wreath decoration. A live band was now playing soothing music from the small stage; further lamps glowed from the back of this stage to preserve the intimate atmosphere which then spilled out onto the wooden dance floor in front. The remnants of their meal – brought in by caterers – had now been cleared and Cal was finally enjoying some time alone with his new wife. All around them, guests swayed along to the calming beat.

"Definitely," she whispered, her beautiful eyes glowing as she looked up at him. "It went perfectly."

"Yes, it did," he agreed, "and you know the most perfect part?"

She shook her head.

"I get to take you to bed tonight and every single night for the rest of our lives." He placed his hand gently on her bottom and pulled her closer, allowing her to feel his arousal.

Lexi giggled. "We're in a room full of people," she whispered, "you're going to have to behave yourself for a little while longer."

"Hmm…" He glanced around, "…the room is, however, emptying.

He pulled her up against him once more and this time ground his hips into her stomach to ensure she was in no doubt as to his feelings and intentions.

"Is this what it's all about for you – sex?" she asked and Cal nodded.

"Of course. Marrying you was the only way to guarantee I could have sex on tap. Which, of course, any self-respecting man in their mid-twenties considers a rite of passage."

He felt her chest move as she chuckled lightly. "You're such a romantic," she teased, "and here I was thinking it was about true love and companionship."

Cal smiled down at her. "Well, of course there is that, but companionship is so much easier to achieve when both parties are naked."

Lexi snorted and abruptly buried her head in his dress shirt. "I can't believe you just said that," she responded once she'd come back up for air. "Anyone here could have heard that."

"So?" Cal looked around in mock innocence. "Any male under the age of forty in this room is wishing they were me right now and those of an older persuasion are enjoying our display." As the words left his mouth Cal experienced a moment of concern, wondering if he'd taken the teasing banter a little too far. To counteract, he pressed his lips gently against hers, but she pummelled his chest, pushing him away a little.

"You," she said with mock affront, "are shameless."

"And you, Mrs Strudwick, love that I am. If it was up to me I'd be doing a damn sight more than just dancing with you right now."

She fixed her eyes on his. "So, it really is all about the sex then."

Cal smiled, loving their easy relationship. "Of course. The fact that you're intelligent, smart, funny and beautiful just adds to the benefits."

"Intelligent and smart?"

"Yes, Lexi. You've just proved you have both of those qualities by marrying me."

Encircled in his arms, she laughed. "Add vain to *your* qualities."

"Oh, I will. I love that you think I have qualities. Some would say you only married me for my money."

"Which would show how little they know," Lexi quipped back and again, he smiled. Who would've thought, four months ago when their lives changed forever, they would have got to this point.

"Actually, that reminds me," Lexi added as she pulled away from his arms a little, "what's happening with your training?"

"See," Cal reached his arm up from around her waist and looped a strand of hair behind her ear, "it's all about the money. I knew it."

Her eyes shone as she looked back up at him. "You know that's not true."

He pulled her close again and dropped his head onto the top of hers, swaying to the still-gentle music. "I know. I love you so much, Lexi. I hope you know that."

"I do," she murmured into his chest. "Luckily, I love you too. Now, just tell me more about the damn training."

He laughed again. He'd finished his day release course in the summer and now Zach was working on training him to do more of the quotes and site visits. "Zach thinks I'm ready to go out and price a few of the smaller jobs. If it all works out then I should be able to move onto the bigger stuff and maybe take on more of the design work. All of this will help me get my own firm later down the line. It feels good to know that I can really have my life in my own hands now. *Our* life."

She lifted her head away from his and he felt the warmth of her palms as she placed them one on each side of his face. "You'll do it, Cal. I know you will. And I'll support you. I only have a few months left at uni before I qualify and with my business degree we're going to do this. We're really going to make the perfect life."

Cal dropped a kiss onto her nose and then pulled her back into the security of his arms as they danced out the song. Lexi still retained an air of naivety, which was part of what he loved about her. Despite what he'd told her about his past and their recent experiences, she still held onto a beautiful, untainted view of the world. There was no such thing as a perfect life, he knew that, but he was going to make damn sure they did the best they could. Getting married was just the start and, even though they'd avoided the subject, he was certain they would try for another baby. Soon. To see her belly swollen with his child was the stuff of dreams and fantasies.

They danced in silence for a few moments, his head full of her, his groin painfully aware of her nearness yet, when the song ended, they drifted apart by mutual consent. Guests were still lingering and Cal knew Lexi wanted to spend some time with her parents. Colin and Bren, against all expectations had stayed the entire day; Colin had even been gracious enough to shake Cal's hand. He knew he'd never have a great relationship with his in-laws, but at least they could learn to live with each other – for Lexi's sake.

Standing to one side Cal watched as Lexi floated from one group to another, laughing, hugging, talking and he shook his head. He had no idea how he'd got so lucky, yet he had. She was his wife – his – and only a damn fool would mess up what he'd got. Together they'd weathered the storm of his past and dealt with the crap of the present and now there was no reason for this marriage, this life, not to be everything he'd dreamed of. It was in his hands now. Everything. All he had to do was be the person he was today and leave everything else in the past where it belonged. That he knew he could do.

* * *

"Hey, man."

Cal turned to see Zach standing beside him, watching as the last of the partygoers departed.

"Hey. Thanks for today." He shook his friend's hand. "I appreciate it."

"You're welcome. Glad you finally made an honest woman of her."

"Yeah," Cal agreed as they both watched Lexi on the other side of the room chatting to Mel. "How the hell did I get so lucky?" he mused and Zach laughed.

"Buggered if I know – just don't mess it up. That's my only advice."

Cal smiled and leaned against the wall. "Don't worry, I don't intend to. Shit though. Me. Married. Who'd have thought it?"

Zach copied his movements and leaned against the adjacent wall. "Yeah, you did have a somewhat interesting start to life."

"Tell me about it."

"What do you reckon he'd say?" Cal asked after a moment of

silence had passed between them.

"Why're you even thinking about him?"

Cal shrugged. "Don't know. I didn't realise I was until now. You know what though – I don't feel anything. It's like even if he were here, I wouldn't care. I finally think I'm free of him."

"That's good, man, real good," Zach clapped him on the back, "just keep looking forward. That's my advice."

"Yeah, I plan to. Zach?"

"Yeah?"

Cal hesitated for a moment. There was something bothering him, lying dormant in the back of his mind. He pulled out a chair at one of the nearby tables and indicated for Zach to do the same. They sat.

"Am I going to be okay, Zach? You know?"

Across from him Zach blew out a breath. "Shit, Cal. You don't ask the easy questions."

"No, I know. But you were there, Zach. You saw me then. You're the only one who did. Can I really do this and never go back there?"

For a moment Zach regarded him and then slowly, he shook his head. "I can't answer that question. Yeah, I saw you then and yeah, of course you've changed. You're about as far from that person I first met than you could be, but I can't say you'll never be tempted."

Zach held up his hand when Cal went to speak.

"You're worrying about it which means you're still aware of it. My hunch says you'll be okay. Just now you told me your father didn't have any hold over you any more so the only person who can jeopardise this marriage is you. Stay in control. Stay aware. That's the best I can tell you right now, Cal."

He nodded as he listened to Zach speaking. He was right of course. It was in Cal's hands.

"I don't ever want to be that man again, Zach. If you think, for one moment, that I might be in trouble, will you – you know?"

Zach leaned forward and grasped his hand. "I got your back, mate. You know I have and as long as I have breath in my body, I always will. But there's something else you need to do, Cal."

"What's that?" He leaned back as Zach released his hand.

"Be an adult."

For a split second Cal thought he'd misheard his friend. Be an adult? What the hell was that supposed to mean? Zach continued to regard him steadily though and so he voiced his confusion.

"I don't understand."

Cal watched as Zach idly drew circles on the table with his forefinger. "It's not just about you anymore, Cal. You have a wife, someone who's depending on you and the only way you can support her, is to be an adult."

He shook his head. "I still don't follow. I'll be supporting Lexi with every fibre of my being. I don't see the difference."

"No," Zach agreed, "you won't. But let me tell you this. There'll be a time in your life when your relationship is tested. I'm not saying that because I want it to be, but, in my experience, even the strongest of relationships have storms to weather."

"We've weathered ours," Cal stated.

"You've had some crap to deal with sure, but life has a way of handing out shit cards, just when you think you've got all your ducks lined up."

Cal frowned. "You saying there'll be more crap?" He wasn't sure he liked the direction this conversation was headed.

Zach shrugged. "I dunno, man, you just need to keep your eyes open."

He shook his head. "We're strong, me and Lexi. We're good."

"You are now, but who knows what's around the corner?"

Cal began to feel his ire rising. "What're you trying to say? That we're not going to make it?"

"Nah, of course not. Look, forget I said anything."

Cal watched his friend for a moment. Apart from the direction of conversation, something else seemed off.

"You okay, man?" he asked. He could barely remember a time when Zach had been so sombre.

"Yeah – I'm good."

"You sure?" Cal wasn't convinced by his friend's tone.

"Yeah – look, just ignore me. All I'm sayin' is if the proverbial hits the fan, be prepared to act like an adult. It's not just about you anymore. Okay?"

"Okay." Cal still wasn't entirely sure what Zach meant but he had a feeling the other man was holding something back. "D'you want to talk?" he asked.

Cal watched as Zach's fingers continued to drum a rhythm on the table, waiting for his friend to answer. After what seemed an eternity Zach looked up and then, fixing Cal with his gaze, he finally spoke.

"She left me. Couple of weeks back. Things got messy and she got out. Left me nothing but a shit big pile of debts. I don't even know half the people we owe money to. As fast as I was making it, she was spending it and now I've crashed and burned. Truth is, Cal. I don't know if the business is going to survive this – much less whether I will."

Cal widened his eyes. "Bloody hell, Zach. Why didn't you say anything for fuck's sake? I just made you stand up next to me at my bloody wedding and witness my oath and commitment whilst yours has gone up in flames."

"We weren't married," Zach responded, "and I didn't tell you because I wanted you to have your moment. You deserve it. You don't need to be worrying about me."

"Jeez, Zach. Of course I'm going to worry about you. You should've told me. What can I do?"

Across from him Zach shrugged. "It's in the hands of the legals at the moment. Even though we weren't married there's some common law agreement. I'm not sure how much of the debts I'm going to have to pay but bottom line – I lose the business."

Cal felt a wave of nausea hit his stomach. "Bitch," he muttered under his breath. Zach heard him.

"Yeah, maybe. But I loved her. Christ, I still love her. Even after all the crap she's left me with. If she was to walk into this room now..."

Cal stood up and shunted his chair to the side so he could sit next to his friend. "No way," he said. "No way do you let her have anything. D'you even know where she is?"

"No," Zach shook his head. "She has family here, but they've not seen or heard from her. She left everything behind, just took her passport and a bag of essentials as far as I can tell."

"She's left the country?" Cal asked incredulously.

Zach nodded. "Maybe. That's one theory the police are working on."

"Which means…"

"If she's gone, there's nothing I can do," Zach concluded.

"Shit." Cal ran his hands through his hair. "You don't deserve this, mate. I'm sorry. And you had no idea?"

Zach dropped his head onto his hands briefly and then looked across at him. "Nope. We'd had a few arguments, sure, but who doesn't? I never thought she'd just up and leave. Went to work one day, came home and she was gone, almost as if she'd never been there. Twenty years, Cal. Twenty fucking years of my life."

Cal shook his head. "Who the hell would do that?" He cleared his throat as a sudden thought struck him. "I don't suppose…"

"What?" Zach prompted.

Cal cleared his throat again. "The police. Have they, you know, looked into foul play?" He hated to ask, but if she'd just disappeared like Zach said, it would have to be a possibility.

"It's not foul play. She took her personal items and left a list of contacts, all of which it turns out I owe money to. She's done a runner, Cal, and there's fuck all I can do about it."

Cal slammed his fist on the table angrily. "Who the hell does she think she is? Twenty years and then she just fucks off leaving a list of debts? How the hell can you be so calm, Zach?"

Zach offered him a resigned smile. "Because there's no point being angry. It wastes far too much energy and right now, I need all I have to keep me afloat. And keep the business. She's done what she's done and yet, the fool I am, I still love her. I would take her back in the blink of an eye. That's what I'm talking about, Cal. Don't be like me. Don't let someone have that much power over you so they can ruin you without even looking back. It hurts more than I can tell you – twists me in the gut every single time I think about it. Every single morning when I wake up alone, for a moment I forget she's not there and then it all comes back. And the hurt and pain is fresh all over again."

Cal stared at his friend. He could tell the man was doing it tough and who could blame him. She'd done a number on him and left him to pick up the pieces. If she walked into the room now, loving her would be the last thing on Cal's mind. He clenched his fists on the table.

"No point in you getting angry," Zach said.

"For fuck's sake, Zach, she screwed you over. How the hell am I not supposed to be angry? No one deserves what she did to you."

"No." Zach's voice was calm and patient, a fact that Cal just about managed to register. "But it's happened and you getting angry is not going to make any difference. Same as me getting angry won't either. Besides, if you get angry you've got a life to lose, it doesn't matter what happens to me, I've got nothing left to lose. It's out of my hands."

Cal blew out a breath. "You're way calmer than I'd be."

Zach shrugged. "That's what I meant about being an adult, Cal."

Cal frowned at him in confusion.

"If you got mad in the past and you couldn't handle your feelings, what did you do?"

Cal widened his eyes. "We both know the answer to that."

"Right. But that's not what adults do. Adults accept the cards they're dealt and learn how to cope. Move on. And they do that without ruining the lives of everyone around them. What good would I be to you or the guys if I went off the rails?"

Cal shrugged.

"Exactly. It's not just about me, you and the guys are depending on me and you're my family. Whatever I feel, whatever I want to do to her, none of that could excuse the devastation it would cause all of you. So, I'm choosing to be an adult."

Cal felt the beginnings of tears prick his eyes and rapidly he brushed them away. He didn't understand how anyone could hurt Zach, let alone someone who was supposed to love him.

"You're a good man," he said, "too damn good for the likes of her."

Zach was watching his finger continually swirling patterns on the table. "Doesn't matter," he said, "I have to learn how to deal with this so I never go back. You must never, ever go back, Cal." Zach pointed an index finger at him. "You need to man up and learn how to deal with things because..." Zach paused.

"Because what?"

The other man shook his head. "Because," he said simply, "if you don't, you'll lose her. Just like I did." Abruptly Zach pushed back from his chair and stood up.

"Wait." Cal put his hand on the other man's arm. "What do you mean? Just like you did...don't say you...?" He couldn't possibly be like Cal? Could he?

"Leave it, Cal," Zach muttered, his voice low but his meaning clear. "That's all I'm going to say, so leave it. Okay?"

Cal shook his head. "No, Zach. It's not okay. What did you mean?"

Zach pulled his arm free. "I didn't mean anything. Just leave it."

"I can't," Cal replied, "you can't say something like that and then walk away. Did you help me because...?"

Zach shook his head angrily and leaned down towards Cal. "I helped you because I could and that's all you're ever going to get from me. So, be smart, and – leave – it."

Cal stared into Zach's eyes for a moment and then dropped his gaze. He didn't want to leave it, but he could see when he was defeated. With a final nod of his head, Zach turned and walked across the dance floor before disappearing through the exit door and out into the darkness.

Cal remained seated, rooted to his chair as the conversation played over and over in his mind. He had no idea how to start to make any sense of it and, unless Zach talked, he figured he never would which left two questions as far as he could tell. One – could he leave it alone and never ask Zach about what had just happened, and two – could he really man up and become an adult?

As he rose wearily from his chair to go and join his wife on their wedding night, Cal acknowledged that he didn't have the answer to either of those questions. Moreover, the way he felt right now, he doubted if he ever would.

Chapter Twenty

May 2015

They were starting a new session. Eventually they'd needed to call time on the previous one and Cal had returned home mentally drained. According to Matt they were making good progress but, as they'd yet to address any of the reasons why he was there in the first place, Cal remained dubious. To his mind, all they'd done was dredge up the past and rake it over and once he was out of the intensity of the counselling room, he failed to understand how that was ever going to benefit him.

"Cal," Matt greeted him and indicated the same worn armchair from a week ago. Cal sat.

"How've you been?" Matt asked as he seated himself opposite.

"Yeah, okay I guess."

"What's happening with work?"

Cal looked at Matt aghast as his anger instantly rose. What kind of question was that? "My ex-wife is fucking the managing director of the company Zach sold out to. What do you think is happening with work?" He held his hand up in apology. "Sorry."

Matt inclined his head. "It's fine. Just remember though, even though it's okay to be angry, it's not always helpful."

"Sometimes, it feels damn good to be angry," Cal said. "Numbs the guilt and all the other crap running around in my head."

"Do you want to explore that?" Matt asked and Cal looked at him in question.

"Feeling angry?"

"Yes. We can talk about your feelings of anger if you like."

Cal shrugged. "I don't mind. I told you what Zach said, didn't I?"

Matt nodded. "He told you to make sure if you got angry, you never went back to that dark place. I remember."

"Yeah."

"What do you think Zach would say if he were here now?"

Cal looked at the landscape painting hanging on the wall opposite. "I don't know if I'm ready to go there. Zach I mean."

Matt nodded and then took a moment before he spoke. "That's fair enough. We don't have to talk about Zach right now, although I think it's important we do soon. Some of what you experienced and why you're here is, I believe, because of Zach."

Cal dipped his head. "Yeah, I know it is. I'd be stupid to think it wasn't. But right now I don't think I can go there." He dragged his gaze from the mountain scene and looked directly at Matt.

"It's totally fine," Matt replied. "These sessions are about you. You lead. You tell me what you need. I'm here to listen and help you work through your experiences. I'm not here to set an agenda or guide you. We take it at your pace."

"Thanks," Cal nodded. "You know," he said after a moment, "I remember one of the lads on the site, not long after I started, talking about his therapist. We laughed about it at the time – poor lad got a right ribbing. Never would I have put myself in his shoes, but it just goes to show. This life – this crap – you never know what's around the corner."

"No, you don't," Matt agreed.

Cal stared off into the distance once more. "I don't want to be angry. That's not me. It's not who I want to be. That's him. Not me."

"Him?"

"My father. The role model to whom I owe my eternal gratitude." If Matt noted Cal's sarcasm, he chose to ignore it.

"I don't know that anyone wants to be angry really. The fact you can acknowledge it though is so much more than a lot of people can do. You need to be proud of yourself for that."

"Proud?" Cal shook his head. "I don't think that's a word I'll be using on myself for a long time."

Matt regarded him. "What happens when you get angry, Cal?"

He shrugged. "The usual. Builds up inside of me, pressure, right from my toes to the top of my head, I can't think straight and then I explode. Bam."

"And do you have any control when you're feeling like this?"

Cal considered the question. "Some. At least, I used to. Before it all happened."

"What about now?" Matt prompted.

Cal shook his head. "Not so much now. To be honest, I'm not sure I even try to control it now."

"Okay." Matt made a note on his ever-present pad. "So, let me just clarify. You said you don't want to be angry?"

"Yeah."

"But, you've just admitted you're not attempting to control it right now. Do you have any idea why that might be?"

"Simple," Cal responded. "I've got nothing left to lose."

"Is that how you really feel?" Matt asked. "I mean truly – deep down, that there's nothing left for you to lose?"

"I told you what I've lost. You tell me."

Matt smiled. "It doesn't work like that. Like I said earlier, this is about you."

Cal sighed. "Okay, I guess that's not entirely true. I've got my business – the bit that's not related to that bastard."

Matt threw him a look and Cal shrugged.

"Right. Well, let's focus on your business then," Matt said after a moment, "Zach sold out to Jae's company when he could no longer keep the business going?"

"Yeah. Jae. That bastard."

This time Matt merely smiled. "And you and the other guys became Jae's employees?"

"Yeah. That bastard."

"But Zach got you a deal," this time Matt ignored Cal's comment, "so that you were free to work on independent projects and build up your own client base? Zach wanted you to be able to capitalise on the work you'd already done?"

"Yeah. That's right."

"Okay – so where are you at with that?"

"After I walked out on the bastard you mean?"

Matt shook his head but remained silent.

187

"I have a couple of requests for quotes."

"Outside of Jae's company?" Matt asked.

Cal nodded. "Yeah. I've got a bit of a client base."

"That's great. Have you worked on them?"

He shook his head. "No. I can't focus."

"That's perfectly understandable after what you've been through although it might be helpful to try. Maybe getting out there again, in whatever capacity, will help your recovery."

"You make it sound so simple," Cal observed. How could he possibly get out there again with so much guilt weighing him down? "Even if I had the confidence to work again, the guilt would kill me. You're talking to me like I'm a normal bloke, like what I've done is okay. But it's not. Trying to tell me to do every day things again – I don't deserve that. That's why I don't want to control the anger. Because I don't deserve to have any kind of life." He leaned forward and placed his elbows on his knees, gaze focused down.

Matt didn't respond and so eventually Cal looked back up. They regarded each other for a moment until Matt spoke.

"Okay," the therapist said at length, "there's something I'd like you to try to get your head around. Remember when we first started these sessions and I told you it wasn't my job to judge?"

Cal nodded.

"That hasn't changed. When I look at you, I see a client – sure, but I also see a man. Someone who's in a bad place right now but who's essentially good. Now," Matt held up his hand, "you can choose whether or not to believe that, but you told me Lexi isn't going to press charges. So, that means, what happened is going to remain a private matter between the two of you and only those you've chosen to involve. You have a chance, Cal. A lifeline. You might not be proud of yourself and you might not feel you deserve it – but that's exactly what you've got. You're swinging from one extreme to the other here and that's what we need to try and level out. Does that make sense?"

Cal thought for a second. A lifeline? He'd never thought about it like that. He knew Lexi had agreed not to press charges, but he'd figured that was purely for her own benefit – because Jae was involved.

"I never thought of it as a lifeline before," he voiced. "I knew I was lucky she wasn't going to pursue it, but I thought it was because *he* was on the scene." Cal couldn't help the inflection, "I guessed she didn't want everyone to know her business."

Matt shrugged. "That may well have been her motivation but that isn't really important. What matters is you have this chance now and it's my job to try to help you grasp it with both hands."

"By getting back out there?" he asked.

"It's a start. If you feel up to it."

Cal leaned back in the chair and considered for a moment. He'd not worked for almost three months. The only thing he did every single day was visit Zach's grave. The rest of his time was taken up dealing with the fallout from his life and wallowing in self-pity. Now and again he saw Tami, but he knew if it wasn't for those daily visits to Zach, he would've thrown in the towel a long time ago.

"Maybe," he agreed.

"Good."

"You know it's not just about Jae being with Lexi?"

"Sorry?" Matt asked. "You've lost me."

"My issue with Jae," Cal clarified. He had no idea why he'd just blurted that out. Talking about Jae had been the furthest thing from his mind.

"No. I don't think I do," Matt said, "there's still a lot of ground for us to cover."

Cal nodded. "True. Do we need to go back over every single detail though?"

Matt shrugged. "It's up to you. We can talk about your past in as much or as little detail as you want to. If you feel that going back over things isn't helping anymore, then we can change tack."

Cal clasped his hands together. "I'm not sure what is or isn't helping right now. I mean, talking about my past is tough, really tough, but at the same time, it's a relief too. To be able to talk about everything that happened and know you're actually hearing me – that's pretty powerful."

Matt smiled. "I once had a client who told me the reason she enjoyed talking therapy so much was that she got to spend a whole hour with someone who listened to her. You're right, Cal. It is powerful and, if we can unpick things or identify ways forward, then it's even more beneficial."

Cal nodded. He could see how that would work. "Should we talk about Jae?"

Matt watched him for a moment. "If you want to talk about Jae then of course, but let me ask you something. You mentioned Lexi wasn't the only problem you had with Jae, so I'm guessing there are things that need to be aired?"

"Yes."

"However, Jae wasn't around initially, when things first started to go wrong, was he?"

Cal thought for a moment. In his mind it felt like Jae had been around poisoning his life forever. "No," he admitted at last. "Not at first."

"I was just thinking, maybe it would be useful to understand what happened to start with, what the catalyst was that led to you being here today – or, at least, part of what it was."

"That means going back again," Cal stated.

"Yes," Matt agreed, "it does. Would you be willing to carry on and piece this together as we've been doing or do you want to go straight to Jae, or maybe even Zach? As I said, it's entirely up to you. I take my cues from you and we go at your pace. All I ask is that you think – honestly – about what's going to help you the most right now."

Cal dropped his head between his knees once more. "I have no idea. I've gone from having a wife, a career and a best friend to having almost nothing. Part of me doesn't even know if I want to get it back. Part of me just wants to give up and stop fighting. Especially when I don't know what I'm fighting for. I mean, sure, I have this 'lifeline', but what am I going to do with it? Go out and quote for a couple of jobs but then what? I've never worked without Zach – I wouldn't even know where to start," his voice broke as he thought about the best friend he would never see again.

"I understand," Matt's voice was calming. "I get there are times when the fight seems tougher than the value of the end prize."

"You selfish bastard, Zach," he muttered to himself, "why did you have to leave me?"

"Cal?"

He looked up. He knew his eyes were full of unshed tears and that Matt would notice.

"You're being incredibly brave, Cal. I need you to believe that. What…" Matt said and then paused, "…what would Zach tell you to do?"

Cal half smiled. "He'd tell me to get a grip. He was never one to show emotion."

Matt smiled. "Okay. That's good."

"And he'd tear me off a strip for being here in the first place. Zach didn't really do talking. But if only he'd talked to me…" his voice broke again. "Sorry…it's just…"

"It's okay." Matt's voice was reassuring. "How long has it been, Cal?"

Cal took a deep breath and closed his eyes. "Four months. Feels like yesterday."

"That's tough. I'm sorry."

"Yeah, me too. I mean, for a while, I tried to carry on. I went to work, propped up the guys, carried on the business, but it was too much. With Lexi and Jae and then with Zach gone…" Cal's voice trailed off.

"That's why I told you you're being brave," Matt said. "It's only been a few months since you lost your best friend and your marriage broke down. Regardless of how you feel, you are being brave. Trust me."

"Maybe." He still didn't feel anything remotely close to brave. "Zach would tell me to suck it up," he said after a moment. "He'd tell me to do whatever the hell I needed to get myself back out there. He wouldn't want me to give it all up. Despite being such a selfish bastard and doing precisely that. He was a great one for giving everyone else advice and never taking any himself."

Matt nodded. "There are a lot of people like that. That's the second time you've called Zach selfish though. Do you really think he was being selfish?"

"What else would you call it?" he asked. "He took the cowards' way out. Pills for fuck's sake. He left me. He left everyone who cared about him. Why? Why would he do that?" Emotion, still raw, rose to the surface. "He had friends, he had me – he had people who loved him. Why the hell couldn't he see that?"

Across from him Matt remained silent, watching as the tears now flowed freely down Cal's cheeks.

"Have you grieved for him?" Matt asked eventually and Cal shook his head.

"No. I was too busy being angry with him for leaving me and consumed with Lexi and that bastard." The tears flowed faster and he watched as they began to plop onto the awful grey carpet. Dark rings appeared where they landed.

"You need to grieve for him, Cal. And I believe that's what's happening now. You're allowing yourself to acknowledge that he's gone."

"He took the selfish way out, Matt. Why would he do that?"

Matt leaned forward and passed him a tissue. "I can't answer that, Cal. But I want you to hear what you've just said if you can. Can you do that?"

"What?" Cal looked up and focused on his therapist. "What did I just say?"

"You told me that Zach had people who loved him – friends – people who cared about him and you were angry he'd chosen to leave you all. You're in exactly the same place right now. You have those people too. You're angry with Zach for the decision he made. Think about that and think about how your friends will feel if you allow what's happened to dictate your future. You can change it, Cal. You have the power – the lifeline – to start again. What would you tell Zach to do if he were you?"

Cal shook his head and offered Matt a watery smile. "You're still one hell of a poker player."

Matt dipped his head to the side. "What would you tell Zach to do?" he repeated and Cal shook his head before briefly closing his eyes.

"I would tell him not to leave me. I would tell him to fight and I would tell him to take every chance he possibly could. That his life was worth so much more."

"And what would he say to you?" Matt asked softly.

Again Cal shook his head. "You're damn good at your job," he commented, acknowledging that Matt had expertly turned the situation around.

"I try."

"He would say to me," Cal paused as he swallowed over the emotion in his voice, hearing the same words now that he heard every single day as he sat beside a grey lump of stone in a cold, damp cemetery. "He would say everything I just told you now. And he would have my hide for even thinking about giving up. He would tell me to fight, Matt."

"I'm sure he would," Matt agreed.

Cal shook his head. "Man, this therapy stuff's tough."

"No one ever said it was easy. Hopefully it's helping you to see things more clearly though?"

"I guess." He took a deep breath in and then let it slowly out. "He left me, but I owe this to him, Matt. I knew that from the very first day I visited his grave, but I didn't have the courage. Sure, I did the deal because I knew he would've wanted me to, but the rest of my life, it's been on hold. Now I know I have to do this, not just for me, but for Zach – the only father I ever had. I'm going to deal with my demons – all of them – and I'm going to go on and make the best life for myself I can. I owe that to Zach, the only true gentleman I've ever known."

Matt nodded although he didn't speak. That was okay though. Cal knew what he needed to do. The therapist had done his job – for now.

"Let's go back to where we were," Cal said determinedly, "and let's put this crap to bed once and for all. For me and for Zach."

Matt leaned back in his chair and crossed his legs. "Sounds good, Cal. Just tell me whatever you feel comfortable with – I know this is going to get tougher from here on in."

Cal shook his head. "It's going to be tough, but you know what, I'm looking forward to it. I have to be free. Not in the way Zach is, but in my own way and if that means going through it all again, then so be it. Bring it on."

Across from him Matt smiled and, lifting a small bell on the table, he rang it. The tinny sound echoed around the room and Cal looked at him questioningly.

"I think we're going to need coffee," Matt said and Cal nodded.

Coffee sounded like a good plan.

Chapter Twenty-One
Cal

June 2014

Cal thought his heart would explode with pride. A few metres in front of him he watched as Lexi climbed the three small steps to the podium, her black gown billowing out behind her. Graduation. She was now the bona fide holder of a business degree. Cal clapped loudly as she accepted her certificate from the Dean. Beside him, Zach did the same. In deference to the warm weather, the graduation ceremony was taking place in the university grounds and the podium that Lexi had just mounted led to a makeshift stage erected on the main lawn area. On the stage stood several distinguished guests, each of who shook Lexi's hand as she passed them by.

"They made it," he said to Zach, "they actually made it."

He and Zach were seated in the theatre style rows of fold up chairs that had been lined up to face the stage.

"Yup. They did." The other man beamed as they both watched Mel make the same journey as Lexi.

"Fully qualified. I guess we better watch our backs now," Cal commented and Zach laughed.

"I never thought I'd see anyone graduate. This is up there as one of my proudest moments."

Cal glanced across at Zach and saw moisture in the older man's eyes as he spoke. The road for Zach over the last six months had been harder than he would have wished on his worst enemy, but somehow Zach was still standing. Getting together recently with Mel, though a surprise, seemed to have given him a reason to try again – a new focus on life. Cal clapped his friend on the back.

"It's special for all of us," he responded, "it's the start of the next chapter."

"Yeah," Zach echoed, "it is."

"So, what are you and Mel doing tonight to celebrate?" Cal asked.

His friend shrugged. "I don't know. I said I'd leave it up to her – see how she feels. How about you and Lexi?"

"Same. I was gonna book a swanky dinner, but then I figured it would be a full on day. Might just chill out at home – if you know what I mean." Cal winked across at Zach and the other man laughed. After they'd got married, Lexi had moved into Cal's flat. Keith, his lodger, had left a few months earlier to take a job up north thus Cal's former bachelor pad was now their marital residence. Less bachelor, more home.

"Yeah. I guess I could be in that too," Zach responded with a smile.

This time they both laughed and then lapsed back into silence as they watched the next class receiving their graduation certificates. To their right, Cal could see Lexi and Mel chatting with their respective parents. They were waiting in line to have their official photographs taken and catching Lexi's eye, he waved. She waved back, her smile beaming. Cal felt his heart constrict. Never had he felt more in awe of his wife than he did right at this moment. To hold it all together and still graduate after what she'd been through amazed him. She was a tough cookie and he loved that she was his. No one else's. His and his alone.

After the next class had completed their graduation the crowd began to disperse. They were at the halfway interval of the presentations and as Lexi and Mel had already received their degrees, Cal and Zach got up to leave. They had no reason to remain there for the rest of the afternoon. Slowly they made their way to where the official photographs were still being taken.

"You know what I find weird," Zach commented as they waited for the girls to finish their duties, "seeing Mel with her parents."

Cal looked at him questioningly. "How come?" he asked.

Zach smiled. "Aside from the fact I'm almost as old as them?"

Cal tutted. "You know no one even remotely thinks like that."

"I know, I know – but it does kind of bring the age thing home when I see her with them. Although that's not what I find weird."

"No?" Cal asked.

"No," Zach confirmed. "It's the fact she actually *has* parents."

Like Cal, Zach had never known a stable childhood.

"Yeah," Cal nodded. "I know what you mean. I found that weird with Lexi to start with too. When we first got together and they wanted to know our every move – that was really tough. I was so used to just doing my own thing."

"I know," agreed Zach, "and that's why it's so weird. To know Mel has other people out there who care for her like I do. Love her like I do."

Cal did a double take. "Whoa...you *love* Mel? Since when? I thought this was just a casual thing?"

Zach smiled at him. "Yeah, so did I. Kind of creeps up on you though. I never for one minute thought she would be into me and now, three months later, I'm hook, line and sinker. I still can't decide if that's a good or bad thing."

"I guess it depends how Mel feels," Cal replied carefully. "Although..." he hesitated.

"What?" Zach asked.

"It's just..." Cal began.

"What?" repeated Zach.

"Are you sure it's not a rebound thing? I mean you just got out of a pretty heavy relationship. You wouldn't be the first to find love somewhere else in record time."

Zach tipped his head to one side as he watched Cal. "You really think this is a rebound thing?"

From his tone it was hard for Cal to read Zach's mood so he decided to answer his friend honestly. "I think it could be. You were with that bitch for twenty years – no one would think any less of you if it was. You know. A rebound thing."

He watched as Zach closed his eyes and remained perfectly still for endless minutes. A persistent tick pulled at his friend's jaw though and at length Zach exhaled heavily as he opened his eyes.

"You're right, Cal, I did spend twenty years with that bitch and now she's gone. And one thing I've learned is that I don't do being alone. My reality is crap right now, but Mel has helped me to see it doesn't have to be that way. We enjoy being together and I know my feelings for her are stronger than they ever were for…" he stopped and Cal waited, knowing it pained Zach to speak her name. The bitch. "…so I don't know," he continued. "Maybe you could say it's a rebound, maybe I'm an old man who's deluded about his feelings but right now, she makes me feel better than I have in a hell of a long time and it's the only good thing I have going on."

Cal regarded his friend for a moment. He wasn't great with emotions and when it came to Zach, who was the most closed up person he knew, Cal had no idea how to handle it. "It's not the *only* good thing you have going on – " he decided to opt for a safer subject given that talking about Zach's relationship with Mel was way out of his comfort zone, "you have that meeting next week."

Zach tilted his head towards Cal. "We done with the touchy feely stuff then?" he asked and Cal saw the twinkle in his friend's eye.

"You know I'm crap with that stuff – business, I can do."

Beside him Zach laughed. "Yeah, I know. How the hell you ever managed to romance Lexi is beyond me."

"Anyway," Cal continued his train of thought, "talking about your love life only ends one of two ways. One, we talk about 'the bitch' and I get seriously angry, or two, you tell me how much sex you're having and I get seriously uncomfortable."

Zach guffawed. "You're jealous!" He pointed his finger at Cal. Rigorously Cal shook his head.

"Erm…no. Thanks. My sex life is just fine."

Zach continued to laugh. "Okay, okay. Whatever. But you know what happens when you get married. Everything gets all cosy and comfy and you forget to have fun."

Cal could feel his hackles beginning to rise, even though he knew Zach was teasing. "How would you know? It's not as if you ever got married."

Zach looked at him quizzically and Cal wondered if his friend had picked up on his tone. "No – but we were together long enough. Hey, I've not upset you have I? You know I was only joshing."

Cal shook his head again, trying to rid himself of the doubt that had begun to manifest itself. It was something that had been burning in the back of his mind but up until now he'd not allowed it air. Not until Zach had suggested he might be jealous. He didn't think he was but…

"It's true," Cal shrugged, "things aren't as active as they used to be but it's okay. We love each other and that's all that matters."

Zach clapped him on the back. "I was only joking. I know you and Lexi are sound, you only have to see the two of you together to know that."

"Yeah, but…" Cal turned to his friend, "look, do you really think it's normal?"

"Okay," Zach pulled him to one side, a little away from the crowd. "D'you really want to talk about this now?"

Cal shrugged. He didn't think he did but, now that the nagging thought had been unlocked, he didn't know if he could not talk about it. "I just want to know," he said after a moment, "I mean, we can go a week sometimes. She's tired, I'm tired – but I still want her. She doesn't always want me though. I figured it was normal but…"

He felt Zach grasp his arm. "It's normal, Cal. Okay. Any negative thoughts you're allowing to brew in that head of yours, you need to get rid of. Now."

"I know," Cal shook his head, "but the other day you told me you'd never been so *active*…and you're older than me. Am I turning into some kind of middle aged pipe and slippers guy?"

At this, Zach laughed again. "Cal, there's no way you're ever going to be a middle aged pipe and slippers guy. I promise you that."

"So how come my sex life is going down the pan?"

Zach shook his head. "Seriously, don't do this. You still want Lexi?"

Cal nodded. "More than anything. If it was up to me we'd be at it every opportunity…"

"Women are different though, take it from someone who knows."

Cal looked at Zach doubtfully. "Maybe. I don't know."

"They are," Zach reiterated. "After a while the sex becomes less 'important' I guess."

Again, he looked at his friend dubiously. "She's young, Zach. Why the hell would sex not be important?"

"That's not what I said. You're twisting my words."

Maybe he was, but all Cal heard was that sex became less important. "So, she's not attracted to me anymore – is that what you're saying?"

Zach shook his head. "Seriously, Cal. You need to wise up and listen, not hear what you want to hear. No – of course isn't because she's not attracted to you. Women are different. That's all."

"But not Mel it would seem," he muttered.

He heard Zach sigh. "Mel and I've barely been together five minutes compared to you guys. We don't live with each other so it's still new. You and Lexi are in that phase when you're so comfortable and happy with each other, the sex is an act of love – not just desire."

"Like you and that bitch?" Somewhere deep down inside Cal knew he was acting like an ass, but it was as if Pandora's box had been opened. His relationship with sex had never been straightforward and to hear that his mate was happily screwing at every opportunity was messing with his head.

"Okay," Zach took his arm once more and began to steer him back towards the girls, "we're not having this conversation. Not here and not today. This is their day, Cal. If you want to compare sex lives – fine, but you don't do it today. Okay?"

Cal shrugged out of his friend's hold, instantly resenting that Zach had gone into 'father' mode. "Don't haul me around," he hissed out of the side of his mouth.

"When you act like a petulant child, you get treated like one."

Cal stopped short, aware they were only a matter of metres away from where the girls stood waiting. "What did you just call me?" He could feel his teeth grinding together as his fists clenched at his sides.

"You heard." Zach turned to face him. "I've told you what the problem is, I've reassured you that Lexi still loves you and I've explained why it might *seem* like my sex life is currently better than yours – yet you refuse to hear it. You're acting like a petulant child, Cal. Grow up and be damn grateful for what you have."

Cal stood rooted to the spot, hands and jaw clenching in time with each other as he looked at his friend. He could scarcely believe that Zach was chewing him out.

"I get that we don't talk about this now," he ground out as he saw the girls approaching from the corner of his eye, "but I don't get why you think you have the right to call me a petulant child. This is my life, my marriage and you don't get to tell me how I do and don't feel about it." As the words left his mouth, Cal regretted them. He knew Zach was right. Deep down he knew he was being ridiculous and old insecurities that had been fed by his bastard of a father were resurfacing, but he felt powerless to stop.

Zach eye's widened and then, as Cal watched, his friend slowly relaxed his face and his stance. "I'll let you have that one," Zach said, "call it a free pass – but you need to stop and think. Your words, your actions, they have consequences. You need to think about what those consequences might be. There's nothing wrong with your marriage or your sex life, Cal, but your head…that's another thing entirely."

With a final clap on his shoulder Zach walked away and Cal watched as he greeted Mel, engulfing her in his comforting arms. Briefly Cal closed his eyes. He knew he'd overstepped the mark.

Beside him he felt Lexi materialise and so he turned to her, breath hitching as ever as he looked at her beauty. "Everything okay?" she asked as her gaze briefly took in Zach.

Cal nodded as he too engulfed his woman in his arms. Damn she felt good. "Everything's cool," he said as he dropped a kiss into her hair, "I'm so proud of you, baby."

He felt her pull closer, melt into him and as ever, his erection responded. With a sigh he gathered her as close as he could, moving his lips down the side of her face and into the warm crook of her neck.

"I love you, Lexi Strudwick," he whispered as his lips journeyed up past her ear, "and I fancy the fucking pants off you."

He felt Lexi giggle in his arms and rapidly he banished his thoughts from only moments before. He'd been an ass. Of course she still wanted him, of course she still loved him, of course Zach was right. He'd overreacted, taken a small thing and blown it right out of the water and he cursed his moment of immaturity. Emotionally Cal struggled at times and the doubts his father had drip fed into his brain over the years still tripped him up occasionally. This was one of those occasions. He was a grade-A fool. He had the most amazing woman as his wife, he had a job he loved and the best friend any guy could want – what the hell could he possibly achieve by trying to sabotage that with unfounded, negative thoughts?

Mind made up Cal pulled slightly away from Lexi and dropped a kiss onto her waiting lips. "Let's get out of here," he said softly and she nodded her assent. Tucking her beneath his arm he began to direct them to the exit.

Zach looked up as they passed and Cal caught his eye. He offered his friend a rueful smile and Zach nodded. Cal knew he understood. The demons, the lies, the challenges – Zach understood them all because some days he was there too.

"See you Monday," he said and again, Zach nodded. They were good. They would always be good.

Because that was what true friendship was about.

* * *

She was glorious. Laid out before him, every sinewy inch of her body his for the taking. Cal licked his lips as he dragged his eyes up and down, devouring her with his heated gaze.

"You're so fucking beautiful," he murmured, watching as she smiled in return. Slowly he lowered himself on top of his wife, fitting himself inch by perfect naked inch to her as hungrily, he claimed her mouth.

Beneath him Lexi responded and Cal revelled in the moment, enjoying that she was as turned on as he. His conversation with Zach only hours before was but a distant memory as he turned his full attention to his wife – the only woman in the world he would ever want.

Carefully he began to caress her, letting his hands wander wherever they wished as he maintained contact with her mouth. She groaned and he swallowed it, feeling her hips fidget restlessly. His erection pressed harder into her stomach and he broke away for a moment, allowing himself a second to compose. He didn't want this to be over too quickly. Not tonight. Tonight he wanted to celebrate his love for her in the best way he knew how.

"Cal," Lexi murmured his name and once more he caught her mouth in his, sucking on her bottom lip before plunging his tongue deep inside. Her hips bucked and he grasped her wrists to steady her.

"Slow down," he said into her mouth as he dragged his teeth away and around to the side of her neck, nipping tiny pieces of flesh as he did so. Lexi turned her head away to allow him better access and he took it, nuzzling into the sensitive curve of her shoulder. She bucked again and this time he grabbed both of her hands with his, lifting her arms above her head and securing them together, one of his own hands easily encompassing her small wrists. Lexi moaned and he looked down into her eyes.

"It's okay," he said gently, "I won't hurt you."

"I know you won't," she replied, eyes huge, desire evident.

"But I want you to keep them there," he instructed, watching her face carefully for a reaction. He'd never restricted her in all the time they'd been together, yet for some reason today, he wanted to. No – needed to. Right now he didn't want to examine why that might be.

Lexi nodded and he watched her for a moment longer, making sure she was okay with what he was suggesting. She nodded again and, with a small smile, he re-captured her lips; this time though he was gentle, showing her how much he loved her. How much this meant to him.

With one hand on her wrists above her head, Cal shuffled to the side to allow himself full access to the rest of her body. His free hand roamed from shoulder to hip and across her thighs before reaching its destination and resting at her core. Lexi closed her eyes and he felt her body stiffen as she braced herself for what she anticipated was to come. Cal didn't disappoint. With one determined move he caressed her in the most intimate of ways with his hand whilst he used his mouth to trail kisses over her taut stomach. He lingered there for a moment as he remembered their child that had so briefly been nurtured by Lexi's body. Dropping one kiss directly over her womb he looked up and met her gaze. She was remembering too – he could see it in her eyes.

For a moment he allowed them to connect, eye to eye, soul to soul and then he continued with his ministrations, pushing her ever closer to the edge. His left hand fought to hold her wrists as she began to wriggle, trying to set herself free, but he maintained her position, his superior strength winning out.

"Cal," this time her voice was urgent, higher in pitch and he could tell she was getting close – reaching her limit.

Rapidly he removed his hand and then shimmied back up her body, placing his mouth over hers once more as he drank his fill. He kissed her endlessly until his body became taut with desire and then, with no warning, he positioned himself and pushed, hard and fast. She screamed and he pushed further, burying himself until there was nowhere else to go. Still her wrists fought against his hand, but he was determined she wasn't going to escape. Impatiently he broke into a punishing rhythm, plunging backwards and forwards, feeling her meeting him as she responded. It was rough – harder than he'd ever been with her before – but Cal needed it and he felt Lexi respond.

"Jesus, Cal." Her head thrashed from side to side and he groaned, building the speed and the pressure ever faster as he neared his end. She felt incredible, her warmth welcoming him, absorbing him as their actions merged into one fluid movement. He was close, so damn close. He pummelled into her, his body slick with sweat, gliding easily against hers.

"Fuck, Lexi," he ground out between teeth clenched against the inevitable. He felt her contract around him and throwing his head back he growled. "Fuckin' hell."

Cal felt her ripples explode around him and with one final push he let himself reach his own nirvana, spilling his seed deep inside of her. His left hand still held her arms above her head and as he positioned himself deep for the last time, he took his right hand up to meet it, their hands joined above Lexi's head as closely as their bodies were joined below.

"Cal," Lexi said on a breath as she pushed her hips up against his one more time. He pushed back, emptying himself until there was nothing left, feeling the last of her warmth engulf him. He swallowed. Her eyes were closed and he watched her for a moment, waiting for his breathing to calm, waiting for her to see him. He kept their bodies joined enjoying coming down slowly, together, inextricably linked body, hands, heart and soul.

"Shit," she said as finally she opened her eyes and gazed at him. As ever they pierced straight into his and he smiled, letting her see everything that he was. Cal had no secrets from her. He was hers for all eternity.

"That was – different," she said hesitantly as at last he released her hands and rubbed her arms briskly to get her circulation going again.

"Are you okay?" he asked. With a small movement he separated their bodies and shifted to the side, watching as she turned to face him.

"Yeah. I think so."

Cal smiled. "I hope so. I wanted it to be different tonight. A celebration. This is the next chapter in our lives, Lexi. You and me moving on together. You sure you're okay?"

He watched as Lexi nodded again. "You took me by surprise," she said after a moment and he reached across to gently caress her cheek.

"Good surprise?" he asked.

Lexi inclined her head. "Yeah. I think so."

Cal laughed softly. "That's about the only thing you've said – 'yeah, I think so'. If you're not okay then you have to tell me. I'm sorry if it was too much – I just needed you so badly. You have no idea."

Lexi grasped the hand he'd rested on her cheek. "I'm good – I promise," she said as he felt her drop a kiss into his palm.

"Okay." Cal looked deep into her eyes and kept his hand secured to her cheek. "It just felt right tonight. I can't explain, but I needed you to know how much you mean to me. I needed to show you."

Beside him, Lexi smiled. "I already know that, Cal. You tell me every single day."

He smiled. "Yeah, but I've never shown you. Not like that."

"True," she turned her head to one side and smiled back at him. "I would tell you. If it was too much."

"Good. I hope so because you can tell me anything. You know that." He dropped a gentle kiss onto her lips. "I love you so much, Lexi."

"I love you too," she responded and Cal bracketed her with his arms, embracing her once more.

"Go to sleep," he whispered into her hair as he snuggled her back up against his chest, "I've got you."

He felt her relax in his arms and then a moment later her breathing deepened as she gave in to sleep. It'd been a long day for her and he knew she was tired but he'd needed to have her, to prove to her how much she meant to him.

As he lay behind her, listening to the gentle sound of her breathing he felt contentment like he'd never felt before. For some reason tonight, things had changed for him. Maybe he'd fallen more deeply in love with her if that was even possible? He didn't know. But after tonight and how intense their love-making had been, he knew their relationship had changed.

Cal smiled as he finally allowed the fronds of sleep to claim him. She loved him and she was fine with what had happened here. In his mind, life could get no better and if part of him had acted the way he had to prove to himself that their sex life was fine – then he completely ignored its presence. Any small part that might be entertaining that thought was pushed resolutely to the outer limits of his mind.

Things had changed tonight. For him their lives had just become even more enriched and as far as he was concerned, that meant only good things ahead.

Chapter Twenty-Two

Lexi

August 2014

Something had changed. Lexi had no idea what, but things in her relationship with Cal had shifted. Whenever she tried to puzzle it out, she always came back to the day of her graduation, but as yet she'd been unable to piece anything together. He was still as loving and attentive as ever, more so even, and he was her biggest supporter when it came to her career. There was nothing specific that she could identify, but Lexi just sensed, deep down, something had changed.

"Hey, can you get this spreadsheet done by four?"

Lexi looked up from her computer, which was situated within a bank of similar desks in the main office area. "Sure."

She took the paperwork from Fraser, the accounting runner who'd just approached her. "Big boss needs it by four, so make that three-thirty." Fraser winked and Lexi nodded.

"No problem."

"Good luck." Fraser began whistling tunelessly as he walked back in the direction from where he'd come.

"First piece of work for the big boss?" Adam asked from the desk opposite and Lexi nodded.

"Do you need any help?"

Quickly Lexi scanned the papers. "No – thanks. I think I should be okay."

"Sure? Well, just holler if you do."

"Thanks," she nodded at her colleague.

Lexi had been working at JaceEnterprises, a multi-national construction firm, for almost two months. After graduating she'd been fortunate enough to secure a paid internship that allowed her to work in all sectors of the business and use her newly acquired skills to their full potential. Currently, she was situated in the accountancy department, which was on the ground floor of the large, modern, open plan office. From the outside the building looked like something out of a sci-fi movie, all angled lines and reflective glass rising over four floors. Inside, the building was just as futuristic; each employee had their own personal metal desk and cabinet along with the latest specification computer. The building also boasted its own basement. This provided parking for the two hundred plus employees of JaceEnterprises.

The spreadsheet seemed fairly straightforward and it took Lexi less than an hour to complete. Glancing at her watch she noted that it was half past two and so she picked up the phone to call Fraser.

"Hi, it's Lexi," she said when he picked up. "The spreadsheet's finished – do you want me to email it to you?"

"Actually, we need a hard copy of this one, can you bring it up to me?"

"Yeah, sure. Erm…you're on the first floor, right?"

"Yep," Fraser confirmed, "next to the lift. Can't miss us."

"Great, thanks." For the first time since she'd started working there, Lexi felt a moment of trepidation. Although she'd been shown around the building on her first day, rarely did she have cause to go anywhere other than her office on the ground floor. This would be the first time she'd ventured outside of her own environment alone.

"I have to take a hard copy up to the runners," she said to Adam as she walked past him to collect the spreadsheet from the printer. "Is that normal?"

Adam looked up from the document he was studying. "It can be, depends what it is. Although I've no idea why they can't print it out up there."

Lexi shrugged. "Maybe it's easier to get us to do it if we're already working on the document."

Adam smiled. "I love your naivety of all things office politics. Wait 'til you've been here a year or more – I guarantee you'll feel very differently."

She laughed. "Hmm… you could be right." Adam was a great source of information – both good and bad, but he was yet to sway her to any real negative thinking. She was enjoying her job so far and had no cause for complaint. At thirty years of age, Adam was older than her and thus, more experienced. He'd been working at JaceEnterprises for three years and had the rather dubious honour of being her mentor.

"You know where you're going?" he asked as he watched her collect the file to go with the paperwork.

"Yes, first floor. By the lift?"

"Yup. See you in a few."

"Okay – wish me luck." Lexi walked away from her desk towards the bank of lifts in the centre of the building. As she waited for the doors to open she took a moment to straighten her knee length pencil skirt. Office wear was vastly different to the Jeans she'd lived in at uni and she was still getting used to the formality. A moment later the doors opened and she stepped inside, relieved to see the carriage empty. As a new employee Lexi had met only a handful of people and most of those she barely had any contact with. Her focus had been on getting to grips with the work and what was required of her – the social side, she figured, could come later. At the first floor the doors swished open and she spotted Fraser instantly. Skirting the first couple of desks she approached the runner who was bent over some paperwork.

"Here you are," she said as he looked up.

Taking the file he glanced over it. "Looks great. Thanks."

"No problem." Lexi turned to retrace her steps.

"Actually, while you're here," she spun back around at Fraser's voice, "would you like to see what we do up here?"

"Sure – erm…will that be okay though? Shouldn't I go straight back to work?"

Fraser laughed. "It'll be fine, I promise."

"Okay."

He pulled up a chair from the adjacent desk. "Now," Fraser said as he tapped out a few instructions on his computer, "I'm not sure if you'll spend any of your rotation with us but we're the cogs that keep things going, yet are amazingly easy to forget."

"Speak for yourself," one of his colleagues called across and Lexi laughed, enjoying the atmosphere.

"What exactly do you do?" she asked.

"We're pretty unique. This is the only company I've worked in that has a department like this. So, what we do," he continued as he pulled a file from the top of a large stack, "is essentially, allocate the work."

"All the work?" Lexi asked. To her that sounded like a huge undertaking.

Fraser laughed. "No, just the work that's specialist or urgent, although some days it feels like that *is* all the work. I usually deal with all the accountancy stuff. The jobs come from the management team and then it's our responsibility to make sure the right bits end up in the right department."

"Wow – that sounds tough," she commented. "You must have to know every employee in this place."

Again, Fraser laughed. "I do – but it's really not as hard as it sounds. Usually the files have instructions attached so I just pass them on. I do, however, need certain other skills at times."

"Such as?" Lexi asked.

"Well, not everyone is as accommodating as you were earlier. Sometimes they're so pushed I have to negotiate to get the jobs done in the right order – or rather, the order Jae wants them done. And sometimes we have to do research, make sure that all of the background data is up-to-date before it gets passed on."

Again, Lexi frowned. "That sounds like a lot of people all doing the same job. Counterproductive."

For a second Fraser regarded her. Lexi noted his dark brown eyes, puppy like, as she waited for him to speak. "Just be careful who you say those kinds of things around," he said eventually and she looked at him quizzically. "I don't mind," he continued. "For a while I thought the same thing, but Jae's very specific how he wants things done and he's not big on listening to anyone else's advice. Guess that's how he's so successful. If he hears you questioning his methods, you could find your time here cut dramatically short. And besides," he winked at her, "you'd be talking me out of a job."

Mentally Lexi berated herself. "I'm so sorry," she said hastily, "I said the first thing that came into my head. Guess I still think I'm in uni – I forget you can't just say whatever you like in the corporate world."

Fraser patted her hand and smiled. "Don't worry, you haven't said anything we've not all thought at one time or another, but this is how Jae likes things done and it works. All you need to do is learn when to keep your counsel – there are people here who wouldn't appreciate someone as young as you criticising the way things are."

"Office politics?" Lexi asked.

"Office politics," Fraser confirmed. "A whole new world and not always a great place to be. But don't worry – I've got your back. Anytime you need advice, just give me a call."

"Thanks," she said awkwardly having no idea what else to say to someone she'd effectively insulted on first meeting.

"Are you liking it here?" Fraser asked after a moment and she nodded, relieved he'd moved the subject on.

"Yeah. It's not been long but I'm really enjoying it so far. Well, anyway," she said as she began to stand up, "I best get back to it."

"You'll be fine, Lexi," Fraser said as he watched her. "We're all pretty friendly here."

"As long as I don't go against what Jae wants?"

He nodded. "Pretty much. But he's not that bad once you get to know him either. He just knows how he likes things done."

"I'll try to remember that. He's the overall boss?"

"Yes," Fraser confirmed. "This," he swept his arm around the office, "is Jae Leonard's baby and now you're part of that."

"I am?" she asked. "I'm just an intern."

"Technically, but that spreadsheet you did today means you made it onto the big guy's radar."

"He knows who I am?" Rapidly Lexi sat back down.

"Jae knows everyone. Every single employee. Nothing gets past Jae. Even new, green, uni graduates."

"Wow," she swallowed.

"In fact, he was the one who asked for you to do that sheet. Said something like *'give this to the new girl, I want to see what she's made of'.*"

She stared at Fraser with wide eyes. "Is that a good thing?" If Jae was as powerful as she was rapidly discovering, did she really want to be in his orbit?

Fraser smiled.

"Don't worry, it's standard practice. At least where Jae's concerned. You haven't been singled out. He likes to see what every employee is capable of. So you can stop panicking." Fraser smiled at her and Lexi swallowed.

"Are you a mind reader or something?" she asked and he grinned.

"No. The stricken look on your face pretty much said it all."

She laughed, partly in relief. "Cal – that's my husband – is always saying he can read me. It gets annoying sometimes."

"You're married?" Fraser asked and Lexi nodded.

"Yup. Young I know, but when you know, you just know. You know?" Crap. That sounded really defensive. Why did she feel the need to defend her marital status?

"I've never heard anyone construct a sentence quite so badly," Fraser teased. Thankfully he appeared oblivious to her automatic defence. "Was it Derek Moss who hired you?"

She nodded

"I think I need to have a word with Mr Moss – suggest he might want to review his decision."

Lexi laughed. "Yeah, maybe not a bad idea."

Beside her Fraser joined in. "I think, Lexi, you and I are going to get along famously."

"Really?" She breathed a sigh of relief as she tried to bring her mind back into focus. It was still tied up with the defence of her relationship with Cal. "So far I've insulted your job and shown myself unable to string a sentence together. You must have low standards." With determination she closed down every other thought and focused on the present conversation – and then realised what she'd just implied.

"Crap," she allowed, "now I'm calling you tasteless. I need to go back to work and quit while I'm ahead."

Fraser smiled and placed the file he was holding in her hands. "I'm not that much older than you," he said. "And I remember what it was like to have foot in mouth – permanently. There's one thing you can't do, and that's insult me. You can try, but it won't work because I like you. In a totally non-sexual completely platonic way," he winked as he added the last line and Lexi couldn't help but laugh.

"We only met five minutes ago," she said, "how can you possibly know if you like me?"

Fraser shrugged. "I'm a fast worker. In a totally non-sexual completely platonic way."

Lexi laughed again. "Well, for what it's worth, I like you too. In a…"

"…totally non-sexual completely platonic way?" Fraser added and Lexi nodded.

"Yes."

"Great. Well, now we've got the awkward stuff over, should we discuss when we're going to meet parents? I'm free this weekend."

Lexi burst out laughing and quickly dropped her head down to the desk as several of Fraser's colleagues looked over.

"Stop it," she said as she felt a stitch begin to grip her side. "I really don't think this is the professional persona I'm supposed to be projecting."

"Hmm…three 'p' words in one sentence. I'm definitely going to talk to Dennis. That man really needs to vet you newbies better."

Lexi turned to face him, seeing his eyes twinkling. This banter felt good.

"I've never had a male purely platonic non-sexual friend before," she commented.

"I'm not surprised," Fraser responded and she frowned.

"That's not nice."

Fraser tilted his head to one side and she waited as he regarded her once more. He was so different to Cal physically. His hair was black, buzz cut style, which seemed at odds with the gentleness of his eyes. Day old stubble wound around his mouth and his chin completing his edgy, almost military look.

"That's not what I meant," he said after a moment, "but on the basis that I've only known you for a matter of minutes and I would like us to be friends...let's just leave it there for now."

Lexi frowned at him again but, when he failed to elaborate further, she rose from the chair once more. "Okay, well thanks for showing me what you do." She smoothed her skirt and turned in the direction of the lifts.

"You're welcome." Fraser remained seated. "And Lexi?"

"Yes?" She inclined her head towards him.

"I'm looking forward to being your blah blah blah male friend."

* * *

"Everything okay?" Adam asked as she returned to her desk. Lexi nodded, thankful that he at least seemed to be straightforward. Whilst Fraser was undoubtedly good fun, there had definitely been an odd moment there and she was still perplexed about her vociferous defence of her marriage.

With a sigh she logged onto the computer and began to work again. Cal was the most important person in her life and whatever was happening between them was something she needed to address, but Fraser, no. She'd only just met him, he was a colleague, maybe a friend in time, but no one she needed to waste any headspace on right now. She needed to talk to Cal though, that much she knew, and, as Lexi worked solidly through the rest of the day, she came to a decision. She was going to talk to him tonight. There was something off. Something not quite right with them and if she was going to be able to dedicate herself to her married life as well as give her career a chance, then she needed to identify what it was. And fast.

* * *

There were two things Lexi hadn't bargained on in her decision to talk to Cal that night. One, that an 'important' football match would be showing on television and two, Zach would be visiting to watch said match.

"You don't mind do you?" Cal asked as she cornered him in the kitchen during half time.

"No, of course not. You know I love Zach."

Cal growled. "Not too much I hope."

Lexi laughed and pushed him playfully in the chest. "That's not what I meant."

Cal grabbed her around the waist and pushed her against the work surface. She felt the cool wood press into her back as he planted a firm kiss on her lips. Immediately her insides melted and she began to respond. He tasted faintly of beer and she embraced it as she allowed him to deepen the kiss. Her desire for Cal had changed over the course of their relationship, but he still had the ability to turn her insides to mush when he wanted to.

"Umm...you taste good," Cal mumbled as he pulled away.

She looked up at him, loving his eyes, the intensity and the desire she saw there. "You taste of beer," she responded and Cal held up his hands in mock surrender.

"Guilty. But you know you can't watch footie without a beer."

Lexi smiled. "I don't know that and I'm pretty certain there's no law to that effect but hey..."

Cal growled again and pinned her against the work surface once more. "I'm thinking that inviting Zach over here was not my smartest idea today," he whispered as she felt him grind his hips into hers. The ridge of his erection pulsed against her and she felt herself respond once more.

"Hmm...actually, I wanted to talk to you," she said and Cal pulled marginally away. For a moment, Lexi felt bereft.

"You did?"

She nodded. "Yes. But it's okay. It'll keep."

Cal frowned at her. "You sure?"

Lexi nodded again. "Yes, it's fine. I promise. We can talk tomorrow. Or another time. You go and enjoy your match."

Again, Cal frowned. "I can ask Zach to leave?"

Lexi held up her hands. "No. Seriously. Just go and enjoy your match and I'll do whatever it is that women do when they're football widows."

Cal laughed and leaned closer once more, securing his lips right next to her left ear. "They wait, naked in bed."

Lexi giggled and then shoved at him. "In your dreams."

"I really think I should ask Zach to leave," Cal said, his expression serious. Lexi planted another kiss on his mouth and then manually turned him around and shoved him to the door.

"Go," she said, "and I'll bring you some more beers."

He stopped at the doorway and turned back to face her, head on one side. "You sure?"

She nodded.

He continued to regard her and then, after a moment, his face broke into a smile. "Beer or you naked in bed? Hmm...tough choice..."

She threw the tea towel she'd just picked up across the room and he expertly ducked.

"Guess I'll settle for the beer then," he said as he turned and walked jauntily away.

Lexi smiled at his disappearing back. That exchange, that moment in the kitchen had been so normal, so Cal. She shook her head. Perhaps she was imagining everything. Perhaps there was nothing wrong with her marriage after all. She shrugged and opened the fridge to retrieve a couple of beers. After taking them into the lounge she went into the bedroom but, contrary to Cal's request, she remained fully clothed, deciding instead to call her parents. It'd been a while since they'd talked and even though their relationship was no longer as easy as it had been, there was something true and grounding about knowing they were always there. Safe, comfortable, loving. When her mother answered the phone Lexi knew she'd been right to make the call. Hearing her mother's voice, listening to her speak, feeling that cocoon of love that was unique to her parents and something which they'd all worked so hard to get back, was exactly what Lexi needed tonight. Absently she filed her planned conversation with Cal as she listened to her mother talk. That conversation with Cal – that could happen another day. If indeed, she reflected, it actually needed to happen at all.

* * *

215

Returning to the lounge a while later, Lexi noted that the football match had finished and the two men were discussing the game.

"Good result?" she asked and Cal nodded.

"Definitely. Although that last foul..."

"I know," interjected Zach, "lucky the ref saw it the same way we all did."

"Don't tell me they were diving for attention again?" she asked as she sat down on the sofa beside Cal. Football was beyond her. With the exception of enjoying the visual spectacle of several fit men running around a pitch, she could take it or leave it. Usually leave it.

"They don't dive...well, not all of them," defended Cal.

"If you ask me – "

"Which we didn't," interrupted Zach.

"...it's a pointless game," she finished.

"That's because you and that friend of yours haven't bothered to study the finer points of the game," Zach spoke again.

"Where is Mel anyway?" Lexi asked. "I could've done with some female solidarity."

"She had to work," replied Zach. "They have her doing crazy hours over there."

"Yeah, sounds like it." Mel had decided to try her hand at journalism and had secured a similar internship to Lexi, only with the local newspaper. By all accounts she was effectively the general dogsbody and without a formal journalistic qualification, Lexi suspected Mel was going to find her journey up the ladder pretty tough.

"How was your day?" Cal asked. "Sorry, I totally forgot to check in with you earlier."

Lexi smiled at him. "It's fine. I know you were pre-occupied. My day was good. Thanks. I made a new friend. Or, at least I think I did."

Zach laughed. "You sound like a school kid coming home and telling Daddy about your day. *'I made a new friend,'*" he parroted.

Lexi threw him a look. "I don't see what's so funny."

"Nor do I," said Cal. "Are you suggesting I'm old enough to be her father? That's rich coming from you."

Zach waved his bottle at them both. "Teasing, you guys. You know that."

"Anyway," Lexi continued, "his name is Fraser and he works as one of the runners. When he was showing me what his job entailed, I just kept saying stupid things. In the end I had no idea what he thought of me. This corporate stuff is so hard."

"Is this your new friend?" Cal queried and she nodded.

"Yeah. I told him I was married and so he said he would be my non-sexual completely platonic male friend. I think I got that right." Lexi smiled as she remembered Fraser making her laugh.

"Okay, whoa. Hold on a minute. Back up," Cal said. "You discussed me with him? Or rather, you discussed the fact that you couldn't be anything other than friends because of me? Does that mean you want to be?"

"Cal," Zach spoke sharply whilst Lexi looked at her husband in utter confusion.

"What the hell are you going on about?" she asked.

"Did you want to be something other than purely platonic blah blah crap friends with him?"

Lexi continued to stare at him incredulously. So much for her gut telling her that her marriage was okay after all. What the hell was going on?

"Cal. No. Of course not. I told him about you – the same as I tell anyone – and he just said that. It was funny at the time. It doesn't mean anything. And it sure as hell doesn't mean I want to be anything other than friends with him. For fuck's sake, Cal. Where's this coming from?" She stood up and moved to the armchair across the room. Somehow being next to her husband felt wrong right now.

"Yeah, Cal. Easy. You're overreacting, mate," Zach weighed in.

Lexi watched as Cal turned to Zach. "You saw her. She told us she'd made a new friend. A male friend. What's wrong with making female friends? Why does the first person she talks about have to be male?"

"I am here you know," Lexi commented, "and for the record, Cal, you're being really childish. Seriously? You're seriously going to have attitude because I happen to tell you I talked to a guy at work? Have you any idea how many men work there? It's a construction company. Take a wild guess."

Cal's face clouded and for a second Lexi wondered if she'd gone too far. He watched her for a minute and then gently placed his beer bottle down on the coffee table.

"Sorry," he said, "I'm so sorry, Lexi." He got up from the sofa and came to the armchair, kneeling down and nestling his head into her lap. "Ignore me. I've had a couple of beers. I didn't mean anything by it. I just love you so much you know. I can't bear to think of anyone taking you away."

Lexi sighed as across from her, Zach coughed lightly.

"That's what comes of the crap upbringing you had," the other man said. "You never know when to trust or who to trust, but you have to trust Lexi, man. She's your wife and it's obvious to everyone how much she loves you. Seriously. The only one who's going to ruin your marriage is you."

"I know," Cal shook his head in her lap. "I'm so sorry. I just…I don't know…"

Gently she placed her hand on his head. She knew he couldn't help this side of him – the mistrust, the lack of emotional maturity. Most times he was across it but not, it would appear, today.

"It's okay, Cal. We've been through this so many times though. I have to be able to tell you about my life, whether it's good or bad, whether I have male or female friends – whatever. That's the way it works. We're a partnership and if you can't trust me, then we don't have a partnership that's worth anything."

"I do trust you." Cal lifted his head and she could see the moisture in his eyes. "It's them I don't trust."

Lexi sighed again. "Cal, not every man I meet is going to want to be with me. Just because you want me, doesn't mean anyone else does and even if they did," she held her hand up as Cal went to speak again, "I would tell them to go to hell. I love you, Cal. You."

"Exactly," Zach echoed. "So get it into your thick head, man, and quit giving her a hard time. Of course she's going to make new friends and meet new people – that's part of life. Deal with it."

Lexi laughed at Zach's tone. "You're the only person I know who can get away with talking to Cal like that," she observed and Zach laughed.

"He gives as good as he gets, I can assure you," Zach replied and she smiled.

"I bet he does."

"Have you two quite finished?" Cal asked as he began to shift away from Lexi. "Because if so, this prize idiot is gonna make some coffee."

"Go for it," Lexi said as she searched out his eyes once more. "I do love you, Cal. Okay?"

He nodded and leaned towards her. Lexi lifted her head up to receive his kiss. She knew in the back of her mind that she should be more angry but, at the same time, she totally understood why he'd reacted the way he did. She watched in silence as he walked into the kitchen.

"Where did that come from?" she asked Zach once Cal was safely out of earshot.

Zach shook his head. "No idea. He mentioned something to me a little while back, but I figured it was sorted."

Lexi frowned and, standing up, she crossed the room to sit beside Zach. "What do you mean, he mentioned something to you?"

"He didn't say?" Zach asked and she shook her head.

"Nope. Otherwise I'd know what you were talking about."

"Then forget I said anything. It's not my place to get involved. God knows I've got enough crap in my own life without walking into yours."

"You can't say something like that and then retreat," Lexi said. "I've been thinking things have shifted for a while, but I thought it was my imagination. If you know something, Zach…"

Zach shook his head. "I don't know anything. We had a difference of opinion when you and Mel graduated, but he's not mentioned it since."

"Graduation?" Shit. That tied up with her idea of when things had started to change. "What happened at graduation, Zach?"

"I can't tell you, Lexi. It's not fair to him. If he's sorted it all out then it's not my place to bring it up again. Forget I said anything."

"Forget you said what?" Cal asked as he exited the kitchen carrying a tray with three steaming mugs. Inwardly Lexi cursed. Now she was more concerned than ever. Earlier, when she'd been able to convince herself she was imagining things she'd relaxed but now, even though Zach had said precisely nothing, her nerves were on high alert again.

"Oh, I was going to tell her about the plans for the company and she was worried what it might mean for you."

Lexi had to hand it to Zach. He was a quick thinker and a masterful liar.

"You know something?" Cal asked Zach as he placed the tray on the table. "I thought you had another meeting later this week?"

"I do."

"So...?" Cal prompted.

Lexi shifted on the sofa to allow room for Cal to sit. After a moment though she stood and returned to the armchair. Sitting three in a line felt awkward and with her renewed concerns, snuggling into Cal like she would normally have done, didn't feel right.

"I have another meeting," Zach continued, "and that's pretty much all I know right now."

"Who're you meeting with?" Lexi asked. She didn't particularly care but, if she didn't join in with Zach's lie, then she feared Cal would notice something odd.

"Jae Leonard," Zach said. Lexi spat out the mouthful of coffee she'd just sipped from her mug. Cal and Zach looked across at her simultaneously.

"Jae Leonard?" she asked. "As in JaceEnterprises?"

Zach nodded and frowned at the same time.

"Wait. JaceEnterprises – that's who you work for, Lexi." Cal frowned at her too.

"Right," she confirmed. "I had no idea they were the company you were in talks with though."

"Well, I'll be damned. Small world," Zach said.

"Hold on a minute," Lexi placed her coffee cup down. "Let me get this straight. You're thinking of selling out to JaceEnterprises?"

Zach nodded. "It's not a done deal, but it's the best one on the table. He likes that I have local contacts. JaceEnterprises is a multi-national and he wants to bring some community feeling back into his company."

"I know how big they are," Lexi commented, "I just can't get my head around the fact you're willing to sell out to a multi-national. Hasn't it always been your baby?"

"Of course it has," Cal responded, "but you know Zach has to sell. God knows I'd buy him out if I could but..."

Lexi shook her head sadly. "Jeez, Zach. I'm so sorry. Not that JaceEnterprises isn't a good choice – I mean, I'm doing fine there – but to have to sell out to someone that big. I guess I just thought you'd be able to keep it local, you know, the job that Cal and the guys love."

"I wish I could, Lexi," Zach brushed at a tear as he looked across at her. "If I could find any other way then I would. But it's the wrong time for anyone other than a huge company to take on a small business like mine. I hate the thought of Cal and the other guys being swallowed up and becoming one of a number, but I just don't see I have a choice."

Lexi watched as Cal dropped an arm across his friend's shoulder. She knew how much Zach meant to Cal and she knew how much the company and the guys meant to Zach. If having his heart broken by his ex wasn't bad enough, now he was selling out what remained of his pride. Suddenly Lexi felt sick. JaceEnterprises had been good to her, but Zach was like family and now she felt as if she was betraying him by working there.

"I'll get another job," she said as she swallowed down the bile that had risen in her throat.

"What? No way," Zach said firmly.

"I don't want to work for a company that's going to swallow up your dream, Zach. You're like family to me."

"Lexi," Zach stood up and walked across to the armchair. Carefully he sat down on the arm. "I had no idea you worked for Jae Leonard but even if I had known, I would still have talked to him. I have to be realistic. I can't keep the firm going, my debts are too high, and no one else can afford to bail me out. I'll make sure the guys get a good deal. I promise. And anyway, having you there might be a godsend.

You can keep an eye on things from the inside."

Lexi shook her head. "Hardly. I'm as junior as they come. I understand what you're saying, Zach, but it just feels wrong. If your dream has gone then I don't want to go to work every day and see the evidence of it."

She felt Zach lean into her and within moments she was engulfed in his comforting arms. Across the room, Cal remained silent.

"You can't fight my battles, Lexi," Zach said, "no one can. Not even Mel. It's okay. I'll be okay. I'll deal with it. I promise."

"But," she began and Zach hugged her harder.

"It's fine. I knew this day was going to come sooner or later. When the deal's done then at least all this will be over once and for all."

For a moment she let herself be held by him, knowing how important he was to her and more so to Cal. She should be comforting *him*, not the other way around.

"What are you going to do?" she asked as she finally pulled away, "will you carry on running the company?"

Zach shook his head. "No, Lexi. This will be the end of the road for me. I'll pay off my debts and then see what happens. No plans right now."

"Shit, Zach." Cal finally spoke. "How can you be so calm? You're going to be losing everything because of that bitch. How the hell is that ever fair?"

She felt Zach disentangle himself and then shrug. "It's not, Cal. Life isn't fair, but being bitter wastes energy. I have to do what needs to be done and I'm okay with that."

Lexi shook her head. Life sucked. "Zach, if you want me to leave Jace…"

She watched as the older man vigorously shook his head. "Don't even think about it. You deserve this and you said yourself you're getting on well. There's no reason for that to change. This is a business transaction. That's all. I've got my life, my friends, Mel, my health – it'll be fine. Okay. So stop worrying you two."

Lexi looked across at Cal and saw her expression mirrored in his eyes. They hated what that woman had done to Zach and now it seemed she was literally removing the shirt from his back. Seeing Zach tonight and hearing him so resigned to his fate, it was almost more than she could bear.

"To think I encouraged you to talk to this Jae guy," Cal mumbled. "I thought he'd invest, not take over."

"It doesn't matter. Either way I was going to lose my company. At least this way I know I can guarantee jobs for you and the guys. That's the most important thing."

Cal stood up and Lexi watched as the two men met in the middle of the room.

"You're one in a million," Cal said as he leaned forward and embraced his best friend. Zach embraced him back and quietly, Lexi stood up. She could see the emotion, feel the emotion and she knew that the two men needed a moment.

On light feet she exited the lounge and made her way back into the bedroom, a place where only an hour before she'd felt happy and loved after the talk with her parents. Now though, she felt empty. Her head was churning, thoughts of Zach, of her job, about how she could face the people who were going to take his dream away and then worries about Cal, about what Zach had been going to say before Cal returned to the room. For the first time since Bobby's death, Lexi felt as if she was walking on quicksand, sinking slowly with every step she took. Whichever way she turned she saw sadness and confusion. She saw a friend broken, she saw her husband in pain and she felt a marriage that was no longer stable. The foundations of her life were crumbling all around her and she felt powerless – terrified. She was still so young and yet she was sinking, slowly, slowly sinking and the worst part?

With only quicksand beneath her feet, Lexi had no idea how she was ever going to be able to rebuild.

Chapter Twenty-Three

Cal

For Cal, it seemed like the perfect solution. Watching Zach last night had crystallised something for him that in reality, had been there for a long time, he'd just not recognised it. Not until he'd seen his best friend facing up to losing everything. After Zach had left the previous evening, he and Lexi had barely talked but Cal was okay with that. He knew she had some processing to do and so did he but, now that he had, Cal was ready to tell her what was on his mind. It made sense whichever way he looked at it and given their history, he couldn't see how Lexi would disagree. It felt right and it was right. All he had to do was wait for Lexi to come home and tell her, and it would be perfect. Life would start to make sense once more.

They'd cleared away from dinner and were sat on the comfy green sofa together. In the background soft music was playing and Cal pulled her closer to him. Although he'd not orchestrated it that way, the dynamic was perfect.

"I've been thinking," he said carefully as he ran his hand gently up and down Lexi's outer arm, "we should make some changes."

He felt her stiffen beneath him and he frowned. "Good changes," he clarified and instantly she relaxed.

"What did you have in mind?" Lexi asked as she swivelled to face him.

"It was after Zach left last night. It all kind of made sense."

"Okay," Lexi's response gave little away.

"Well, you know how we always said we wanted a family," he swallowed, "I think we should try. Now."

Cal watched her face closely. Surprise flickered across her beautiful features.

"Now?" she asked. Her tone mirrored her expression. "You think having a family is what we need? Now?"

In his head, Cal admitted, it had sounded like a master plan, but he could kind of see why she would be surprised. Shocked even.

"Look," he shifted so they were facing each other. "I figured things are different between us now. We've been through so much, moved on, grown up and I can't think of anything more perfect than bringing a child – our child – into this world."

Lexi's mouth formed a rounded 'o' and belatedly Cal realised this had been the last thing she'd been expecting. He waited. It was important to him that she have her say, without him pressuring her. After a moment she closed her mouth and then swallowed.

"Wow. Left field."

As responses went, it wasn't quite what he'd hoped for.

"I know – although we have talked about it before."

"Yes," she agreed, "but for our future. Not right now. I've only just started work, my career. I don't think I'm ready to give all of that up just yet. And your job – we don't know how stable that's going to be."

This was one of those occasions when Cal cursed her level-headedness.

"I understand all of that, Lexi," he responded, "but I feel like we need that deeper connection. Something that will be just for us – not something anyone else can take away. My job, your job – they're just jobs, but we're about so much more. We're about me and you, how we feel about each other and our lives together. What could be more perfect, more beautiful, more permanent than creating a whole new life together?"

For a moment she stared at him. "I don't disagree," she said after a while, "but I'm still so young and so are you. This isn't something we have to rush into."

"I know, I know," he clasped her hands. "But things have changed between us. I sense it and I think you do too?"

He watched as she nodded.

"And I figured it's because we've fought so hard to get here. Now we need the next thing, the next commitment. And for me, that's a family."

"You think things have changed because we don't have a family?" she asked and after consideration, he nodded.

"Zach is alone, Lexi. We saw him last night."

"He has Mel," Lexi interrupted and Cal held up his hand after releasing hers.

"Yes, but he has no family. No one to turn to. Nothing to show, if you like, for the life he's led. I don't want us to end up like that. I want us to show the world who we are, I want us to create the family I don't have. I want us to be together forever and I want to make our bond impenetrable."

Lexi shook her head and he frowned. "That's a huge ask for one small baby," she commented. "You know that having a child has to be right for both of us and I'm just not sure it's right for me."

"Because of your career?" he asked. Cal could feel himself becoming impatient. He'd not considered that she wouldn't be totally on board with his idea.

"Partly, but I'm still so young, Cal. There's so much for me to do before I settle down into family life."

"Whoa. Hold on," Cal shuffled a little away from her. "We lost our baby and neither of us recovered from that. Not really. This is our chance to make a new life for all of us. Put all of that behind us."

Again, she shook her head. "Having a baby is like putting a sticking plaster on a gaping wound. It won't make things better."

Cal did a double take. "Wait – are you saying we have a problem? A gaping wound?"

"No," she countered, although her tone sounded unconvincing. "I'm saying that having a baby is not the answer to everything. If things have changed between us, then don't you think we owe it to ourselves to work out why that is, before we go rushing into the whole family deal?"

As Cal listened to her words he felt a dagger slowly begin to advance towards his heart. She wasn't on the same page with the family idea but more than that, she was suggesting there was a problem – something that needed to be fixed. Although he knew things had changed between them, never had he categorised it as a problem. In his mind, they were stronger than they'd ever been. Apart from the sex.

"Is this about sex?" he blurted out before he had chance to censor the thought.

"What?" Lexi looked at him in complete shock. "Sex? What the hell are you talking about?"

Cal swallowed as realisation dawned. Zach had been right. Lexi had no issue with sex or lack thereof. Mentally he cursed.

"Well?" she prompted when he remained silent.

Lightly, he coughed. "It's just that...we aren't as 'active' as we used to be." He could feel himself cringing, yet he schooled his head high. "I thought maybe you didn't want me anymore. Maybe things had changed? We always had this intense connection. Physical. And it's not there like it used to be. I figured we needed a new focus."

"And you thought of a baby?" Lexi's voice was barely a whisper, the surprise in her tone evident.

Slowly, he nodded. Somehow, sitting here, with all of his concerns out in the open, he felt like a small child again. Confused, lost and way out of his depth. "Yes," he said quietly, "but not as a sticking plaster. As an affirmation of our love."

He watched as Lexi ran her hands through her hair. "Jeez, Cal. You confuse the hell out of me. Two seconds ago you were talking about having a baby to what – cure our lack of sex life? And now you say just about the most romantic thing you've ever said. Damn you."

Cal allowed himself a small smile. "I didn't mean to confuse you. Hell, I just say whatever comes into my head – but the part about our love. I meant every word."

She smiled back at him, a tiny curve of her beautiful mouth and Cal released his breath. "I know you did."

They both remained silent, their eyes doing the talking, the moment suspended in time.

"I love you so much," he said as eventually he broke their connection. "I know we need to talk and yeah, maybe we do need to talk about sex, but I promise you, this baby idea? It was never about sex. It was about you and me. You're everything to me and I just wanted to prove that by giving you something more precious than anything. A baby. A part of you and a part of me, forever joined." Cal felt his eyes mist over. Damn. Before he'd met Lexi he'd considered himself to be wholly lacking in emotion. Now though it overflowed – on a daily basis. He let his love for her shine through his eyes as he waited for her to say something.

"We can talk about it," she said at length, "it's not fair for me to blow your idea out of the water, I'm just not convinced now is the right time."

Cal saw his love reflected back to him in her eyes and he relaxed. As long as she still loved him, he was good.

"It's okay. I understand. I guess I didn't really think it through." He smiled ruefully. "Maybe we should just sort the sex stuff out first?"

Lexi nodded. "Okay."

He took a deep breath. "I've been thinking…that you don't want me anymore."

Her eyes widened in shock. "Cal, I love you," she said as she reached for his hands, "of course I still want you. It's just so full on with everything else. I'm tired and some days, sleep wins. That's all."

"That's what Zach said," he replied and watched as she frowned.

"You talked to Zach?" she asked.

"Yes. At your graduation. I wanted some advice."

"You talked to Zach about our sex life?"

Cal couldn't pin down her tone. "Yes. Shouldn't I have done?"

"No, no…" she replied hesitantly, "it's just…"

"What?"

"He mentioned something yesterday. About how you thought there was a problem, but he didn't have time to tell me what it was. He said he figured you'd sorted it out. Now I know what he was talking about, it all makes sense."

He shrugged apologetically. "Sorry. I didn't know what else to do. I found myself getting angry when you turned away or when you were asleep. I thought you were pulling away from me – from us. I had to talk to someone and Zach is the only one who knows where I've come from. I knew he'd understand."

"And did he?" she asked.

"Not really. He told me it was normal. Just like you said."

"In which case it sounds to me like he did understand," she countered.

"Yes, he understood your point of view. Mine, not so much." Cal remembered the conversation vividly. It was the only time he and Zach had ever had words.

"You don't believe me?" Lexi asked after a moment. "You think it's more than life getting in the way?"

For a second Cal considered. Again, when he'd thought about it, in his mind it had all made sense. She'd pulled away from him, turned away from him and he couldn't equate it to any other logical reason. The fact it was supposedly 'normal' didn't cut it with him.

"I believe you. Or I believe that's what you believe. But I'm not convinced. You turn away from me, Lexi. You pull away sometimes too. How can that be normal? How can that not be personal?"

Lexi stood and paced to the other side of the coffee table, the worn oak furniture providing a barrier between them. "Because it's not," she said and she held out her hands as if to emphasise the point. "I'm still as attracted to you as I was when we first met, but we've been together for a long time now. Things change. We've become different as a couple, more comfortable I suppose. And I'm tired. I should have known this was what it was all about. The baby. The way I was feeling. Sex."

Cal stood too as he felt his ire rise. "Hold on, Lexi. You just heard me say that a baby had nothing to do with sex. The lack of physicality in our relationship has been bothering me, sure. But that's not why I want to have a baby and you said you understood that."

"I do, I..." Lexi shook her head. "I knew something had changed between us. Why didn't you just ask me? Is that what the scene was all about last night when you found out about Fraser?"

"Fraser?" For a second he was perplexed. And then he remembered. The guy from the office. "No." Was it?

"Are you sure?" she asked. "You completely overreacted when I told you about him."

"Yes, and I apologised for that," he stated as he strove to keep his voice calm. What the hell was she doing bringing a stranger into this conversation? This was supposed to have been a beautiful moment, but Cal could feel it turning sour, everything he'd hoped to achieve slipping further away from him.

"I know, but I don't think you have this sorted. You don't think I want you anymore – do you?"

Cal looked across at her, eyes wide. He didn't think she did and her body language, on occasion, concurred with him but for the sake of their marriage and because it was supposedly 'normal', he decided to let it go. "I believe you still want me," he said simply as he tamped down his frustration, anger and negative thoughts. "This isn't about Fraser or any other guy," he added, "we're stronger than that."

"Absolutely," she agreed. "I still want you. I've always wanted you and we're strong."

Cal felt his heart begin to thaw for the first time since the dagger had entered. He could read it in her face, see it in her expression, watch it in her beautiful eyes. She did want him…but then she'd hit a nerve. He'd denied it today and he would deny it for evermore, but he had to acknowledge it to himself. Fraser was an issue. Not Fraser specifically, but men. Other men. She was so beautiful and he had zero faith in anyone of his gender being immune to that. They couldn't be. So was it possible, he tried to reason, that this was all about sex after all? That when he felt her pulling away and heard her talking about her work, her life, he felt threatened? And, as basic as it was, sex, or the lack thereof, was his evidence of that?

"Cal?" she asked softly and he broke out of his thoughts, but not before he'd allowed a tiny spear of jealousy to enter his mind.

"You want me?" he clarified as he tried to shelve the destruction raging in his brain. She wanted him. She was his. She had said so. He had to believe her. Had to let that go. Had to move on.

"Yes. I want you," she repeated. And Cal nodded. He was going to believe her. He had to.

"And," she moved around the table so she could stand toe to toe with him. As ever, her nearness affected him and he felt his erection stir. "I want to have your baby."

He looked at her in utter confusion. "What? Now?"

With a small smile she nodded.

Cal took a breath. His brain had just done a complete three-sixty and in some kind of odd parallel they were back exactly where they'd started. Talking about having a baby.

He shook his head. "I'm lost," he said. "We just discussed all the reasons why it wasn't a good idea. You don't even think I believe you want me anymore. Why would you say something like that?"

Briefly Lexi closed her eyes and Cal watched as she opened them again. "Because," she said slowly, "when it comes down to it, it really is simple. I love you. I want you. And I can't think of a more precious way to affirm that. Like you said."

Cal shook his head again. "Man – women really are from another planet. You could've just said 'yes' first time around and it would've saved a hell of a lot of time."

He looked at her, allowing their eyes to connect and she smiled. "True. But where would the fun have been in that?"

He leaned forward and briefly placed a kiss on her lips. His body was telling him to do so much more, but there was no way he was going to obey. She might be able to move on and end up back where they started, but he was still playing catch up.

She took another step towards him. "I've just been really tired, I promise. I love you, Cal. And I want you. And now, I get to prove it."

He felt her shimmy closer and his arousal jumped. Damn his traitorous body. He was trying to do the right thing here, yet, she was too beautiful and his body knew it. His body was her slave. If she had this effect on him, though, his meddling brain spoke, who knew what effect she had on other men? It had never troubled him when she'd been at uni, it was only now, since she'd been at work, he'd felt the shift. All those men looking at her day after day, did she really think that being married would protect her? Did he think it would?

With a final shake of his head he attempted to banish the thought. He'd promised to believe that she wanted only him and to trust her. Now all he had to do was trust every other man on the planet. Sounded easy enough but with his ugly past advancing perilously close to his present, Cal wasn't so sure. Trusting every man Lexi ever came into contact with would be impossible.

With those thoughts burning in his brain Cal swept her up in his arms and carried her to bed, but not before he had one final thought, one final realisation.

His problems from here on in – they were only going to get worse.

Chapter Twenty-Four

Lexi

Three months later – November 2014

Lexi felt her stomach churn as she checked her watch. The second hand ticked around, its pace pedestrian as she waited. Nerves got the better of her and her stomach flipped again. This time it was accompanied by a wave of nausea that gripped her, robbing her of breath. Lexi opened her mouth and slowly inhaled. She could do this...only one more minute. One more minute until she knew the answer that would change her life. Their lives. Hers and Cal's.

Trepidation caused her breathing to quicken and she glanced down at her watch. Thirty seconds to go. The inside of the tiny toilet cubicle felt stifling as she began to count in her head, beating time with the second hand on her watch. Nearly there. Nearly, nearly there.

A final glance revealed that the time had elapsed. With shaking hands she lifted the simple white stick from the top of the toilet cistern where she'd carefully placed it minutes before. Taking a deep breath she turned the stick over, her eyes focusing immediately on the small window about halfway along its length. One line. Shit. She looked closer, peering into the window, getting as close as she could, trying to identify even a faint second line, but there wasn't one. Still only one line. Shit. For the fourth time in a row, there was no baby.

An odd mix of emotions ran through her as she disposed of the stick and composed herself, ready to return to her desk. Carrying out the test at work wasn't ideal, but when, on previous occasions, she'd done them at home, Cal had prowled around impatiently making the situation more tense. Naively, perhaps because they'd conceived before, they had both expected it to be a breeze. They were rapidly realising, however, becoming pregnant was a lot harder than they'd first imagined.

Adam looked up as she returned to her desk. "Fraser's got some more work he wants to send your way. Any chance you could go up and collect it?"

"Sure." Lexi dropped her bag underneath her desk and then retraced her steps, mounting the stairs and walking the short distance to Fraser's desk on the first floor.

"Well, if it isn't my favourite NSCP," Fraser greeted her as she arrived beside him. Their agreed method of friendship – non-sexual completely platonic – had long since been shortened to NSCP which kind of gave them a code, a definition to their relationship.

"You wanted me?" she asked, her tone level and lacking in emotion. As much as she liked Fraser, her latest discovery hadn't left her in the most buoyant of moods.

"Hey, you okay?" Clearly she'd not hid her low mood well.

"Yes, sorry. Ignore me. Bad day. What can I help you with?"

Fraser regarded her for a moment and she waited, expecting him to press further. Thankfully, he didn't.

"I've got a couple more files for you. From Jae." He handed her a pile that contained four blue-bagged files. Blue-bagged meant big clients.

"Are you sure these are the right ones?" she asked. Up until now she'd been restricted to green-bagged files. Small to medium clients.

Fraser glanced down and checked a list. "Yup. Seems he wants to test you again." He winked at her and she managed a small smile.

"Does he give this much work to everyone?" she asked as she tidied the files into a pile ready to be carried downstairs. Since that first one almost four months ago, she'd found herself working on at least two cases a week for him. Oddly though, she'd yet to meet him in the flesh. The files either went back to him via Fraser or, on occasion, Derek Moss, the manager who'd hired her.

"Actually," Fraser answered, "you're getting off pretty lightly. He has most of the interns run ragged in their first few months."

"Oh," Lexi felt her heart drop to the floor. "That can't be good. He obviously doesn't trust me." Kind of topped off her morning.

"Whoa, hold on, Lexi. It doesn't mean anything of the sort," Fraser responded. "It all depends what work needs doing. Some months are heavier than others."

"I understand that," she countered, "but you said yourself he usually runs the interns ragged. How come not me?"

She watched as Fraser shrugged. "Timing, maybe. The run up to Christmas can be chaos, but sometimes it's our quietest time of the year. I don't think it's anything to do with the quality of your work, otherwise I would've heard about it. So don't stress. Okay?"

Lexi shook her head. "It's hard not to. Maybe he thinks I can't handle the pressure?"

Fraser held up his hand to her. "Lexi, please don't overthink this. I promise you. There's nothing wrong with your work. I would know if there was. And even if I didn't, which is a big *if*, then Derek would know about it. So just take it as it is. A nice quiet time. It won't last. You can be sure of that."

She felt her heart begin to pick up off the floor and move somewhere closer to her chest. She was, however, still unconvinced. "Is there anything I can do? Extra work? Something to show him what I'm capable of?"

Fraser pulled a chair across to his desk and gestured for her to sit. "Please, Lexi. You have to believe me. You're doing okay. Better than okay. I have no problem with the work you're producing and neither does Derek. I've not had any bad reports about you at all. If there was something wrong, I really would know about it."

She tilted her head to one side for a moment. "It's just, my career is important to me."

Fraser nodded.

More so now, she added in her head as a vision of the faint, single line swam in front of her eyes. If she couldn't get pregnant then her career would be all she had left.

"What are your plans career wise?" he asked and Lexi shrugged. Somewhere between starting this job and deciding to try for a family her career goals had got lost, as had the idea of running her own company. That desire had paled following the complications with her parents and their revelations. Somehow its importance was no longer at the forefront of her mind.

"I'm not sure," she answered honestly, "I was just going to see how the internship played out and then weigh up my options. I enjoy the accountancy work, but I don't think it's where my passion lies."

Fraser laughed. "I can understand that. The word passion and accountancy aren't often linked."

She laughed along with him. "Yeah. I've noticed how people tend to switch off when I tell them I'm specialising in accountancy right now."

"At least they know what you're talking about. Try telling someone you're a runner. To the world out there I'm either a fitness freak or a criminal on the run for committing heinous crimes."

Lexi laughed again. "I guess I never thought about that. I bet you've had some really interesting corporate dinners."

Fraser smiled. "Oh, yeah. Some you wouldn't believe. One woman was convinced I was on the run from my wedding and kept offering to make me feel better – if you know what I mean."

She giggled. "And were you? Running from an ex-fiancée?"

He shook his head. "Nah, never got close. And don't tell me I need a dating website. I'm very happily single thank you."

Lexi smiled. "I wasn't going to. Marriage isn't for everyone and I'm sure the single life has its perks."

"That it does," Fraser agreed, "which reminds me, a bunch of us are going for drinks after work. Fancy coming along?"

Automatically she shook her head. She had to get home and break the bad news to Cal and then they'd have to re-group and focus on the next month. Even though they'd only been trying for four months, the pressure Lexi was feeling was almost overwhelming. And though her attraction to Cal and their chemistry hadn't waned, performing at almost every opportunity in a bid to conceive, was feeling mechanical now, rather than the loving experience it should be.

"Lexi?" Fraser waved his hand in front of her face and she snapped back to the present. "Where did you go?"

"Sorry, deep in thought. Thanks for the offer but I can't."

"No worries," Fraser responded good-naturedly. "Another time."

"Sure," she smiled. "Thanks though, for thinking of me."

"Hey, I only have one NSCP friend – gotta look after her."

Lexi smiled at him again as she rose from the chair and collected the files. "I'll get these done as soon as," she said, "and, if there's any more work going…"

"Yes," Fraser finished for her, "you'll be the first to know."

"Great, thanks." With the files clasped to her chest she made her way back down the stairs, stopping at the coffee machine to grab a hot drink before returning to her desk.

"At last," Adam commented as he watched her drop the files down. "You got blue files. I've been telling Fraser for weeks you were ready."

"Really?" Lexi asked in surprise.

"Yes. I don't know why it's taken so long. You're good at your job, Lexi, and you're fitting in well. Makes sense to me that they try you with more complex cases."

"I hope you're right," she responded as she opened the top bag and withdrew the first bunch of paperwork. "Fraser told me I'm not getting as much work as they usually give interns. Do you think I need to be worried?"

She glanced up and looked at Adam. With his sandy, chin length hair and stubble to rival Fraser's, she often thought he looked like he should be in a rock band, although not the bad boy kind.

Adam shook his head. "No. You're doing fine. I promise. I'm sure Fraser explained it really does vary – depending on what work's around?"

Lexi nodded. "Yes, he did. I was just worried. I want to make sure I'm progressing."

"You are progressing, Lexi. We have your review coming up and I'm certain that Derek will attend. He'll be able to give you all the feedback you need, but you really have nothing to worry about. I promise."

"Okay, thanks." Both Fraser and he had said the same thing so Lexi shrugged and decided to quit worrying. If there was a problem, they would've told her.

Directing her attention to the file in front her, Lexi noted the instructions on the now familiar paper pinned to it. It detailed that the account was to be closed and that JaceEnterprises were required to make a final payment to the client. Lexi frowned. That didn't sound right. Usually the client paid JaceEnterprises, not the other way around. Carefully she re-read the note. No, it definitely said that JaceEnterprises had to make a payment and the amount was not insubstantial.

"Adam?" she asked. "This file – it says we have to pay the client a large amount. Is this right? Shouldn't it be the other way around?"

Adam reached across the desk and she passed the file to him. "Let's have a look."

Lexi waited as her colleague leafed through the file, reading and checking documents. After a few minutes he handed it back to her. "No, it's right. This is for a take-over. Unusual, but not unheard of. Most of the paperwork will be filed already, this is just the last payment to the client. All you need to do is facilitate the payment and then the account can be closed."

"Ah, okay," she replied as she took the file back from him and tapped the client number into her computer. Waiting a moment for the screen to load she idly tapped her pen on the desk, her mind wandering back to that damn white stick. A fresh feeling of disappointment hit but it wasn't as great as it had been earlier. Maybe it was just because she was getting used to it now although, was trying unsuccessfully to become pregnant, something you ever got used to?

Her computer pinged indicating the file was now open and so she glanced at the details, making sure that the amounts on the paperwork tied up with what was on the computer records. Automatically she looked at the client's name and, as she did so, her heart stopped.

It couldn't be.

Lexi looked again. Shit. It was.

The client that JaceEnterprises was taking over was Zach's company. The final payment she was about to process would mean that Zach no longer had any hold over the business – one he'd built from the ground up. Lexi went hot and cold as she struggled to drag in a breath. She'd known it was coming, but to see it here in black and white was difficult to process. She knew first-hand how much the company meant to Zach and to the men who worked for him – Cal included – and to know that today, with one click, she was going to be responsible for taking it away from him, it was too much. Sickness engulfed her once more and rapidly she pushed her chair away from the desk and ran towards the toilets.

"Lexi? You okay?" Adam asked as she dashed past him and she nodded. There was no way she could formulate any words.

Arriving at the cubicle just in time she bent over the toilet bowl and emptied the contents of her stomach, retching like she'd never retched before. Ever since she'd found out that JaceEnterprises was going to buy out Zach's company it had been difficult, but, with it going on in the background, nowhere she could see, she'd been able to deal with it. Forget that she was working for the company who would destroy her friend's livelihood. She understood that JaceEnterprises weren't responsible for Zach's downfall, but it still felt as if she were working for the vulture, picking over the wreck of a decent man's life and now that the reality was staring her in the face, she could no longer deny it. What was more, the absolute gut wrenching irony was, she was going to be the one who was ultimately responsible. She was going to press that button, make that payment and dissolve all of Zach's rights to the one thing that had always remained steady to him. His company.

Taking a deep breath she grabbed a tissue from the dispenser and wiped her face, barely able to comprehend the enormity of what she had to do. She could ask Adam to do it, or one of the other staff of course, but then how would that go down with a boss who was already giving her a light workload? Would that show weakness if she asked another member of staff to do the work she'd been specifically tasked to do?

Lexi flushed the toilet and exited the cubicle, stopping at the washbasin to rinse her face with cold water. As she regarded her reflection in the mirror, something Fraser had said only a few moments before replayed in her mind. He'd said that Jae was testing her again.

Testing her? Her mind whirred at a hundred miles an hour as she tried to make sense of her thoughts. Testing her? Was it possible that Jae knew about her connection to Zach? Was it possible he really was testing her? Giving her the ultimate test to what? Prove her loyalty? She shook her head. No. That couldn't be true. She'd never met Jae and as far as she was aware, he knew nothing of her. She was just another intern, one of a number. Why would he deliberately give her a file he knew would mess with her head and her loyalties? He wouldn't, she reasoned. It had to be a simple case of bad luck.

Once she'd planted the seed of doubt, however, her mind refused to let it rest, and, unable to continue with her work without knowing what had happened here today, she climbed the stairs once more and sought out Fraser.

"Hey," he greeted her, "back so soon?"

"How does Jae decide who gets what work?" she demanded.

Fraser frowned. "What do you mean?"

"How does he decide?" she repeated, her tone strong, her words measured.

"I have no idea, Lexi. What's going on?" His face was a picture of confusion.

"That file, one of the ones you just gave me?"

Fraser nodded.

"Is it possible Jae would give me that file for a reason?"

Fraser shook his head. "Lexi, I have no idea what you mean. Of course there's a reason. He knows what needs doing and he knows who's capable of doing it. Beyond that I don't know what else he considers."

"Yes," she said agitatedly, "but these files, the ones that come direct from him, do you sort them?"

Fraser shook his head again. "No, Lexi. Look, why don't you tell me what's going on?" He pushed the chair that she'd vacated only a few minutes before towards her. Reluctantly she sat.

"So, if he decides personally who gets the work, then there must be something in the thought process. Right?"

Fraser looked at her bemused. "Of course. I already told you. He knows what needs doing and who'll be best placed to do it. As far as I know, that's all there is to it."

"Okay," Lexi wrung her hands together in her lap. "So, if I happened to know one of the clients he's given to me, it's nothing more than a coincidence?"

"You know one of the clients?" Fraser asked and she nodded. "Then yes, it would be a coincidence. I don't imagine Jae has the time to look into every employee and work out whom they might know. Is there a conflict of interest here? Do you need to pass on the file?"

Lexi shrugged. "Maybe. But I don't want him to think I'm weak or incapable. He already gives me less work."

Fraser reached to her lap and grasped her hands. "Lexi, stop. Stop, stop, stop. We already covered this. If there's a client you can't deal with for personal reasons, then no one is going to think less of you if you pass it to someone else. Ask Adam to deal with it. Okay?"

His tone was soothing, but Lexi felt far from pacified. The thought that Jae knew something, that he'd deliberately given her this test wouldn't recede and she jiggled her feet restlessly. "But what if he did know, Fraser? What if he did this on purpose? What if it was a test? You said he was testing me again…"

Beside her, Fraser sighed. "Because he's moved you onto bigger clients. I didn't mean anything other than that. If there's any possibility that Jae knew your connection to the client, then he wouldn't have given you the file. There would be no point because he would know you'd have to pass it on. Why waste time moving a file around?"

"No," Lexi shook her head. "Something's not right here." She had a gut feeling, a nagging doubt that she couldn't let go. "I want to see him," she said and then stopped as she immediately realised what she'd just asked.

"You want to see him?" Fraser repeated, his expression showing a mixture of shock and admiration. "You do know that he never makes time for interns? And that the chances of you getting an appointment are non-existent? That's why he has a team, people like Derek. Why not go and talk to Derek?"

"Because," Lexi replied, "he'll know even less than you do. Only the man himself will know why he gave me this file. And I need the answer. I have to know, Fraser."

"Why, Lexi? Why's it so important to you? Can't you just pass the file onto Adam and forget about it? It's not like you don't have other work to do."

"It's not that simple," she replied. "What I have to do with that file, the work that needs to be done, it's going to finish off a man I know and love. I can't be the one responsible for doing that and sure, I can pass the file to Adam, but I'd still know it'd been done. And there's this feeling, Fraser. I don't know. My gut is telling me that this *is* a test. That Jae knew exactly what he was doing and if I pass it to Adam, then I fail. I can't afford to fail either, Fraser. I'm in an impossible situation. So I have to talk to him. I have to know."

"And what if you're wrong? What if it's like I said, a coincidence?" Fraser asked. "Don't you think your career will be harmed more by fronting up to him and what – accusing him?"

She sat up straighter in the chair and squared her shoulders. "It's a chance I have to take. This company that's being taken over, it's where my husband works. He'll be fine, I know they've worked out a deal for him, but the owner, Zach, has been left with no choice other than to sell. Everything will be gone. It's breaking his heart and I have to know if the man I work for, if Jae Leonard, is sick enough to make me, someone who's going to witness Zach break, be the one to finish it off. And, if he is," she ended, "then I'm pretty sure I don't want to be working for him anyway."

Fraser watched her in silence for a moment, his dark eyes searching her face. After a while he spoke quietly. "You know what, Lexi, you're one hell of a woman and I wish I had you fighting for me. Your friend is a lucky man. You are, of course, about to commit professional suicide, but I can't deny your motivation. If you really want to talk to him, if you're sure you need to do this, then I'll see what I can do."

Lexi closed her eyes briefly and let out a long, slow breath. "I'm sure, Fraser. I know it seems crazy, but you've not seen him. Zach. He's lost, broken. It's not Jae's fault, I know that, but if he's so sick and twisted as to..."

Fraser held up his hand. "I get it, Lexi," he said softly, "I really do. Leave it with me."

With another deep breath she nodded and then on legs that could barely hold her weight, she began the now familiar walk back to her desk. Inside she acknowledged that this could be the last time she made this journey, but right now she couldn't bring herself to care. She wasn't pregnant, she had to go home and trample on Cal's hopes and now, it seemed, she was going to be the one putting the final nail in Zach's coffin. However she spun the events of the day, Lexi knew deep down in her heart there was no way any of this was going to end well.

* * *

She'd been back at her desk for less than five minutes when the phone rang.

"It's me," Fraser said as she answered it. "He's agreed to see you but..."

"But what?" she prompted.

"It has to be tonight. When we all go out."

"But I'm not coming out with you tonight. I can't. And what kind of person conducts a meeting like this in a pub?"

On the other end of the line she heard Fraser sigh. "It's the best I could do, Lexi. He won't agree to see you unless it's tonight. Apparently he was intending to come out with us and he figured it would kill two birds with one stone. His words, not mine."

"Yeah, right." Her mind raced as she tried to work out what to do.

"Is there no way I can see him here, before you go out?" she asked.

"No. He was definite. This was the only way he would agree to see you. I promise, Lexi, I did try. The ball's in your court now. If it's that important to you, then you're going to have to change whatever plans you have for tonight. I'm sorry."

The line went dead and Lexi frowned at the phone for a moment. Whether he'd intended to or not, Jae had skilfully backed her into a corner and after the serve she'd given Fraser upstairs, she could hardly not agree to Jae's terms. If she didn't go she would look like an utter fool, but more than that – it would appear she didn't care, which was about as far from the truth as it got. Damn him. Damn Jae and

243

his manipulation. Without so much as lifting a finger, he had very firmly put her in her place.

Dropping her head into her hands she rubbed at her eyes. She could feel Adam's gaze burning into her from across the desk, but she refused to look up. He'd asked if she was okay when she'd returned and apart from answering, she'd said nothing else. It was way too complicated.

The phone rang again and she picked it up, expecting it to be Fraser. It wasn't.

"Lexi?"

"Yes?" she responded. The voice on the other end was not one she recognised.

"This is Jae Leonard."

Lexi felt her heart stop for the second time that day.

"I understand I'll be meeting with you tonight?" he continued. His voice was smooth, yet she could still hear the rough behind it that spoke of his origins. He, like Zach, she'd been told, had built his construction company up with his bare hands. Literally. The only difference was – he'd been a hell of a lot more successful.

Lexi swallowed. "Er, yes. I think so."

"You think so?" she could hear the surprise in his voice.

"Well, no. I'm hoping to be there tonight, but I have plans. I haven't got around to cancelling them yet."

"You're hoping to be there?" This time she detected more than surprise. Sarcasm perhaps? "You're the one who requested this meeting," the steel in his voice was unmistakable, "so, I would suggest that you cancel your plans. If you want the meeting, you'll be there."

"I will – er…" she stuttered but, before she had time to finish her sentence, the line went dead. With a shaking hand she replaced the receiver. He'd got the better of her again and the corner into which he had backed her was now rapidly decreasing in size.

* * *

Cal answered on the second ring. "Hey, how's your day?"

"Don't ask," she mumbled, "look, about tonight…"

"Yeah, actually, I need to talk to you. I have to go out tonight.

244

With Zach."

"You do?"

"Yeah. I know you said we needed to talk though, so if it's not okay with you then I can let him know."

Lexi swallowed. "No, it's fine with me," she took a deep breath. "Actually, I have to go out too, that's why I was calling."

"You have to go out?" She could hear the surprise in Cal's voice.

"It's a work thing. A meeting."

"Tonight?" Cal repeated and Lexi nodded as she spoke into the phone.

"There's a group going out for this meeting. Apparently it's the only time it can be arranged. I don't want to go but it's really important and if you're going out too..." she let the sentence hang.

"Zach's take over got finalised today," Cal said slowly, "that's why I need to go out. Be with him. He says he's okay but..."

"He's not," she finished.

"No," Cal agreed, "he's not."

"I'm sorry," she said.

"What've you got to be sorry for?"

"I work for them. It can't be easy for Zach knowing that." That and the fact I will be personally pressing the button to close his company down, she added mentally.

"You know he doesn't think like that," Cal commented. "It would've been difficult however it had played out. At least this way you and I are working for the same company now. That should have some benefits."

Lexi heard him smile and she smiled in response. "It's good to hear your voice," she whispered, aware that several members of the accountancy team were tuned into her every word.

"I love you," Cal said, "and it's okay, we'll go our separate ways tonight but tomorrow..."

"Tomorrow we'll talk," she concluded. Not having told Cal she was doing the test today gave her a day's grace. That particular piece of devastating news could wait until tomorrow. If that meant she carried the burden alone for one more day then so be it. In the scheme of things, it really didn't seem important.

"Are you coming home first?" Cal asked and she shook her head.

"No. They're going straight from here. Hopefully means I won't be too late home. I'll be back before you for sure."

"Okay. I hope it goes well. Take care and don't forget, I love you."

For the first time that day Lexi smiled a genuine smile. "Back atcha. See you later."

"Yeah. Bye, babe," Cal said softly and she heard a click as he disconnected the call.

Lexi cradled the receiver for a few moments before replacing it. Thank God for Cal and the love they shared. He made her world a better place and right now, she needed all the good karma she could get. Having a meeting with Jae Leonard filled her with both anger – for Zach and the part she'd been asked to play – and trepidation. Her gut kept telling her she wouldn't get out of this evening unscathed and, if she was being completely honest, the thought of what was about to come, terrified her.

* * *

The clock ticked around to five-thirty pm and Fraser appeared beside her desk. "You ready?" he asked and she nodded.

With a final click she shut down her computer and then picked up her bag from beneath the desk.

"It'll be okay," Fraser said reassuringly as they made their way out of the building and walked towards the pub. "His bark really is worse than his bite."

Lexi remained silent. It didn't matter whether he barked or bit. In not one scenario that she'd run through did this end well and, regardless of Fraser's reassurances, she knew she was heading into the lion's den. The only real question that needed an answer was in what state would she emerge? Would she leave the pub tonight with her job but more importantly, her dignity, intact?

Lexi knew only time would give her the answer.

Chapter Twenty-Five

Lexi

The pub wasn't one Lexi had visited before. Formerly a paper mill, the outside was square and uninspiring although hanging baskets and garish lights adorned each of the uniform window ledges running horizontally across its front. Above the brick porch entrance, large, gold letters proclaimed the name of the establishment, this having also been engraved onto the glazed doors within. Inside, dimmed mood lighting revealed several low-level tables scattered around the central bar area dominated by the huge, circular, dark oak bar structure. A mixture of booths dotted around the far edges provided more secluded seating, each of which was sited beneath a window hung with a luxurious burgundy velvet curtain. As they entered, a backdrop of chatter fought with current pop music, the sound engulfing them along with the mouth-watering smell of freshly cooked chips that lingered in the air.

"Over here," Fraser took her arm and directed her to a couple of tables which had been pulled together just beyond the bar. A few familiar faces were already seated and after doing quick introductions for those she didn't know, Fraser left to get the drinks. Grabbing the stool nearest to her, Lexi sat down and tried to make herself as inconspicuous as possible. Large gatherings had never been her thing and this was her first outing with work colleagues. She would have been nervous enough just being here, even if she wasn't expecting Jae to appear at any moment.

"Does Jae usually come to these things?" she asked Sonya. The girl sat beside her was someone that Lexi recognised.

"No. I've never known him to come. Mostly you're lucky if you see him from one month to the next," Sonya replied as she turned towards Lexi. "Why?"

"Oh, nothing," Lexi shook her head as she tried to mask her surprise at Sonya's answer. When Fraser had told her the meeting was tonight, she'd figured it was the norm and that Jae was making her fit in with his existing plans. "I've not met him yet, that's all," she finished. Which was true. She hadn't.

"He can be elusive, our Jae," Sonya replied, "don't worry, you'll know when you've met him."

"I've spoken to him," she blurted out and then mentally kicked herself. Whatever he'd done to Zach, Jae was her boss and Lexi knew enough to understand that she shouldn't be gossiping about him. She had no idea how close these people were to Jae.

Sonya looked at her oddly for a moment. "You'll meet him eventually," she said and then turned away.

Feeling effectively dismissed, Lexi began to frantically search the pub looking for any sign of Fraser returning. She spotted him making his way back to their table and so she shifted to allow him to take the stool on her other side.

"I'm so glad you're back," she whispered as he placed a tall, white-wine spritzer in front of her.

"Aw, I didn't know you cared," he quipped and she smiled.

"I don't really know these people and I think I upset Sonya," she whispered.

Fraser peered around her so he could see the other woman sitting beside Lexi. "Uh-oh. You didn't ask her about Jae, did you?"

Lexi nodded. "I asked if he usually came to these things – if he was going to be coming along tonight."

"But you already know the answer to that," Fraser replied.

"I know," she hissed, "I was trying to make conversation. But then she said he doesn't usually come to these things and got all funny."

"Oh, Lexi," Fraser shook his head. "I can see I'm really going to have to give you that lesson in office politics, sooner rather than later."

"Why? What did I do?" she asked as she leaned forwards to take a sip of her drink.

Fraser mimicked her and took a slug of his pint before placing it down on the beer mat in front of him. "Let's just say that Sonya has a thing for Jae. Unrequited as far as I can tell."

Lexi frowned at him. "Isn't she married?"

Fraser laughed. "Yup. You really do need that lesson."

"No, seriously," she said, "I thought she was married."

Fraser nodded. "She is."

"So why would she have a thing for Jae?"

"When you meet him, you'll probably understand."

"Okay," Lexi frowned again, "but that's not really what I meant. If she's married then she shouldn't be having a thing for anyone other than her husband."

She watched as Fraser picked up his pint and took another sip before placing it back down and turning to her. "It doesn't always work that way, Lexi. The real world isn't always picket fences and roses."

"I know that," she defended, "Zach, the guy I was telling you about? He lost everything because of the woman he loved. Ran off to who knows where, presumably with someone else, and left him nothing but a mountain of debts. Skipped the country – never to be seen again."

"Ouch, that sucks," Fraser replied. "No wonder he's a mess."

"Yes, but that's still not the point. They weren't married."

Fraser tilted his head to one side. "I'm not sure I understand. Are you saying that because they weren't married, it's okay she ran off with someone else? But if they'd been married then it wouldn't have been okay?"

Lexi thought for a moment as she realised the stupidity of what she'd just said. "No, wait. I – oh crap, I don't know what I mean. I guess I was just thinking that I'm married and so I wouldn't be looking."

Fraser took a deep breath and she watched as he slowly turned to face her. His chocolate brown eyes searched hers and for a second she felt herself drawn in as she allowed their gazes to meet. He was communicating with her and she felt a jolt as something passed between them, like it did with Cal. She felt helpless to break the communication and so she allowed it to continue, their eyes sending messages unheard. Anticipation built and time stood still as the background noise dimmed to a lull. This was just like with Cal, she reflected and finally, as that thought broke through, good sense prevailed and she closed her eyes to sever the connection. She had no idea what'd just happened but, whatever it was, she knew it had to be terminated – now. When she opened her eyes again a moment later, Fraser was still watching her. Waiting. Unmoved. He ran his gaze across her face and she could feel herself burning on every path his eyes traced.

"Don't be so sure of that, Lexi," he said at length and after one last, lingering look, he too turned away from her.

* * *

The evening had gone from bad to worse and there was still no sign of Jae. Sonya to her left was pointedly ignoring her and to Lexi's right, so was Fraser. With nothing to occupy her hands other than her rapidly disappearing drink, which oddly Fraser had replaced, Lexi decided to visit the toilets. The last thing she wanted to be, when Jae finally did decide to arrive, was drunk.

Peering at her reflection in the mirror she noted the dark circles that were starting to form around her eyes. Lack of sleep – which was no great surprise given they weren't doing a hell of a lot of sleeping in bed these days. Instinctively she patted her stomach, remembering back to this morning when she'd done the latest test. At the time, whilst she'd been waiting for the result she'd been anxious, nervous even and, when it had been negative once more, she'd felt disappointed. Now though, the emotions seemed more complex than that. Part of her was still disappointed, but, if she was being completely honest, that part was significantly smaller than it had been on day one. There were other emotions mixed in there too and, although it pained her to identify it, one of those emotions was relief.

She shook her head at her reflection, watching as her blonde hair swished from side to side. What kind of wife did that make her? What kind of person felt relief at a negative pregnancy result when they were actively trying for a family? And, whilst she was doing the whole self-reflection thing, what the hell had happened with Fraser back there?

250

Rinsing her hands she splashed some cold water on her face. Today had been right up there as emotional roller coasters went and she was finding it virtually impossible to work out how she felt about anything right now. Perhaps it wasn't the best time to be searching for answers. She still had the meeting with Jae to get through – assuming he ever showed up – and she knew that was going to take a hell of a lot of emotion out of her. Talking about Zach and everything he'd lost was going to be tough but more than that, determining if she was working for a man with sick and twisted morals was really going to push her limits.

After a quick brush of her hair she snapped her handbag closed and opened the door to exit the ladies' room. A small corridor, secured by a door, led from the toilets to the bar area where they were seated and it was in this corridor that she found Fraser, lounging against the wall. Clearly he was waiting for her.

"Hi," she said as she went to walk past him. Thinking about what had transpired between them earlier was just one of the things she was putting in mothballs for now. "I'd better go and see if Jae has arrived yet." Talking to Fraser, especially alone, was not on her agenda.

"He hasn't," he replied as gently he touched her arm. "Lexi, wait. Please."

She stopped but didn't turn around. He'd been ignoring her for most of the evening and the mood she was in, he didn't deserve any pleasantries.

"Will you let me explain?" he asked.

Lexi shrugged. "I have no idea what happened and even less idea why you've been ignoring me all night. As far as I'm concerned, there's nothing to explain. Let's just leave it and deal with this meeting with Jae." She spun around to face him. "Okay?"

Fraser shook his head. "No, I need to explain."

Lexi sighed. "Fraser, today so far has been pretty crap and I'm only expecting it to get worse. Please can we just leave it? It really doesn't matter."

Slowly he shook his head again. "It matters to me, Lexi. I really want a chance to explain. At least let me tell you why I've been ignoring you."

251

She let out a breath. "Okay, fine."

"Not here," Fraser said as he began to guide her back towards the bar area. "I got us another table away from the others. So we can watch for Jae."

"Is he even going to turn up?" Lexi asked as she glanced at her watch. Seven-thirty. Had she really only been enduring this hell for two hours?

"He'll be here. One thing Jae always does is what he says."

"There's a first time for everything," she commented as she followed Fraser back out towards the front of the bar where he'd secured a small table in an alcove.

"It's a bit more secluded here," Fraser said as he gestured for her to sit down. "I thought it would be better – for when Jae arrives."

Lexi nodded. "I hadn't even thought of that."

"Why would you?" Fraser replied as he settled himself on the plush velvet bench seat opposite her. "You have this beautiful air of naivety which I find completely refreshing. To you, meeting Jae here, it's a business meeting but to others…" he nodded his head towards the table where the rest of the staff still remained, "…it could be interpreted as so much more."

"Which is what I really don't get," she said after a moment. "I'm married. I have a ring on my finger for heaven's sake," she flashed her left hand at him. "Just because some people might be tempted to break their vows, it doesn't mean everyone is."

Fraser sighed. "Which is why I need to explain what happened earlier, Lexi. There are some things you need to know."

She looked across at him and then reached forwards to pick up the fresh drink that had magically appeared. Fraser must have got it for her when she'd been in the bathroom.

"Just so you know," she said as she replaced her glass on the table having taken a sip, "I don't get what happened earlier, either. I don't get why it caused you to ignore me which, in my opinion, was heartless given you're the only person I really know here."

"I know. And I'm sorry. I am. I was being an ass. But…" Fraser dropped his gaze to the table and began to play with a beer mat.

"But, what?" Lexi prompted as he remained silent.

Slowly he raised his head and looked at her. "You said you weren't interested in breaking your vows."

"And I'm not," she defended. "I love Cal. Why would I break them?"

Fraser shook his head. "No, that's not what I'm saying. The fact that your head says you don't want to break them is not in doubt. The problem is – sometimes your body tells a different story."

Lexi shook her head. She was beginning to feel uncomfortable with the way this conversation was going. "You're crazy," she said. "When have I ever given anyone cause to think I would break my vows?"

She watched as across from her, Fraser swallowed. "Intentionally," he began, "you never have, but sometimes … sometimes when you look at me – at people – your eyes say something different."

Lexi regarded him in shock. "Are you serious? My *eyes* tell you – and others it would seem – that I'm willing to stray? You know what, Fraser? This conversation is over. I don't care what happened earlier and I'm just about done waiting for Jae. I have a home and a husband to go to. I don't need this crap." She shuffled along the bench seat and out of the cramped alcove. "This," she said as she gestured around the pub with her hand, "never happened and nor did this conversation. And as for Jae, I find that I no longer care if he's sick and twisted because if he is, it appears he's in good company."

Lexi began to back away from the table as she continued to glare at Fraser.

"The good company I don't dispute," said a voice from behind her and Lexi jumped, "but I would prefer it if you decided how sick and twisted I am once you've got to know me. It never pays to be judgemental."

As if in slow motion Lexi watched Fraser's eyes move beyond her shoulder and she knew, without even turning, that Jae Leonard had finally arrived. Not only that, he'd clearly heard every single word she'd just thrown at Fraser. Slowly she released a long breath and then began to pivot on her heel; she knew that when she completed the one-eighty-degree turn she would come face to face with him – Jae – the man who thus far had been conspicuously absent in her working life.

Eventually, as his face finally swam into view, she heard Fraser speak from behind her offering a somewhat unnecessary introduction.

"Lexi Strudwick, meet Jae Leonard."

Lexi Strudwick, meet Jae Leonard.

Five words. Five really simple words, yet, as she regarded the man stood resolutely in front of her, Lexi felt the world stop and then slowly, ever so slowly, restart. Their gazes collided and a feeling of impending doom began to thread its way to her soul. Somehow, Lexi knew that with those five simple words her life had just changed inexplicably. Jae Leonard. A man who she unfathomably knew was about to challenge her world in the most damaging of ways. Call it a sixth sense, call it whatever, but when their eyes finally disconnected Lexi's heart began to beat once more.

The only problem was…

She hadn't even realised it had stopped.

* * *

The alcove suddenly seemed so much smaller as Jae settled himself on the bench seat next to Fraser. With a gesture of his hand he indicated that she should sit back down and, in deference to his authority, she did.

"Lexi," the voice was the same, earthy drawl she'd heard on the phone that afternoon, "it's great to finally meet you."

He extended a hand towards her across the table and automatically she reached out and shook it. His hand was large, much larger than hers but warm, the resulting handshake firm. Lexi nodded. She said nothing in response, not trusting herself to speak. Was it great to meet him too? Only time would tell.

"You have something that you wish to talk to me about?" he asked and again, Lexi nodded before finally finding her voice.

"Yes," she said, "I do."

Jae angled his head to one side and regarded her for a moment. It felt strange, like she was being studied under the microscope and beneath his gaze, she fidgeted. Lexi fixed her eyes on his shoulder, hoping his perusal would end soon.

"How long have you worked for us?" he asked and she allowed her gaze to move to his face.

"Almost five months," she responded watching as he arched his brow. A dark brow, black, the same colour as his nearly too long, wavy hair.

"I'm sorry I've not met you before today," Jae apologised.

"It's fine. I know you're a busy man."

"Indeed," she watched as he moved his head back to centre, noticing that his eyelashes were long too, sweeping down over eyes almost as dark as his hair, "although it's not acceptable for me to wait five months before introducing myself to an employee. You therefore have my sincerest apologies for the oversight."

"Thank you," Lexi nodded although given her unerring feeling of impending doom she would have preferred to wait another five months to meet him.

"Are you enjoying your time with us?" Jae asked and again, Lexi nodded.

"Yes. Very much thank you. Fraser's been very kind." She indicated the other man who had yet to speak. "As has everyone else of course," she added. Surreptitiously she glanced in the direction of the other table and as she did so she felt, rather than saw, Jae follow her gaze.

Turning her head back she took a moment to look at him in profile. In addition to the dark features she'd already catalogued, Lexi noted that his nose was a little pointed and his chin had a small cleft, both of which gave him a proud air. His presence in the cramped confines felt overwhelming. He exuded confidence and power and Fraser, sitting to his left, almost paled in comparison.

Jae turned his attention back to their table and then smiled at her before looking sideways towards Fraser.

"Is everyone here?" he asked.

Fraser nodded.

"Is she here?" Jae asked again, his voice lowered. With the distance between them being so small, however, Lexi had no difficulty in hearing what he said. Thanks to Fraser, she also knew to whom Jae was referring.

"Yes," Fraser responded.

Jae nodded slowly. With his head turned towards Fraser, Lexi was able to examine the opposing profile view. She saw the same pride as she'd seen before but, in addition, she saw the faint remains of an ugly scar running up the entire length of his right cheek. As if he could feel her looking, Jae moved his right hand up to cover his cheek and turned back to face her full on. His eyes, when they focused on her once more, were arresting and Lexi immediately understood how Sonya had been tempted to stray down a troubled path with him. When he gave someone his undivided attention, as he was doing to her now, his presence was all encompassing. She knew she was going to need to be strong to come out of any association with him completely unscathed.

"What was it you wanted to talk to me about, Lexi?" Jae asked. The question, after the initial pleasantries, was direct and it caught Lexi off guard. Rapidly she took a sip of her drink, grateful Fraser had been thoughtful enough to replace it.

"It's about work," she said eventually as she swallowed over the lump in her throat. For all her bravado when she'd asked Fraser to organise this meeting, Lexi recognised that the reality, when faced with her boss, was vastly different. She hadn't changed her mind, she still wanted to find out what Jae knew about Zach, but she felt much smaller than she'd thought she would. He made her feel humbled – and nervous – which caused her to recognise that she did in fact care about her job. Her earlier protestations of not working for him should he turn out to be twisted, were beginning to feel somewhat empty. If she cared about her job, her thought process continued, then that meant she cared about Jae Leonard or, more precisely, what he thought of her. This was all totally new to Lexi, but she understood she was going to have to be careful how she played this. One wrong move and she could very well be sacrificing her career and possibly her future.

"Go on…" He watched her, those dark eyes never wavering from her face as he waited for her to answer.

Lightly she coughed. "There was a file, this morning," she said, her voice more tentative than she'd hoped and quickly she took another sip of her drink. Perhaps getting drunk in order to have this meeting would've been a better plan after all.

"Okay." His eyes were still boring into her and Lexi shifted in her seat.

"One of the files you allocated to me – I know the client." She watched for any hint of a reaction but there was none.

Across from her, Jae shrugged. "That's not entirely unusual. Did you hand the file to someone else?"

She shook her head. "Erm…no, not yet. I wanted to wait until I'd spoken to you."

"Why?" he asked. "You didn't need to speak to me for a matter as trivial as this. Fraser or Adam could easily have dealt with it. You know the client, you hand the file over. Basic business protocol. Don't tell me I've come all the way down here for this?"

His tone hardened and Lexi wondered why. Was it because he genuinely thought he was on a fool's errand or was it because he knew more than he was letting on?

"I know," she spread her hands on the table in front of her, "and of course Fraser advised me to hand over the file." She looked in the other man's direction and he smiled weakly at her. "But it's not that simple."

"Rarely is business simple and life, even more rarely. How old are you?"

Lexi looked up at him in surprise, the question coming out of nowhere. "Twenty-two next month," she answered and Jae smiled, although it failed to reach his eyes.

"In which case you still have a lot to learn, Lexi, both about business and about life. Yet, I understand that you're married?"

Immediately she felt herself bristle. "Yes, I am," she answered simply. She felt no need to elaborate. This was, after all, a business meeting.

"Do you plan to have children?" he asked and Lexi's eyes flew straight to Fraser. He couldn't ask that kind of question – could he?

"It's not really relevant, Jae," Fraser mumbled, but the other man dismissed him with a wave of his hand.

"In a business environment I would agree with you, Fraser," Jae commented, "but we're not in a business environment. This is a public place, a place for socialising."

"I still don't think it's appropriate," Fraser repeated and Lexi smiled at him, thankful that despite what she'd thrown at him before Jae arrived, Fraser was still there supporting her.

Lexi watched as Jae turned his head towards the other man. "Do I always do what's appropriate?"

She saw Fraser shake his head. "No, I guess not." His voice sounded resigned and Lexi began to wonder what else Fraser knew. What other inappropriate things Jae had done that he knew about.

"It's fine," Lexi held up her hand, "I don't mind answering the question. Yes, I plan to have children sometime. But then most people do. That's no big secret."

Jae turned his head back towards her and she saw him frown. "That's a huge generalisation for someone so young. On what authority can you make a sweeping statement like that?"

Lexi frowned back. "I don't...I have no authority..." her voice wavered and she took another deep breath. "But that's how it works – marriage and kids. That's the deal."

Across from her, Jae burst out laughing. Feeling affronted she looked at Fraser who just shrugged.

"What's so funny?" she asked.

Jae shook his head. "Fraser told me you were somewhat naive, but I never realised he was being serious."

Again, her hackles rose. "What's wrong with wanting the prescribed life? What's wrong with wanting to follow the path our parents did? And their parents before them? Surely it's our own choice and a person's belief shouldn't be laughed at. Regardless."

Jae tilted his head as she spoke and then, when she'd finished, he nodded. "He also told me you had spirit. I didn't believe that either, but it seems I was wrong on both counts. I apologise. You are of course, right. It's entirely personal what we choose to believe and how we choose to live."

His words were sincere but his tone told her otherwise and Lexi raised her guard further. The atmosphere felt odd, uncomfortable perhaps and coupled with the dominance of his presence, she was starting to regret wanting to meet him. When they should have been talking about Zach and his company, they were talking about her life, her marital status. Again.

"I want to ask something," she began. The fact that Jae had laughed at her beliefs made her feel emboldened and some of the anger she'd felt earlier when she'd first seen Zach's file, began to return. "Why is my marital status such a fascination?"

Fraser had just sipped his beer and as she asked the question he choked, rapidly putting his hand to his mouth before he spurted the contents all over the table. Lexi looked over at him, as did Jae.

"You okay?" Jae asked and from behind his hand, Fraser nodded. Lexi dug around in her handbag and retrieved a tissue that she handed to Fraser. Jae watched the exchange with amusement.

"You have tissues in your handbag?" Jae asked.

Lexi sighed as she looked back towards him. "Don't tell me, that's hilarious too?"

He shrugged. "Not especially. But ten years ago I didn't know too many girls who carried tissues in their bags. You seem very – domesticated – for one so young."

"And we're back there again," she commented, "my age, my marital status. Look, I asked for this meeting because I wanted to talk to you about a work related matter and I apologise if this seems forward, but I'd rather we focused on that." Her tone was blunt and for a moment she wondered if she had indeed been too forward, even though the way they were going it would be midnight before the subject of Zach ever got raised.

Jae's dark eyes focused on her once more and again, she had the feeling she knew how Sonya felt. Shaking her head she raised her eyes defiantly to his. "Please?" she asked again. "You're a busy man and I'm sure you have better things to be doing. Can we just talk about why you're here and then we can all go home?"

His eyes remained unmoving, but slowly he nodded. Inside, Lexi began to squirm under his scrutiny. The depth of attention he was giving her was starting to feel uncomfortable.

"Great," she blew out a breath. On the other side of the table Fraser had finished mopping himself up and was now relaxing further back into the bench, almost as if he was removing himself from the conversation.

"You knew the client?" Jae prompted as he too settled a little further back in his seat.

"Yes. Zach Jackson?"

Jae's eyes flickered and she knew he recognised the name, but he remained silent.

"He's Cal's – my husband's – best friend. I've known him a while. He's the kindest man I've ever met."

Jae waved his hand. "That may be so, but I still have no idea how this relates to me. Hand the file over. Simple."

Lexi took a moment to compose herself. "Normally I would. I would've just handed the file to someone else and this would never have been brought to your attention but...the file..." she hesitated.

"Yes?" Jae arched his eyebrow. "The file?"

"It's to close down his business. After your take-over. After JaceEnterprises took over his company."

This time his eyes definitely flickered.

"We're a large company, Lexi. Buying out other companies is what we do occasionally. I'm sorry your friend has lost out, but I'm sure he'll have been well compensated."

Lexi frowned at him. "Are you saying you don't know the case?" she asked incredulously. "You allocated the file to me – surely you must know the case?"

Once more his eyes flickered and instinctively, Lexi knew he wasn't being entirely honest. "I knew it was a take-over, yes. The finer details were negotiated by my management team."

"But you allocated the file to me?"

"Yes. You're an intern who is more than capable – so I am led to believe – of closing down a file and paying the necessary funds."

"So this was like any other case to you?"

"Yes."

Out of the corner of her eye Lexi saw Fraser turn to gaze out of the window. More proof that he wanted nothing to do with this conversation.

She took a moment to gather her thoughts. "So, you're saying you had no real knowledge of this file and no idea that I was in any way connected to it?"

On the table, Fraser clenched his fist. A small movement but one that Lexi didn't miss.

"It was a file that crossed my desk in the same way thousands of others do, Lexi," Jae responded. His voice was back to being smooth, the way it had been when he'd first sat down. "I merely checked the contracts had been signed. I trust my management team. I knew they would've done their job properly."

Lexi shook her head, barely able to believe what she was hearing. Fraser had always impressed on her how Jae knew everything. How he knew every client, every employee – and yet here he was dismissing Zach as someone he didn't know, hadn't even met?

"Wait a minute," she said as she remembered something Zach had said previously, "you had a meeting with him, a couple of months ago. I know because he told me. That's when we realised I was working for the company that was going to buy him out. You must know this case."

Jae's dark eyes bored into her. "I know the name. That's all." This time when he spoke there was an edge to his voice. Almost like he was warning her not to say any more.

"You met with him though. I know you did."

"Because this Zach told you?"

"Yes," Lexi defended. "He told me he had a meeting with you."

"And were you present at this meeting?" Jae asked.

She shook her head in an attempt to maintain her cool. "No, of course not. What a ridiculous question."

Jae shrugged. "Not really. If you weren't present at the meeting, then how can you possibly know it was me he met with? It could have been anyone on my management team. I trust them to represent me at all levels, Lexi."

Helplessly she looked across at Fraser, sure that the other man

261

would have her back. He glanced away from the window briefly before shaking his head and resuming his study outside.

"All I'm saying, Lexi," Jae continued, "is that you have no way of knowing for certain if I was at that meeting. It's entirely possible I do indeed know very little about this takeover."

She almost laughed. Almost. "You seriously expect me to believe you know nothing of a takeover? However small? And yes, of course it's possible you weren't at that meeting, but I know Zach will tell me you were and out of the two of you, I know who I believe."

Opposite her she watched as Jae's eyes darkened. Absently she marvelled at how it was possible for them to become darker than they already were. "I would be very careful, Lexi," he said at length. "You are an intern, someone who is eminently dispensable. If you value your job, you might have to think about where your loyalties lie or, at the very least, think about what you say *before* you say it. I do not appreciate my honesty being questioned."

For a moment his words hit the mark and instinctively she recoiled. Perhaps she had overstepped, but then she ran his words over in her head one more time. By inference he was suggesting Zach wasn't being honest. Bravely she raised her eyes to his once more.

"I stand by what I just said," she reiterated, "I don't know if you're telling me the truth or not, but my money is on not. I have no idea why you would be lying to me and even less idea why it matters right now, but it does. There are reasons why I wanted to understand your involvement in this takeover," she continued, aware that with every word she was almost certainly hammering a nail into her professional coffin, but honesty mattered to her. So, she had principles. So damn what? "...and those reasons haven't changed. I would still like answers from you, although it would appear you're not going to give them to me. At least not now." She reached forwards and lifted her glass to her lips, taking one final sip. Across from her Jae remained stony faced.

"I'm sorry this meeting didn't go to plan," she said as she slowly stood, "and I totally understand if I no longer have a job. But you've ridiculed me, laughed at my beliefs and, I'm certain, lied to me. Somehow, losing you as my boss, doesn't seem that great a sacrifice."

Lifting her handbag from the bench seat she walked towards the exit door and away from the two men. She could feel both sets of eyes penetrating her back as she walked, but she held her head high and kept on going. As first meetings with your boss went, Lexi knew she'd been completely unprofessional. She knew she'd been out of line and she understood he wasn't the kind of person you spoke to that way – especially if you valued your career. Moreover, she had no idea where that Lexi had come from, the person who had just stood up for what she believed in in front of her boss. It wasn't a Lexi that she knew, but, as she carried on out of the pub and headed towards the taxi rank, she decided she actually kind of liked that Lexi. Perhaps this was what her parents had meant when they'd talked to her about growing up – about how she would know when she got there and that things would feel right. It'd been unplanned and unprofessional, but it had felt damn right – the timing, the words, everything. Used to never being alone Lexi had often struggled to find her own identity in the past, but there, in that pub, in that moment, she'd found it. She'd found her own identity and she'd found a new Lexi, a Lexi she was proud of. A Lexi that she knew would be strong and who would guide her in whatever direction she took from here, and she needed that Lexi. Because, in the process of discovering herself, she'd almost certainly lost her job.

Chapter Twenty-Six

Cal

Cal's evening out with Zach had not gone according to plan. On arrival at the pub – the same one near the university where Cal had first met Lexi – Zach had taken two pints in quick succession, which had loosened his tongue. After that the floodgates opened and rather than joining his best friend in drowning his sorrows – which was what Cal had been expecting – he found himself way out of his depth.

"Bastards," Zach observed as he began on his third pint of the evening.

"Who?" Cal asked since his friend could've been referring to any number of people.

"Debt collectors."

"Oh," Cal shrugged his shoulders in acknowledgement. "No argument from me there."

"Bitch," Zach said and this time Cal knew exactly who Zach was talking about. She who would never be named again.

"Yup. No arguments," he agreed.

"D'you know," Zach waved at him with his half empty pint glass, "those debt collectors have taken almost as much in interest as the amount I owed in the first place. Correction," he said as he placed his glass down with a thud, "the amount that bitch owed."

"Are you clear now?" Cal asked.

"Yes." Zach stared morosely into his beer glass.

"Well, that's something," Cal said. "I mean you get to start again. That's good."

His friend turned to face him and Cal instantly knew he'd made a poor choice of words.

"Start again?" Zach asked. "I've just spent the last twenty fucking years building up my business, why the fuck would I want to start again? At my age?"

"I didn't mean with the business," Cal replied calmly, "you got enough out of the deal to go wherever you want. Start your life again – could be liberating."

Beside him, Zach snorted. "Right. And you know so much about life and how it works."

Cal shook his head and remained quiet for a moment. He knew Zach wasn't really angry with him. He'd had a rough deal and he was lashing out. Cal, it appeared, was the current punch bag.

"I don't," Cal said at length, "I think life sucks and I hate that that bitch doesn't even have to pay for what she's put you through. You've lost your business for fuck's sake. I'm not alright with that and nor will I ever be. I was just trying to be positive. I don't know. I'm not a philosopher or anything, but I figure hope is pretty much all you have left. And me." He added as an afterthought.

"You're shit with words, man," Zach said, "if that was supposed to make me feel better..."

"Agreed. I drink better than I talk," Cal said as he signalled to the barman who topped up both of their beers.

"Is it wrong," Zach asked after they'd taken another drink, "to feel completely empty inside? No – more than empty. Dead?"

Cal considered for a moment. He'd known that feeling before he met Zach. "It's not wrong, but it's a hell of a place to be. I get it. I was there too when we met, but I don't want to see you there. It sucks."

"I don't wanna be there," Zach replied, "but I am and in some ways, it actually feels pretty good."

"Whoa," Cal looked across at his friend in alarm. "You think the way you feel right now, feels good?"

He watched as Zach shrugged. "Yeah, in a way. It's like I already hurt more than I thought I could, so now I don't feel anything anymore, I don't hurt anymore. So I'm empty. Dead."

Cal clapped his arm around Zach's shoulders. "You gotta stop talking like that. I understand how you feel but you taught me life could be better than that. Remember?"

Again, Zach shrugged. "Yeah. But I talked a lot of bullshit in those days."

Cal pulled his arm a little tighter around Zach's shoulders. "You did not. I don't wanna hear you saying stuff like that. You straightened me out. I would never have had this life – Lexi – without you. You gotta toughen up. Like you told me to do."

"You were young. You had your whole life ahead of you. I don't. I'm middle aged, Cal. What have I got left to look forward to? Old bones and a council retirement flat? Nah. That's not for me."

"Zach?" Cal asked. Suddenly he began to feel concern for his friend. Real concern. "You okay?"

Zach laughed. "Shit, Cal. Seriously? You seriously ask if I'm okay? I lost my business today. Pfft. Gone. Puff of smoke. All those years I worked, only for some bitch to put a match to it. I lost the woman I thought I loved and my business – the only life I've ever known. And I've got nothing to show for it. You really need to ask if I'm okay?"

"That's not what I meant," Cal replied. "I know it's shit, but the way you're talking… are you okay? Are you gonna be okay?"

Again, Zach laughed. "You're crap at this, Cal. Why not just come out with it. Ask me the question."

Cal shook his head. "I don't know what you're asking me, Zach. I'm worried about you. I've never heard you talk like this. Are you financially destitute now?"

"No," Zach turned to face him, "I'm not destitute."

"Okay," Cal breathed out, "so you can start again. Get another place? Work?"

"Yeah, I can, but you know what, Cal? I'm tired. I don't wanna start again. I want my life exactly like it was. This – this idea of a new beginning – it's all shit. Things people say to make you feel better. Well, I've got news for you. It doesn't make me feel better. That's why dead inside is good. Because now I don't feel it anymore and believe me, that's good."

"I get that, I do," Cal dropped his arm from around Zach and picked up his pint, "but there has to be a way out of this. What about with Mel? What does she say?"

Zach shook his head. "Over."

"What?" Cal looked across at Zach. He was shocked. Over? "Lexi never said anything. When did that happen?"

"Well, technically we're still together, but it's not working. She's too young. It was never going to be a long-term thing."

"Shit, man. When it rains it really rains. I'm sorry." He clapped his hand on Zach's back again.

"To be honest," Zach said, "it's a relief. Trying to be the man she wanted was bloody hard work. Like I said, I'm tired. I don't have the energy anymore."

"Why not take a break – get away for a while?" Cal suggested.

Beside him Zach snorted. "On my own? Yeah. Like I'm such good company."

"I know it's crap, but maybe being somewhere different would help. You know? Perspective?"

Zach shook his head. "No. This is all I know. This place. My friends. You. You're my family. If I take off then I lose what remains of my sanity."

"Okay, I get that," Cal agreed, "but you wouldn't be gone for long. Just a couple of weeks maybe. Enough time to realise there's something out there other than blackness."

Again, Zach shook his head. "Nope. Not happening. If I went somewhere else I'd have to pretend to be someone again. Talk to people. Communicate. Hell, it's all I can do to get washed these days."

At that, Cal smiled. "I didn't know how to mention the smell."

Zach threw him a look. "You really think I'm in the mood for humour?"

He shrugged. "No. I guess not. I'm here for you, you know that. You taught me to be strong and to understand I could be better, live in a good place. Now you have to take your own advice."

His friend laughed, although the sound was hollow. "That's the trouble with giving crap advice. People think you're some kind of wise man – truth is, I talked bullshit then, just like I talk now."

Cal could feel his anger rising to the surface. "You saved me, Zach," he said quietly, "and I don't care if you want to acknowledge that or not. Your advice, the way you supported me, no one else has ever done that. Quit selling yourself short, okay? I can help you. Let me help you."

"You got a twenty-year-old established business you wanna give me?"

Cal shook his head.

"Then there's nothing you can do."

He shook his head again. "It's about so much more than that. C'mon. I've never heard you talk like this before. It'll be okay. You'll get through it. I know you will."

Cal watched as Zach turned towards him and dropped his head to one side. "Yeah," he said after a pause, "I don't doubt I'll get through this. Or rather, that I could get through this. But you're forgetting one thing. I don't know that I *want* to get through this."

"What?" he frowned at his friend, "what the hell is that supposed to mean?"

Zach sighed. "Haven't you been listening to anything I've said? It's good feeling like this. I already told you. I feel lighter than I have in a long time knowing that nothing else can get me now. I'm officially at the bottom. So, I figured, I may as well enjoy the ride."

"You think this is living?" Cal asked as he watched Zach signal for another pint.

"Nah." Zach shook his head. "Living wasn't all that hot though. Right now I don't mind sitting here. Existing. Yeah. Existing. That feels good."

When he'd first met Zach, Cal had been low. He'd known he was using women to make him feel, because inside he was dead – like Zach was now. Cal knew all about existing. He knew how it felt to live a half-life where you simply functioned and then took the odd moment of pleasure. Zach had shown him that life could be different though. He'd shown Cal that he could trust, that he could be someone and that he could learn to love. The way he lived now was a million miles away from the nineteen-year-old Zach had first met and, despite some trying times, he never wanted to go back to that half-life again. Seeing Zach in exactly the same place, tore at his heart. He knew the numbness and the blessed relief, but he also knew the cost. There was no way he wanted that for his best friend.

"Tell me what I can do, Zach," he said. "What do you want? I mean, what do you really want? If you could have anything, what would it be?"

"To be left the hell alone," Zach grumbled.

"If that were true, you wouldn't have called me."

"Now I wish I hadn't."

Cal sighed. Zach was in a worse place than he'd first thought. "I don't believe that. I think if you wanted to be left alone, you wouldn't have bothered to call me."

"Yeah?" Zach turned to him and Cal could see his friend's eyes were red and a little unfocused. The alcohol was taking effect. "Well, how about you leave me the hell alone now?"

He shook his head. "Not gonna happen, mate. You picked me up. I'm not letting you go through this alone."

Cal jumped as Zach slammed his fist on the bar. "When the fuck are you going to let up about how I saved you? Huh?"

"You did save me," he argued.

"No. No, I didn't." Zach's words were becoming slurred, each one more carefully enunciated than its predecessor. "You saved yourself."

Cal shook his head. "Now you *are* talking bullshit. If it hadn't been for you, I wouldn't have found my way."

Zach laughed and with the addition of alcohol, the sound was ugly. "You really believe that? You really think that me," Zach indicated himself with a finger that was less than steady, "that I, saved you?" The finger pointed towards Cal.

"Yes," he stated firmly. "I do."

Again, the ugly laugh.

"You're so full of it. Man. Really?"

"Zach," Cal held out his hand towards his friend, "I think you've had enough. Let's get out of here. We can go back to mine. Have a coffee."

Zach shook his head. "Let me tell you something," he slurred. "I never saved another person in my life, cos that's not who I am.

This," again he pointed at himself for emphasis, "this is me. A nobody. With nothing."

"No, Zach. No. I'm not going to hear you talk like that. You've saved me and the other guys too. You helped us. All of us. You'll never be a nobody – that's just the alcohol talking. Let's get out of here."

Zach snorted. "Sorry, Cal. I ain't going nowhere. I just realised that feeling of being dead – it's way better after a few beers. You can go. I'm stayin'."

Cal shook his head. "Okay, this isn't you. You've had a rough day and you've had a few too many. That's all. Let me help you." He moved forwards and put his arm around the other man's shoulders. "C'mon." Despite Cal's best efforts though, Zach refused to budge.

"I told you," he pushed Cal away, "I'm stayin'."

Cal glanced at his watch and noted that it was still early. Letting out a breath he spoke again. "I'm stayin' too then. But you've had enough, okay? Let's get some coffee." He signalled to the barman.

"Coffee?" Zach scoffed. "Shit, man. You've gone soft in the head. Too much time with that chick."

Cal froze and then frowned at his friend. In all the time he'd known Lexi, Cal had never heard Zach call her anything other than by her name. Zach considered Lexi a lady; he'd told Cal on many occasions. To hear Zach refer to her so casually now, threw him.

"You mean Lexi?" he asked surprised.

"Yeah," Zach turned bloodshot eyes his way. "Why? How many others you been screwin'?" There was a sickening laugh.

Cal swallowed over his immediate anger as mentally he calculated how much Zach had had to drink. Five pints, which, by Zach's lads' night out standards, was a drop in the ocean. He was way more wasted than five pints.

"Have you had anything else to drink?" Cal asked.

Zach laughed again, the sound still ugly. "No. What? You think 'cos I've got nothing I'm turning to drink?"

Confused, Cal shook his head. "No, of course not."

"Thought you were going," Zach spoke carefully.

"Nope. I told you. If you stay, so do I."

Two cups of steaming coffee appeared in front of him and he pushed one in the direction of Zach. His friend regarded it with disgust and then using his arm he forcefully sent it down the bar and away from him. Scalding black coffee made a trail down the oak beam as the cup teetered and then eventually fell, the liquid that had remained in the receptacle now dripping onto the beer taps and eventually the floor behind the bar.

"Shit, Zach." Cal grabbed a couple of napkins and began to ineffectually mop at the mess as the bartender reappeared. "Sorry, mate," Cal said as he indicated the spilt drink.

"No worries." With a cloth the bartender skilfully remedied the damage. After assuring the man that he didn't want a replacement, Cal returned to his seat beside Zach and sipped at his own cup.

"I don't get it," he said as he allowed the first swallow of the hot liquid to run down the back of his throat. "You can handle your drink way better than this. Are you gonna' tell me what's going on?"

Zach turned sideways and once again, Cal marvelled at the lack of focus in his friend's eyes. Never had he seen him so wasted on so little and in such a short space of time.

"I told you. Nothing to tell."

For a moment Cal held Zach's eyes, trying to stare him down, trying to read something in what was left of his friend's dead gaze, but there was nothing. He shook his head.

"So, what happens now?" he asked with a brightness he was far from feeling. "Have you thought about what you're going to do?"

Again Zach looked at him but remained silent.

"What about buying a property? Renovating? Maybe a smallholding?" Cal knew he was clutching at straws, but his meagre skills at managing this situation were evaporating – fast. "Smallholding can be big business these days. Organic this and non-GM that."

"She's really done a number on you," Zach said finally and Cal looked at him confused. "Before her you wouldn't have known what those words meant let alone tried to tell me they were my future."

Cal began to wonder how aware Zach was of what he was saying.

If, as Cal suspected, the other man was completely gone, then talking about anything of magnitude was pointless. Plus he was getting rather tired of the flippant way in which Zach was referring to Lexi.

"Never mind."

He watched as Zach shrugged before taking another slurp of his disappearing pint. For his part, Cal finished up his coffee, knowing he needed his head to be clear. For a few minutes they sat in silence, slurping, sipping and, as far as Cal was concerned, thinking. Something about Zach and the way he was behaving was bugging him. It was too far out of the ordinary.

"Thank fuck for painkillers," Zach mumbled and for a moment, Cal paused – waiting.

"What do you mean?" he asked after Zach offered nothing further.

"Painkillers," Zach slurred. "Strong ones. Thumping headache. It's gone now."

Cal frowned. "That's good." He thought for a second. "You've taken strong painkillers today?"

"'S what I just said."

"When?"

"How the fuck should I know? A while ago."

Automatically he glanced at his watch, but since Zach didn't know when he'd taken the pills, the action was pointless. "What kind of painkillers?"

Zach looked across at him, his face creased in a frown. "What the fuck does it matter? I had a headache, now I don't. And I feel empty and it feels bloody good."

"Okay, fine." Cal held up his hand. "Where did you get them from?"

Zach slurped the last of his pint before slamming it down on the oak bar. "Doctor. For my ankle."

"Your ankle? Wait a minute…Zach, you hurt your ankle over a year ago. You still have some of those painkillers?"

"Yup. Found them in the drawer."

Cal took a deep breath. "How many have you taken?"

"What the hell is this?" Zach lifted his glass in the direction of the bar tender. "You my mother or something?"

"No, of course not. But if they're old then they could be out of date. They might be hitting you harder than before."

Zach laughed. "Shit, man. You've become so bloody domesticated. What happened to the Cal I knew?"

Beneath the bar stool, Cal clenched his fists. This was the beer and now, it would appear, the meds talking. He had to stay calm.

"I think you might be having a reaction. To taking the meds and drinking," Cal clarified. "I've never seen you like this before and we've had our share of big nights in the past."

Zach's bloodshot eyes regarded him. "So what? I feel better than I have in ages."

Cal nodded. "I'm not surprised. I think you should stop drinking. Let me take you home to sleep it off."

Another pint appeared in front of Zach and Cal grabbed at it quickly, moving it out of his friend's way. "C'mon, let's get home. You'll feel better tomorrow and then we can talk some more. Okay?"

Zach reached across in front of Cal in a bid to grab the new pint. "Gimme my beer," he slurred, but Cal was faster and moved the glass further out of reach.

"No," he stated firmly, "we're going home."

If looks could kill, Cal would've dropped dead on the spot as Zach attempted to stare him down, but steadfastly Cal held his ground.

"Gimme my beer," Zach tried again, but this time Cal reached over and placed it behind the bar, well out of reach.

"We're going," he said to the bartender as he threw a couple of notes on the bar. Zach lunged forward as he stood from his stool and Cal expertly caught him. He'd been prepared.

"Get your fucking hands off me," Zach shouted as Cal began to move him in the direction of the door.

"All in good time," he said as he used his youth and superior, non-drink induced strength, to get his friend out of the pub and into the cool night air. Beside him, Zach swayed.

"Get your hands off me," Zach said again as he began to push against Cal. The combination of the meds and the drink were really hitting though and Cal knew better than to release Zach. Propelling the other man forwards, he opened the door of a waiting taxi and with Zach rendered weaker than a newborn kitten, he pushed him easily onto the back seat. Quickly he shuffled in beside his friend and gave the driver Zach's address.

"Too bloody nosey for your own good," Zach mumbled as he gazed out of the side window. "Why couldn't you leave me alone?"

Cal ignored him. This was old ground and the answer was the same as always – because he was Cal's best friend. That and the fact Cal owed him, regardless of what Zach, in his current state, felt.

"Where we goin'?" Zach asked. This time Cal replied.

"Yours. Cold shower, coffee and bed."

Beside him, Zach snorted loudly. "You're my fuckin' mother."

"Whatever."

They rode in silence for a few moments.

"My mother," Zach's voice was a little less slurred and Cal turned towards him. "Did I ever tell you about my mother?"

Cal shook his head. "No." In truth Zach had never told him about any of his family. To Zach, the guys were his family.

"She loved me," Zach said.

"Of course she did," Cal responded when it was obvious his friend wasn't going to say anything more.

"Did your mother love you?" Zach asked.

Cal knew this question was prompted by the drink/meds cocktail still zinging around in Zach's veins. Never, in a sober state, would he have dared to bring up the issue of Cal's parents. It was a closed subject. For a second he shut his eyes.

"In her own way," he responded after a moment.

"'S good. 'S good that our mothers loved us."

"Yeah," Cal agreed quietly as he continued to stare out of his own window. The lights of Brufton stretched out before them as they negotiated their way around the outskirts of the city and on towards Zach's home.

"She killed herself," Zach commented and at this, Cal whipped his head around to face his friend. The way Zach delivered it in such a matter of fact way alarmed him almost as much as the words themselves.

"Shit, Zach. I'm sorry."

Zach shrugged. "I was five so it must have been...fuck, I don't know. A bloody long time ago."

Cal remained silent. He was way, way out of his depth now.

"He laughed," Zach said again and this time Cal slapped his hand over his mouth, afraid of what might come out yet instinctively knowing who Zach was referring to.

"My father," Zach confirmed and Cal kept his hand firmly in place as bile rose up in his throat. Shit. And he thought he'd had a crap start.

"She was on the floor. I saw her there when I got home from school. In the kitchen. I tried to wake her up. I tried. But she wouldn't wake up. Nancy from next door came around. Nancy..." Zach said as he let his voice trail off.

Cal shook his head and swallowed. This was too much. Way too much and yet Zach was opening up to him, telling him about his past and he knew he had to say something. Support his friend in some way.

"I'm so sorry," he said. It felt wholly inadequate, but he had nothing else to offer.

"They called my dad." Zach was staring out of the window and Cal knew his friend's mind had gone to another place – he was reliving the moment as if it were happening now. "And the police. Dad got home first. He walked into the kitchen and saw her, the same as I'd done and I ran to him. I ran to him. I wanted him to pick me up and tell me it was okay but he didn't. He looked down at me and then he started to laugh. And he carried on laughing and he didn't stop. Not even when the police took her body away. Not even when they took him away too. And Nancy, she stood with me on the doorstep and she held me close as we watched them leave. My mum and my dad. Both of them. Gone."

Subconsciously Cal registered that the cab had stopped and they were sitting outside Zach's block of flats. He reached forwards and handed the driver the fare.

"Zach?" he said quietly. "We're home."

His friend turned to look at him, his eyes blank almost as if he'd forgotten that Cal was there.

"Right," he said as he shoved at the door and began to leave the cab. Cal rushed around to help him, knowing that even if the effects of the alcohol had worn off some, Zach would still need support. Especially after what he'd just told Cal. Together they negotiated the short path up to Zach's front door, which, thankfully, was on the ground floor. After finding the keys in Zach's pocket, Cal unlocked it, encouraging his friend to move in ahead. Zach took a few paces and then stopped, turning back to face Cal.

"I'm sorry, man," Cal said. "So sorry."

Zach shook his head and as he did so, he pointed a shaky finger towards Cal. "If you *ever* breathe a word of what I just told you to anyone…"

"I won't." It was the least he could do.

"Not even Lexi."

Cal nodded. "Not even Lexi." He crossed his heart with his hand and, after a moment, Zach turned away and walked in the direction of his bedroom.

"See yourself out," he said as he disappeared into the room beyond.

For a moment Cal stood rooted to the spot and then, as he heard a thud followed by a loud snore, he spun around and retraced his steps to the front door.

It had been one hell of a night and even though there was a good chance Zach wouldn't remember much of it, Cal knew that what had happened here tonight would remain burned in his memory forever.

* * *

Lexi wasn't home which, given that it was only nine-thirty pm, was no great surprise, and in many ways he was relieved. He needed some time alone to process what had just happened. For the first time since Cal had known Zach, the other man had opened up about his past. At times during their friendship, Cal had privately speculated on what may have happened to Zach in his early years, but never, in his wildest imagination, would he have considered the scenario that Zach had just so painfully described. His mum had died when he was five and his dad had what? Killed her? No. Cal shook his head. Zach had said his mum had taken her own life. Whatever. However you looked at it, whatever had happened, it was seriously fucked up. No wonder his friend never talked about it.

He leaned back into the comfort of his favourite green sofa and glanced around the living room of their newly bought house. He and Lexi had moved in less than a month ago after selling Cal's flat. The house gave them the extra space they'd wanted to start their family and its location, in a small cul-de-sac in an up and coming suburb of Ledgeworth, was perfect. It had been empty for some time; the formalities were therefore completed with relative ease, and before he knew it, Cal had moved from a small, cramped flat, into a modern house. He shook his head. He could barely believe he owned a property like this coming from the background he'd had. Although small, it was more than he could ever have hoped for and he knew he and Lexi would be able to raise a beautiful family here. Upstairs were three bedrooms – the third being little more than a box room – and a family bathroom. Downstairs the house had a kitchen, cloakroom and lounge/diner, which was were Cal now sat in contemplation, running over the events of what had transpired to be a troubling evening.

With a sigh he kicked off his shoes and stretched his long legs out in front, curling his toes into the luxurious rug Lexi had insisted on buying. For a moment he reflected on his past, his childhood. Even though he no longer cared whether or not his parents were alive, it didn't mean he never thought about them. Only recently he'd been forced to tell Lexi what had happened during his childhood, the memories of which still burned, but this, what Zach had just described – man, that really sucked. With another shake of his head he rose from the sofa and walked into the kitchen to switch the kettle on. Coffee. He needed more coffee.

An hour and a half later, Cal sat nursing his third coffee and still there was no sign of Lexi. He'd tried to watch some television, but his mind wouldn't let go and in the end he'd just sat in the quiet of the living room, waiting. He could have gone to bed, of course he could, but Cal wanted to see his wife. He needed to feel her arms around him and to take his comfort from her. So, he waited.

Eventually, after another half an hour, he heard Lexi's key in the lock and desperate to see her, he leapt up from the sofa to greet her in the doorway.

"Hi," Lexi said as she almost collided with him. Cal noted the surprise in her tone.

"Hi, yourself." He reached forwards and pulled her into his arms, feeling her familiar warmth and comfort, knowing that waiting up for her had been the right decision. "How was your evening?" He pulled away to look into her eyes, eyes that, for a moment, shifted sideways before meeting his.

"Yeah, good. Yours?" She pushed away from him and walked into the kitchen, switching the kettle on herself. Cal followed her.

"Not so good. Zach was a mess."

"Right." Lexi's answer lacked emotion and so Cal waited, sure she would question him further. She didn't.

"He lost his company today," Cal clarified. He was sure he'd told Lexi when they'd spoken earlier, but he reiterated the fact just in case.

"I know." Again that emotionless tone.

"So," Cal continued, "he was a mess."

Finally she turned away from the kettle to face him. "I can imagine. I wasn't expecting you to still be up," she commented and Cal shrugged.

"I wanted to see you. It's been a tough night. How did you get home?"

"Taxi." Lexi turned back towards the kettle and filled her mug with boiling water. "Want one?" Cal shook his head.

"I left my car at the office," she continued as he watched her spoon in coffee. "I'll get a taxi in the morning."

"Yeah, I didn't drive home either," he added. "Gonna end up being an expensive night by the time we've both covered our taxi fares."

Lexi whirled towards him, coffee in hand. "What the hell is that supposed to mean?"

Cal shook his head, perplexed at the irritation in her tone. "Nothing. It was a joke. We can afford the taxi fares. Are you okay?" he asked. It was becoming increasingly apparent to him that Lexi

278

was not.

"Yes, fine." She brushed past him and walked into the lounge. He followed her, sitting beside her as she claimed his former seat on the green sofa.

"Many there?" he asked as he watched her slowly sip her coffee.

Lexi gave him a sideways glance. "Does it matter?"

He shrugged. "No. I guess not. You're later than I expected," he added.

"I know." Lexi nodded. "Took a while to get a cab. This time of night."

Cal tilted his head to one side and frowned. "Really?" One of the things that had always impressed him about Brufton was the number and availability of cabs. He and Zach had needed to use them on plenty of occasions in the past.

"Yeah. Anyway, I'm tired." She took another swallow of her drink and dropped the mug onto the table. "I might go on up."

"Okay."

She stood up and then, as he watched her begin to disappear from the room, something inside of him gave way. He'd been sat there for over two hours waiting for her to return and the best she could come up with was transport issues.

"Lexi?" he called and she turned. "I was waiting for you because I need you. I know," he held up his hand, "that's really selfish, but if you could've seen Zach tonight…" He shook his head. "I need you, Lexi," he finished quietly. "Please, just be here for me."

Her beautiful eyes regarded him and he watched them, wholly unable to decipher any of the messages or emotions that were running through them. "It's been a long day," she said eventually, "I really am beat."

Briefly Cal closed his eyes. "I know. For me too. I just need to hold you, Lexi. That's all. I just need to feel you near me. Your comfort."

The warring emotions continued to chase across her face and Cal remained where he was. Something wasn't sitting right with him but he couldn't work out what. Was it the way Lexi was behaving or just the remnants of a really rough day? If her day had been anything like his, then it was understandable that she was off form. Having to ask her to comfort him though, that wasn't something for which he'd been prepared. Slowly, carefully, she made her way back to the sofa and sat down beside him once more. In a way that was so achingly familiar, Cal reached out for her and tucked her into his side. Lexi swung her feet onto the sofa and for a moment they stayed there, unmoving, silent, he taking what he needed from the only person he ever wanted it from. After a while he dropped a kiss into the silky strands of her hair.

"Thank you," he said. In response, Lexi snuggled closer.

"Sorry," she said a moment later, "it's just been one of those days."

"I know." Cal pulled her tighter to him and dropped another kiss on the top of her head. "I understand. Do you want to talk about it?" He felt her shake her head.

Lazily he began to draw circles on her arm with his fingertips as he inhaled her unique citrus scent. Even though she'd been out all day, she still smelled like heaven to him and Cal knew he would never tire of her fragrance.

"I need to tell you something," she said after a moment and Cal shifted his position so he could look at her.

"Sure, anything," he replied quietly. Lexi's eyes sought out his.

"I did a test. There's no baby."

Cal felt an ice-cold dagger hit his heart and then move downwards, stopping to rest in his stomach. "I didn't know it was time," he said, "to test."

She nodded. "Yes. It's time."

"Jeez." Cal pulled himself away from her a little. "Why the hell does this have to be so hard?"

He looked back up at Lexi and she shook her head. "I don't know."

"Are you okay?" he asked. At least now he had a plausible explanation for her mood.

"Yes," she nodded. "I'm okay."

"But it's another month. Another chance," he said. "Are you sure? What do you need? What can I do?"

"Cal," Lexi raised her hand and somewhere in the back of his mind he registered that it was the first time she'd spoken his name that night. "I'm fine. I promise."

He took a moment to look at her, regard her, see for himself that she really was okay, and, after spending a few seconds studying her, he concluded that she was.

"Okay," he said, "well then we can just keep trying. If you're okay then we can carry on and hope that next month we'll be lucky. It's gonna happen, Lexi. I know it is."

"Sure," she responded, but Cal didn't miss the reluctance in her tone.

"You want to keep trying?" he asked, relieved when she nodded her head.

"Of course. It's just been a tough day all around."

"I know." Cal leaned towards her and grasped her hand in his. "I'm sorry," he said as he used his other hand to lift her chin upwards allowing their eyes to connect, "I'm sorry it couldn't be better news."

Lexi smiled. "It's fine. Honestly."

Cal lifted her hand towards his lips and placed a gentle kiss in her palm. "Okay," he mumbled as he nipped at her sensitive skin.

She remained silent, but Cal's body had reacted predictably to his contact with Lexi and so he began to increase the pressure of his kisses, moving up from her palm to her inner arm and then he used his leverage to pull her onto his lap. He felt her resist, just for a moment, and he frowned. "It's a cuddle," he whispered as he dropped his lips to the nape of her neck, "I know you're tired." He felt her sigh.

"Sorry, Cal. I'm not in the mood." She placed her hands on his shoulders and gently, but firmly, moved away from him. Cal frowned up at her again. This was new. Never had she resisted his affection so finally.

"It's a cuddle," he reiterated. "We've both had crap days. We're both tired. I figured we could use the comfort."

"Don't think for me, Cal," she said as she began to stand up. "I know what I want and I know that I'm tired." Irritability laced every word she spoke.

Cal stood too. "What's going on?" he asked. "You seem – different."

Lexi stepped around him, shaking her head as she passed. "I'm tired, Cal. I already told you that. And we didn't get pregnant. I'm not different. I'm just done in."

Cal nodded. "Yeah, sorry. I'm not used to this, that's all." He gestured between them to indicate the distance and as he watched, Lexi's expression softened.

"I know," she said as she took a couple of steps back towards him, "but trust me. I'm okay. I need sleep. That's all."

He felt her place her hand on his cheek and he leaned into it. "I didn't mean to be insensitive," he whispered and she traced her hand from his cheek across his lips.

"I know."

Cal remained standing where he was for a moment, her hand on his lips, his eyes closed. When he opened them she was still there. Waiting. Watching. Gently he removed her hand and dropped it back down to her side.

"Goodnight," he said and she smiled.

"'Night." Lexi turned and began to walk away from him for the second time that evening.

"Wait a sec," he called and she stopped.

"I love you," he closed the distance between them and walked around to stand in front of her. "I love you," he repeated and leaned forwards to place a soft kiss onto her lips.

Lexi didn't move and, taking that as a sign, Cal shifted closer towards her, encircling her with his arms. The soft kiss was doing crazy things to his body and so he applied a little more pressure, asking the question, waiting to see if she would answer. After a few seconds she opened her mouth and he swept inside with a groan. She tasted so good, a flavour that was pure Lexi and he drank it in, deepening the kiss, crushing her closer with his arms, pushing his erection into the softness of her stomach.

He felt her arms go around him and he drank more, revelling in the primitive feeling of this age-old connection. Her arms were tight, banded around him and he pushed deeper, further, moving his hands, dropping them down her back and then lower to caress her buttocks. He felt her respond, her hands digging into him and he smothered a groan at the brief surge of pain. She wanted it rough? He could do rough. He gathered her to him using all of his strength and ground his mouth as deep as it would go, teeth clashing as he continued to devour her. Still he felt her fingers pressing against his arms and, encouraged, he allowed his hands to move around to her front, feeling for her beautiful breasts, knowing he needed to move this to the next level. Inside of his mouth he felt her speak, but he swallowed the words. Blood was coursing through his veins and his arousal was out of control as he massaged her breasts through the thin fabric of her blouse. Again she spoke and again he swallowed it, moving his fingers to her nipples and pulling on them, bringing them to their peaks, his movements rough and effective. He groaned as her body responded to him and he bucked forwards, needing his hardness to be as close to her as possible.

He slanted his mouth and continued to kiss her, knowing his stubble was rough but not caring. She was digging her fingers into him so hard, he knew she needed this as much as he did and he was more than willing to comply. He carried on with the exploration of her breasts, pulling, massaging and pinching, everything else insignificant to him as he made love to his wife. Suddenly and without warning he felt a searing pain in his mouth followed by a sharp, metallic taste and instantly, Cal freed her lips.

"Ow, shit. What was that?" He moved his tongue around the inside of his mouth, alarmed to realise that the taste was blood and the source the very same tongue. He poked it out and dabbed gently at the tender spot on the front with his fingers. "What happened?" he asked in confusion.

Lexi regarded him, face stony, and suddenly Cal felt fear. Her expression was murderous, her face wreathed in anger, not the passion he'd been expecting. "I bit your tongue," she stated matter of fact and Cal blinked.

"Okay," he sucked a little on the injured member from inside of his mouth. "Why?"

"Because I said no, Cal," she said simply.

"What?" he looked at her in utter confusion. "You said you were tired, but when I kissed you – you wanted more. I felt it. You were grabbing me, your fingers were pressing into me…"

"Yes. I was pushing you away."

"Pushing me away?"

"I said no, Cal," Lexi repeated. "No, means no. It's not negotiable."

He couldn't bear the way she was looking at him. Her expression, if he was reading it right, was bordering on disgust.

"When?" he asked, the question lame given the magnitude of what she was suggesting. "When did you say no?"

She took a deep breath and then let it slowly out. "Before and then twice when you were kissing me. Twice I tried to tell you. And I pushed you. Hard. But you didn't stop."

As he watched he saw her eyes mist over.

"Shit, Lexi," he rubbed at his forehead. "I didn't realise. I'm so sorry. Fuck. I would never do anything you didn't want me to. You know that."

She sniffed and shook her head. "Do I?"

"Yes. Of course. I would never, hurt you. I love you too much. I'm so sorry. I thought you were responding, I…"

Lexi shook her head. "I told you I was tired," she said, her voice monotone, "I told you I'd had a crap day and I told you I didn't want comfort. I told you that. And then, when you kissed me, I told you again. And I pushed you away. You didn't stop, Cal. How the hell can you have thought I was responding?"

"Because…" Cal began and then stopped. Arguing, trying to make the point that he thought she'd been as caught up as he, was fruitless. He recognised that. She'd said no and he hadn't listened. Devastation engulfed him as Lexi continued to regard him as if he were a stranger not her husband, and certainly not as the man she loved.

"I'm so sorry, Lexi," he said again.

"I know you're sorry," she said quietly and he chanced a brief look up at her, hating that her beautiful face was streaked with tears. "But that still doesn't change the fact I said no."

She turned and walked out of the room and he heard her mount the stairs. Cal didn't move. He had no explanation for what had just happened, no understanding of how he could have got it so wrong, how he could have misread her signals, how he could have believed that she was coaxing him on when all of the time she was pushing him away. Never, since he'd been with Lexi, had he known her to push him away but that, he knew, wasn't the point. She'd said no.

Fuck. He kicked at the wall, feeling a surge of pain as his toes connected but he barely acknowledged it. Walking backwards he collapsed onto the sofa from which he'd risen only moments before. Dropping his elbows onto his knees he put his head into his hands, feeling the tears well up behind his eyes. He'd made a monumental mistake and he didn't have the first idea how to fix it. The thought of losing Lexi terrified him, made him sick to the stomach and knowing he could be the one responsible for that loss made it impossible to bear. Needing the release he allowed the tears to fall, watching as they dripped through his hands and onto his bare feet, uncaring of the dampness soaking its way into the carpet. Compared to losing Lexi, nothing else had any meaning and he was consumed with utter desolation. What had he done? How had he got it so wrong?

Cal shook his head; he was terrified. He felt as if his chest was being squeezed in a vice. How could she stay with him now? Lexi was a precious commodity, someone you treated right – not like the women from his past.

Suddenly an even more terrifying thought struck Cal and the nausea increased, clawing at his stomach and begging for release. Rapidly he ran from the room, making it to the cloakroom just in time. He retched until he had nothing left, emptying his body and his soul as he tried to purge himself of what he'd done to his beautiful Lexi.

As Cal sat on the cold, tiled floor, a mere passenger to his life whilst it dissolved around him, he realised there was another question that needed to be answered – one that didn't involve Lexi. There was a question he had to find the answer to if he was going to have any hope of surviving this. Whatever happened now, how was *he* going to live with himself?

For, as he'd sat on the sofa, head in hands, he'd had a horrific realisation – a realisation that terrified him almost more than the thought of losing Lexi. A realisation he couldn't even begin to comprehend in terms of his life now but a realisation that was nonetheless, there, front and centre staring him in the face. A realisation he'd hoped he would never have to encounter again.

For when Cal had been kissing Lexi, when she'd been digging her hands into him and when he'd taken it as encouragement, Cal realised now, with sheer terror, that somewhere in the darkest recesses of his mind, he'd known Lexi was pushing him away and, somewhere, in an even darker recess he realised…

…he'd carried on anyway.

Chapter Twenty-Seven

Lexi

Two hours earlier

Lexi had just given the taxi driver her address when the opposing passenger door was wrenched open. Jae swung himself rapidly into the seat and, ignoring her, gave the driver a different address. Within seconds they were moving through the evening traffic.

"Who the hell do you think you are?" she levelled at him. Thankfully, the new Lexi was still present. "Where are we going?"

"I'm your boss," Jae responded coolly, "and we're going somewhere that we can talk." His presence was commanding, even more so now than when he'd monopolised the small booth in the pub.

Lexi snorted. "My boss? Didn't I just give you every reason to fire me? And, like I said, I'm not sure I want to work for you anyway."

Jae looked across at her in the darkness of the car and Lexi dropped her eyes to avoid meeting his gaze. He wore his suit well, the dark grey material stretched across taut thighs which rested a scant distance away on the seat beside her. When he twisted to face her, his shirt stretched across clearly defined abs. He was much larger than Cal both in authority and size and momentarily Lexi's comparison of the two men left Cal out of favour. Mentally she berated herself. How dare she compare anyone to the man she loved?

"Where does it come from?" Jae asked and Lexi frowned, her thoughts scattered.

"What? Where does what come from?"

"The sass."

Lexi shook her head in bemusement. "You've lost me. And you haven't told me what the hell's going on. I don't have any desire to talk to you. I said all that I wanted to say in the pub. Driver…" she leaned forwards to get the attention of the taxi driver, "…Mr Leonard is leaving. Can you pull over please?"

The guy threw her a brief look over his shoulder. "Sorry, Ma'am, no can do." He lifted his left hand to reveal a crisp, new, fifty pound note. She shook her head.

"You bastard."

Jae smiled. "For someone who, according to Fraser, is mild mannered, your language is certainly colourful."

"Yeah?" Lexi knew she'd allowed her tongue to run away with her this evening, but she couldn't show any weakness. Not to him.

"Indeed. I was surprised," Jae continued, "to see so much fight when I met you. Where does it come from?"

Lexi ignored him and turned her head to look out of the window.

"I think you surprised your friend too," Jae commented. "I don't think I've ever seen Fraser so floored." His voice rumbled through the darkness, teasing her emotions.

She let out a deep sigh. "If all you wanted to do was discuss my vocabulary then you've wasted a perfectly good fifty pound note."

"I never waste money, Lexi. Call it a policy of mine. A commandment if you like."

"A commandment?" she sneered. "Like the ten commandments? I can't wait to hear what the other nine are."

Beside her Jae laughed lightly. "And that, Lexi, has just proved I never waste money. You're curious, you want to know more about me and that means you plan to spend more time with me."

Lexi almost choked at his arrogance. "I can assure you I have no such plans," she responded. "My only plans are to get the hell away from you and get home. To my husband." It seemed surreal that her journey – her evening – had been hijacked in this way.

"Ah yes," she felt the seat dip as Jae moved a little on the leather lined bench, "your husband. What is it he does?" His tone was all innocence yet Lexi wasn't about to be fooled.

"You mean you don't know?" she asked sarcastically. Cal was, after all, inextricably linked to Zach. "According to Fraser, you know everything which is why," she continued, "I don't believe you have no knowledge of Zach Jackson's file."

"I don't think I said I had no knowledge of the file," Jae responded. His earthy voice rolled carefully over the words with no hint of emotion.

"But you implied," Lexi countered, "that the name Zach Jackson meant nothing to you."

"Again," Jae's response was smooth, "I think that might be your interpretation rather than what I actually said."

Lexi shook her head. "Whatever. All I know is you're not prepared, for whatever reason, to give me the answers I want."

For a moment Jae remained silent and the taxi continued to bump along. Looking out of the window, Lexi struggled to gain her bearings. She could tell they were no longer in Brufton, but she didn't recognise their current location.

"Where are we going?" she asked again. Oddly, despite barely knowing this man or indeed their destination, Lexi didn't feel concerned. In a strange way, she felt safe.

"My house."

She looked across at him in shock. "Your house? Isn't that against every single corporate rule and probably the other nine commandments?"

Jae laughed, the sound rich in the confines of the taxi. "I see the spirit that Fraser mentioned now. It probably is," he conceded, "but needs must. Relax, Lexi. You can trust me."

"I know nothing about you," she responded, "and trust must be earned. I do, however, believe there are others more closely acquainted?" She was referring to Sonya yet, when Lexi felt Jae tense beside her, she immediately regretted the words. "Sorry," she said as she tried to understand what had possessed her to mention the other woman, "it's none of my business and out of line. I apologise. Put it down to the rather bizarre situation I find myself in right now."

"Apology accepted although for future reference, don't mention that woman to me again." Although his tone remained calm she could detect the steel beneath. The way he spoke and his words told her in no uncertain terms that Sonya, for whatever reason, was off limits.

Abruptly the taxi stopped.

"Keep the change," Jae said as he alighted, moving quickly around the car to open her door. They'd stopped beneath a streetlight and Lexi could see the darkness of his eyes as the lamp cast an ethereal glow over his features. A light dusting of stubble that she'd not previously noticed covered his strong jawline. Everything about this man screamed strength and authority.

"Thanks," Lexi said encompassing both the driver and Jae. Exiting the vehicle she looked around, still unable to get her bearings. They were on a pavement that led to a large iron double-width gate. Jae dug a fob out of his pocket and pressed it up against a flat, square pad mounted on the wall to one side of the gates. As Lexi waited, the gates swung open and after motioning her through, Jae used the fob on a similar pad on the other side to close the entrance.

"Just up here," he said as he guided her along a block-paved driveway that circulated around an impressive three tier fountain. Water trickled over the rocky mountain construction and ended in a square pool at the bottom. Mesmerised by the sound, Lexi stopped for a second to admire it. Jae halted beside her.

"It's beautiful," she said reverently. Blue, green and red lighting alternated on the three tiers providing a feast not only for the ears but for the eyes as well. Lexi had always dreamed of having a fountain in her garden but this – this was something else.

"I like it," Jae said after a moment. "One of my early construction projects."

"Yes, of course," she said as she turned to look at him. "I'd forgotten you started at the grass roots end."

He nodded. "Which is, in my opinion, the only way you can run a successful company. If you don't know what each person is supposed to be doing, or you don't understand every job or role, then you cannot possibly manage them." He began to move away from the fountain and Lexi followed.

"Even accounting?" she asked as she fell into step beside him.

His soft chuckle reached her on the light breeze. "Yes, Lexi. Even accounting."

A few steps further led them to a raised porch, accessed by four small steps, beyond which stood an impressive oak wood door. Using a key from the same bunch as the gate fob, Jae opened the door and once more indicated that she should precede him. Lexi did so, taking a couple of steps inside before stopping, aghast. The hallway was like nothing she'd ever seen before. Everywhere she looked was exquisitely panelled in wood all of which met at a glossy, tiled floor. A large, crystal chandelier rose above her head and she followed its line upwards noting several intricate fleur-de-lys style engravings etched into the generous coving. The centrepiece of the entrance was undoubtedly the staircase; wide, with similar carvings running down the spindles, it stood timeless as it rose proudly from the middle of the hallway.

"Wow. This is…another project?" she asked.

Jae closed the door and walked to stand beside her. For the first time she became aware of the difference in their heights – he had at least eight inches on her. "Not so much. This was my parents' house. My father built it from scratch. With the exception of the fountain, the work is all his. I just make sure it doesn't fall down."

His answer was flippant, but Lexi didn't miss the past tense reference to his parents. "Was?" she asked and then mentally kicked herself. His parents, like Sonya, were none of her business.

Ignoring the question he held his arm out in front of him. "This way," he said as he led her towards a door at the far end.

The room beyond the door turned out to be a kitchen with a large seating area in one corner furnished by two comfortable sofas. It was to these that Jae propelled her.

"Coffee?" he asked as she seated herself on one of the sofas. Lexi nodded.

"Yes, thank you. Black…"

"…no sugar. I know," Jae finished.

Lexi frowned wondering how he knew her coffee preference.

"Fraser told me," he responded and for a moment she wondered if she'd voiced her question aloud.

"Right."

The ensuing silence in the room was broken only by the sound of the coffee machine as it percolated. Jae walked swiftly around the kitchen, his movements lithe. As he changed position, so his suit stretched to accommodate him and Lexi could see that his size was pure muscle. He was clearly someone who not only worked out, but also took pride in his appearance. From the back, his dark hair curled over the crisp white collar of his shirt before being secured at the nape with a band. This surprised Lexi, his hair was longer than she'd initially thought and even though it wasn't a look she'd usually associate with a suit, on him it looked edgy. And it worked. Rapidly she redirected her thoughts. She'd already caught herself comparing him to Cal once tonight and if she continued to watch him, Lexi was afraid she'd do it again. Feeling disrespectful to her husband she turned her attention instead to the kitchen, which, like the man, epitomised sleek design. Stainless steel appliances were matched with black marble worktops, each of these highly polished. Everything was ordered and had its place with the exception of a stack of papers that lay haphazardly on the counter where Jae now stood. He was glancing at them as he finished making their drinks and Lexi found herself picturing him here every morning, making coffee, reading through papers as he drank. Having no idea if he lived alone, Lexi wondered whose responsibility it was to keep everything so immaculate. In some ways the beauty and order of the house was at odds with the ruggedness of its owner, yet, like the hairband and the suit, it worked.

Jae turned and their eyes briefly met. His dark gaze focused intensely on her and she looked away. Being here with him, in his environment, felt uncomfortable. He was her boss and she respected him, but bringing her here at this time of night...she'd been serious when she'd said it broke all of the rules. Even by her limited professional experience, it felt wrong.

"Why am I here?" she asked. "I meant it when I said this broke a lot of rules. I've only just met you."

"A fact of which I am entirely aware," Jae responded as he neared the sofa area holding two steaming cups. "I have very little free time at my disposal and even less when I'm at work. There are never enough hours in the day and, as you were so keen to talk to me, I figured it would make sense we did that tonight – seeing as we were both available." Dark eyes perused her as he handed her a mug. Taking the sofa immediately opposite he folded his long, lean form into a seated position, his eyes never leaving hers.

"What time do you have to be home?" he asked.

Lexi blinked at him. "Home?" She glanced at her watch. It was almost nine pm. "Soon. I told Cal I wouldn't be late."

Across from her, Jae nodded. "What do you suppose Cal would say if he knew you were here now? Do you think he would mind that you're drinking coffee – alone – with a virtual stranger?"

"Of course he would," Lexi responded, "what man wouldn't? But you're my boss and you gave me absolutely no choice in being here. I'm sure he would understand."

"Would understand?" Jae queried. "Strange choice of words."

"Why?" she asked.

"The use of the word 'would' suggests that you don't plan to tell him. If you'd used 'will' on the other hand..."

Lexi shook her head. "That's just being pedantic. Of course I'll tell him. Cal and I have no secrets. We built our marriage on something called trust. Maybe that's not a term you're familiar with."

A shadow crossed Jae's eyes as she watched him. "If you knew me at all, Lexi, you would know that I hold trust and honesty in the highest regard. As you've only just met me, however, I will forgive you that comment. I understand and believe in trust as much as the next man. That would not, however, make it fine with me if you were my wife and I found out you were drinking coffee with a man that was not me, alone at night."

"How dare you judge Cal?" she asked, her anger starting to rise. "You don't know me or him and may I remind you that I had no choice in being here right now. In fact, I could easily call the police and tell them I was brought here against my will. How does that fit with your honesty and trust values?"

Jae sat back and crossed one ankle over his knee. "Are you really here against your will, Lexi?"

"Yes," she replied instantly, "of course. I was on my way home and you hijacked my taxi."

Across from her she watched as he inclined his head to one side, black hair flopping across his forehead. "True. But look at it this way. You requested our meeting. The conversation we had earlier was in no way satisfactory to either of us. This is a continuation of the meeting you requested, therefore, are you really here against your will?"

She shook her head and shrugged. "Spin it whichever way you want. If this is a continuation of our meeting, then let's just get on with it."

"Would you protest," Jae mused, "if this meeting was with another woman in her home?"

"Probably not, but that's irrelevant. Relationships between men and women are always more complicated – and platonic ones, less understood."

"Yet, Cal would understand?"

Lexi ignored the question. "If you're trying to rile me it won't work," she responded.

"I'm merely intrigued," Jae continued. "If you were meeting with a woman alone, you could no more guarantee that lines wouldn't get blurred than they would meeting a man."

Lexi sat back a little further. She'd drained her coffee and now placed the empty mug on an adjacent, black lacquer side table. "Is it just as likely for a woman to be attracted to a person of the same sex as it is for the attraction to be between opposing sexes?" she asked. Although the question was irrelevant, she figured she ought to contribute to Jae's random choice of conversation if she were to have any hope of leaving here soon.

Jae smiled and Lexi noticed how even his teeth were. "I have no idea what the facts and figures are in relation to that particular scenario. All I'm saying is you can never guarantee that any relationship, whether it be between opposing sexes or the same sex, will remain purely professional. It's just not possible. Not anymore."

"Maybe not."

"However," Jae continued, "for the purposes of expediency and your comfort, let me reassure you that my motivation for bringing you here was simply to conclude our business meeting – nothing else."

For a moment Lexi was taken aback. It sounded like a reassurance and an insult, all at the same time. "Great." She gathered her thoughts. "Let's carry on then shall we? I see no reason to delay."

"Nor do I," Jae responded.

"Great," she said again. "By the way, what should I call you? I'm not sure what the protocol is." Now that they'd established the ground rules, she was keen to keep their meeting on a purely professional level.

Across from her he shrugged. "There isn't really a protocol. Whatever works for you. Jae is fine."

She nodded. "Okay – Jae." Short for Jason?

"It's short for Jason," he stated and Lexi looked at him in surprise. Again he appeared to have read her mind. "JaceEnterprises comes from Jason too."

"Right. Good play on your name."

He smiled. "Thank you, although I can't take the credit. That was my father, Jason Senior."

"He was the founder of JaceEnterprises?" Lexi asked surprised. Although she'd never researched Jae, she'd always supposed that the company was his baby.

"Yes. It started with this house actually. Some of the contractors liked his designs and word spread. There are a few more houses with his stamp on them around here. Still standing I believe."

Lexi smiled. "That's good to know. Your father must have been very talented." The detail she'd seen in the hallway alone was exquisite.

"Yes, he was." Jae uncrossed his legs and sat forward, "But we're not here to talk about my father. You wanted to talk to me about Zach Jackson. Shoot."

"Okay," she nodded, "but first I need to know – did you take that meeting with him? The one I asked you about in the pub."

Jae's eyes connected with hers across the distance that separated the two sofas. Again she noted their unfathomable darkness, so different to the beautiful green light of Cal's eyes. The silence stretched and then eventually, he spoke.

"Yes, Lexi. I did take that meeting."

She shook her head. Even though she'd already known the answer, to hear the truth from his lips hurt. Especially after he'd so vehemently denied it earlier. "Why?" she asked. "Why did you lie to me? Why did you make me look like a fool in front of Fraser?"

She watched as he closed his eyes. "I had to, Lexi."

"What?" she almost laughed as her voice rose with emotion. "You who preaches honesty and truth? You *had* to lie?"

He opened his eyes and they focused instantly on her. "Yes. I had to lie," he repeated.

She sat back in her seat once more. This – this was unbelievable.

"Then tell me, Jae, how in the hell am I supposed to trust you or believe anything else that you say?"

Jae stood and closed the distance between the two sofas, settling on the far end of the one Lexi occupied. Instinctively she shifted as far away from him as she possibly could.

"There are several answers to that question," he began, "but I want to explain something to you first. I need you to understand something."

She nodded reluctantly. Why it was important for her to understand anything when he'd flat out lied was beyond her.

"You," he began again, his voice lowered now he was sitting closer to her, "are an intern."

"Someone who is eminently dispensable?" Lexi parroted back his earlier words.

Jae ignored her and continued, "which means you don't get to be in this position. You don't get to spend time with me like this. You don't get to argue with me and you sure as hell don't get to have an opinion. You work. You do your job, you report to Adam and to Fraser and that's it. That's your role."

"It's because of you that I *am* here," she interjected but again, he ignored her.

"You don't get to request meetings. If you want to know something, you ask your colleagues and they ask me – that's the way it works, the way it's always worked. How many people in my organisation do you think get to talk to me the way you have tonight?" He waved his hand. "You don't need to answer that. The point is, you're new, green, inexperienced and yet here you are, in my kitchen, arguing with me like one of my management team. Telling me what's right and wrong. Accusing me of underhand dealing with someone who you claim is your friend."

Lexi looked at him wide eyed.

"The fact that you and Zach are friends is irrelevant when it comes to business, Lexi. If you were more experienced you would understand that. Sometimes, business deals have to be done that are unsavoury. Sometimes decisions have to be made that are not mutually acceptable, but for the most part, I am fair. My management team are fair. The deal I brokered with your friend was fair."

"So you did know about the deal?" she asked as she focused on the crisp white cotton of his shirt. She no longer felt able to meet his eyes.

"Yes. Like I know about every single other deal that JaceEnterprises enters into. I told you earlier, I know every job and every employee. It's the only way I know how to run my company successfully. Similarly, every employee knows their role, their place – and that includes interns. Until you. You," he continued, "have been on my radar for a while. Your work is impeccable, you are trustworthy and conscientious and you are fiercely loyal – something which your devotion to Zach proves. These are admirable qualities and are of interest to me. When we get an intern through our programme with your ability, I get to know about it. I want to know about it. I know about you, and I have done for a while."

"But we've never met," Lexi stated, finally bringing her eyes to his.

He returned her gaze. "You have never met me. There's a difference."

She frowned. "I don't understand? And what does that have to do with you lying about Zach?"

Jae let out a sigh and then shifted a little. "I've been watching you, Lexi. Not," he held out his hand in defence, "in a creepy way. In a professional way. I've been watching how you conduct yourself, how you work with others, how you communicate with your peers and I've been impressed by you. I think you have promise and I would like JaceEnterprises to be the company that benefits from your potential, so, when you asked to meet with me, I agreed. I thought it was time we met properly so I could find out for myself, what you were about. I didn't, however, bargain on breaking so many rules this evening."

Lexi remained silent; she had no idea what to say.

"In the pub," he continued, "you asked me some questions. You were direct and you weren't intimidated by me. At first I resented that but then you showed your spirit, the spirit Fraser tells me about and I realised that actually, I didn't mind. In many ways, the fact that you challenged me was refreshing."

Lexi swallowed. "I don't know what came over me. I'm usually pretty quiet and reserved." She dropped her eyes to her lap suddenly feeling ashamed. The adrenalin that had been fuelled by her nerves and then fanned by her anger was beginning to recede. She felt humble and small. "I'm sorry. Zach's important to me. That's all."

For a moment there was silence and then Jae spoke once more. This time his voice was even quieter. "It's okay. You don't need to apologise. I meant it when I said it was refreshing and I know this isn't the way you usually behave. I've been watching you, remember?"

Lexi smiled. "Oh yeah. Professionally."

Jae returned her smile. "Yes. Professionally. And what you showed tonight, the way you took me on regardless of who I am, that showed passion, guts, spirit and loyalty. You were willing to sacrifice yourself and your job for your beliefs – not many people would do that. You left that pub tonight not knowing if you had a job to come back to, not knowing where your next pay cheque was coming from, not knowing if your reputation had been ruined before you'd even built it up – yet still you left, because you were fighting for something that mattered to you. Seeing that in another person was liberating. I'm sick of ass kissers, people saying what they think I want to hear. You spoke your mind, you showed a glimpse of someone that could be truly powerful and I liked that. I liked it a lot. My only regret is that I lied to you."

She looked up at him and shook her head. "I still don't get that. None of what you've said explains why you lied."

He leaned forwards and braced his arms on his knees, linking his hands: large, capable hands. "I needed to expose that person, the one

I saw a glimpse of tonight. I had to know if she was really in there or if Fraser and I were wrong. I had to know if you had what it takes and the only way I could think to do that was to lie to you. I knew your loyalty would be tested. It was low, but it worked. I saw you. I saw who you could be and whilst it doesn't forgive the lie, I hope you can understand why I did it."

For a moment Lexi didn't move as she listened to his words and then replayed them in her mind. As she allowed them to flow, she allowed them to process and suddenly it all became crystal clear. He'd set her up. Played her. Lied to her. For what? To test her for the good of JaceEnterprises? Every drop of adrenalin that had left her veins surged back through as her fury built. He'd played her to test her loyalty and expose her potential. Angrily she shook her head as Jae remained unmoving, watching her, waiting for her reaction. Lexi didn't look at him – she couldn't. If she'd considered him low before, then this had taken him to the next level. Without warning, everything inside of her erupted.

"You scheming…" she rose from her seat. "You did all of this to test me?" She waved her hand around the kitchen. "You wanted to test my loyalty by making me close down a friend? You're one sick bastard. You knew about the file all along and that I was connected with Zach. You knew it would kill me to close him down. What kind of person does something like that? And Cal? What about him? You knew his connection to Zach too? That it was about more than Zach for me? You sick, sick bastard…"

"Lexi," Jae stood too. "Calm down, please."

"No, no way." She held her palms up towards him and paced to the other end of the room. "You did all of this to test me? And I fell for it. I fell for the whole damn thing. You have no idea what you've done. No idea what Zach has been through, what Cal has been through. No idea what this could do to Zach yet you used his lowest ebb to test me?" She shook her head, "You can never excuse something like this."

Jae remained where he was, his tall form dominant despite the size of the room. "I understand that I'm guilty of not thinking it through perhaps."

"Perhaps?" she spat at him. "You think?"

"I never meant for it to be like this. I wanted a way to show you what you can be, who you can be. I need people like you in my company, Lexi. People I can depend on. People who I know will have my back whatever. One thing money can never buy is loyalty and trust, in fact, it usually buys the exact opposite."

"And I'm supposed to feel sorry for you?" she asked sarcastically.

He shook his head. "No, of course not. I don't want your pity. I want your loyalty. I want you to defend me the way you defended Zach. I want to know I have you in my corner because you have the talent to really be someone. And I want to give you the opportunity to be that person."

She laughed cruelly. "You want me to be someone at the expense of my soul because that's what you're asking. You can rot in hell for all I care and if that means I don't have a job tomorrow – then so be it." Lexi shook her head. "You have no idea what you've done, no idea at all."

Across the other side of the room, Jae stood his ground. "I understand more than you think. I know what it's like to lose everything. It's convenient for you, now that you know about my little indiscretion, to use me for blame. To release all of your anger at the crap hand that life has dealt your friend – and perhaps your husband – and direct it at me. And that's okay. I can deal with that. But don't forget, Lexi, I never asked Zach to sell his company – he came to me. Yes, I bought him out but at a fair price. It was a business deal. He needed the money and I needed his contacts. If you want to blame someone for the way he's feeling right now then you're knocking at the wrong door. I helped him out by giving him what he needed."

Lexi shook her head. "I accept you're not responsible for his situation, but you're the one that asked me – knowing my connection to him – to put the final nail in. For that my anger is more than justified. You lied to me, tested me to see if I was good enough to make it in your world and that's sick."

"I've apologised for that," he responded calmly. "I get that I made a bad judgement call. There were several ways I could have found that person I'm seeing now but regardless, I have no regrets that what happened tonight has exposed her. She can really be someone, Lexi. She has what it takes and that excites me. You might not like the way it happened, but you can't ignore what is staring us both in the face. You have the qualities I need and you're an asset to JaceEnterprises."

She snorted. "An asset? What, like Zach's company is an asset?"

"Yes," Jae moved a few steps closer, "an asset. It's possible for a person to be an asset just as much as an acquisition is. Take it whichever way you want to, but it's meant as a compliment. You can do great things and there aren't many people I can say that about." She could feel his warmth and smell his spicy scent as he continued to advance.

Lexi let out a calming breath and allowed herself a moment. "This evening..." she paused and dragged in a couple more breaths, "...it's been out there." She glanced at her watch. "I alienated a good colleague, I found out my boss is a liar and now I'm late for my husband. I don't think this is a night I'll remember with pleasure."

Jae watched her, unmoving, dark eyes roaming her face.

"I'm disappointed," she continued. "I've heard nothing but great things about you and yet you resorted to manipulation to get what you wanted."

"That's fair," he said as he took another few steps closer. "If it's any consolation, I'm disappointed with myself."

"Which," she said as he stopped within a few feet, "is probably harder to deal with than my disappointment in you."

"Don't be so sure," he responded and she looked at him quizzically.

"Isn't your harshest critic yourself?" she asked. "The one person you can never get away from?"

"Yes," he inclined his head, "but that doesn't mean I'm immune to the feelings of others."

"Even someone as 'dispensable' as me?" she asked.

"Particularly someone as dispensable as you."

The atmosphere suddenly felt weighted. Jae had lowered his voice in deference to the distance by which they were divided and something passed between them as their gazes connected for a brief moment. Rapidly she took a step back and focused on a point over his right shoulder.

Jae cleared his throat. "I want to offer you a position on the management programme," he said as he too moved away. He paced back to the sofas before turning around to face her. "I really do think you have what it takes."

His earthy voice was sincere and despite everything that had occurred this evening, Lexi knew she could trust him. If for no other reason than the fact that Zach had trusted him – or *entrusted* him – to take care of his baby.

"Thank you," she said as she acknowledged the compliment he was offering. "I might not like the way you operate, but I'm flattered at your faith in me – and your offer – but I have no experience. I can't give you what you need from your management team."

"Which is why you follow the training programme," he stated. "I know you're light on experience, but we can give you all the tools you need and expose you to as many situations as we can. It's a fast track programme, Lexi. It's not easy. It's tough, it can be long hours and it requires commitment and dedication. If you think you can't give me that level of commitment, then you need to tell me now."

Lexi thought for a moment, remembering the negative pregnancy test she'd done that morning. It felt like another lifetime. If she were to commit to something like this then there would be no time for babies. Not now. It was a tough call and a decision she needed to make with Cal's backing. True she'd been questioning her desire to have a baby, but she owed it to Cal to talk this through. All of it.

"Can I take some time?" she asked, "I need to talk to Cal."

He inclined his head. "Of course."

"Thank you."

Silence fell and they remained where they stood, each watching the other.

"Can I go home now?" she asked eventually.

Jae smiled. "Of course. I'll call you a taxi."

"Thank you."

Taking his phone out of his pocket he made the call. "It'll be a short while. Would you like another drink?"

Lexi nodded. "Okay. That would be good."

He turned away from her and moved towards the kitchen. "Take a seat," he said indicating the sofas once more.

Now that the atmosphere between them had calmed, Lexi allowed herself to relax and, walking back to the seats, she resumed her earlier position. The smell of freshly brewed coffee reached her nostrils and by the time Jae presented her with another cup, she was more than ready for it. After placing his own mug on the table, Jae took the seat beside her again, rather than the sofa opposite.

"I hope you say yes," he said after a moment, "this really is a great opportunity. For both of us."

Lexi looked sideways at him. "I understand and thank you for giving me the chance." He was studying her, his features relaxed. His eyes were soft as was his voice.

"I'll never lie to you again," he said and she continued to look at him. The sincerity in his expression was clear. His eyes burned deep, their intensity captivating and Lexi knew he meant every word. A thrill ran through her to hear a man such as Jae making promises, allowing her to see his vulnerability. "You're right that being disappointed in myself is bad but oddly," he cleared his throat, "the fact you're disappointed in me – that cuts deeper."

Lexi swallowed and her muscles began to tense. The atmosphere between them shifted again. "I'm only an intern," she began, "it doesn't really matter what I think."

"Maybe not for much longer," he observed. Still they maintained eye contact, neither able to break away. "You might not be an intern for much longer."

There was an undeniable pull; a current running between them and Lexi was struggling to maintain her thought process. She shifted a little further away. Jae's eyes narrowed at the movement and finally she closed her own: a defence against the potent force that was threatening to take her prisoner.

"I'm just going to put something out there," he said slowly as she re-opened her eyes. "This might turn out to be my second mistake of the evening but…" he paused, "I don't think so."

"What?" She looked up at him from beneath heavy lashes as her breaths became uneven and her palms began to sweat. The inappropriate nature of her thoughts and reactions burned in her soul but she felt helpless to fight. She waited, holding a breath she could ill afford to spare.

"I think," he hesitated, "I think there's something here. Between us." He used his hand to indicate his meaning as his voice lowered. "I think you feel it?"

"I'm married," she said as betrayal at even having this conversation stabbed through her heart. "There's nothing here."

Her brain congratulated her as she stood rapidly from the sofa, knowing she had to get out of here, yet, her emotions begged her to stay. She continued moving though, listening to her brain, understanding the only way to make this right was to leave. Now. "I'll wait for the taxi by the gate." She took measured steps towards the kitchen door.

Jae began to move, walking a few paces behind as he followed her out of the kitchen. "I'm right, aren't I?" he said as they neared the front door. "That's why you're running."

She spun to face him. "No, Jae. You're wrong." Her mouth spoke the words she knew she must as the betrayal reached her stomach. "I cannot have this conversation with you." She turned back and paced the last couple of steps to the solid oak exit.

"I don't disagree," he said and momentarily she halted, her hand hovering over the door handle. "That doesn't mean I'm wrong though," he finished. "You're married. I know. You're committed to another man. I know. I'm ten years older than you, I know. But there's something here, Lexi, and if you deny it, you're lying to me. I'm not suggesting it means anything," he added, "but if you believe in the values you've been lecturing me about all night, then you can't deny it."

He was directly behind her; she could feel the warmth of his breath on her neck. Butterflies warred with disloyalty as she closed her eyes, feeling him, smelling him, knowing he was right. There was something here, something had changed between them over the course of the evening and she would be a hypocrite if she lied now. But acknowledging it, putting the words out there wasn't something she could do to herself or to Cal. For the sake of her marriage, she had to lie.

"No," she repeated slowly as she continued to face the door, "you're wrong."

Without warning she felt him place his hand on her shoulder and she closed her eyes ever tighter. It scorched where his palm lay and as he slowly turned her towards him, she felt helpless to resist. She opened her eyes. They stood, inches apart, eyes connected.

"You're lying to me, Lexi," he breathed, "but I understand why."

Awkwardly, she swallowed. "Was this part of your plan?" she asked.

Jae shook his head. "No."

She watched as his eyes darkened.

"I have to go."

He nodded and moved his hand from her shoulder, dropping it to his side. For a brief moment he closed his eyes, hiding the dark orbs from her gaze. She began to turn and reach once more for the door handle.

"Lexi?"

Against her better judgement she spun back.

"Can I...?" he stopped. "This was never part of my plan," he said softly.

She nodded. "I know. Let's forget it ever happened. It was a moment. That's all."

"So you did feel it?" he asked and belatedly she realised she'd walked right into his trap.

"I have to go," she repeated.

Jae continued to watch her. "You have no idea how much I want to kiss you right now."

The butterflies in Lexi's stomach jumped to her throat. The betrayal sat heavy in her heart, weighing her down with fear.

"I have to go," she said quietly one last time and he nodded. She turned around, her movements final, and opened the door. He placed his hand on her shoulder and she paused. The warmth of his breath tickled her neck and then suddenly she felt his lips connect with her skin, the contact brief, but she knew she'd not imagined it. Her neck burned where he'd caressed.

With a determined step she walked out of the front door and back past the beautiful fountain. She kept going, pausing momentarily for the iron gate to swing open, but she refused to look back. As she reached the pavement the taxi pulled in and gratefully she opened the door. Giving the driver her address she faced rigidly forwards. She didn't look back. Not once.

There was no way she could afford to.

Chapter Twenty-Eight
Cal

May 2015

Cal had drained his second cup of coffee and yet barely registered either of them. They were getting close now, really close and it was becoming harder to keep his emotions in check. More than that, the story was increasingly difficult to tell.

"That night then," Matt asked, "is that when things started to go wrong?"

Cal considered a moment and then shook his head. "No. It started at Lexi's graduation – that was when I first began to have doubts that she wanted me and even though we talked about it, it never really went away. I tried, but I just couldn't. It was like those doubts were poisoning me and I became powerless to stop them. I remember," he continued, "that time when Zach told me the only person who would ruin my marriage was me. I thought he was crazy at the time, yet look at me now."

Matt nodded. "It's getting tough, right?"

"Yeah," he rubbed his hand across his face. "That night when she went out though, I should've known."

"How did you feel, when Lexi told you she was going out?"

"To be honest, I didn't give it much thought at the time. Zach had just lost his company and things were going down at work. He needed me and I figured it made sense that we were both going to be out the same night. She said it was work and I believed her."

"What about when she got home?"

Cal sat back in the chair and crossed his ankle over his knee. "She was late home. She got home after me even though she said she'd be home early. I was pissed at her. Not really bad but after the way the evening with Zach had gone, all I wanted was Lexi. I really needed her and I didn't like it that she wasn't there."

"Was that the first time she hadn't been there for you?"

"Yeah, I guess it was."

"Were you suspicious at that point?"

"No," Cal shook his head, "not at all. We talked a little. She told me about the pregnancy, that there was no baby and it made sense then, the way she'd behaved and so I let it go. But, then it all went badly wrong."

"The kiss?" Matt asked.

Cal shuddered. It still killed him to think about it let alone talk about it.

"Yeah," he said, "that was unforgivable." Even now, after everything that had happened since, the memory of that night was still fresh. It had been the beginning of the end.

Matt watched him for a moment. "What went wrong, Cal?" he asked softly.

He took a breath. "I honestly thought she was okay, that she was into it." He coughed.

"It's okay," Matt said, "take your time."

Cal cleared his throat and then swallowed. "I thought she wanted it. I thought she was responding and so I carried on kissing her."

"But she didn't want you to kiss her," Matt stated and Cal nodded.

"I really thought she wanted it…" Again he stopped and shook his head. Damn, this was so tough and if he thought this part of the story was difficult to tell…but he had to do it. He had to face everything that had happened. Everything he'd done.

"You know what kills me the most though?" he asked. His voice wavered as he fought back emotion and shame. "I think part of me knew she was saying no," he added quietly as he dropped his head. "I'm so ashamed. Shit, Matt," he shuddered. "How can you still want to help me? And this is just the beginning."

"No judgement," Matt said. "Remember?"

Cal shook his head. "You're a better man than me. If I heard the story you're hearing…she said no, Matt. And I didn't listen."

He raised his head from where he'd been studying the carpet once more and faced the therapist. This was the first time he'd looked the other man in the eye since his admission.

"I'm screwed up," he said as he felt tears begin to form behind his eyes. "Really screwed up."

Matt leaned forwards and braced his arms on his thighs. "You're facing up to it. That's what being here is all about. Facing up to what happened and learning to move on. Realising your mistakes. Ensuring you don't make them again."

"But what kind of person does something like that?" he asked knowing as soon as he spoke that it was a pointless question. The answer was him. Cal Strudwick. He was the type of person who did something like that – and worse. He was an animal and he deserved nothing. He didn't even deserve to live.

"I've made a mistake," he said suddenly and rose briskly from the chair. "This therapy…" he waved his hand around the room, "it's not for me. It's not for someone like me. I don't deserve to be listened to and I sure as hell don't deserve to be helped. I don't deserve it." He grabbed his jacket off the adjacent sofa and shrugged into it.

Matt watched him. "I'm not going to stop you, Cal," he said. "If you want to leave, that's your choice, but I believe everyone deserves a second chance and by being here and facing up to what you did, that applies to you too."

Cal looked down at his therapist who had remained seated. "Maybe there's an argument for second chances, but I already had that, the day after the kiss. The chance I need now is not a second chance, it's way more than that and *that* is what I don't deserve. I don't deserve anything." He turned and walked in the direction of the office door. "I'm sorry," he said as he neared the exit, "it's not personal."

"I understand," Matt replied, "and it's not unusual for people to find therapy too much, especially when we get to the really difficult parts but, if you go, I want you to think about one thing. Can you do that?"

Reluctantly he turned back to face Matt. "What?"

309

Matt stood slowly and closed the distance between them.

"I want you to think about what happened that night and in the days and weeks that followed," he said. "I want you to think about it as objectively as you can. Try to put aside your feelings of guilt for a moment and watch what happened as an outsider. I want you to think about whether you're solely to blame here – whether, as unforgivable as your actions that night were, was it only you that messed up? You might find," he continued as Cal stood his ground waiting, "the answer, the truth, ultimately surprises you."

Chapter Twenty-Nine
Cal & Lexi

November 2014 ~ The morning after

Cal

Leaving the house early after bedding down on the couch for the night, Cal took a taxi to collect his car. Today was Saturday; that meant no work so Cal drove along the coast, stopping at a secluded car park overlooking the sea. The days were short and grey at this time of year and the view was uninspiring. The waves crested and fell with their time-honoured regularity and for a moment Cal watched them, envying their freedom to form and then re-form, every wave providing a new opportunity. As he sat he reflected on what had happened last night and disgust washed over him anew. He'd done the unmentionable: he'd ignored his wife when she'd told him no and what terrified him the most was his fear that he could have lost control. So easily. Lexi had bitten his tongue, but until then, he hadn't really heard her – had he? The scenario crashed round and around in his head, as it had done during his endless night-time waking hours, yet still he was no nearer to making sense of it all. On the seat beside him, his mobile rang. It was Lexi.

"Hello?" Cal's voice shook as he answered the call. He was both surprised and nervous to hear from her.

"Hey," her soft voice reached him across the crystal clear connection. "Where are you?"

He told her.

"We need to talk," she said and he nodded.

"Yes."

He wanted to say so much more. He wanted to ask her why she was prepared to talk to him, what he'd done to deserve her even calling him, but he didn't. She'd called him, she'd instigated the contact and he chose to consider that positive – at least, until he knew better.

"I'll come to you," she said. "Neutral territory might be best."

"Okay."

Again he could've said more, offered to come and collect her, take her to her car which she'd left at work, but he let her make the plans. She was in control of their relationship right now. Firmly.

"It'll take half an hour to get my car and then come to you so I'll see you then?"

Cal nodded. "I'll be here." It wasn't as if he had anywhere else to go and talking to Lexi was the only thing that mattered to him anyway.

"Okay, bye," she said and he listened as she ended the call.

Cal had no idea what she was going to say to him, no idea if he was sitting here watching the waves wash away his marriage, waiting out the last half an hour of his time as Lexi's husband, but it was out of his control. Completely. Whatever she wanted to say, however she wanted to deal with this, it was up to her. All he could do was sit, his life in pause and then, like a passenger, arrive at the destination of her choosing. Any choice he had in the future of their marriage had been relinquished last night because last night, Cal Strudwick had reverted to form and he knew he could never, ever make that right.

Lexi

Waking to find Cal gone was a blessing, but Lexi knew they had to talk. Last night had been a game changer, a life-shifting event, a period of time that illuminated so much and yet shadowed even more. Cal was her husband and there was no doubt in Lexi's mind that he'd overstepped the mark, but she had to be honest with herself. After the evening she'd spent with Jae and the unsettling way in which it had ended, she'd been unfair to Cal too. When he'd reached for her, asked for her comfort and kissed her, her mind hadn't been on her husband but on a man she'd only just met. The overwhelming guilt she felt paled the line Cal had crossed. Everything became blurred and it was no longer simple, nor was it black and white. He'd done wrong but so had she and it was *her* guilt, *her* fear of what it meant that was consuming her today, not the fact she'd said no and Cal had ignored her. For that reason, and for that reason alone, she knew she owed it to Cal to talk things through.

Lexi looked across at him as they simultaneously exited their cars. He appeared as shattered as she felt. How had they come to this? Less than twenty-four hours ago their marriage had been solid and now it had been rocked by the events of one night, their bond reduced to a meeting in a remote car park with no one but Mother Nature as witness. She shook her head. It didn't make sense but then since graduation, little had and she realised that now. Perhaps this, today, was a symptom of a bigger problem.

They met in-between the two cars.

"Shall we walk?" Lexi asked and Cal nodded. It was cold and breezy, the endless grey overhead matching their moods.

"Lexi," Cal began as they stepped over the low wall and commenced a slow pace along the harbour path. "I'm so sorry. I don't know what to say. I just…" he stopped and Lexi turned to him. They both paused their stride. "I love you so much," he said, his face earnest, "I can't bear to think I did that to you. I swear to God, Lexi. I never meant to hurt you. I didn't hear you, I thought you were happy, okay with what was happening but that's no excuse. I know that. God, how I wish I could turn back time. I'm so sorry."

He stopped speaking, his eyes desperately searching hers.

She watched him for a moment, seeing the sincerity in his features, reading the eyes of the man she loved, yet today, as she continued to scour his face, there was something missing. Instead of drowning in clear green eyes, she found herself wanting to see murky, dark depths and abruptly she shook her head. Taking a stride forwards she resumed walking. Cal fell into step beside her and they continued on in silence.

"I'm sorry I was late," she said eventually. She felt Cal look across at her, but she continued moving. "The business thing – it took longer than I expected."

"It's okay, it's okay," Cal said, his words rushed, "you have no need to apologise to me. Shit. I need to be apologising. Not you."

Bracing herself against the cold she dug her hands deeper into her coat pockets. "You've apologised, Cal. You don't need to say you're sorry again. I know you are."

"Good," he said, "that's good. I'm glad." He paused a moment and she waited. "Is there a chance here, Lexi? Tell me this isn't the end?"

She heard the appeal in his voice and knew she had to give him some kind of answer, but she was struggling to focus. Guilt weighed heavy on her mind and yet all the while, images of Jae raced through her brain. Jae telling her he knew she was lying and that she felt it too. Jae making her coffee. Jae smiling at her, the curl of his mouth tugging upwards as he did so. Jae's warm breath on her neck, the whispered softness of his lips as they connected with her nape.

Lexi closed her eyes as nausea pulled at her stomach. She felt like a bitch, a scarlet woman and she hated herself more than she could ever hate Cal. She'd met her boss last night and now her thoughts, her hopes, her dreams, her plans with her husband were in complete disarray. Yet here she was watching her marriage fall apart and allowing her husband to take all of the blame. What the hell had happened to her? Where was the Lexi that believed in right and wrong? The Lexi that loved Cal beyond all reason? The Lexi that had made her marriage vows with unswerving belief? Again she shook her head to rid herself of thoughts of him. Jae. He had to disappear, he had to.

"I went to Jae's house," she said as she stopped walking once more, "after the pub." Cal stopped too and looked at her. Lexi knew it was the last thing he'd expected her to say. In truth, she'd had little idea she was going to reveal it either, but in order for Jae to go and to leave her brain, she had to be honest with Cal. "I left the meeting to come home and then he hijacked my cab."

"He what?" Cal's voice was outraged and belatedly Lexi realised how she'd made it sound.

"No – no," she said as she turned to face Cal and held up her hand, "not like that. We didn't finish our meeting. I kind of stormed out. He thought it was important we finish it because he wants to promote me. He wants me to take a management programme."

"That's great," Cal said, but his voice was flat, emotionless.

"It's a big opportunity."

Cal nodded. "I'm sure it is." Clear green eyes regarded her and, unable to let him in, she dropped her gaze.

They lapsed once more into silence and this time it was Cal who resumed their pace. Lexi caught him up.

"That's why I was late," she repeated, "we talked about the possibilities that might be available to me – with JaceEnterprises."

"Uh huh," Cal continued walking.

"It could be the start of a great career," she added wondering how the hell they'd got onto this subject. They were supposed to be talking about their marriage.

"Undoubtedly," Cal's voice was wooden.

"It's probably not the best time to talk about this though."

Beside her Cal shrugged. "I don't know what to say, Lexi. I don't know what you want me to say. I'm terrified here." He paused again and turned to face her. "Terrified that what I did to you last has ruined our marriage so, yeah, talking about your career is not top of my list right now."

"I know, I know," she said and she did know that. "I don't know what to say either, this is all new territory for me. I figured I owed you some kind of explanation about why I was late."

Cal shook his head and moved back a little, resting himself against the harbour wall. "You owe me nothing, nothing at all. It doesn't matter that you were late, it doesn't matter that you went to this Jae's house – don't you see? None of that matters right now. All that matters to me is our marriage and if we can't talk about that, if we can't work out if there's anything left to save after what I did…then I have nothing else to talk about. Not now. I asked you if there was a chance and you didn't reply. I have to know, I have to know if there's any chance at all?"

Lexi looked at him, at Cal, at the man she loved leaning against the harbour wall as the winter wind tousled his blond locks. He had no idea what'd been going through her mind only moments before –

who had been going through her mind. Cal was here for her, focused on her, his life on hold for her, his future dependent on her and she wasn't even giving him a chance. She was more confused than she'd ever been in her life. He'd committed a sin against her but he said he hadn't heard her – and perhaps that was true. How could she possibly know for certain when she'd been so screwed up in her own mind at the time? Letting out a long breath, she made her decision.

"There is a chance, Cal," she said quietly, "we still have a chance."

She saw the relief flood his face and watched his shoulders drop as he released the tension he'd clearly been holding. It was one mistake. One time. One situation. Who was she to deny him, to deny their marriage when, in all reality, she herself was not whiter than white? Her thoughts when she'd returned home had still been consumed with Jae and today the guilt weighed heavy as he continually returned to her thoughts. She had to put him in a box, put last night in the past because she knew no good would come of letting him enter her life. The mere fact she was attracted to Jae was more than she could allow and yet because of that fact, because she felt she too had compromised something last night, she owed it to Cal to give their marriage one more try. Surely, after everything life had thrown at them, they owed themselves that?

Cal engulfed Lexi in a hug and she drank in his scent, feeling that safety, the security she'd always felt with him. In reality she didn't know if they could make this work; perhaps too much had happened last night, but she knew she had to be brutally honest with herself. She had to acknowledge the real reason why she was prepared to give Cal another chance. And the real reason was because last night, when Cal had kissed her, Jae had been the man in her thoughts; she had to own the truth. Lexi had tried to stop the kiss not because of Cal but because, for that moment which had been suspended in time, she'd been kissing Jae. It had been nothing to do with Cal. It was all on her because it had all been about Jae. Jae, her boss and the man who last night, had so comprehensively stolen her mind.

* * *

316

The email was brief, but it said what it needed to say.

Dear Jae,

Thank you for offering me the opportunity to join your management programme here at JaceEnterprises.

I regret to inform you that, after giving the matter my full consideration, I have decided now is not an appropriate time for a career move.

I trust you will understand and respect my decision and I thank you for your belief in my ability.

With kind regards,

Lexi Strudwick.

Lexi mailed it as soon as she arrived in the office on Monday morning. She and Cal hadn't talked about it further; Lexi had already decided if she was going to make a go of her marriage, she had to remove herself from Jae's radar as much as possible. So, whether or not to join the management programme had been a decision that had never really needed to be made. She was young – there would be other opportunities. She hoped.

"Hey, how was your weekend?" Lexi looked up to see Fraser approaching her desk and instantly she was reminded of the awkwardness that had existed between the two of them on Friday evening.

"Yeah, good," she replied automatically. The reality that she'd spent it trying to rebuild her marriage didn't seem appropriate to mention right now.

"Get home alright on Friday?" he asked as he leaned himself against her desk.

"Yes. Thanks."

Lexi had no idea if Fraser knew what had happened after she'd left the pub and if he didn't, she wasn't going to be the one to enlighten him. Besides, she had got home alright. Eventually.

"Can we do lunch?" he asked and she looked up at him in surprise. Fraser had never offered to spend lunchtime with her.

"Okay," she said warily. "Have I done something wrong?"

Fraser smiled. "No." He looked around the office and lowered his voice a little. "We need to clear the air – after Friday," he said.

"Oh, right. Yeah, okay," she replied.

"Great." He removed himself from her desk. "See you here around one?"

Lexi nodded and watched as Fraser departed in the direction of the stairs. She was still unsure what had happened with him on Friday. She figured though, if they were going to maintain a good working relationship, they needed to sort it out. Clear the air as he'd said.

One o'clock arrived. Lexi's email had been ominously silent thus far and she didn't know whether to be concerned or relieved. She'd been half expecting a summons to Jae's office or worse, a brisk reply giving her an hour to clear her desk.

Fraser arrived on the dot. "I got us a table at R88," he said, mentioning a relatively new cafe style eatery nearby.

"Sounds great." Grabbing her coat she shrugged into it and followed him out of the door and onto the busy street.

"I hope you don't mind," Fraser said as she fell into step beside him, "but I didn't want there to be any awkwardness between us. I'm not one for letting things lie. If there's a situation, then I like to get it sorted."

Lexi looked at him sideways. "A situation?" she asked.

Fraser smiled down at her. "I'm aware that we didn't part on the best of terms and I wanted to remedy that. Here we are…" he pushed open the glazed door as they reached the cafe. Lexi walked in ahead of him and settled herself into the booth to which they were directed. Fraser slid in across from her and she took a moment to glance at their surroundings. The café hadn't been open very long and this was the first time she'd visited. Occupying a relatively small unit, the café had been cleverly fitted out to make the most of the space. Square tabled booths lined the edges whilst circular tables filled in the central area, some of which extended into an alcove just beyond her sight. Each was covered with a red chequered cloth reminiscent of days gone by and Lexi could see this was the over-riding theme. Several black and white portraits lined the walls proudly showcasing ancestors who, it would seem, had run similar establishments in the past. A large blackboard hanging above the counter dictated the specials; the counter itself being small and similarly covered with a red chequered cloth. Most of this cloth, though, was obscured by a number of glazed domes, each of which contained a mouth-watering selection of cakes. The smell of freshly brewed coffee teased her nostrils and she breathed in the delicious scent.

"Special's usually good here," Fraser said as he indicated the board above the counter, "but you can have whatever you want. I'm buying."

Lexi allowed a smile to form around her lips. "What a gent," she said with a grin, "maybe I'll get you to give Cal some tips."

Fraser returned the smile. "Maybe. Although I'm on my best behaviour right now," he winked at her, "you mightn't want me to influence him on a bad day."

Lexi laughed, suddenly remembering why she liked Fraser so much. He always had the ability to make her relax and laugh, both commodities that were in short supply right now.

"You know what," she said as she glanced at the red, leather bound menu, "I think I'll just have a chip butty."

"A chip butty?" Fraser looked at her in shock. "I bring you to a classy eatery, offer to pay for lunch and you want a chip butty?" his tone was incredulous and Lexi laughed.

"Yup. They have it here on the menu," she indicated with her finger, "and I can't remember the last time I had a chip butty."

"Well, in that case," he said, "I'll have one too. May as well join you."

Lexi grinned as Fraser signalled the waitress over and placed their order. A few moments later she departed.

"So, Friday," Fraser began, "I guess we should clear things up. We didn't finish our conversation before Jae arrived."

Lexi looked across at him. The laughter had disappeared from his eyes, his expression serious, all banter now gone. She nodded. "Okay."

"I think," he cleared his throat, "I think we need to talk about what happened earlier in the evening, or rather, me trying to explain what happened earlier."

She nodded again.

"I was telling you," he continued, "about the way you react sometimes, how your body can give out messages you perhaps don't intend it to." He regarded her warily.

"Yes," she said, "I remember."

"The thing is, you do it a lot. A real lot. Like," he hesitated, "in the pub before Jae arrived, the way you looked at me, your eyes were telling me things, giving me messages."

She blinked at him. "You mean, before you started ignoring me?"

Fraser nodded. "Yes."

Lexi thought for a moment. When she'd been looking at Fraser in the pub she'd been thinking of Cal, thinking of how it felt when she was with him, how there was this communication between them. It had never occurred to her that Fraser would read it otherwise, yet, after what happened later that night with Jae, Lexi was beginning to see how naïve she'd been. That moment with Fraser, she'd passed it off as nothing, but her mind and body had been a traitor that night: a traitor with Jae, a man who was not her husband.

"I didn't understand," she said after a moment, "we're friends, I didn't think anything of it."

"I know you didn't," replied Fraser, "and that's why I need to tell you because you have to be careful, Lexi. The way you looked at me on Friday – some men could take that as an invitation."

She regarded him with wide eyes. "An invitation?" Was she really capable of misleading others that much?

He nodded. "Yes. I know how much your marriage means to you but there are others who wouldn't care about that. They would see you looking at them that way," he blew out a breath, "and they wouldn't care if you were married or not."

An image of Jae flew into her head and immediately she tried to erase it.

"You have no idea what effect you have on men," Fraser continued softly as he leaned closer across the booth. "There are a fair few of us who'd like to be more than just friends with you. . ." he broke off and Lexi looked at him in surprise as she processed what he'd just said.

"You mean you?" she whispered incredulously. She had no idea he felt anything other than friendship towards her.

Fraser nodded slowly.

Lexi shook her head. "Fraser, I…"

He held up his hand. "You don't need to say anything. It's cool."

She continued to watch him, slowly shaking her head. "I'm sorry."

The waitress arrived with their order and they both leaned back allowing their food to be delivered.

"Please don't be sorry, Lexi," Fraser said after the waitress had departed, "it really is fine. I just wanted you to be aware. Not every man will be as understanding as me." He paused and took a sip of his drink, freshly ground coffee served in a tall, red mug. "You have a way about you," he continued, "you're beautiful, talented and vulnerable. It's a hell of a potent mix and not everyone will honour the boundaries."

She thought of Jae again. He hadn't appeared concerned with boundaries on Friday night. Was he one of the men Fraser was warning her about? Swallowing, she forced her mind back to the present.

"I honestly had no idea," she said. "You're such a good friend and I…"

Once more he held up his hand. "Just let it go. Okay? I only told you because I wanted to explain what happened on Friday, but I don't expect anything from you and I appreciate you don't feel the same. I just wanted you to know, that's all."

Lexi's throat constricted as she attempted to chew a mouthful of butty. She was flattered, of course, but concerned too. If Fraser had picked up on her signals then who else had, and moreover, was she giving the very same signals to Jae? Automatically her heart skipped a beat as he once again entered her thoughts. Damn that man. Why did he have to take up so much of her headspace when she had a husband at home who she loved beyond reason?

"Thank you – I think," she responded, "for the advice and the compliment. I'm flattered." Once again she tried to send Jae metaphorically packing.

Fraser laughed. "You're welcome."

They lapsed into silence for a moment and Lexi took another bite of her sandwich. How was she going to explain this lunch to Cal, she wondered? Already she'd skirted the truth when she'd told him about Jae. If she revealed that Fraser had confessed to liking her, she wasn't sure he'd cope.

"That," Fraser interrupted her thoughts, "is good." He pointed at the butty.

Lexi smiled but didn't respond; she was bewildered, confused. A few days ago her head had been full of Cal, now it was full of Jae. Added to that, Fraser's new revelation was begging attention and she felt as if she were on a rapidly spinning merry-go-round with no idea when to get off.

"Do I really give out signals?" she asked. Maybe that part was something she could control – even if it was a bit late; the horse, it would seem, had already bolted in both Jae and Fraser's direction.

She waited as Fraser regarded her. "Yes," he said at length, "you do, but like I said, I know you're completely unaware. Unfortunately though, for some men, that naivety just adds to the attraction."

"So, what am I supposed to do?" she frowned at him. "Should I just not look at anyone?"

Fraser laughed and she frowned at him some more.

"I was being serious," she said.

Fraser nodded. "I know. And that's precisely the naivety that makes you even more attractive. You might be married, Lexi, but you have a long way to go in understanding how the male mind works. I can't tell you what to do all I can tell you is to be careful. This is me, you're safe with me but, like I said, not everyone respects the marital boundaries."

Once more she shook her head. "I'm so sorry, Fraser."

He shrugged. "It's cool. Just understand that you're in the real world now. This is big boys' territory and the protected bubble of marriage – let's just say I've seen that compromised more times than I can remember."

"I know people have affairs," she said after a moment, "I just had no clue I was suggesting I'd be interested in one."

Fraser shrugged. "I've never been married and I can't imagine committing to one person right now but," he indicated her with this hand, "you've found that person in Cal and if he's truly the man you're going to spend the rest of your life with, then just be careful. That's all."

Lexi didn't respond as she considered his words. When Fraser had suggested lunch this had been the last thing she'd expected would happen. Every day, though, it seemed she was encountering new things she didn't understand, imagine or know about. Either she was, as Fraser said, incredibly naive, or she was completely screwed in the head. Panic ripped through her chest as yet again Jae entered her thoughts – in particular what he'd suggested on Friday. Even though she'd not cheated on Cal, guilt hit her square in the gut. She'd been giving out signals, Fraser had said as much. Is that what Jae had picked up on and if so what did that mean? Why was she giving out signals? Did that mean she no longer loved Cal?

Nausea battled with panic and guilt and, pushing her half-finished sandwich away, Lexi grabbed at her sparkling water and took a long slug.

"Why would I do that?" she said almost to herself, but Fraser had heard her.

"You weren't aware…" he began, but she raised a hand to stop him.

"No, but these things, they're subconscious?"

He nodded.

"So, somewhere in my subconscious – does that mean I'm not happy?"

"Whoa, Lexi. No." This time it was Fraser who held up his hand. "You can't over-think this. Men have unreciprocated feelings for women all the time; nothing you did has anything to do with how I feel."

"No," she shook her head, "that's not what I meant. If I'm subconsciously giving out signals, doesn't that mean something? Maybe somewhere, deep down I'm questioning my marriage?" The mere thought of that being the case terrified her but so much evidence was stacking up to suggest she was.

"Don't go there," Fraser warned.

Inside her stomach tied itself in knots as more and more questions crashed through her head.

"I don't understand," Lexi said once more. "What the hell's happening to me?"

"Nothing's happening to you," Fraser began in a reassuring tone. "Everything is just the same as it's always been."

"No," she spoke firmly, "no, it's not. How can it be? I don't care that I don't know I'm doing it. Somewhere in here," she tapped her finger roughly on the side of her temple, "there must be something wrong otherwise why would I act that way – subconsciously or not?"

Fraser took a deep breath and then shook his head. "I'm sorry, Lexi, but you're asking the wrong person. I don't pretend to know how the male psyche works let alone the female. All I can tell you is what I see, but, beyond that, I really can't help. I wish I could."

"Some friend you are," she muttered as the panic began to escalate. How could she doubt Cal – her one true love, her soul mate?

"This is nothing to do with our friendship," Fraser responded. "I can't get involved in your marriage. It wouldn't be right."

"But I love Cal," she defended to herself. "I love him."

Fraser heard her and smiled. "In which case," he replied, "you've nothing to worry about."

She looked at him in confusion. "How can you say that? I've led you on…"

"Seriously. Let it go. If you still love Cal your marriage is fine. You have nothing to worry about." Lexi could hear the beginnings of frustration in his tone but she needed to try and understand.

"Now you sound naive," she responded. "You think marriage is simply about loving someone?"

Fraser shrugged. "How the hell would I know? I told you, I can't imagine committing to one person but I'm sure loving that person is a damn good start."

"Of course it is," she agreed, "but it goes so much deeper than that. There's respect, humility, understanding, attraction, compromise – the list is endless."

"Which," he pointed out reasonably, "is why I said only you can work out what any of this means." He gestured towards her with his hand.

Lexi looked at him quizzically. "Wait. If there's nothing wrong, what am I working out?" She knew she was being deliberately argumentative but everything Fraser had said coupled with her own, largely unacknowledged insecurities, was making her prickly. Every time she considered there might be a problem with Cal, it felt like a spear through her heart. She felt as if she was betraying the one man who she knew loved her above all else. Frustrated, she waved her hands at Fraser. "I'm not having this conversation," she said, "my marriage is fine and that's all you or anyone else needs to know."

"You two obviously don't have enough work to do," observed an unmistakable, earthy voice behind her and Lexi jumped. Not only did she instantly know who it was, she'd also been completely unaware he was there. Frantically she searched her memory banks for the last words she'd spoken, praying he hadn't overheard anything incriminating.

"Jae," Fraser stood to greet their boss and the two men smoothly shook hands. "We were just having lunch," he said, indicating their half-eaten sandwiches. "Would you like to join us?" Fraser's tone gave no hint of the depth of their conversation only moments before. Lexi threw him a glare. Jae joining them was about the worst thing she could imagine.

"There isn't room," she said. The booth, in her opinion, wasn't designed to seat more than two.

"No, you're right," Jae concurred, "there isn't really room."

He didn't, however, make any attempt to move on.

"Well," she glanced at her watch. "We still have half an hour of our break left so we'll be sure to be back in plenty of time. It was good to see you again." Even though Lexi wasn't sure she wanted to continue her chat with Fraser, it was infinitely more preferable in her opinion, than spending the next half an hour with Jae.

Jae's eyes flickered as he focused his intense, dark gaze on her. Lexi closed her own eyes and turned away.

"Ever get that feeling of deja-vu?" Fraser asked after a moment. She looked back at her friend, eyes questioning.

"I seem to remember our conversation ending abruptly on Friday too," he murmured and, gathering his jacket, he began to rise from the bench.

"Wait," she held her hand up to Fraser, "we haven't finished..."

"It's fine," Fraser said as he began to move away from the table. His expression was inscrutable and for the first time Lexi began to wish that he gave out signals too. Everything felt wrong and unfinished. "I'll take care of the bill on the way out," he said as he departed, regarding her one final time, his expression odd. Lexi watched as Fraser spoke to the waitress and continued to follow him as he exited the café. She didn't want to turn to the man stood beside her because she knew if she did, she'd be in trouble. His gaze, though, she could sense, hadn't wavered from her face the entire time he'd been standing there.

"So, it seems we're alone again," Jae commented innocently as he slid into the booth which Fraser had only just vacated.

"That was rude," she said, "and besides, I have to get back to work too."

"I'm your boss," Jae asserted, his gaze unwavering, "and we need to talk." Even though Lexi had yet to meet his eyes, she could feel the heat of his stare. He had still not looked away.

"We have nothing to talk about," she said, as finally, she did lift her gaze. "The situation with Zach is resolved and I covered everything else in my email."

"Perhaps," she watched as he leaned back in the seat and clasped his hands loosely together on the table, "although I'm not the biggest fan of impersonal communication. When we're dealing with those a distance away or even in another country then of course, it has its benefits. When though, we're talking to someone who is in the same building, I much prefer personal communication. It saves there being any misunderstanding. Wouldn't you agree, Lexi?"

She looked at him and shook her head. "No, I don't agree. Email is a very effective method of communication and after what I wrote to you this morning, there shouldn't be anything left for us to talk about. Unless, of course you're going to tell me I no longer have a job?"

Jae remained silent for a moment and Lexi fidgeted under the intensity of his presence. Ever since Fraser had left, the atmosphere had changed. The image of him that had burned in her brain since Friday was even brighter now that she was looking at him anew. His suit of choice today was charcoal black, a look that on some men would've been plain wrong. On Jae it merely emphasised the cobalt unruliness of his hair and the depth of those torturing eyes. Guilt pierced her heart again. This was wrong. So wrong. Focusing she brought her mind back to Cal; the man she loved and the man she was going to continue to build a future with.

"How do you feel about clichés?" Jae asked and she looked at him in surprise.

"Pardon?"

"Clichés," he repeated, "how do you feel about them?"

Lexi shook her head. "I've never given them much thought. Um…in books they can be annoying I guess, and so too in life. If someone uses clichés all of the time then it feels like you can't ever get to the person beneath. So, I suppose, they're okay but in moderation. Why?"

Jae tilted his head to one side. "Have you finished?" he asked, indicating her half-eaten lunch. Lexi looked down at it. The chip butty she'd been enjoying mere moments before looked cold, sad and unappealing.

"Uh – yeah, I guess so."

"Good," he stood. "I have something I want to show you."

Lexi glanced at her watch. "I only have fifteen minutes of my break left."

Jae smiled. "Don't worry, I'll clear it with the boss."

Lexi shook her head. "No, you don't get to do this. Sorry." She walked out of the booth and, pushing past him, headed straight to the door. It was only seconds before he caught up with her on the pavement.

"Do what?" he asked as he adjusted his long stride to fall into step with her.

"Order me around. Organise my life. I want to go back to work. I'm not some puppet you can move around at will. You hijacked my life on Friday night, and now my lunch with Fraser. You don't get to keep doing that."

Lexi knew she was addressing him in a less than professional manner but given the lunch she'd just had with Fraser and the complexity of her thoughts right now, she figured he deserved it. If it wasn't for him, she wouldn't be in this state of confusion.

Beside her he halted and placed a hand on her arm, forcing her to stop. "Lexi," he said as he held her firm, "don't make me do this. Don't make me remind you I'm your boss."

She shook herself free. "No. No, you're not my boss. Not anymore. If you were my boss you would've sacked me by now, torn me off a strip for even speaking to you this way. You can't do this, Jae. I have a life and a husband. If working at JaceEnterprises is going to be like this then I quit. I won't do this. I'd rather work somewhere else than have you in my head, driving me crazy."

He widened his eyes. "What did you say?"

"You heard," she said as she began to move in the direction of the office, "I quit. I'll clear out my desk when I return. A formal letter will be in the mail to you tomorrow."

"No," he stopped again and once more grabbed her arm, "what else did you just say?"

Lexi thought for a moment and shrugged. "That you should have sacked me? It doesn't matter either way; sack me or I leave. I can't work for you. End of."

Jae shook his head, dark wavy hair flopping across his forehead. Lexi remonstrated with herself for noticing. "You're not leaving and I'm not sacking you. *That* is end of," he said. A car drew up beside the kerb and with one swift movement Jae opened the door and manoeuvred her inside. Lexi pushed ineffectually against him but he was too strong and he'd caught her off guard. Once more.

"You don't get to do this again," she said angrily as he seated himself beside her, "just leave me the hell alone."

His handsome face was stony as he stared straight ahead. The car eased away from the kerb. "I told you I wanted to show you something," he stated, almost as if it forgave his actions, "and that's what I intend to do."

"And I," she said as she pulled her phone out of her handbag, "intend to call the police. I don't care who you are: you've once again, taken me against my will."

Beside her she heard him sigh. "If it makes you feel better, Lexi, then go ahead."

She stopped tapping into her phone and turned to face him. "You're okay with me calling the police?"

Jae shrugged. "Not especially, but you seem hell bent on doing it."

"You've taken me against my will," she countered.

"Yep. So it would seem." He resumed staring straight ahead.

For a second Lexi looked at her phone, knowing she only had to press one more button before the police were alerted. She was tempted to connect the call but then realised it was pointless. He wasn't exactly kidnapping her. With an exaggerated sigh, she replaced the phone in her bag.

"Where are we going?" she asked.

"You'll see," he said as he turned slightly and nodded towards her handbag. "Called off the dogs?"

Lexi smiled ruefully. "Yeah, okay. You just – you can't keep doing this."

He nodded and then turned to face forwards again. "So you keep saying."

Sitting back in the seat Lexi took a moment. The car that had picked them up was large and luxurious. A limousine, it had acres of space in the rear and a privacy glass divider between them and the driver up front. Everywhere she looked was polished leather and chrome and momentarily it took her breath away. Never had she ridden in a car this opulent.

"This looks like something the Prime Minister should be travelling in," she commented, "do I need to look for outriders?"

Jae laughed. "I'm beginning to think you have a thing for the police." He smiled sideways at her as he relaxed back in the seat. "No, no outriders. It's just the most comfortable way to travel."

"I wouldn't know," she commented, "this is the first time I've been in anything like this."

Jae turned to face her. "My first car was a Reliant Robin. It belonged to my father and he restored it for me."

Lexi looked across at him. "I don't even know what one of those is," she said.

"You would if you'd seen one," he replied, "only had three wheels. A masterstroke of engineering."

"Three wheels?" she asked aghast. "How does a car travel on only three wheels?"

Jae laughed again. "Oh, Lexi. You have so much to learn."

She frowned. "That sounds like you're mocking me. Just because I don't know what a Robin is, or whatever the hell it was called…"

"I'm not mocking you," he said smoothly, "I promise. I'll show you a photo of it."

"Or I could Google it," she responded grumpily.

"Or you could Google it," he agreed.

They rode for a moment in silence.

"I don't understand your question," she said at length. The distance between them on the back seat had remained the same, but Lexi was beginning to feel overwhelmed by his presence. Much like she had done in the cafe and again on Friday, at his home. She needed to break the silence.

"Which question?" he asked.

"About clichés? I don't get what that has to do with anything."

He smiled, but he didn't respond.

"You're not going to answer?" she asked. "Is this like Zach all over again? Am I going to find out there's a lie in here somewhere?"

Jae shook his head. "No lie, but it's easier to show you than try to explain. Trust me."

Trusting Jae wasn't on her agenda, but Lexi knew she had no choice; at least not if her curiosity was going to be satisfied.

"How was your weekend?" he asked and immediately she stiffened. How did he do that? How did he know just what to ask, which questions would put her on edge?

"Good. Thanks." Her answer was brief by necessity. Guilt stabbed through her again as Cal replaced Jae in her mind. She shouldn't even be here let alone talking to this man; not considering the way he disturbed her equilibrium. She loved Cal with all of her heart. She did. She loved him. "Yours?" she asked out of politeness.

"Troubled," he replied. Lexi merely nodded suspecting it would do

330

her no good to ask what he was referring to. They lapsed into silence once more.

"I don't understand something else," she began.

"What's that?"

"Why you didn't just ask for a meeting, or better still, reply to my email? You didn't need to go to these lengths. Despite how I feel about you, I would've met with you. You are, after all, my boss."

"It was a chance encounter," he replied, "I was in the cafe meeting with someone else; you didn't see me when you came in. I figured I'd take the opportunity I'd been presented with. Far easier than trying to negotiate a meeting time with you."

"Right," she nodded. True, she hadn't been able to see into the side alcove, but she was certain she would've felt his presence or that Fraser would've spotted him. Was that another lie?

"Were you intending to reply to my email?" she asked instead.

Jae nodded. "Yes, but only to arrange to meet with you. As I said, I much prefer to talk in person."

"An email accepting my decision would've been just fine," she responded, "you didn't have to do all of this." She gestured at the interior of the car.

Jae turned to look down at her. "A coincidence, Lexi. Like I said. As for accepting your decision – it's your decision. If you don't wish to take part in the opportunity I'm offering you then that's your choice. It doesn't change the fact that I have something to show you, in fact – we're here."

The tyres crunched as the car pulled over a rough gravelled area and came to a standstill a short distance from what appeared to be a building site. With a frown, Lexi exited the car and walked to the front of the vehicle where Jae already stood.

"What's this?" she asked. Directly in front of them was a large site, mostly cordoned off for safety, but Lexi could see the foundations of a substantial property being laid. Beyond the foundations the land continued for a distance and then dropped away providing a stunning view to a forest below. That then stretched almost as far as the eye could see before finally ending at a large lake. "It's breath-taking," she said.

Beside her she felt Jae nod. "Isn't it?"

"Where are we?" she asked. "Is this one of your projects?"

She turned to face him and he shook his head. "Yes and no."

Lexi frowned.

"It belonged to your friend. To Zach," he said and Lexi felt her heart constrict. "According to the plans, he was building this for his future, his retirement home."

Lexi swallowed over the lump that had suddenly formed in her throat. "And now?" she whispered, almost afraid to hear the answer.

"It formed part of the take-over," Jae confirmed, "it had to. There was no way I could give him the value he needed without this land."

"This was Zach's?" she whispered again. "And now..." she felt sick and automatically grabbed at her stomach. "Why would you show me this?"

Jae took a step away and then turned back so he stood directly in front of her. "I get how much this must hurt," he said, "I really do, and, until Friday, I didn't know what I was going to do with this place. The plans are drawn up, the work has begun and with my capital there's no reason why the house can't be finished – but I don't need another house, Lexi. So, it's been in limbo, waiting for me to decide what to do."

"And have you decided?" she asked as she felt tears beginning to form at the back of her eyes. Cal had never mentioned this place to her, yet he must have known. He must have known Zach was building this for his future. To see something this beautiful being taken away from her husband's best friend was almost as hard as closing down his business. Suddenly, a not altogether pleasant thought struck her.

"Is this...?" she asked, barely able to voice the words, "...is this another test? Is that why you've brought me here? To test me again?" Nausea began to travel from her stomach and up into her throat.

"No. No," Jae held up his hand, "I promise. I brought you here because I wanted to show you this place and because on Friday, you helped me to decide what I wanted to do with it. I figured it was only fair to share it with you." He turned from her and paced a few steps away.

"I'm going to keep it, Lexi," he said. "I'm going to finish construction in exactly the way Zach planned it, every single detail."

"Why?" she asked as she stepped closer towards him. "Why would you do that? You could create anything here."

"I know," he half turned, "it's a huge plot of land with unrivalled views, hell, I could even sell it and make a profit but…I can't. Talking to you on Friday, hearing you stand up for your friend, it crystallised a few things for me, and this piece of land, this is the start. I'm going to honour what your friend began here, Lexi. This will be his house, exactly as he planned it."

"You're going to let him live here?" she asked incredulously. Surely one conversation with her on Friday night was not enough to secure such a future for Zach.

"No. Not exactly," he replied. "If work continues as planned then it'll be around ten months before it can be lived in. During that time I'll be assigning someone to oversee the project, make sure it's completed as Zach wanted it to be. You'll be that person, Lexi. You might not want the management programme, but you have so much potential and I don't want to see that wasted. I want you to oversee this project, not just for me but for Zach."

Lexi swallowed again. This was too much. Way too much.

"You want me to make sure this is completed for Zach?" she asked, barely able to get her head around what Jae was asking of her.

"I want you to get it completed, yes, but not for Zach, for you."

"Whoa, whoa," Lexi took a step back. "What the hell is that supposed to mean? Completed for me?"

Jae closed the distance between them a little. "For you," he repeated. "This is yours, Lexi. This land, the plans, everything – it's yours. Upon completion of the project, it will be handed over to you – what you do with it then, is entirely your decision."

Lexi almost stumbled as she took another step back. "Wait. No way, you can't do that. If you want to give it to anyone then you should give it to Zach, at least give him back something."

Jae smiled as he advanced further. "But that's the beauty of this, Lexi, I am giving it to Zach. I'm completing his project for him and by asking you to oversee it I know it will be done precisely as he wished it to be. I'm giving it back to Zach because, when it's finished, it will be yours and there'll be nothing in the contract to say you can't give it to him. There's no reason why he can't live here and spend his future here exactly as he planned."

"You'd really do that?" she asked, unable to believe what she was hearing. "You'd do that for Zach?"

"No," Jae said as he closed the last few feet between them. Lexi looked up and noted the darkness and intensity in his eyes. Instantly they connected with hers and she allowed it for a brief moment before turning away. Using his index finger he placed it under her chin and gently pulled her head back around to face him.

"No," he repeated as he kept a gentle pressure on her chin to ensure she remained focused on him. "I wouldn't do that for Zach," he said, "but…"

Lexi waited, watching transfixed as his lips formed the last few words.

"I wouldn't do that for Zach," he repeated slowly, every word carefully enunciated, "but I *would* do that for you. And that, Lexi, is the cliché."

Chapter Thirty

Cal

Two weeks later ~ December 2014

It didn't matter how many times he went over it in his head, Cal still couldn't believe his marriage was intact. It had been two weeks since the night of the 'kiss' and Lexi was still his wife. To him, it made no sense. He'd been convinced she would run. As the time went on and Lexi stayed, he'd tried to dwell less on what'd happened and focus on the positives of their relationship. He knew things weren't back to where they had been but the fact that Lexi was prepared to give them time, was more than he could ever have hoped for.

Work was just finishing on the last of Zach's projects and the lads were almost ready to down tools. Despite Zach having made provision for them all, Cal had yet to receive any instructions from JaceEnterprises with new work. They only had until the end of the week on the current job and then, if nothing was forthcoming, they would all potentially be unemployed. For Cal, the last thing he needed was a dent in his income when he was trying so hard to get his life back on track.

"Any news?" Mace asked as Cal got out of his car that morning. Like all the guys, Mace was keen to know where their next pay cheque was coming from. Cal shook his head.

"Can't you ask that wife of yours?" Mace asked. "She works for him."

"Yeah, I already asked. She said it wasn't her job."

"Whose is it then?"

Cal shrugged. "Don't know. I thought someone would've given us the work by now."

"Yeah," Mace nodded. "I hate running this ship without Zach."

"Tell me about it," Cal agreed. Working without Zach was proving difficult for all of them.

"Why won't he come back?" Mace asked. "You seen him?"

Cal nodded as he emptied one of the waste buckets into the skip and secured it to the winch ready to pull back up. "A couple of weeks ago and he wasn't in a good place. I've tried to call, but he's not answering."

"You could go round," observed Mace and Cal threw him a look. "So could you."

Mace nodded. "Yeah, okay. It's just you're closer with him than the rest of us."

"It's been a rough couple of weeks, Mace. I'll try to call over later. Okay?"

"Alright, man. Make sure you tell him we need him."

Cal nodded. "I'll try, but I don't like my chances. He wasn't interested in coming back last time I saw him."

Mace shook his head. "Such a waste. If I could get my hands on that bitch…"

"If we could all get our hands on her…" Cal agreed. "No one deserves to suffer like that. Especially not Zach."

Cal didn't know how much the other guys knew about Zach's past. The only time he'd really opened up to Cal was during their recent night out and even then, Zach had told him to forget what he'd heard. Zach was a private person, yet it still hurt Cal to think his friend was trying to cope alone, even if that was by choice.

The ringing of his phone interrupted Cal's thoughts and he pulled it out of his pocket, surprised to see it was Lexi. As a rule, they never called each other at work.

"Hey, you okay?" he asked, instantly concerned.

"Yeah, yeah, I'm good, listen…" she said, "you know you were asking about work for you and the guys?"

Cal nodded. "Yeah…"

"I think I might have your next project."

"Seriously?" Cal asked. The news couldn't have come at a better time. "What kind of project?"

"Well, I need to show you really. Can you come to the office later today? We'll take you out to the site and you can see what you think."

"Of course," Cal said. "What time?"

"Erm…" He heard her tap on a keyboard. "About four pm?"

"Sounds good," he looked around at the rest of the men. "Is it a big enough project for all of us?" he asked.

He heard her tap on the keyboard again. "How many men?" she asked.

"Ten," Cal replied, "mixed trades."

"Yeah," she said after a moment, "it should be big enough for all of you."

"Thanks," he said, "that'll mean a lot to them."

"You have to approve the job first, Cal, so don't get telling them anything just yet."

"No, I won't," he agreed.

He heard her intake of breath. "This is a special project. I think it could be just what we all need."

Cal smiled into the phone. "In which case, I can't wait."

"See you at four," Lexi said, her voice soft on the other end of the line. After a second, he heard her disconnect. Cal replaced the phone in his pocket.

"Good news?" Mace asked and Cal nodded.

"Could be. Lexi has a job to show me. If it comes off, there'll be work for all of us."

Mace frowned. "I thought you said it wasn't her job to deal with this kind of stuff?"

"No, it's not. I don't know why she called. Anyway, doesn't matter. Work is work. Let's hope it comes off."

"Keep me posted," Mace said as he disappeared into the building beyond.

"Will do," Cal called after him. For a moment he waited outside, running his eyes over the construction work they'd completed on this project, checking for any obvious flaws. He could see none. The guys Zach had hired and trained, they were good guys and Cal hoped that whatever came of his meeting later, he'd be able to give them some good news. Christmas was less than two weeks away and Cal, as much as any of the other guys, needed some seasonal magic.

* * *

Lexi was waiting in the foyer when Cal arrived at JaceEnterprises.

"Hey," he walked up to greet her with a smile on his face. Even after all this time her beauty still took his breath away. Lately she'd bought more suits for work and she was dressed in one now, the slim fitting navy jacket and short length skirt outlining her slender figure. She'd left her exquisite blonde hair long today and the strands brushed across her shoulders as she turned.

"Hey," she greeted him as he approached. Reaching her, Cal leaned forwards and dropped a kiss on her cheek. Lexi pulled away.

He frowned at her in question as he watched her stiffen.

"It's my place of work," she said by way of explanation, "everyone knows everything that goes on. I need to be professional."

Cal glanced around the deserted reception area. "There's no one here," he said, "and in any case, I'm your husband. I don't think it matters."

She flicked her hand at him and he watched as surreptitiously she looked around, her eyes hovering on the first floor balcony that afforded a view of the area in which they stood.

"It matters," she said, her eyes fixed to the balcony. Cal followed her gaze. A man stood on the gallery, he was tall, corporate looking and Cal could tell from Lexi's expression it was someone of note. The man waved his hand in a greeting that Lexi acknowledged.

"Who's that?" Cal asked.

Lexi's eyes remained on the other man as he descended the stairs that led to the reception area.

"That's Jae," she said quietly, "Jae Leonard."

"As in boss, Jae?"

"Yes."

"Great. I can't wait to finally meet him."

Lexi talked about Jae often. He was, by all accounts, both successful and fair and Cal had been keen to meet the man for a while. For the benefit of both himself and the other lads, Cal wanted to make sure he created a positive working relationship with their new boss.

Jae stepped off the bottom stair and covered the short distance to them in long, economical strides. Cal wasn't in the habit of noting much about other men, but Jae had a commanding presence, one that was hard to ignore. He could immediately tell why Zach had been so keen to sell out to this man. There was definitely something about him.

"You must be Cal," Jae said as he approached, hand outstretched. "Lexi's told me a lot about you."

Cal caught Jae's hand and shook it. "Likewise," he said as he withdrew from the greeting. "I'm glad we finally get to meet."

Jae inclined his head. "So, did Lexi tell you anything about this project?"

"No," Cal responded, "she said it was best to show me?"

"Yes," Jae smiled, "it's a hell of a lot more effective. Let's go."

He began to move towards the exit, Cal and Lexi automatically fell into step behind him. Jae reached the large glazed door first and held it open. Cal's eyes immediately alighted on the large, black car that was waiting for them by the kerb and he swallowed a measure of disappointment at its predictability. The whole *I have to have a limo because I have money thing* didn't do anything for Cal. In many respects he would've preferred to see something old and restored, maybe even a flatbed truck. Something practical.

A uniformed chauffeur opened the door and Cal slid inside followed immediately by Lexi and finally, Jae. Despite his prejudices, once he was inside the car, Cal couldn't fault its luxury and he whistled. This sure was some way of travelling.

"Jae's first car was a Reliant Robin," Lexi said and Cal looked at her in surprise.

Jae smiled at Cal from the seat opposite. "A car your wife had never heard of."

"No," Cal said as he tried to wrap his head around Lexi knowing something that personal about another man. "Bit before her time."

"Indeed," Jae agreed. "We visited this site a while back and her reaction to this vehicle was similar to yours."

"Ah, okay," Cal nodded. "It's not the type of transport we're used to," he said. "You never told me you'd been out to a site? Or that you'd been in one of these," he turned to Lexi.

Beside him Lexi shrugged. "I guess I must've forgotten. There's always something new happening. It's hard to remember what I have and haven't told you."

Cal dipped his head as he considered. Her argument held water to a point, but to forget something as memorable as your first trip in a limo? Rapidly he archived the thought. They were only just getting back on track. If she'd forgotten to tell him, then that's what had happened. No good would come of him letting his brain run away in other directions. He reached across and snagged her hand, squeezing it gently.

"So, what's this site all about then?" he asked. Beneath his hand, Lexi's fingers were unresponsive. Inwardly he frowned.

"It's a fairly new acquisition," Jae informed him, "a project which I've asked Lexi to assist with."

"That's great," he smiled at the other man. Lexi's fingers remained wooden and cold and so he squeezed them again. "Can I ask," he said, "do you plan to use all of Zach's guys on a long term basis?"

Jae nodded. "Yes, of course. My hope is to utilise your colleagues to their full potential. It was part of my agreement with Zach and I'm not one to renege on agreements."

"Thank you," Cal said, "it's just that without Zach on board the men have been worried. Lexi's call today came at just the right time, particularly with Christmas around the corner. Most of the men have families."

"It can be a difficult time," Jae agreed.

Beneath his hand Lexi's fingers stiffened further and then, with a sharp tug, she freed them. Cal looked across at her in askance, but she kept her head deliberately averted. A feeling of dread began to creep into his soul. He'd thought they were okay but since he'd met her today, her actions had said otherwise. Was she having second thoughts about staying with him? Suddenly he wished Jae Leonard wasn't in the car so he could have his wife to himself. Talk to her. Find out what was going on.

"Do you have a family?" Jae asked.

With difficulty, Cal returned his attention to the other man.

"Er, no, not yet." He felt Lexi stiffen beside him. "You?" He didn't particularly care what Jae's answer was, but he felt obliged to ask. The confines of the car necessitated they make small talk at least.

"No. Actually, I'm not married. Never met the right woman."

Cal smiled. "I was damn lucky to meet Lexi," he said. "When you find the right woman there's nothing like it."

Jae smiled at him. "I can imagine."

Abruptly Lexi turned to face Cal. "I am here you know," she said. He struggled to pinpoint her tone.

"As if I could forget." For a moment she allowed his eyes to connect with hers and he drank from their familiar core before she rapidly closed them and turned away again. Cal frowned.

"How long have you two been married?" Jae asked.

"A year," Cal answered.

"Ah, still in the honeymoon phase then."

"You could say that," Cal hedged. "It's been something of a whirlwind ride for us."

Jae nodded. "Life has a tendency to be unpredictable, that's why I truly believe in taking every opportunity that presents itself. Wouldn't you agree, Cal?"

"Absolutely."

Lexi remained silent and once more, Cal reached across to grasp her hand. Once again she pulled it away.

"Never been close?" he asked Jae. "To getting married?" His mind was whirring as he tried to make sense of the way Lexi was behaving. Was it simply because he wasn't being professional? After all, that was what she'd chastised him about when he'd first arrived at the office.

"Once," Jae said and suddenly Lexi moved, turning forwards to face their boss.

"I thought you said you'd never met the right woman," she commented and Cal looked at her in surprise. It seemed an odd conversation to join considering her silence thus far.

"And I haven't," Jae answered. "If she'd been the right woman, then I would've married her."

"Right," Lexi said and immediately turned her attention back to the view outside.

"When you know, you know," Cal said. "You'll find her, mate." This time he placed his hand on Lexi's thigh. He felt her flinch.

"Here we are," Jae said after a moment and Cal looked out of the window. The familiar hoardings of a building site came into view and, as the car pulled to a standstill, he saw the metal safety barriers in place, which told him the site was a long way from completion.

"Has work started here?" he asked Jae as they all filed out of the car.

"Some work. Foundations mainly. It's essentially a complete build."

Cal nodded as he looked around. The location was stunning and the view was out of this world. He walked as close to the barriers as he could.

"What a place," he said as Jae materialised beside him. "What's the development?"

"One house," Jae said and Cal looked at him in surprise.

"You could easily get three or four on here."

"I know, but the plans had already been drawn up when I acquired it."

"Surely you could submit new plans?" Cal asked, his mind temporarily filled with the sight before him.

"I could," Jae agreed, "but I've decided to continue with the existing plans. Lexi?"

Cal turned at the same time as Jae, watching his wife as she made her way carefully across the site towards them.

"Care to tell Cal what this is all about?"

Lexi stopped in-between them. "This was Zach's," she said and Cal looked at her in shock.

"Zach's? Are you serious?" Zach had never mentioned anything like this to him.

He watched as both she and Jae nodded. "It formed part of the take-over deal," Jae said. "The plans were for a retirement property.

For him. I thought you might have known about it."

Cal whistled. "No way. Zach never mentioned anything to me about a retirement property. Some land. Wow."

"It belongs to JaceEnterprises now," Lexi said unnecessarily, "but as Jae said, he wants to develop it according to Zach's wishes. He's asked me to oversee the project, make sure it's just so."

Cal nodded, his mind full as he tried to take in the information he was being given. "Does Zach know?" he asked.

Lexi shook her head. "No. When the building's complete, the property will be handed over to me."

"To you? Why? Surely it remains his property," he indicated Jae, "or Zach who, in my opinion, is still its rightful owner." None of this made sense to Cal.

"I came to realise," Jae said, his tone even, "this property means more to Lexi and to you than it can ever mean to me. It makes sense for me to hand it back."

"You're giving my wife a house?" Cal asked incredulously.

"I'm giving Zach's dream back to those who care about him," Jae said.

"I want Zach to live in it," Lexi stated, "it *will* be given back to its rightful owner, but not until it's finished. His vision will be there for him to physically see, not just on paper."

"You sound remarkably calm about this," Cal observed as he spoke once more to Lexi.

"I've had a couple of weeks to get used to the idea."

"You've known about this for two weeks?" His voice raised an octave, "and you didn't think to tell me about it?"

"No," Lexi turned to him, "I wanted to tell you, but I needed to get my head around what Jae was proposing. I had to make sure it was right for me to get involved before I told you."

"Shit, man. Jeez." Cal shook his head. "Not only do I find out my best friend has an entire plot of land I didn't know about, but my wife has kept it secret for two weeks. Talk about left field."

"It took me by surprise too, Cal," Lexi said, "but when I thought about it, I realised how right it was. Can you imagine you and the guys working on this for Zach and giving it back to him? What kind of gift would that be?"

Cal felt his eyes begin to mist over. "He sure as hell deserves it," he said, "but this is big. Huge." He shook his head again.

"We estimate there's about ten months work here," Jae said, "it would get all your guys through Christmas and beyond. I can't think of any other contractors I'd rather have work on this project."

Cal nodded and then frowned as a thought struck him. "What do you get out of it?" he asked. "If you're giving the completed house away, what do you get out of it?"

The other man turned to face him. "That's a valid question," he said. "Initially I was going to sell the land as four separate plots which would have generated a profit, but then I found out about Lexi's connection to Zach. After hearing her talk about him, I changed my mind. To answer your question, Cal, I don't get anything out of this – other than knowing I did the right thing. Sometimes, knowing that – well, it's worth more than money."

"Decent," said Cal, "really decent."

Jae remained silent.

"So," Lexi turned to him, "are you going to do this?"

"Of course," Cal responded immediately, "I can't believe you had to ask. If I can give that man back anything..." He shook his head once more. "It'll be a beautiful thing."

They all stood in silence for a moment, looking out over the land and the view beyond.

"How's this going to work?" Cal asked after a while. "You said you're overseeing the project, Lexi?"

"Yes. Jae will be passing the plans to me and then it'll be my job to make sure everything is done according to them."

"And the finances?"

"I will provide the necessary capital," Jae said. "Lexi will submit the invoices to me for payment."

Cal nodded. "Okay. What about sourcing materials, do you want me to do that?"

"I'd like to source the internal fixtures," Lexi said, "but the building materials, yes. I was hoping you could do all of that."

"No problem. Hey," he said as he realised something, "we're going to be working together. That's cool."

"Yeah," she replied, although he noted her voice lacked emotion. Something was off with her today.

"Hopefully it won't be too much of a good thing," Cal said awkwardly, "living and working together."

"I'm sure you'll be just fine," Jae interrupted, "but, to make sure there are no conflicts, I'll be bringing in a project manager, someone impartial."

"Why?" Lexi asked and Cal watched as she turned to face Jae. "Don't you think I can do this?"

Cal's heart constricted for his wife knowing she felt her skills being called into question.

"No, of course I think you can do this, Lexi," he heard Jae respond. "Otherwise I wouldn't have asked. And," he added, "I have every confidence in Cal and the team too but, as Cal just pointed out, you'll be spending an inordinate amount of time together and you're both intimately connected with this project. Whilst I know you'll do the right thing by Zach, I still need you to do the right thing by me. I want someone who can offer an outside perspective. It's merely a professional contract, Lexi. Nothing personal."

Cal saw Lexi relax a little and he breathed out on a sigh. He knew what Jae was saying and understood the other man's reasons but for Lexi, she was still so new to all of this and the last thing Cal wanted was for her confidence to be dented. Thankfully, it would seem, Jae didn't want that either. He was grateful to the other man for giving his wife this opportunity and grateful too, that he was being sensitive to her feelings. Given what Jae was doing with Zach's dream and the opportunity he was giving Lexi, Cal had to conclude that on first meeting, Jae seemed like a respectable man.

"Who're you using?" he asked Jae.

"One of my newest, yet most trusted managers. She's been with me a little over a year; this will be her first major project."

"She?" Lexi asked. "Your project manager is a she?"

Jae nodded.

"I've met a few in my time," Cal interjected, "the world is full of females in roles that were previously dominated by men. Look at what you're doing, Lexi. It wasn't all that long ago the mere presence of a woman on a building site would've been frowned upon."

"I know that," Lexi replied, "I was just surprised. I naturally assumed it would be a man."

"No. She's definitely a woman," Jae confirmed, "in fact, I asked her to meet us here. Hopefully she'll be here anytime soon. So, when do you think you'll be able to start?" he turned to Cal.

"I'll go over the plans later this week and get the materials ordered – say the week before Christmas? We can hopefully get the foundations safe even if the materials haven't arrived."

"Sounds good," Jae agreed. "Confirm your proposed timescale with Lexi when you have delivery dates for the materials and she can let me know. I don't want this to run on too much longer than planned."

Cal nodded. Neither did he. To be able to give this back to his friend was a huge incentive. Never had he felt more passionate about a project.

"Thank you," he said as he reached forwards to shake Jae's hand, "you have no idea how much this will mean to someone very special to me."

"No thanks needed," Jae pumped his hand in return. "Like I said, it feels good to be doing the right thing."

The sound of a car arriving caused them all to turn and, after coming to a standstill alongside the limousine, its occupant alighted. Dressed in a similar manner to Lexi, the woman approached the three of them. A brunette to Lexi's blonde, she was smaller in height yet slender like his wife. From what Cal could see, she also curved in all the right places. Mentally he berated himself for noticing.

"Hi," she spoke first to Jae, "thanks for the opportunity. Is this the land?" Jae nodded and indicated the area with a sweep of his arm.

The woman nodded. "You were right when you said it was pretty special. Hi," she extended her hand towards Cal, "I'm Tami."

Cal took her hand and shook it. "Cal," he said as he looked at her for the first time. "Contractor."

"I know," Tami released his hand and for a second, he missed the contact. "You must be Lexi," she turned to his right and Cal watched as Tami and Lexi exchanged greetings. Side by side their looks were unnervingly similar despite the difference in their hair colour and height.

"Tami?" Lexi asked.

Cal watched as the other woman nodded. For a moment he monitored Lexi's face, surprised to see her expression had turned to a frown.

"Wait, I know you," Lexi said after a pause.

Jae and Cal turned to Lexi in unison.

"University." Lexi said. "You were in the Student Zone giving Perce grief. My friend Mel gave you money for your electric. That was you – right? Brufton uni?"

Cal turned to Tami, watching her face as she processed Lexi's words. There was a small flicker of recognition.

"Brufton uni?"

"Yes," Lexi replied her face animated. "Don't you remember? You accused Perce of short changing you and Mel helped out. Never saw you again after that though. Small world. How the hell did you end up here?"

Tami slapped her forehead. "Wait, yes, I do remember. Wow. Yeah, small world. I was full of attitude back then."

Lexi laughed and Cal was pleased it sounded genuine. For some reason it seemed important these two women got along. "Yeah, you weren't the easiest customer. Where did you go?"

"Oh, I had to leave uni suddenly. Long story." As Cal watched, her eyes slid sideways to him and he couldn't help but notice their unusual tiger shade of brown. Jae turned to encompass both women.

"So you two know each other?" he asked.

Tami nodded. She turned her focus to Jae and oddly Cal felt bereft.

"Not really. We met in the uni bar once. I needed some cash and they helped me out." She extended her arm in Lexi's direction.

"Small world indeed." Jae responded.

"That doesn't explain how you ended up here?" Lexi asked.

Tami shrugged and Cal noted the delicate rise and fall of her shoulders. Again he chastised himself. He had no business thinking of another woman. He needed to get his head back in the game.

"Jae and I met at a mutually convenient time," Tami was saying. "I've been working for him ever since I left uni."

"So," Cal cleared his throat, "Jae tells me this will be your first major job?"

She turned her gaze from Lexi to him. "Yes, but don't worry. I won't let you down."

"I hope not," he responded, "this is a special project – they don't get much more precious than this."

"Understood," Tami said with a mock salute. Cal couldn't decide if she was being cute or rude so he decided to ignore the gesture. "When are we due to start?" she asked.

"Week before Christmas," Cal replied. "We were just discussing the schedule."

Tami moved a little closer to him and Cal felt an odd kind of pull. "Have you looked at the plans yet?" she asked and he shook his head, suddenly unnerved by her proximity.

"I'll look over them later this week." To his left he noted Lexi had moved away a little and was now deep in conversation with Jae.

"I hear you know the guy?" Tami asked. Cal struggled to bring his mind back into focus as he watched his wife and Jae. Whatever strange sensations he was experiencing around Tami, they were not enough to negate a small frisson of jealousy. They looked so close. Jae and Lexi. So in tune.

"Yes," he responded as he dragged his gaze back to Tami, "Zach. He's one of the good guys."

Tami smiled and he noticed the even whiteness of her teeth. Again he inwardly cursed. Lexi was in a cosy tete-a-tete with Jae and he was noticing the whiteness of another woman's teeth. What the hell was happening?

"And you think it'll be a ten month build?" Beside him Tami continued with her questions.

"I don't know without seeing the plans but Jae," he indicated the other man who was now standing even closer to his wife, "reckons that should be about right."

Once again his mind whirred. Lexi had been odd all afternoon and now she was standing much closer to Jae than he would've liked. Yet, if he was noticing things about Tami that he never normally would, it was entirely possible his mind was just screwed. He settled on that as an explanation and looked out again across the land he hadn't known about. It was a stunning location.

"Nice, huh?" Tami said and he nodded.

"I can't believe he never told me about it," he commented.

"You knew nothing about it?" she asked in surprise and he shook his head.

"Nope. Not until today. If I had a piece of land like this, you can be damn sure I'd be telling the world."

"So would I," Tami agreed.

Cal caught a faint whiff of her perfume on the breeze. Spicy. He liked it. Shit. He looked across to where Jae and Lexi had moved even further away and were now almost at the car.

"You worked for Jae long?" Tami asked.

"No. Lexi – she's my wife – she's been working for him a few months now, but I only met him for the first time today. He took over Zach's company by some kind of divine coincidence."

"Jae mentioned you two were married," Tami looked across at where the others were stood. "I like coincidences," she said after she'd turned back to him. "I like to think they're planned."

Cal laughed despite his inner turmoil. "That's a contradiction, surely? How can a coincidence be planned? If it was planned then it wouldn't be a coincidence."

Tami smiled and this time he noted her two small dimples, one either side of her generous lips. Dammit. He remonstrated with himself – again.

"I used to think like that," she said, "but not anymore. Take today for example. I think it was planned that we should meet."

"We're working in the same field for the same company," he stated, "it's inevitable that we should meet."

"Yes," Tami inclined her head, "but to be working on such a unique project together..." she let her sentence trail off and Cal decided not to pursue it. He didn't believe in coincidences but if it worked for her, who was he to disabuse the notion?

"Have you seen everything you need here?" he asked. He had a sudden impatience to return to the car.

Beside him she inclined her head. "Yes, I think so. I have a copy of the plans too, so shall we arrange to meet once you've had chance to go over them?"

"Yeah, sounds good. I'll organise a time with Lexi."

"Great. I'm looking forward to working with you, Cal." Tami said.

"Likewise." He shook her hand again as they began to walk back in the direction of the cars.

The pull he'd felt when she first stood beside him enveloped him once more. It was an odd sensation, something he couldn't put his finger on, almost like he knew her, but he'd never met her before. He would've remembered.

Their shoes crunched on the gravel as they approached the limo and Lexi and Jae both turned. They were still standing close together, closer than Cal would've liked and his feeling of unease deepened. They seemed comfortable together, more than he would've expected for a professional relationship. As he and Tami neared the large, black vehicle Cal saw Jae's arm move swiftly to the side and he narrowed his gaze. Had the other man had his arm around Lexi? It was impossible to tell.

"Okay, see you soon," Tami said as she shook hands again with both Lexi and Jae.

"Right," Cal waved awkwardly as she got into her car, all the while watching Lexi and Jae. They had by now separated to a professional distance and for a second, he wondered if he'd imagined it all.

He heard Tami start her car and then watched as the vehicle disappeared from view. Out of habit he read the registration plate – CLA 1R3 – and, as the numbers landed in his brain, he realised it was a private plate yet he couldn't work out what it said. To be fair, he didn't need to know.

"Ready to go?" Jae asked from beside him and he nodded.

"Sure."

As he entered the limousine Cal's feeling of unease intensified. He sensed a change in the atmosphere and he knew it wasn't just his imagination.

Lexi and Jae continued a professional conversation, but Cal remained silent, preferring instead to keep his own thoughts. He knew this afternoon would be a moment he'd replay sometime in the future, and not because it was the first time he'd been introduced to Zach's dream. Three thoughts continued to rotate with equal regularity as he sat in the car in his self-imposed silence. Outwardly he appeared calm, yet, the feverish activity of his mind allowed no such luxury within and Cal felt as if his head was spinning out of control.

The first thought of the three, and by far the least troublesome, was the unshakeable feeling he'd met Tami before. Even though he was certain he hadn't, Cal couldn't dismiss the odd kind of familiarity he sensed with her.

The second thought was burning much deeper than the first, hitting him right in his gut and causing his breath to constrict. Dread and fear ran through every vein because his second concern was Lexi and Jae, and the way they were around each other. No matter how he looked at it, there was something strange between them and Cal recognised it. He was no fool. What he didn't know though was the exact nature of their relationship and that led to the third and most unsavoury thought – the one actively tearing him apart inside. As it gathered momentum it pulled at his heart and slowly broke off piece by piece until nothing but crippling fear remained.

If, the third thought taunted, he discovered Lexi and Jae were more than colleagues then Cal had absolutely no idea how he was going to cope. Yet coping wasn't the worst he'd have to face. Cal knew he'd lose his sanity and possibly his mind and that scared him more than anything.

Because he had no idea how the hell he was going to deal with it.

Chapter Thirty-One

Lexi

In the end it had taken her two weeks to decide how she felt about Zach's project and today was the culmination of that decision. A decision that had been made by a brain Lexi knew was beyond scrambled. The visit to the site had been more awkward than she could ever have imagined and Cal had not been fooled, she knew that. His manner, particularly on the return journey had cooled, and she hated herself for the way she'd treated him. The problem was she was out of control, living on her wits and acting on her instincts and with each passing day, the gulf between her and Cal widened. Lexi knew she was the one to blame, but in her addled mind, she could no more make the two sides meet than she could remove Jae from her head. He'd taken up permanent residence and Lexi knew, having seen the two men together today, she was in serious trouble. She loved Cal, but she desired Jae and the latter situation was something over which she was rapidly losing control.

Arriving back at the office Cal immediately departed and Lexi finally allowed herself a moment to breathe. That had been the hardest thing she'd ever done and all she wanted was a darkened room to lie down in.

"Lexi?" Jae called to her as she began to walk back to her desk. She turned.

"Can I see you for a moment?" he asked. She nodded. It had been foolish of her to think she could run away and hide. Silently she followed him to the first floor and on into his large office, automatically sitting in one of the visitor chairs to the front of his desk. He moved around for a moment, locking the door and closing the blinds. Lexi didn't bother to look at him. She'd known this day would come.

"We have to talk," Jae began, "that – that was one of the hardest things I've ever done."

Lexi nodded in agreement.

"This is crazy," he said as he took the beige, padded office chair adjacent to her, "we have to work out what the hell is going on here."

Lexi remained silent.

Jae sat back and she could feel him looking at her, his dark eyes boring into her in the way they always did whenever they were alone. She kept her eyes averted.

"I gave you two weeks," he said after a moment. "I backed off, I deliberately avoided all contact with you so you could think."

"And I'm grateful," she said as she looked down at her palms. "It gave me time to decide about the land and whether or not to work on the project."

Jae swished his hand to the side. "I don't give a damn about the land, Lexi. That's not why I gave you space."

Lexi didn't respond. She didn't know how to.

"Look," he began again, "this thing between us, I have to know where I stand."

This time she raised her head and looked up at him. "There is no 'thing' between us."

Angrily he shook his head. "Dammit, Lexi. When are you going to admit there's something here?"

She continued to watch his face. "There isn't anything here, Jae. There can't be. I'm..."

"...married," he finished, his tone curt. "Don't you think I know that? I've just spent the afternoon with your husband, watching him fawn all over you. I'm more than fucking aware you're married."

Instinctively she shrank back in the chair.

"Sorry," he said and held up his hand, "that was harsh." He let out a sigh. "Okay, cards on the table. I'm attracted to you in a way I've never been attracted to a woman before. At first, I thought it was just physical, but the more I see you, the more I watch you, I know it's bigger than that. I want to be with you, which I understand is as complicated as hell for you, but for me it's blindingly simple. There's something here, you know there is and you have to admit it. You have to, Lexi."

For a moment she closed her eyes. She had admitted it to herself in her own private moments but the thought of admitting it to him – it would be like signing her marriage away. Making it public. Putting it out there.

"We hardly know each other," she said at last. "We've spent time together on only three occasions – you can't possibly know you want to be with me from three occasions."

"I can," Jae said and she watched as he stood, moving so he was positioned directly in front of her. "I can," he repeated more quietly.

Lexi shook her head. "How? How can you?"

He took a breath and then leaned his muscular form back against the desk: a larger version of the modern metal one she herself worked from. The fabric of his navy trousers stretched across his thighs and Lexi schooled herself not to look. "I'm older than you, Lexi, by ten years – a fact of which I'm very aware. I've been around for longer than you and I've met many women during the course of my life. In all of that time I've never met anyone who makes me feel the way you do. That's how I know I want to be with you. I don't want to be alone anymore. I want to be with someone who makes me feel alive and that someone, is you."

"What about the woman you nearly married?" she asked.

Jae smiled. "How can you deny there's something here when that was the only part of the conversation you picked up on? I guess you thought I wouldn't notice? Too bad, Lexi. I notice everything about you. Everything."

The way his deep voice moved over the words sent shivers down her spine. He knew he affected her, *she* knew he affected her, but she couldn't bring herself to finally admit to it. That felt like the ultimate betrayal and she couldn't do that to Cal. He didn't deserve it.

"You didn't answer my question," she said as she desperately played for time. "What about the woman you almost married?"

Jae inclined his head. "I'll do you a deal," he said. "I'll tell you whatever you want to know about her – and about my life – if you'll admit there's something here. Admit you feel it too."

She looked up at him and swallowed. His shirt and tie were dark grey – a perfect companion to the navy suit jacket that matched his elegantly tailored trousers. His black hair, as ever, was secured in a band at his nape and his dark eyes were intense, focused on her face. Lexi wondered how much it mattered to her to know about the woman he'd nearly married. Did it matter enough for her to voice those words out loud and seal her fate? Even though her mouth watered at the temptation he presented, she made her decision.

"Never mind," she said, "it's not important."

"Dammit, Lexi," Jae slammed his fist on the desk. "What do I have to do to get you to admit to this?" he asked.

Lexi looked into his eyes, their dark depths tugging, pulling her down. She knew how easy it would be to get lost in them, to get lost in him, but she would not only lose herself, she'd lose Cal too. Right now that seemed like too high a price to pay.

"It's too much," she said quietly, "I can't admit to anything. The price I'd pay is too high and for what? An affair? A bit of fun until you get bored? I would lose Cal. I would lose my home, my life, possibly my job – everything, Jae. I would lose respect. It's too high a price to pay. I can't."

Jae clenched and then unclenched his fists, dropping them to his side. "I understand, Lexi, believe me, I do." His voice had calmed a little. "I know you have so much more to lose than me but right now, all I'm asking is for you to admit to it. Admit there's something between us. That's all."

His words captured her, his request so simple and slowly, something inside began to stir. The butterflies she'd experienced before, at his house, gently awoke, their fluttering wings beginning a nervous dance in her stomach. Her breath hitched a little and she allowed their gazes to mesh as she catalogued every feature of his handsome face. The roughly styled black hair, the shadow around his jawline, the teasing half-smile formed by his full lips, the proud styling of his nose, the faint scar running down his right cheek and those damned dark eyes. It was wrong, so wrong, but she was helpless to break the contact and pull away. Her eyes revealed too much; to lie to him now, to not give in and tell him what he wanted to hear, would be futile. Finally she knew she had no choice. She had to say it. She had to utter the words despite knowing that once they were out there, she couldn't call them back. Her resistance would be over, but she had no other choice.

"I feel it too," she said slowly, her voice small in the stillness of the room, "I'm attracted to you too."

His eyes darkened further and a flush crept up his cheeks. He remained exactly where he was, leaning against the desk. Lexi watched, waiting, not knowing how this would play out. For endless moments their eyes held and then finally, after what felt like an eternity, he broke the silence.

"Thank fuck for that," he whispered.

"What happens now?" she asked, dropping her gaze to the floor. Admitting it had been one thing, looking at him now it was out there – that was another thing entirely.

She felt him shake his head. "I have no idea, Lexi. In an ideal world..." he stopped and reluctantly she returned her eyes to his.

"It doesn't matter," Jae said. "You've done what I asked you to do. I can't ask for more than that. You're right. You have too much to lose."

"In an ideal world...?" she prompted. "You made me admit to it, you can't just pretend it never happened."

Jae's eyes pinned her to the chair. "The last thing I want to do is pretend. Hell, if I could, I would take you over to that sofa right now and show you how much I want you." He nodded towards the matching beige, comfy looking two-seater positioned on the opposite wall.

Her eyes widened in shock.

"Yes, Lexi. That's how much I want you. I would do everything I've dreamed of and more, right here, right now."

She continued to gape at him, her breath coming rapidly as his words ignited her fire.

"You have no idea how much I've dreamed of being with you, Lexi. Of showing you what you do to me. Every fucking night since the day I met you. So you can be damn sure I don't want to pretend this didn't happen. I'll remember this moment for the rest of my life but," he stopped and for the first time Lexi noted his breathing was ragged too, "and here's the absolute killer…I can't do a bloody thing about it."

Again she heard the anger in his voice and once more his fist hit the desk. Hard. "It doesn't matter how much I want you, how much I believe that we have something special – because you're married. Off limits – and even if that weren't the case, you're ten years younger than me, it's practically cradle snatching. And, this is just such a cliché it makes me sick to my stomach – wealthy boss meets inexperienced intern. Seriously, Lexi? Who buys into that crap? So, now, even though I pushed you to admit to this I'm left wondering why the hell I did because now I know you feel it too, it makes it fucking impossible to walk away, yet we both know there's no other choice."

Lexi remained unmoving, watching the emotions chase across his face as he summed up their situation so succinctly. For her part she had no idea why he'd made her admit to it either. Now the words were out there though, Pandora's box had been opened and she could no longer deny her attraction to Jae. The problem with opening Pandora's box was that it was incredibly difficult to close.

"I don't get why the hell you made me admit to it either," she threw at him. "I can't take those words back and you've just reiterated how pointless this is. What can either of us have possibly gained by acknowledging our feelings?"

Jae stood and closed the couple of paces towards her chair, "I needed you to say it. I needed to hear you say it."

"Why?" she asked, her voice raised as she lifted her chin to look up at him. "Before we could pretend but now… this is madness."

She rose from the chair and grabbed her handbag. Their proximity meant their faces were mere inches apart as he looked down at her.

"I need to go," she said as she made to step around the chair, "I need to work out what the hell this means for me."

"It can't happen," Jae stated.

Lexi felt his warm breath brush over her face and she nodded in agreement. "It can't happen." She took another step and began to move away from him towards the safety of the door. She'd barely cleared the chair though when she felt his hand grasp her left arm and she turned back. Instantly, their eyes connected.

"It can't happen," he said one more time, his voice soft.

She nodded.

His eyes dropped and focused on her lips. Lexi could feel them begin to burn.

"Dammit, Lexi," he said. His voice was low, barely audible. Again, she felt the whisper-softness of his breath caressing her face. Lexi closed her eyes. This was too much. It was too much to handle and too much to bear.

"I have to go," she said as she opened her eyes, unsurprised to see his gaze still firmly fixed on her. "I need to go, Jae."

He inclined his head. "I know." He made no move to release her arm, however, and Lexi made no attempt to free herself. She was a prisoner, caught by her attraction and held by her emotions. She was helpless. There was nothing she could do.

Time stood still as they remained where they were, both fighting battles that could neither be seen nor won. It was wrong, it couldn't happen, there was no way out of this and there was no resolution that would avoid unimaginable hurt and destruction. Like two enemies drawing battle lines they held their position, unmoving, barely breathing, each waiting for the other to show weakness, feeling, wanting, seeing and yet knowing they had to walk away.

Lexi continued to regard Jae, looking deep into his eyes, watching as they flicked over her face and paused on her lips once more. The atmosphere intensified and she began to feel light headed, her need for cool air to blast her with reason becoming ever greater. The distance between them closed. Slowly Jae dropped his head, his eyes never leaving her lips and Lexi stood mesmerised as his dark, wavy locks flopped over his forehead, his mouth getting closer, ever closer. She swallowed. Her mind told her to flee, run as fast as she could, leave this office, leave this place and go back to her husband, back to the life she was supposed to live. Her heart told her to stay. Its rate picked up to an impossible speed as his lips came ever nearer and with every breath a struggle, she remained motionless. There was no battle to be won. Her head and her heart may be at war, but the fight had been over a long time ago. In all honesty, the fight had been over the first time she'd met Jae and this, here and now, this was her white flag moment. Her ultimate surrender.

Jae's lips finally touched hers and instinctively she closed her eyes. Gently he pressed into her, moving his lips, kissing her slowly, his pace unhurried and Lexi responded as a small moan escaped from her throat. Jae dropped his hand from her elbow and pulled her closer to him, bracketing her with his arms as he begged to deepen the kiss. His lips pressed harder, and, unable to resist, she allowed him entry. His taste was strong and masculine and she drank him in, their teeth clashing as they both pulled closer together. His arms were powerful and safe and for a second Lexi forgot herself as she permitted him this moment, this shared experience, her head blissfully unscrambled for the first time in days. He was like water to her dehydrated soul and she closed her arms around his neck, pulling him ever nearer, their connection unbreakable as they finally gave in to their passion, their mutual attraction.

Time was suspended as hands began to caress, his moving carefully down from her waist to rest on her hips. Lexi pushed her own hands beneath his jacket, running her fingers over a shirt warmed by his solid body beneath. Everywhere he touched, she burned and another moan escaped. It was too much and yet it was not enough. Only moments ago he'd been telling her how much he wanted her and Lexi needed to feel that from him now. She needed proof he wanted her enough to make this right, enough to allow them both to salvage something out of a situation they had no hope of reversing. This was it for her; she'd already compromised everything for him by being here and allowing him to kiss her. She had to know he was in this too. Gathering a strength she didn't realise she possessed, she pulled away.

"Wait," she said as he looked at her in askance, "I have to know what this means to you."

Jae regarded her, his eyes dark, his face flushed, his lips moist. "I told you how much I want you, Lexi," he replied.

"Yes, yes, I know," she said quietly, "but this is it now. We've crossed the line, Jae. I have to know we can salvage something out of this."

"We can," he said, "I know we can."

"My life – it will never be the same again. This is huge. I have to know you're in this too, that when everything comes out, you'll be here for me. I need to know this is not just some fling to you. You have to tell me what this means."

Jae leaned back from their embrace a little and, using the pad of his thumb, he brushed it along the side of her cheek. "I don't know what the future holds any more than you do. I want you in my life, I already told you that and yeah, when it hits the fan, of course I'll be here for you. You're not the only one with something on the line here."

Lexi frowned. "You're not married."

"No, I know. But I have my reputation too, Lexi. I work with a lot of people who would frown upon our association. We might live in a more liberal society now, but there are some who wouldn't understand this. Marriage is sacrosanct and oddly, that's something I believe too. I can't tell you how much I wish you weren't married. I hate that we're breaking your vows and I hate what we're doing to Cal. He's a good bloke. He doesn't deserve this."

At the mention of Cal's name, Lexi took a step back. Jae was right of course. Cal didn't deserve this and the guilt pierced her anew. Just because she was attracted to Jae didn't make it right or her deception any easier to bear.

"What if we don't have a future?" she asked. "You said you almost got married before. What if I'm the same as that woman? Someone you thought was right but wasn't? What if I – we – sacrifice everything on a whim?"

Jae dropped his arms from around her and shoved his hands into his pockets. "I can't answer that. No one can. All we can do is act on the information we have here and now and hope the future takes care of itself."

Lexi shook her head. "I don't know if that's enough, Jae. Right now, what we've done here," she indicated the office with her open palm, "it's not too bad, we can come back from this. We both can. I can put this behind me and carry on with my marriage. I can pretend it never happened and so can you. We can close Pandora's box and maybe that's what we should do because I don't know if just letting the future take care of itself is enough for me."

She watched as he rocked back on his heels and once again leaned against the desk. "Would you leave Cal? For me?" he asked.

Lexi swallowed and widened her eyes in shock. It was a valid question, yet, hearing it so black and white…she took a moment to consider her answer. Where only minutes ago her mind had been clear, now, with the dulling of passion, the confusion returned along with the unbearable pressure of guilt.

"I love Cal," she said, "and I hate the way I'm feeling right now. I hate that I've done this to him and I hate that I'm capable of doing this to him. When I got married, he was my life and I could never see a time when he wouldn't be. This – you," she pointed at him, "I don't know what this is." She took a deep breath. "So, no, I wouldn't leave Cal for you but, if this carries on, if we explore this attraction between us, then I would have to leave him. Not for you but because I couldn't live with myself if I stayed. The only way I can stay with Cal is if I walk out of this door right now and learn to live with what we've just done."

He stood watching her and then slowly, he shook his head. "It doesn't work like that. What we did here, sure, you can walk away, go home and try to pretend it didn't happen and we can never speak of it again. But how long do you think it would be before you met someone else? Not me, but someone else you were attracted to?"

"That wouldn't happen," she defended, "you, me, that's just a freak situation."

Jae smiled at her. "No, Lexi, it's not. Men and women meet people they're attracted to all the time. The difference between what happened here and all those other people is that we chose to reveal it and then we chose to act on it."

Vehemently she shook her head. "No. I would learn from this. I'd walk away and I'd learn from this. I would become a better person and I'd make sure this never happened again."

"You can't, Lexi." Jae moved away from the desk and, gently taking her elbow, he guided her over to the sofa. They sat, side by side, not touching. "You can tell yourself it won't happen again but it will. I can guarantee it. You've only been married for a year, that's no time at all. For you to be kissing me like you just did after only a year – that tells me this will happen again, regardless of what you tell yourself."

"No, I'm not that bad a person," she reiterated, "it's you and the circumstances."

Beside her she heard him sigh. "At the end of the day it doesn't really matter what you believe. If you walk away now then yes, you can pretend and yes, you can go on with your life, but is that really what you want? Can you really do that? Can you play happy families and pretend that you didn't do this here?"

"I can try," she said. Now that the passion had burned out she was feeling stronger, the message was clearer and she knew what she had to do. She'd been unwise to act on her attraction. With the passion in part satiated, the cold reality was seeping in. She had a life, she had responsibilities and she had a husband. The war was not over, in fact, the battle had only just begun.

Slowly she got up from the sofa and made her way to the office door. "I've made my decision," she said as she turned back to face him, "this can't happen again."

She watched as a flicker of emotion crossed his face and then he schooled his features. "As you wish."

Lexi began to make her way to the door again and then suddenly she remembered something. "Does this affect Zach's project?"

Jae shook his head. "That's a professional decision. It won't be affected by anything that happened here."

"Thank you," she said.

Pivoting back she completed the last few steps to the door and slipping the lock she began to pull on the handle.

"Lexi?"

She stopped, but she didn't turn around.

"In answer to your question," he said, his voice low and soft, "what happened here today…it meant everything to me."

With a small cry she swallowed over the lump in her throat and, using hands far from steady, opened the door. Closing it behind her she walked back in the direction of the main office, drawing on every ounce of strength she possessed to keep going. She wiped at eyes heavy with tears yet they weren't the only part of her body struggling under an unwelcome weight.

Even though leaving Jae's office and putting their encounter behind her had been the right decision, a feeling of desolation washed over Lexi. Her heart, she realised, weighed heavier than her tears and, as she collected a file and began to continue working, she acknowledged it weighed heavier now than it had ever done before.

In fact, it felt as if it were barely functioning.

Chapter Thirty-Two

Cal

Present Day – June 2015

Cal had returned. Despite his angry protestations he'd come back to his counsellor's office. Matt, he'd realised had been right and, given time to think, Cal finally understood there were other factors involved in his break-up with Lexi, not just those manufactured by him. Not that any of those factors made what he'd gone on to do in any way acceptable, but at least it meant he could identify the triggers now. He could deal with why he'd done what he'd done and he hoped that would mean he could heal. And never do it again.

"How've you been?" Matt asked as Cal once again settled into the overstuffed leather armchair.

"Up and down," he responded.

"I wasn't sure you'd come back."

"No," Cal replied, "neither was I."

"I'm glad you did though," Matt said, "I think we still have some important work to do."

Cal nodded. "I agree."

"It takes guts you know, Cal – to come back."

He shrugged. "I had no choice. After I left I couldn't stop thinking about what you said and the more I went over it, the more I realised you were right."

Matt dipped his head. "Go on…"

Cal coughed. "Well, when I did what I did…I couldn't get past that – and nor should I," he added with sincerity, "but because I was so screwed up, all I could remember was what I'd done and it never occurred to me there might have been another trigger."

From the opposing armchair, Matt looked at him. "And you've been able to find other triggers?"

"I think so," he replied hesitantly. "I tried to remember distinct things that happened around that time because I want to get through this. I want to be able to hold my head high again and have some kind of life and so I figured you were right and I needed to try to see what else was going on."

"Makes sense," his therapist agreed.

"The thing is," Cal continued, "I realised that because I couldn't get past the guilt, I couldn't see anything other than what I did – and I'm not trying to excuse my actions because I would never do that. There can never be any excuse for what I did."

"I understand."

Cal took a breath. "I started to remember other things, odd things, things that had happened with Lexi around that time. Things about the way she was, about her and Jae and suddenly the trigger hit me. I'd been so absorbed in myself and my blame I'd forgotten the point of our argument. All I could remember was what happened afterwards but now it's clearer." He stopped. "We argued about her and Jae. I remember it all now."

"What exactly do you remember?" Matt asked.

Cal took a deep breath. "It started just before Christmas when we got the chance to work on Zach's project."

"Okay," Matt said.

Cal swallowed. Reliving everything wasn't getting any easier for him. "So, when we went to the site for the first visit, that's when I thought she and Jae were close. Like, closer than they should be. I asked her about it and she said there was nothing. She told me they'd worked together on a couple of occasions – that was all. I believed her. I had no reason not to." He swiped his palms across the tops of his thighs. "I also wanted to make sure she was okay with what happened – you know, with the kiss?"

Matt nodded.

"She told me it was fine. Forgotten. That we'd both been in another place at the time and we should just move on. She said we'd already got through so much together and she was committed to getting through this too. She told me she loved me and that she valued our marriage and I believed her." Again, he paused.

"Am I right in guessing she wasn't being entirely honest?" Matt asked.

He nodded. "I didn't realise it at the time though. A couple of days later things hit the fan with Zach," he swallowed as he felt the tears begin to well up. "Sorry…" he said as he awkwardly cleared his throat.

"It's okay," Matt said quietly, "take your time and if you're not ready to talk about Zach, it's not a problem."

He nodded. "Okay." Again he blew out a breath before continuing. "We got through Christmas and the next couple of months somehow. We had the situation with Zach to deal with and we were both busy with work. After what'd happened, we wanted to make sure we did justice to the project and so we settled into a routine. It wasn't perfect but we got by. I figured we were both dealing with our grief in our own way."

"That's understandable," Matt commented, "everyone deals with grief in different ways and until we're faced with it, we can never really know how we're going to cope. So, you made it through to when, March?"

"Yes. Beginning of March. This year."

"Okay." Matt jotted something on his notepad. "What happened in March?"

Cal closed his eyes as the memories re-surfaced and his hands shook as he rubbed them across his face.

"There was something not right," he said, opening his eyes. "When Zach…" he paused a moment to gather himself, "I took to drinking a little. Not much but more than I should've done. For a while Lexi didn't say anything. I was sober for work and I never drove when I'd had a drink, but as time went on, I think it began to be a problem for her."

"What makes you say that?"

"She used to make comments, just stupid things about me needing my drink and I noticed she was less interested in being close to me –

physically. I asked her about it and she told me it was the drink, that I didn't smell so good."

"Did you stop drinking?"

Cal nodded. "Not completely, but I cut way back to where I was when we first met. I tried to find other ways to deal with my grief."

"Other ways?" Matt asked.

"I read somewhere that one of the best ways to deal with emotional trauma is by using distractions. I know," he held up his hand, "that doesn't sound like the kind of stuff I'd read, but I was in the dentist and the article was sitting there, staring at me. So, I read it."

"There's nothing wrong with using distraction techniques," Matt said, "and I'm glad you read the article. It's useful to have as many coping strategies as we can."

"It made sense to me," Cal continued, "so I tried to think of something I could do, besides work, that would occupy my mind. I decided on photography. Nothing fancy, just my phone and a walk outside now and again."

Matt nodded. "That all sounds great, Cal."

"Yeah, I thought so. That's what I did when I cut back on the drinking. I went out for a walk and I took photos. At first it felt like a poor substitute, but I didn't want to lose Lexi. I knew I was being unfair to her and so I was determined to get back to how I was."

"Did it work?" Matt asked.

Cal braced his forearms on his knees. "To a point. It helped me to cut down on the drinking, but Lexi still seemed odd, distant. I talked to her about it again and she said she was happy I'd cut back but that was all she said. She still kept her distance physically; she said work was tough."

"And is that when you started to get suspicious?"

"No," Cal shook his head, "not really. I was still dealing with my grief and I was consumed by the job too. It wasn't until Tami got involved that things changed."

"Tami?" He watched as Matt glanced at his notepad. "Your girlfriend?"

Cal shrugged. "I wouldn't call her that but yeah, I see her from time to time."

"Okay. So Tami got involved. How come?"

"She was working on the project too, overseeing everything. At the beginning of March there was some company function and Tami had gone along. Lexi went too, but I stayed at home. I didn't want to be somewhere I'd be tempted to drink and I wasn't really in the party mood. I was happy for Lexi to go, though. I wanted her to have a good time."

Matt nodded. "That's fair, although given your earlier concerns with regards to her and Jae…"

Cal shook his head. "I know it sounds crazy, but I was overwhelmed with grief and in a bad place. I didn't want Lexi to miss out just because I wasn't coping. Anyway," he continued, "a couple of days after the party I had a meeting with Tami about the project. When we'd finished with work she told me she'd seen Lexi with Jae at the party and that they'd seemed very friendly. At first I was angry with Tami and I told her to get the hell out of my business but then I remembered all those months ago when I'd first thought something was odd. I couldn't see what Tami had to gain by telling me all of this so I asked her to explain."

"And did she?"

"Yes." He wrung his hands together and focused on the floor. "I was terrified, Matt. The more she said, the more she told me, the more I believed her. I felt sick to the stomach and I could hardly breathe. I didn't want to listen and I didn't want her to be right, but everything she told me made sense. In a way, she was only confirming what I already knew but had been too frightened to see."

Matt remained silent for a moment. When he spoke, his voice was quiet. "What did she tell you, Cal?"

Cal dropped his chin to his chest and shook his head from side to side. "She said…" he cleared his throat, "that she'd seen them. Kissing. Outside. Where they thought no one would see." He kept his head down.

"I'm sorry, Cal. That's rough."

He nodded. "I didn't want to believe her, but I couldn't understand why she was telling me if it wasn't true. She told me, she said, because she valued me as a colleague and she didn't want to see me cheated." He shook his head again. "I didn't know what to think. I felt sick and angry and hurt and betrayed. I could barely keep control, but somehow I did. Somehow I finished that meeting and then I went home."

"Did Tami say anything else?" Matt asked.

Cal shook his head. "No. She didn't need to. Only that she wasn't lying." He ran his hands through his hair. "You know the worst part? I think I already knew. I wasn't even surprised. I think I knew from that moment when I kissed her months ago. I don't know who I was more angry with: Lexi for cheating or me for being so stupid as to think I could behave like that, kiss her like that, and get away with it. I was so angry, Matt. So angry." He clenched his fists as he relived the emotions. They felt as real now as they'd felt back then.

"Are you okay to carry on?" Matt asked and Cal looked up at him.

"I know we're getting to the really tough stuff now, Cal," the therapist clarified, "and I want to make sure you're okay to go there."

He thought for a moment. Was he? In reality, no. But then he could never see a day – at least not in the foreseeable future – when he would be ready to go there. "Now's as good a time as any," he said eventually and watched as Matt nodded.

"Okay, Cal. As long as you're sure."

He closed his eyes. "Yes, I'm sure," he said carefully.

He knew where they were going to have to go now and he knew he never wanted to go there again, but he needed to heal. And in order to heal, he had to face up to everything that had happened. He had to face it, acknowledge it, deal with it and learn to live with it. If he wanted any kind of future, he had no choice.

"Alright, Cal," Matt said, his voice barely audible in the quiet of the room. "Take your time. I'm here and we can stop whenever you need to. Okay?"

He nodded slowly. "Okay."

He was going to do it. He was really going to do it. After all of these months, after all of the hurt and the pain, he was really going to do it.

"Just one thing before I start," he said as he lifted wretched eyes once more to Matt.

"Sure, Cal."

"I still love Lexi," he said, "I've never stopped loving her and what I did to her – I'll never forgive myself. It was wrong and no matter what happens now, there'll never be anything anyone can say to make it right. So I need you not to try. Okay?"

"Okay," Matt replied, "whatever you need."

Cal closed his eyes momentarily as he gathered his thoughts for what felt like the last time. Finally he was going to do it. Finally he was going to tell another living soul what had happened on that fateful night in March.

And never, with the exception of that night, had he been more scared in his life.

Chapter Thirty-Three

Lexi

Saturday March 7th 2015

Lexi was nervous. She felt like her life had been in a holding pattern for the last few months and for some reason today, tonight, felt like doomsday.

Her relationship with Cal was different and for her, broken, yet she knew she'd owed it to him to try. It wasn't about the fateful kiss, that time she'd said no, it was more about how she felt and who she was inside; it was also about Jae and her guilt. The guilt that still riddled her whenever she relived that moment in Jae's office. The guilt that had kept her here with Cal – yet she was beginning to realise guilt wasn't enough. She felt as if she was walking through treacle, her feet stuck, her mind a million miles away and she knew the time was approaching when she and Cal would have to face facts. They'd lived through the devastation of Zach's death and she'd supported him as best she could, but deep down inside she knew they could never get back to where they'd been. Too much had happened to both of them.

Lexi had stayed clear of Jae since that day in his office. Any work related communication had been carried out through Fraser and even though avoiding Jae had been the right thing to do Lexi felt restless, dissatisfied and unhappy. Whenever she thought of Jae she felt like she was tiptoeing along a fuse wire and getting ever closer to the point of detonation. Lexi knew something was going to happen between them eventually – it had to – but she had no idea what and when. All she knew was that when it did she would be utterly helpless and there would be no way to prevent the irreversible outcome.

Cal had been sat on the bed watching her for the last half an hour.

"Why don't you come?" she asked. It wasn't the first time Lexi had suggested he join her at the annual company ball. Though their relationship, for her, was coming to an end, there was still something hugely comforting about Cal's presence. That motivation, though, made her a prize bitch. She knew it did. She was being wholly unfair to Cal. Lexi needed to deal with their situation and her feelings and she needed to do it soon. D-day. Doomsday. Whatever.

Cal shook his head. "No. I'm not in the mood. I'd only spoil it for you. You go. Have a good time. There'll be other evenings."

She nodded as guilt turned her stomach inside out. The fact he was being so good to her, wanting nothing for her but happiness made what she was going to have to do even harder to contemplate. He didn't deserve this, which was in part why she had to let him go. He needed to be loved completely and Lexi knew she was no longer able to give him that. She loved him, but she was no longer *in* love with him. Finally acknowledging that had been one of the hardest things she'd ever had to do. Her fire for Cal had burned out and now there was nothing left but cooling ashes.

She walked across to where he sat and stood in front of him. "Are you okay?" she asked and he nodded.

"It's been almost three months. I'm getting there," he replied.

Losing Zach had torn Cal apart and she'd watched him travel a dark road ever since. He was on his way back, slowly, which is why it had taken her until now to finally understand that her marriage was over. That it had to be over. Ending it whilst he was still in the depths of despair was just too cruel and so she'd distanced herself. And with that distance had come clarity as well as an increased hatred for what she was doing to him. She'd been maintaining a pretence; a watered down image of what their lives had been like before. To face up to the reality and do what was needed had felt like a mountain too high – until now. Now she knew everything was about to change and she was as terrified as she had been on the day Bobby died.

"I don't want to be tempted," he said as she moved back to the mirror and tried to quell the uneasiness rising in her stomach. She looked at him over her shoulder.

"To drink," he clarified.

Lexi remained silent. He'd worked so hard to get his drinking back under control and she knew she and their marriage had been his motivation. He'd been heading towards a dangerous addiction and she'd hated to see him like that. At the time, she'd honestly believed if he could come back from that then they'd be okay. It was only now she understood how wrong she'd been.

"You look great," he said to her reflection and, awkwardly, she smiled. The deep blue silk, full-length dress was new; she'd bought it last week. With a fitted bodice and flared skirt, it was a dress in which she felt comfortable and elegant. Up until tonight she'd deliberately avoided thinking about the fact Jae was likely to be there, yet, the unvarnished truth? She'd chosen the dress with Jae in mind. She wanted to look good. For him. But now she had to face up to her motivation and for a moment she halted her preparations as she considered backing out. What kind of person was she? Outwardly she may look the same but inside Lexi barely recognised herself. Where was the Lexi who talked about truth and honesty and placed so much value on those qualities in everyone else? When had she become the very person she disliked above all others?

Cal must have noticed her hesitation. "What's wrong?" he asked.

Lexi shook her head. "Nothing." Rapidly she searched for an excuse, a plausible reason for the look of panic she knew had shadowed her eyes. "I was thinking it might be awkward going alone."

He smiled, still communicating purely with her reflection. "I can understand that, but I doubt you'll be the only one alone. Not everyone has partners."

No. But not everyone had been propositioned by Jae.

"No, I guess not," she agreed.

"You'll be fine," Cal said and she watched as he lounged back on the bed. His complete faith and trust knifed through her. The guilt became oppressive and she swallowed down another wave of nausea. She had to tell Cal. She had to end this. He didn't deserve to be lied to for a moment longer.

She walked to the bed and sat down beside him.

"Cal?" she said, her voice wavering.

"Uh huh...?" he remained reclined.

"We have to talk about something," she began. Her heart pounded rapidly and her palms started to sweat. He didn't respond.

"Cal?" she looked across at him and saw his eyes were closed. "Cal?"

"What?" he mumbled.

"I need to talk to you about something," she repeated. Her throat went dry.

"I've been thinking about Zach's project," Cal said in response and she looked at him in confusion. Slowly he opened his eyes. "What do you think we should do with it once it's finished?"

Quickly she shook her head. She needed to get the words out and fast, before she lost her nerve. "I don't know, look – we have to talk."

"We could set it up as some kind of charity centre, you know, for kids with difficulties. Like Zach. Like me," he finished quietly.

Lexi stared at him once more. "Sounds good, but that's not what we need to talk about."

"There would be plenty of room, we could have dedicated spaces for different activities – like some kind of drop-in centre. And then with the land, we could get some animals. I don't know, sheep, that kind of thing. Give the kids something to focus on."

Again she shook her head. "Cal," she said, her voice becoming frantic. If he carried on for much longer she knew she'd never be able to form the words she must. "That's not what I need to talk to you about."

"Oh, okay." He opened his eyes fully and sat up, shifting a little so he was beside her. "Sorry. It's just the idea came to me today and I can't stop thinking about it. How cool would it be to actually build some kind of legacy? Other kids could be helped. Like he helped me. Even make it some kind of training centre, you know, for trades."

Lexi nodded. "It's a beautiful idea," she said as she felt her earlier courage begin to evaporate.

"I mean, there's probably lots of red tape and obstacles, but we could do it, Lexi. We could look into it. I know it's yours, but we both wanted it to go to Zach so I figured maybe this way, we could give it

374

back to him. What do you think?"

She sighed. Cal was animated. More so than she'd seen him in a long time. "We can look into it," she said hesitantly, "but…"

Cal held up his hand. "I know. There'll be legalities and stuff but I really think this is what Zach would've wanted, to go on helping people. The more I think about it, the more right it feels and it'll help me to heal too. I can focus on doing what he would've wanted me to do and I won't feel like I've let him down."

Lexi turned to face him. It was the first time he'd really spoken about Zach's death.

"You think you let him down?" she asked in surprise.

Cal nodded. "Yeah, I do."

"How come you've never told me that before?"

He shrugged. "I couldn't. It's been so hard to come to terms with the fact he left us all and to know he did that by choice…I should've been there for him. I should've been more of a friend to him."

Gently Lexi placed her hand on Cal's thigh. Now was not going to be the right time to say what had to be said. She shelved her rehearsed speech. "You were a friend to him," she reassured softly, "you were the best friend he had."

"Then how come he left, Lexi? Huh? How come he left without even saying goodbye?"

Sadly she shook her head. The hand that he used to cover hers trembled. "I don't know, Cal. I wish I did."

Beside her she heard him take a deep breath. Lexi waited.

"Anyway," he said after a moment, "I figured even though I wasn't there for him when he needed me, the least I could do was be there for others. Help others. Somehow it makes what he did make some kind of sense."

She closed her eyes and swallowed. She'd never been as close to Zach as Cal had been, but she'd still loved the man. His death had hit everyone hard and now she understood more of what Cal had been going through, what he'd been feeling, the way he'd reacted in the months afterwards, began to make more sense. Finally she understood why he'd needed to travel that dark road.

Tears sprung at the back of her eyes. She couldn't tell Cal about their marriage right now, he was still too vulnerable. She'd been selfish in her desires and hadn't given enough consideration to the effect her leaving would have on Cal. On top of everything else it would be too much. She couldn't leave him. Not now. It would finish him and no one deserved to be finished. Not like this.

"We can talk some more about it later," she said softly as she pressed a gentle kiss to his temple and rose from the bed.

He nodded.

"I have to go." She consulted the slim gold watch adorning her wrist. "The taxi will be waiting."

Cal looked up at her and she could see the light that had gone out the day he'd found Zach, beginning to shine in his eyes once more. Now he'd confided his idea for the project to her, she could see he had hope.

"It'll be okay," Lexi said and he nodded.

It would be okay because it had to be okay. Grabbing her bag she slowly walked towards the bedroom door. Her feelings hadn't changed; her marriage was over, but there was no way she could act on that now or any time soon.

"Lexi?" Cal called to her as she exited the room.

She turned back. "Yes?"

"Have a good time," he said and she gave him a watery smile.

"Thanks."

It wouldn't happen; there was no way this evening was going to be anything other than difficult but, as she was rapidly discovering, nothing in her life was easy right now. Especially if she continued to be impossibly attracted to a man that was not her husband.

* * *

Despite her best intentions, Lexi noticed him the second she walked into the ballroom. Decorated in purple and black, the 1920s style room shrieked glamour, which aptly befitted its location in one of the most costly local hotels. Large round tables filled the room, each being concealed beneath a purple cloth. Gold-framed chairs with extravagant black covers provided seating around the tables and everywhere Lexi looked, black and purple balloons floated. In the far corner, resplendent in black dinner suits, a male, four-piece band played soft music and a few couples swayed on the gold edged dance floor in front of them. In the opposite corner was the bar, this staffed by smartly dressed hotel employees. Several waiters carrying large, silver salvers, glided effortlessly between the tables and assembled guests. It appeared little expense had been spared on the trimmings and even though she glanced around taking in every detail, Lexi's gaze was still hopelessly drawn to the man standing on one side of the dance floor. Surrounded by several colleagues with whom he was actively conversing, he didn't appear to notice her arrival. With a sigh of relief, she made her way to the table on which Fraser was seated. She may have avoided Jae for now but Lexi was certain it was only a matter of time before their paths would cross. Thankfully, she acknowledged as she reached her table, she'd no longer be alone when it happened.

Fraser, in the absence of Cal, had promised to be her pseudo date and she didn't plan on allowing him to leave her side. His feelings for her, Fraser maintained, were well under control and now that she was finally here, Lexi realised she was looking forward to spending the evening in her friend's company.

"Looking good, partner." Fraser let out a low whistle as she arrived.

Lexi smiled and allowed some of her earlier anxiety to dissipate. She could do this. It would be okay. She would get through this evening.

"Thanks," she tilted her head as she ran her eyes over him in a quick inspection. "You don't scrub up so bad either." Wearing a traditional black tuxedo complemented by his dark hair and permanent day old stubble, Fraser looked almost Mediterranean. "Not bad at all," she concluded as she finished her perusal.

He laughed. "I aim to please."

Their table seated six and Lexi was relieved to see Adam was also there with a woman who she presumed to be his wife. The other two seats were currently vacant.

"Hi, Lexi, this is my wife, Tory," he confirmed. Lexi smiled at the pretty redhead seated beside him.

"Great to meet you," she said as she slid into the chair adjacent to Fraser.

"Lexi's one of our interns," Adam explained to his wife.

"Adam's very patient with me," Lexi responded and Tory smiled.

"Why d'you think I married him? We redheads have a reputation for being hot headed."

Lexi laughed. "You mean it wasn't his money?"

The other woman grinned. "Well, that too. Only thing is I'm having trouble finding where he's stashed it."

Lexi laughed once more.

"I am here," Adam said. Tory reached across and tweaked his bow tie and then dropped a brief kiss onto his lips. For a moment Lexi was overcome with sadness as she mentally replaced Tory and Adam with Cal and herself. That would've been them not so long ago, joking with each other, giving of loving gestures. She wished she knew how it had all gone so wrong and not for the first time she began to doubt herself. Maybe if Cal had come tonight, then perhaps they would've been able to get back on track. What if she was imagining it all? What if the love was still there?

"You okay?" Fraser asked and mentally Lexi shook herself.

"Yes," she reassured him, "I'm fine. So," she asked brightly, "anyone know how the evening works?"

Across from her, Adam spoke. "Dinner, dancing and a raffle," he said. "Did you get to see the menu?"

"No," Lexi shook her head, "I was something of a late addition."

Fraser smiled. "Yes, it took a bit of persuading I can tell you."

"So, have you two been together long?" Tory asked and Fraser laughed.

"No, we're not a couple," he said, "just friends. Lexi's married."

"Ah, oops. You could've told me," she turned to her husband and Adam shrugged.

"It didn't seem important."

Tory raised her eyebrows at Lexi. "Men," she said.

Lexi smiled back. "My husband didn't want to come," she clarified. "Not really his thing. I was going to give it a miss too, but apparently," she turned to her right to indicate Fraser, "it's too good a night to miss."

"And so it is," Fraser stated. "You won't be sorry."

Instinctively Lexi knew she would be.

"Have you been before?" she asked Tory. The woman was seated on the other side of Fraser and next to Adam, which meant the two empty seats were in between herself and Adam.

"No. This is my first time. *Our* first time," she amended as she looked at her husband. "He's avoided it every other year claiming two left feet, but you know how it is. I wanted to come at least once so I got him to take dancing lessons."

To Lexi's right, Fraser snorted. "No way, man. You've taken dancing lessons?" he asked Adam.

"Not by choice," the other man grumbled as Fraser continued to laugh.

"Hey," Lexi said, keen to defend her mentor, "there's nothing wrong with men having dancing lessons. You only have to turn on the TV to see how cool it is."

Fraser began to laugh harder. "Oh my God. If you think it's cool too then we're in for a seriously awkward night. Lexi, my dear, there's nothing cool about men wearing tight trousers and sequins."

"If you're a woman there is," Tory interjected. "If you're allowed to ogle the women in their next to nothing clothes, then it works the same way for us. Nothing wrong with a buff man in tight trousers."

Lexi began to laugh. "Amen to that," she said enjoying the banter which had temporarily taken her attention away from her worries. "If Adam has taken lessons to please his wife then I think that's romantic, Fraser. Maybe that explains why you're still single?"

"Now watch it you," Fraser nudged her good-naturedly. "How many times do I have to tell you I'm happy being single?"

Lexi leaned across in front of him so she could speak to Tory. "Apparently he likes to keep his options open," she said sotto voce, "but I think that only works when one has options." Tory giggled.

"Okay, ladies," said Fraser, "now I'm beginning to feel like my man Adam over there. I am here, you know."

"Ah," Lexi said, "so he's your man now is he? A moment ago he was a freak in tight trousers and sequins."

Across from her Adam smiled. "I should give up, mate," he addressed Fraser. "One is bad enough, but you're never going to win with two of them on your case."

"And here I was thinking that two women would be seriously hot," Fraser quipped, "little did I know."

The four of them all erupted into laughter. "That, my friend, would only ever happen in your dreams," Lexi responded when she could finally catch her breath. Getting out tonight was doing her good.

"Actually," Tory said, "that's something that always seems unfair on our gender. How come it's perfectly acceptable for men to vocalise their fantasies about two women, but when it comes to us – God forbid if we mention other men."

Lexi watched as Adam swivelled his head towards his wife. "You think about other men?" he asked and Lexi swallowed. This was cutting a bit too close to the bone.

"No, of course not," Tory responded, "that's not what I meant. But if I'd just said something like Fraser did, except changed the women for men, I have a feeling we'd be heading for the divorce courts right now."

"Fraser can't get divorced," Adam pointed out reasonably, "he's not married."

Again, Lexi swallowed.

"I know," countered Tory, "that's not really the point though. Help me out, Lexi?"

Lexi felt her palms begin to sweat. There was no way she could formulate any useful argument when it came to other men and divorce. It was way too close to home.

"I think," she said carefully, "what Tory's trying to say is that there's still some inequality when it comes to what's acceptable for men and women."

"Really?" Adam asked his wife. "You think that?"

Tory shrugged. "In some ways, yes. I mean, take wages for example. Aren't they always proving that a woman doing the same job as a man, still earns less?"

"That's because physically women are not as capable," Fraser interjected and Lexi scowled at him. "In manual jobs," he added.

"That's so not the point," Lexi commented. "It doesn't matter what type of job it is, if a woman is doing it to the same capability as a man, then their pay should be equal."

"I agree with you, Lexi," Adam concurred, "but with women, don't you always have to consider that they may leave to have children?"

Lexi looked at Adam wide-eyed. "Of course, but have you any idea how sexist that sounds?"

"Yeah," Tory said as she nudged her husband playfully in the ribs.

"I didn't mean it to be sexist," Adam responded, "it's a fact. Men are never going to have children so by default, they represent a more stable workforce."

"Oh, Adam," Tory said, "I had no idea you still lived in the dark ages. Men have as much right to time off as women where children are concerned now. I don't think it matters what sex you are. As Lexi says, if a woman's doing the same job as a man to the same capability, then the pay should be equal."

"I agree," Fraser said, "but that doesn't mean it's going to change any time soon."

"I remember," Tory continued, "when I went to my very first full-time job interview the guy that interviewed me, he asked all the usual questions and then, right out of the blue, he asked me if I was planning to have children. I nearly died. I was only eighteen."

"That's not young these days," Fraser commented. "Look how many kids are having kids."

"Why did he want to know that?" Lexi asked ignoring Fraser's comment.

"Well, he said he wanted to make sure I wasn't going to leave as soon as he employed me."

"That's outrageous," Adam said. "You can't ask someone that kind of question."

"Ah," responded Tory, "so you're not so dark ages after all."

"I can't believe you weren't offended," her husband said.

"It didn't occur to me to be offended. I wanted the job. It was that simple."

"Did you get it?" Lexi asked.

Tory nodded. "I did, although I later found out he had a bit of a reputation this guy, if you know what I mean. A few years later he had a harassment case brought against him."

"Serves him right. I can't believe you never told me this before," Adam said.

As Lexi watched, Tory placed her hand on her husband's arm. "Never came up in conversation."

Adam inclined his head. "Guess not."

"So," Lexi said, "do we know who's joining us?" The two seats between herself and Adam were still empty.

"Nope," Fraser shook his head. "I just got told this was us when I arrived. I didn't see a table plan anywhere." He looked around. "The big wigs are over there," he pointed to a larger table with even more purple and black embellishments, "so it'll be another pair of minions, just like us."

"Speak for yourself, Fraser," Adam said, "there's nothing minion about me." He winked at Lexi and she laughed.

"That's true. If he can mentor me then there's no way he's a minion. He's a King minion at least."

"Emperor," Adam corrected.

"Yeah, whatever," Fraser waved his hand. "If it wasn't for me, no one would know what the hell they were doing anyway so if anyone is an Emperor then it's me. And you know it." He emphasised his point by angling his finger towards Adam.

"Oh God," Tory said from beside Fraser, "please don't tell me we're about to have a pissing contest."

"Language," Adam berated his wife.

"What?" she asked innocently and Lexi giggled. Tory was funny and down to earth – precisely the kind of company she needed right now.

As the conversation naturally lulled, Lexi gave herself chance to scour the room for anyone else she recognised. At least, that was what she told herself, however, she knew she was only looking for one person. Her eyes alighted on the area where he'd been standing previously, but he was no longer there. Some of the management team were seated at the larger table Fraser had pointed out, but he wasn't there either.

"It's a shame your husband didn't want to come," Tory addressed Lexi and rapidly she brought her mind back to the present.

"I, for one, am glad," Fraser responded. "If Cal had come then I would've been officially dateless."

"Which," Lexi said, grateful for his interjection, "is something you claim to love. Keeping your options open."

"How long have you and Cal been married?" Tory asked and for the first time, Lexi resented the other woman's interest. She knew the question was innocent and perfectly natural but, feeling the way she did, talking about her marriage was not a comfortable place for her.

"A little over a year," she replied keeping her tone neutral.

"Still in the honeymoon stage then," Tory said.

"Something like that," Lexi mumbled. She felt, rather than saw, Fraser look at her questioningly. As far as he and everyone else were concerned, she had the perfect marriage.

"Do you remember our first year?" Tory asked Adam and he nodded.

"Yup. The first year of the ball and chain. Not likely to forget that."

Tory lightly punched him.

Fraser threw his hand out in Adam's general direction. "See," he said, "that's precisely why I remain happily single. Not a ball and chain in sight."

"You do know that's a myth?" Tory asked Fraser.

Lexi remained silent. Once again the conversation was veering into dangerous territory.

"The ball and chain?" Fraser asked. "Then how come every self-respecting stag night features a man chained to something?"

"Naked," Lexi added and then immediately chastised herself. She would've been far better keeping quiet.

"What?" Fraser looked at her.

"Naked," she repeated. "When the man is chained on his stag night then he's usually naked."

383

"Okay," Fraser responded, "so what did you get chained to, Adam?"

The other man took a moment. "A road bollard. In the middle of the A173."

Fraser burst out laughing. "No way?"

"Way," Adam confirmed.

"And he was naked," Tory whispered at which Fraser laughed even harder. Lexi tried to control herself as she imagined her mentor chained to a bollard in the middle of a major road, but in the end she gave in and burst out laughing too.

"How did you get out of that?" Fraser asked.

Adam shrugged. "A night in the cop shop."

"The only blemish on his otherwise immaculate record," Tory added with pride before she dissolved into giggles herself.

"It's not funny," Adam said. "I was mortified."

"Well, you shouldn't have drunk so much, then you would've known what was happening."

"Yeah, yeah," Adam replied to his wife, "easy for you to say now."

"So did you get charged?" Fraser asked.

"No," Adam shook his head. "It happens a lot. Lexi's right. A slap on the wrists and told to be a good boy in the future."

"Have you never been to a stag do?" Lexi asked Fraser and he shook his head.

"Nope. My mates are all still single too."

"Ah…" Adam winked at Lexi again, "that explains so much…"

Unable to stop herself, Lexi dissolved into a fit of giggles.

"I hope you're not suggesting what I think you're suggesting," Fraser said to Adam.

"Of course not," the other man replied innocently. "You were the one who started this conversation."

"No I wasn't," defended Fraser, "it was Lexi."

"Nope," she said as she held up her hands, "I only added the naked bit. You and Adam were talking about balls and chains."

"Aha," said an unmistakably deep earthy voice from behind her, "it seems, Sonya, that we've found our table."

Instantly Lexi froze as every single part of her body went on high alert. He couldn't be sitting here, could he? And with Sonya?

Beside her, Fraser turned.

"Jae, what are you doing here? Aren't you supposed to be up there?"

"No," she heard him reply. "I'd much rather sit with people who aren't going to spend the entire evening talking shop."

Lexi caught a whiff of strong perfume as, out of the corner of her eye, she saw Sonya settle herself next to Adam.

"And, from what I just heard," Jae continued smoothly, "it seems I've found the perfect conversation to join. This must be my seat."

His large hand grasped the back of the chair to Lexi's immediate left. She felt him pull it back.

"What makes me think this was planned?" Fraser whispered into her ear and she looked at him her eyes wide. "It's obvious," he continued in the same hushed tone, "whenever you're around, so's he."

Lexi shook her head. "No. It's a coincidence."

The chair to her left scraped towards the table and she knew that in a matter of seconds, she would be in impossibly close proximity to Jae Leonard.

"I'm not sure I believe in coincidences," Fraser whispered back before he turned his head towards Tory.

He'd dismissed her, again. Fraser had dismissed her in exactly the same way he'd done in the pub all those months before. Scarcely able to believe it she clenched her hands in her lap. She'd known she'd have to see Jae, but never, in any of the scenarios she'd imagined, had he been sitting right next to her.

"So," Jae said to her left, his warm breath brushing over the part of her shoulder left bare by the bodice straps, "here we are again, Lexi."

Rapidly she closed her eyes. She'd known something was going to happen tonight, she'd sensed it. There was going to be a catalyst to detonate the fuse wire. What she hadn't anticipated was that it would come in the form of Jae and Sonya.

On the one hand she was glad he'd not come alone, at least he would need to be attentive to Sonya which would give her opportunity to create some distance between them but, on the other hand, his choice of Sonya as a date seemed strange. The snippet of conversation she'd overheard between Jae and Fraser in the pub regarding the other woman, had suggested Jae was not Sonya's biggest fan. Perhaps some of her disbelief at their pairing came from jealousy – an emotion she neither liked nor welcomed – yet the result, if added to her ever-present nausea and guilt, was a ticking time bomb, slowly creeping ever closer to mass destruction. Mass destruction of her life.

She let out a deep breath. She could do this, she could hold it together. It was only one night. Taking every ounce of courage she could muster she turned to her left, unsurprised to see Jae's dark eyes already boring into her.

"So, it would seem," she said, her tone clipped and cold. "I have, however, spent the last few months actively avoiding you so don't expect that to be any different this evening simply because we're sitting next to each other."

Lexi turned her head away and focused on Fraser's back. The other man was still deep in conversation with Tory.

"Oh, Lexi," Jae responded and once again she felt his breath whisper across her bare skin, "I'm well aware you've been avoiding me, in fact, I can tell you exactly how many days it's been since we last spoke."

Lexi swallowed and closed her eyes.

"Tonight though, regardless of what you say, it will be different," he continued. "I can assure you that before this evening is done you will no longer be ignoring me. And that, Lexi, is a promise."

She felt him move away and heard him talking to Adam. She had a reprieve – for now, but as she drew in a ragged breath, she knew it was only temporary. Jae was right. There was no way she was going to be able to ignore him all night and that, ultimately, was what terrified her the most.

The catalyst had arrived. The fuse wire was almost done. The bomb was due to detonate.

And, as Lexi desperately tried to compose herself one thought kept running round and round her head.

How many pieces was she going to be left in when finally, the bomb exploded?

Chapter Thirty-Four

Cal

Saturday March 7th 2015

Cal hadn't moved since Lexi had departed. In truth, he barely acknowledged she'd gone, so consumed was he with the idea he could really make something of Zach's project. He didn't know why it hadn't occurred to him before because when he thought of it now, it just seemed so simple. And so right.

It had been three months and, contrary to what he led others to believe, Cal was not over the death of his friend. Not by a long way. His childhood ensured that he'd witnessed much, but never would he forget finding Zach. Never would he erase the image of his friend in repose, cold and rigid. Never would he blot out the sight that had greeted him only three months earlier. No. He told everyone he was okay, that he was recovering, because that was what they wanted to hear. He stopped drinking, he brought himself back from the brink of addiction, but only because that was what Lexi had wanted from him. In all honesty, Cal was beyond caring. Lexi remained the only person of value in his life and that included himself. If it hadn't been for her and the very real chance he could lose her, then Cal knew he would likely have followed Zach on his journey. She'd become the only reason for living – until today. Today he'd hit on an idea that gave him hope again. An idea he knew, if executed right, would help countless children like himself and Zach. And if he couldn't support Zach any more, then he was damn sure he was going to support others. It was, Cal knew, the least he owed his friend.

Closing his eyes he concentrated on blackness, on letting nothing imprint itself in his mind. He was getting better at it. Better at chasing away the images, but with Zach's project so fresh, today was challenging. The images were there and no matter how much he tried to send them away and conjure up the blissful darkness he'd come to rely upon, they steadfastly refused. With a sigh, he allowed them to come – the images and the memories. He allowed them in. He allowed the familiar feeling of devastation to overwhelm him, yet today he took comfort in the fact it was tinged with a small glimmer of hope. A glimmer he was going to grab with both hands, just as soon as he'd let the memories play out one more time.

* * *

December 2014

It had been a couple of weeks since Cal had seen Zach. After their evening out when Zach revealed what happened to his mother, his friend had gone underground and Cal had heard nothing. Consumed, though, with his own troubles, Cal figured Zach needed space and had allowed him it. Times were tough for his friend and whilst Cal wanted to support him, he also knew that sometimes, men were better just left alone.

Recently though, Mace had been on his case, asking if he'd seen or heard from Zach and so Cal decided he'd pay him a visit. Even if Zach turned him away at the door, at least Cal could check his friend was still doing okay.

His knock went unanswered so he tried calling Zach's phone. He heard it ring inside the flat. It went unanswered. The curtains were drawn which Cal thought odd considering it was still light outside. Punching in another number, he tried Zach's mobile. Again, it went unanswered. Cal frowned. Usually Zach answered one or other of his phones. He tried the door again. Still nothing.

Zach lived in a ground floor flat so Cal walked around the side and to the communal gardens at the rear. There was a door from the flat to the gardens and Cal knocked again on this. Still no one came. Through a small gap in the curtains Cal tried unsuccessfully to see inside. As a last resort he tried the door handle, surprised to find that beneath his hand, it opened.

Pushing the door away from him he negotiated the full-length curtains, fighting through them and into the small lounge beyond.

"Zach?" he called. "Zach? Are you here?"

Slowly Cal moved through the lounge and on into the kitchen. The sink was piled with washing up and Cal frowned. Zach had always been a stickler for tidiness both at work and at home. For the first time since he'd entered his friend's flat, Cal became uneasy.

"Zach?" he called again.

The kitchen led onto a small hallway that in turn led to the front door, the bedroom and the bathroom. Making his way to the bedroom he called out again. "Zach?"

The bedroom was empty, the bed unkempt. Cal's feeling of unease deepened. It was only a few strides from there to the bathroom and, as he pushed open the door, Cal immediately retched at the smell. He knew instantly the man was dead. Even for someone who had never seen a body, he could tell Zach had gone. He stood frozen in the doorway, looking at his friend, curled up on the floor. He retched again.

Taking the phone out of his pocket he dialled with a hand that was far from steady.

"Police," he said when the call was answered. After giving the address he hung up.

He walked to the front door in a daze and opened it. He had no idea how long it would take the police to arrive, but he knew they would need the door open. Dragging in a few breaths of crisp December air he grasped at his throat. It felt as if every ounce of oxygen had been drained from his lungs. Ahead of him lay the pathway to the pavement. He could walk that pathway and retrace his steps to the pavement and then on to his car. He could do that. Or, he could go back inside. Cal moved on autopilot, his thoughts no longer conscious. Somehow his legs moved, somehow his hands found the keys inside of his jacket pocket and somehow he managed to drive himself home.

He'd given himself an early mark that day on account of visiting Zach and so he took the time to shower. Endlessly. The water turned cold and still he showered, trying to rid himself of the images he knew would haunt him forever. Eventually he stepped out of the shower and

389

back into a world that did not yet know of Zach's passing.

The story was reported the following day. It appeared in the local newspaper and Lexi showed it to him. Her face, when she passed him the paper was stunned yet she tried to be gentle with him when she broke the news.

The police concluded that a neighbour must have found the body, the cause of death an overdose of SSRI's – anti-depressants. Cal hadn't even known Zach was taking anti-depressants.

He mourned with everyone else. He went through the motions. He attended Zach's funeral and gave a eulogy. He kept the other guys going, he worked tirelessly on Zach's house and he put one foot in front of the other every single day. Yet he kept his counsel. He spoke not a single word of that day to anyone and, when Mace asked if he'd been to visit Zach, he simply said no. That he'd not had time.

Everyone accepted what he said. No one asked any questions and, after the initial mourning period, people talked of Zach less. He'd left a gaping hole in their lives, but they were moving on. The guys were moving on, the house was moving on but Cal was not. He was the only one who travelled that road of despair, the only one who could barely find the will to live himself. Yet still, he kept his counsel.

* * *

Zach had been everything to Cal. The father he never had and the inspiration to be a better man. Even when he'd been troubled, Cal had never considered Zach would take his own life. He'd always been so strong, held things together so well and yet, he'd taken the coward's way out.

There were days when Cal couldn't forgive him for that. Days when he hated Zach with a passion for leaving. Days when Cal ranted at a God he barely believed in, for taking the one person on whom he could depend. And then there were the days when he hated himself, the days when he relived every single moment of the time when he'd found Zach. Days when the road to despair seemed the only one worth navigating and days when he hated himself more than he could ever hate Zach.

Today was one of those days – a day when he hated himself – and that was mostly why he hadn't gone with Lexi. Yes, the drink was a factor, but it was about so much more than that. Until, that was, he'd hit upon the idea. Now he was able to see some hope on the horizon, a hazy vision of a different road he could travel and Cal wanted to grab that. He was tired of hating himself, even though he knew the hatred would never go away because, when Zach had needed him the most, Cal had let his best friend down.

When Cal had found Zach cold and alone curled up on the floor, Cal had let his best friend down. He hadn't stayed with him. He'd left him there to be found by strangers. He himself had taken the coward's way out and left his best friend behind. That, Cal knew, that single action, made him a bigger coward than Zach would ever be.

* * *

The other man picked up on the first ring.

"Mace? It's Cal."

"Hey, man. Kinda late to be callin'."

"Yeah, sorry," hastily Cal consulted his watch. "I've had an idea," he continued, "about Zach's place?"

"Okay," Mace responded.

Cal took a moment to outline his thoughts. "D'you reckon we could make it work?" he asked.

"Don't see why not," Mace replied. "I like it. I think Zach would've liked it too."

"Yeah, that's what I thought," Cal agreed. "Listen, do you know anyone who might be able to help us with all the red tape?"

Mace had been in the industry a lot longer than Cal and he figured the other man might have some useful contacts.

"I'm not sure, lemme give it some thought."

"Okay, thanks." Cal nodded. "He left such big hole," he added, "I just wanted to try and fill it somehow."

"I hear ya," Mace responded. "Say, is Lexi okay with this?"

"Yeah. I ran it by her tonight and she was on board."

"Great." On the other end of the line, Mace was silent a moment. "I haven't been to see him in a while," he said at length.

Cal grasped the receiver more tightly. "Me either," he said.

"I was thinking of going. Wanna join me?"

Cal thought for a moment. Visiting Zach's grave had always been his solace but lately, the hatred he felt for himself had overwhelmed him. In truth, he'd not felt worthy enough to visit.

"Yeah, maybe," he replied. "When were you thinking?"

There was a short silence. "Now," Mace said eventually and again, Cal consulted his watch.

"It's dark. It's late. You really want to go now?" he asked. Oddly, the idea didn't spook him.

"It's almost ten pm," Mace responded, "you remember what ten pm is?"

"Of course." Ten pm had been beer o'clock to Zach. Every night at ten pm Zach would drink a beer, no matter where he was. It'd been a long running joke that you could set your watch by Zach.

"You wanna go to his grave and drink beer?"

"Why not?" Mace responded. "Can't think of a better time to go."

Cal considered for a second. "Okay, I'm in."

"Alright," the other man said. "I'll grab the beer and see you there."

"Sure." Cal hung up and frowned at the phone. He'd always known that out of the men, Mace had taken Zach's death the hardest, but he'd never considered that anyone other than himself could be affected enough to want to drink beer at Zach's grave. The fact Mace wanted to do that now surprised him.

It took Cal less than ten minutes to drive to the graveyard. Grabbing the torch from the glove box of his car he made his way up the dark church path, passing by headstone after headstone. The torch barely lit his way, but it didn't matter. Cal knew exactly where Zach's grave was. He could've found it blindfolded. Mace was already there. Seated on the bench adjacent. In the silence, an owl hooted.

"Hey," Cal greeted the other man.

"Hey."

Wordlessly Mace handed him a beer and he popped the top of the can.

"Cheers." In unison they raised their cans to the small headstone that adorned Zach's resting place.

"I come here to think sometimes," Mace said after a while.

"Really?" Cal asked. "I figured I was the only one that ever came."

Mace turned to him and Cal could just make out the other man's eyes glinting in the shadows. "You didn't have the monopoly on him you know," Mace said.

For a moment, Cal was taken aback. "I never said I did," he defended.

"You didn't need to," Mace responded. "The way you've been acting says it all."

Suddenly Cal sensed tension radiating from Mace.

"Wait, whoa. What's the problem here?" Cal asked.

In the dark he saw Mace shake his head. "Forget it. Doesn't matter."

"No," Cal said, "there's something on your mind. Spill."

He heard Mace take a deep breath. "It's been tough on us all," Mace responded eventually, "that's all I'm sayin'."

Cal shook his head. "You think I don't know that?" he asked.

"I think you know, but you're too wrapped up in yourself to care."

Angrily Cal stood. "Where the hell did that come from?" he asked. "You know I care about all the guys. I know it's been tough for everyone."

"Do you?" Mace asked. "Cos' from where we're all sat, it seems like the only person you care about is yourself."

Cal clenched his hands at his sides and paced away from the bench. Never had he considered Mace would launch at him and he was completely unprepared.

"How dare you?" he asked, careful to keep his tone hushed out of respect. "How dare you suggest the only person I care about here is me? I lost my best friend, Mace. I think I'm allowed to find it a little tough to cope."

He watched as Mace shrugged. "No one's sayin' you don't, but we lost him too. Most of us knew him a hell of a lot longer than you did and we've had to watch you drowning in self-pity. You don't have the monopoly, Cal. It's time you realised that."

"This," Cal spat out as he paced back towards Mace, "is Zach's final resting place. Do you really think this is where we should be having this conversation?"

"Maybe, maybe not. But I can't think of a better place. You know damn fine that Zach would be tearing you off a strip for the way you've been carryin' on, like you're the only one allowed to mourn him. We've all had to put up and shut up, keep things goin', while you drowned your sorrows."

"I've worked every bit as hard as the rest of you," Cal defended, "you know that."

"Yeah, but how much good you been. Really?"

Cal raised his eyebrows in shock. "Why are you attacking me, man? I don't get what the hell I ever did to you." He crunched the empty can up in his hand.

Again he saw Mace shake his head. "I'm not attackin' you, you'd know if I was. I'm just givin' you a healthy dose of reality. Whilst you've been in that dark place, shouting at anyone who even mentioned Zach's name, we've been working to keep us afloat. Correcting your mistakes, holding it together and some of us – we've had enough. It's been three months," Mace pointed out needlessly, "you have to get it together, man, and you have to allow us to mourn Zach too. We can't hold both of you up."

Cal snorted in disbelief. "You know I've worked like a dog."

"Yeah," Mace stood, pulling himself to his full height. "But I also know you've screwed up. Little things, nothing major, but you've slipped up, man. We've covered for you, but you have to get a grip. You've got an idea for Zach's place? Well, great. But you have to make it work, Cal. You have to get back on the horse and quit giving the rest of us a hard time. We loved him too. We're allowed to mourn him too. And," Mace took a breath, "we're allowed to talk about him."

For a moment, Cal stood speechless. Although similar in height to Mace, Cal was of a slighter build and standing here, in the dark depths of a graveyard, the other man's presence was intimidating. He allowed the random thoughts to ricochet around his brain until finally he grabbed onto one.

"I've screwed up?" he asked quietly.

"Yeah," Mace said. "A couple of times."

Cal shook his head. "I had no idea."

Opposite him, Mace let out a sigh. "Look, I didn't tell you this stuff to make you feel bad. The slip-ups, they were small, okay. Nothin' big."

"But I screwed up," he stated, his tone flat.

"We understand," Mace said, "but it's been tough. You've either shut us down or yelled at us."

"I have?" For the first time, Cal realised that much of the last three months was blurred. If he'd yelled at the men as Mace said, then he had no recollection.

"You have," Mace affirmed quietly.

"Shit," he said as he walked back towards the bench and slowly sank down. "I'm sorry." He dropped his head into his hands.

He felt the weight of the bench shift as Mace sat back down beside him.

"You don't need to be sorry, man," Mace said.

For what felt like the hundredth time, Cal shook his head. "I never realised until now, but I actually don't remember much of what happened since he went." He nodded his head in the direction of Zach's grave.

"Figures," Mace said. "You've been all over the place."

"He believed in me, Mace, when no one else did."

"He believed in all of us, Cal," Mace said softly.

"How long did you know him?" Cal asked, suddenly realising he knew next to nothing about the other man's relationship with Zach.

"Twenty years, give or take."

"Christ. Really?"

"Yup. We earned our stripes together if you know what I mean."

"Shit, man," Cal said. "I'm sorry."

"It's okay." Mace clapped him on the back. "We all knew you and he had somethin' special."

"I never had family," Cal said quietly, "not til I met Zach."

"Same for most of us," Mace said. "He was our family and," the other man took a breath, "we felt like we'd let him down."

"No way," Cal shook his head. "You guys were there for him. It was me who let him down." He watched as Mace grabbed at a nearby blade of grass, pulling it out and then flicking it towards the path.

"See," Mace said after a moment, "that's where you got it all wrong. I been thinkin', if someone's set on doin' what he did, then there's nothin' any of us can do."

Cal scuffed his boot into the ground. "I don't know."

"Look," Mace said, "if anyone should feel bad, it should be that bitch who cleaned him out."

Cal inclined his head. He couldn't disagree. "You just said you and the guys thought you'd let him down though."

"Yeah, past tense. We did and then we got to talkin'. We figured we'd done everythin' we could. Zach knew we were there for him but, in the end," Mace paused, "it didn't matter. We couldna' done a damn thing even if we'd known."

"And that's it?" Cal asked.

Mace nodded. "Pretty much."

He dropped his head into his hands again. "I don't know if I can do that. Forgive myself."

Again the other man clapped him on the back. "You have to, man. It was his choice and there weren't a damned thing any of us coulda' done."

"Yeah," Cal said, "but you weren't the one who found him."

"Neither were you," Mace commented, "a neighbour did."

Cal lifted his head and sat back against the bench. Slowly he took a deep breath. "No," he said carefully, "the police got it wrong. It wasn't a neighbour. It was me." He felt the bile rise up in his stomach.

"What you talkin' about, man?" Mace turned a little so he was facing Cal. "The report, it said it was a neighbour."

Slowly he shook his head. "No. I found him, Mace." Through a throat suddenly constricted, he dragged in a lungful of air. "I went round," he continued, "like I said I would. He didn't answer. I got in through the back and I found him. Lying on the floor." Cal swallowed. The memory was as vivid now as if it had happened only moments before. "I called the police and then," he stopped, ashamed to admit to his actions of

396

that day. "I drove away," he said finally. "I got in my car and I drove home. I left him, Mace. When he needed me the most, I left him."

With a small cry he dropped his head into his hands again, feverishly rubbing at his eyes in an attempt to erase the memory. For a moment, Mace said nothing.

"You found him?" he asked eventually. "You?"

From within his hands, Cal nodded.

"Shit, man. It don't get rougher than that."

"But I left him, Mace." He turned his head towards the other man. "I walked out. I left him to be found by strangers. I should've stayed. And I'll never forgive myself for that."

Mace stood and then paced a few steps away from the bench before slowly returning. "If it means anythin'," Mace said softly, "I woulda' done the same."

Angrily Cal shook his head. "No you wouldn't. No one would."

"Look," Mace said, "you don't get to decide what I would or wouldna' done in that situation. I would've freaked."

"I didn't freak," Cal replied, "I was calm and yet I walked away. What kind of man does that make me?"

"One who cares," Mace replied.

"No," he reiterated, "I should've stayed."

"And done what?" Mace asked. "I'm sorry, but he was gone. What could've been done by stayin'?"

"Nothing," Cal said, "but at least he wouldn't have been alone."

He watched as Mace shook his head, the inky black obscuring much of the other man's features. "When he chose to go that way, he chose to be alone."

For a moment, Cal considered Mace's words. He'd never thought of it like that before. He'd always assumed he'd let Zach down by running out on him, but Zach had chosen to leave the world that way. He'd chosen to end his life alone. "I guess."

"Like I said," Mace continued, "me and the guys, we've talked and we're okay now. But we wanna talk about him. We wanna remember the good times. We've forgiven him and we've forgiven ourselves for what happened."

Cal took a deep breath and suddenly, as he sat in the dim light of the graveyard, it was as if a weight lifted from his shoulders. Mace was right. Cal couldn't have done anything differently. Zach knew he and the other guys were there for him but he'd chosen an alternative path. He'd chosen the path he thought was best and Cal blaming himself for Zach's single-minded choice gained nothing. Cal had to forgive himself too.

"You know what," he said carefully as he stood and approached Mace, "you're a wise man."

In the silence, he heard Mace chuckle. "Nah, I just know Zach wouldna' want to see any of us like this."

Cal nodded his agreement. "No, he wouldn't."

In unspoken unison the two men began to walk away from the bench. After a few steps Cal turned back and offered a quick salute to Zach.

"So long, mate," he whispered. He stood a moment, looking at the small black obelisk in the distance and then, with assured steps, he spun around and carried on walking. He was going to keep putting one foot in front of the other and, from now on, he was never going to stop.

Chapter Thirty-Five

Lexi

She was officially a bitch, Lexi reflected as she sat watching Jae expertly manoeuvre Sonya around the dance floor. Her head was full of thoughts of Cal and the truths she was going to have to tell him and seeing Jae tonight had crystallised what she already knew. It wasn't about Jae per se, the fact Lexi could develop such an overwhelming attraction to another man told her everything she needed to know. Her life was screwed up, she was about to destroy her husband and she understood that ultimately she was the only one to blame. If Lexi could run now she would. Get in her car and drive, and keep on driving until she could drive no more. The hatred she felt for herself was immense as was the guilt, but she knew she deserved nothing less. She deserved no sympathy or empathy, nor did she deserve the understanding of others. She deserved a lightning bolt to strike her down where she sat for in her mind she was committing one of the most shameful of sins. In her mind Lexi was committing adultery and she knew that for as long as she lived, she would never be able to square that with her conscience.

"Dance?" Fraser asked from beside her and she shook her head. At some point during the evening he'd decided to talk to her again. Lexi wasn't sure if he'd simply run out of things to say to Tory or, if he'd realised he'd overreacted. Either way, it wasn't important enough for her to care right now.

"Look, I'm sorry," he said as if he'd read her thoughts.

Lexi waved her hand. "It's fine." Although Fraser had no way of knowing, she had much bigger concerns to contend with.

"It is odd though, isn't it?" he asked.

"What is?" Lexi responded, even though she suspected she already knew the answer.

"Jae," Fraser confirmed. "Whenever we're together, he appears."

Lexi inclined her head. "Coincidence."

"Yeah, you said that earlier," he commented, "but I don't believe in coincidences any more now than I did then."

Lexi let out a sigh. "I have no idea why he's sitting at our table, Fraser."

"He should be up there." Fraser pointed again to the larger table at the front of the room.

Lexi shrugged. "Well, he's not. I don't like it any more than you do, but there's nothing we can do about it." Somehow she kept her voice calm and her tone neutral. The last thing she needed was for Fraser to get even the smallest hint of her real thoughts.

"We can dance," Fraser tried again.

"Jae is dancing," she pointed out.

"Yeah, I know. No, it's not that I have a problem with Jae," Fraser said, "it's just he's always around."

She shook her head. "I'm confused. If you don't have a problem with Jae, then what do you have a problem with?"

"Him being around," Fraser repeated.

Unable to help herself, Lexi laughed. "That makes no sense. So Jae is around. So what?"

"I don't like it," he said. "I don't like him being around you."

Rapidly Lexi swivelled her head to the side. "What the hell is that supposed to mean?" she asked even though again, she suspected she already knew. She drew on her stock defence as the now familiar knife plunged into her heart. "Jae knows I'm married."

"I know, I know," Fraser held up his hands in surrender. "It's not about me if that's what you're thinking; I'm simply looking out for you as a friend. He's so much older than you."

Her throat restricted as once again, she thought of Cal. She shook her head. "Fraser…"

"Yeah, I know, it's just…oh, whatever…" Fraser raised his hands. "I don't know what I'm saying."

"Okay," she responded, "so, let's just move on."

"Sure." Beside her, he nodded. "I'm going to get a drink, can I get you one?"

Lexi shook her head. "No, thanks. I'm good." She indicated the glass of water on the table in front of her. Wine had been served with the meal but after that, she'd stuck to water. The last thing she needed tonight was alcohol dulling her senses.

"Okay." Fraser scraped his chair away from the table and walked off in the direction of the bar leaving Lexi alone. Both Adam and Tory were also dancing so she allowed herself a moment to breathe and collect her thoughts. With a weary sigh she rubbed her face with her hands.

"Dance?"

Lexi jumped and then, as she recognised the voice, she felt her heart begin to pound. Dragging her hands away from her eyes she looked up. As she'd known would happen, her gaze immediately collided with a pair of deep, dark eyes.

"No, thanks." Somehow she kept her voice steady.

"You haven't danced all night," Jae observed as he smoothly pulled out the chair adjacent to her.

"No," she replied.

His woody aftershave tickled her senses as he sat down beside her.

"It's good exercise," he observed.

Lexi kept her gaze forward, focusing on Tory and Adam, admiring her mentor as he showed the skills he'd recently learned. "I'm fine for exercise," she said.

They lapsed into silence.

"Where's Fraser?" Jae asked after a moment.

"Drink," she said. Limiting her answers to one word felt like the safest option.

"We really have to talk," Jae spoke directly into her ear.

"Where's Sonya?" she asked. Beside her she felt Jae shrug.

"Not sure. Lost her on the dance floor somewhere, but I have no doubt she'll return."

"That's not very chivalrous of you," Lexi commented. "She's your date, surely you shouldn't allow her to simply disappear?"

"Is Fraser your date?" Jae asked. This time it was Lexi who shrugged.

"Pseudo date," she responded, "Cal didn't want to come."

"Strange," Jae mused.

"What?"

"That Cal didn't want to come."

"Why?" she asked. "It's not really his thing and after what happened to Zach…" she let her voice tail off. "He's thought about what to do," she said after a pause, "with Zach's project."

"Great," responded Jae although there was little enthusiasm in his tone.

"He wants to open it as a centre to support kids with difficulties. Those that have a hard time at home, that kind of thing."

Jae nodded. "Sounds noble."

"That's how he and Zach met," she explained. "Zach pulled him through some tough times when he was younger and Cal figured it would be a great legacy."

"It's your place," Jae commented, "it's up to you what you do with it once it's finished. If you want to give it to Cal and make it into some kind of centre, that's your call."

"I know," Lexi said feeling slightly irritated at Jae's lack of interest. "I just thought you'd like to know."

"Thank you," he replied, but she could tell he had little regard for the plans. Again they lapsed into silence.

"Shouldn't Sonya be back by now?" she asked. The tension between them was almost unbearable, not least because their conversation so far had been stilted and uncomfortable.

"Probably," Jae replied.

"Maybe you should go and look for her," she suggested.

Jae remained seated. "Maybe you should go and look for Fraser."

Lexi clasped her hands in her lap. "I imagine he's got talking to someone."

"Which," Jae said, "is what I imagine has happened to Sonya. I don't think either of them needs us to find them right now."

Lexi sighed.

"Let's dance," he repeated and again, she shook her head. Jae stood. "I'm not taking no for an answer this time, even if I have to drag you onto the floor."

"I said no," she responded, but Jae ignored her. Grasping her hand from her lap he began to gently tug on it.

Even though they were alone, the other tables were all in close proximity and the majority were still well populated. Lexi weighed up her options. As much as she didn't want to dance with Jae, the resulting scene if she refused was likely to be much more damaging and so, with forced resignation she stood and pushed her chair out of the way. Jae gripped her hand tighter.

Her midnight blue dress dropped to its full length as she followed Jae to the floor and she allowed herself a moment to enjoy its feel as it swished around her ankles. In no time Jae had secured them a spot to one side of the dance floor and Lexi allowed herself to be drawn into his embrace. Fighting him would have been futile.

The band were playing a slow, jazz number and Jae pulled her close. Their bodies were separated by only the tiniest fraction and every nerve in Lexi's being began to tingle. Finally, reluctantly, she allowed herself to raise her head and look directly into Jae's eyes. Predictably, he was already watching her.

"You look beautiful tonight," he whispered.

"Thank you," she said. Jae looked impossibly handsome in a deep navy tuxedo, but Lexi held her tongue.

"So," Jae said after a moment, "we need to talk."

"We said everything there was to say last time," she replied.

Jae shook his head. "I don't believe we did." His right hand slid around her waist and secured her ever more firmly to his solid length.

"There's nothing to say," she reiterated, "nothing between us. There can't be." Even though Lexi knew her marriage was over, she also knew that to run straight into Jae's arms would be beyond cruel. If there was going to be a future for her and Jae, then it needed to be once the situation with Cal had been resolved.

"You see, that's the thing," said Jae, "I'm not sure you truly believe that."

The music continued to play in the background and gently they swayed in time. Lexi didn't respond. She had far too many muddled thoughts in her brain and being in such close proximity to Jae was making it even harder to formulate sensible views.

"Okay, let's try something else. I want to tell you something, Lexi, and I want you to tell me honestly, how it makes you feel."

She frowned up at him. Jae dipped his head so his breath whispered against her left ear.

"I haven't slept with anyone," he breathed, "since the day we met."

Instantly Lexi recoiled and stared at him with wide eyes. "What?" she spluttered.

"You heard. Now, tell me honestly, Lexi, how does that make you feel?"

She continued to regard him in shock. "I – I…"

"Take your time, we can always dance to the next song," he said smoothly.

"You can't just say that kind of thing to someone," she responded at last.

He tilted his head. "Why not?"

"Because – because…it's not the kind of thing people generally share."

Jae smiled. "If I'd announced that at a board meeting then I would agree with you but, as it's something that will remain purely between the two of us, I fail to see what the issue is," he said with frustrating reason. "All I want to know, Lexi, is how the knowledge I've remained celibate since the day we met, makes you feel."

Lexi could feel the heat creeping up her cheeks. "That could be for any number of reasons," she hedged, "so maybe I feel sad for you."

Jae shook his head. "Nope. Not good enough. You know perfectly well why I've not slept with anyone and it has nothing to do with a shortage of offers."

Lexi swallowed and, at the same time, Jae dropped his left hand and bracketed the other side of her waist pulling her directly against his groin. She felt the hard ridge pushing into her abdomen and helplessly, her femininity responded.

"It also has nothing to do with equipment failure," he whispered as he jerked her sharply forwards ensuring she was in no doubt of his aroused state. "So, I ask again," he said, "how does what I've just told you, make you feel?"

For a moment she closed her eyes and then swallowed again.

Her womanhood was tingling and every nerve ending had started to come alive as her own arousal began. Her breath was coming in shorter pants now and quickly she pressed her head into his shoulder in an attempt to hide what was happening to her body. Jae lifted his right hand up from her waist and tangled it into her hair.

"That's what I thought," he said softly and Lexi cursed her traitorous body and mind. "The truth is," he continued, "I haven't even looked at another woman since the day we met. You've consumed me, Lexi."

She nuzzled her head closer into the crisp fabric of his suit as tears began to prick at her eyes. This couldn't be happening, yet it was. And it felt so damn right. Bitch, she said to herself, bitch, bitch, bitch, bitch, bitch.

"Let's get out of here." Jae moved her away from him slightly and then, with a firm hand, guided her out of a rear door she'd not previously noticed. It led them into a quiet lounge area through which they walked until Jae stopped at a secluded plush velvet bench, situated in the far corner. Wordlessly she sat. Jae settled to her left. In the distance they could hear the muted sounds of the band.

"There's something here," Jae began as he grasped her left hand with his right. "We both know it. You can't keep denying it, Lexi."

She shook her head, knowing that beneath his, her hand was trembling. "What good would it do for me to acknowledge it?" she replied. "I told you last time I was attracted to you and it ended up with us pushing a boundary, crossing a line. Whilst I'm still married, I can't do that."

"What do you mean 'whilst you're still married'?" Predictably Jae had read between the lines.

"Precisely that," she hedged. "Whilst I'm still married to Cal I can't entertain thoughts of being with you. I believe in my vows, Jae."

He gripped her hand tighter and then, using his other hand, lifted her chin up so she was looking directly at him. "Do you believe in happiness?" he asked. Lexi nodded. "Then surely you owe it to yourself to be happy," he said.

"I am happy," she stated, even though inside she knew that wasn't entirely true.

"I don't believe you." Jae dropped her chin and she looked around the room. They appeared to be the only ones here.

"Tell me about yourself," she said by way of distraction.

Jae turned his head towards her and she noted his expression of confusion.

"We're alone here," she explained, "and if we keep talking about whether or not there's anything between us, we'll go around in circles."

"You want to talk about me?" he asked, his tone injected with disbelief. "We have an evening to ourselves, the opportunity to explore what's going on here, and you want to talk about me?"

She nodded. "I know next to nothing about you."

For a moment he continued to watch her. Bravely, she raised her eyes to his and allowed the silent communication. After a few seconds he shrugged. "Okay, if you want to talk about me, let's do it."

"Thank you."

Jae still held her left hand and she squeezed his. In response he curled his thumb into her palm and began to draw gentle circles. Lexi tried not to shiver.

"You already know the business is a family business?" he asked.

Lexi nodded.

"I inherited it when I was twenty-two."

"Wow," she responded. "I can't imagine inheriting that kind of responsibility at my age."

"I had no choice," he said, "my parents were killed in a plane crash. I'm an only child so..." he stopped.

"Oh God," Lexi slapped her right hand to her mouth. "Jae, I'm so sorry. That's awful."

He nodded. "It was ten years ago now. They were in a private plane. Dad had a new contract in Jersey and they'd chartered a flight. No one really knows what happened, but it came down in the sea. My parents, along with three crew, were lost."

Lexi looked at him wide eyed. "How the hell did you cope?" she asked.

"I don't know," he said. "In all honesty I think I fell apart a little but I had a duty to keep things going. I just ploughed everything I had into the company, and eventually, I began to heal. I still think about them every day."

"I can imagine," she said as she felt a huge wave of sympathy for him. "My parents are still alive and well," she added. "We have our moments, but I couldn't begin to think what it would be like without them. I'm so sorry."

"Thanks." His thumb continued to trace distracting circles in her palm. "You know the worst thing?" he asked after a moment and she looked up at him. "They never found anything. No wreckage, no bodies, nothing."

Lexi shook her head. "That's terrible. So you didn't even get to bury them?" she asked quietly.

"No," he said. "There was an investigation and each day I waited and I hoped. I knew they'd gone, but I still wanted to see them."

She nodded.

"Eventually they closed the investigation and I had to accept I was never going to see them again. They have stones," he said, "at the church and I planted a tree on the coast, where the plane took off. I go and visit it sometimes."

Lexi gripped his hand tighter, wondering if she had the courage to let him know she completely understood. In the end she decided she did.

"I lost my brother," she began hesitantly, "when I was twelve."

"Shit, Lexi." Jae caressed her cheek with his left hand and then turned her to face him. "That's rough. Really rough. At least I was an adult."

In his eyes she could see sympathy and understanding. He'd been there too. He knew how it felt.

"His name was Bobby," she said, "he got knocked down. I saw it happen."

"Fuck," Jae let out the expletive and then rapidly pulled her to him and enveloped her in his embrace. "Jesus, Lexi." He continued to allow his warmth and comfort to consume her.

"That was ten years ago too," she observed ironically as she drank in his essence and took the support he offered. He pulled her impossibly closer. "I miss him so much," she said as she screwed her eyes closed. "He would've been twenty-four now. A man."

"I hear you," Jae whispered quietly. "My parents – they would've been nearing retirement. In a way just starting life."

"So would Bobby, be just starting." Lexi observed solemnly. "He was brilliant. I know he would've been successful at whatever he did." Using the back of her hand she wiped at her eyes and then pulled away a little so she could focus on Jae's face. "It sucks, doesn't it?" she asked and slowly he nodded.

"But you," he said as he cupped her face in between his hands, "you saw it happen. How the hell does a twelve-year-old begin to process that?"

On a deep sigh, she closed her eyes. "In reality, I don't think I ever did. My parents," she opened her eyes again and looked into his opposing dark depths. "They blamed me. I mean," she held up her hand as she saw anger cross his face, "they never openly blamed me as a child but I knew they did. It all came out – recently." Rapidly an image flashed into her mind. She saw herself lying in the hospital bed after losing Cal's baby. She saw her parents visiting. Lexi swallowed.

"Shit," she said aloud, "when does the pain ever go?" Not only had she lost her brother, but in her short life she'd also lost her child. The pain from both losses still burned. Lexi wondered if she should tell Jae about the baby too, but it didn't seem right. It was her and Cal's private grief.

Jae reached forwards and brushed a tear away from her cheek. "It doesn't," he said simply, "at least it hasn't for me."

Lexi managed a watery smile. "What a pair we are," she observed. "This is supposed to be a party and look at us." Removing her hands from his shoulders she sat back a little.

Jae smiled. "Yeah." He reached across and tucked a tendril of her hair behind her ear. "It just makes me feel that we have even more of a connection," he said softly as he pulled his hand away. Lexi felt the warmth of his breath caress her cheek.

"What were your parents like?" Lexi asked.

"Full of life," Jae sat back in the seat too. "Dad worked really hard

to get the business going. I remember him always being at the yard."
Lexi watched as he smiled fondly. "Then, things took off in a big way.
He began to get international clients, people looking for an English
touch to their buildings. There was a lot of travelling."

"Did you travel too?" Lexi asked.

"Sometimes. He took me to New York once. It was the most
unbelievable city. I must've been twenty maybe. I remember thinking
I would go back one day. I never have."

"No?" she asked surprised.

Jae shook his head. "No. After Mum and Dad died it was all I could
do to keep things going here. I had to put in managers overseas."

"But you still have interests over there?" she asked. "I mean, you
could visit again."

He shifted on the bench, turning his torso so he could face her.
"I'd like to take you one day," he said softly.

Lexi inclined her head. "I'd love to go," she said, "but we both
know it's not going to happen."

"Why not?" he asked and she detected a hint of stubbornness in
his tone. "C'mon, Lexi. We have something here. You know it and I
know it."

Lexi sighed. "Jae, we've been through this so many times…"

"Dammit, Lexi."

Without warning he closed the distance between them and
grabbed at her chin. Her eyes widened in shock, but he gave her
little time to process as his lips, curved and dangerous, descended
towards hers.

"Jae," she said on a small cry, but he ignored her; his eyes pinned
hers in place as he allowed his lips to complete their descent.
Automatically she closed her eyes as she received his lips. She knew
this had always been on the cards. This moment, tonight, this was
when the touch paper was going to be lit and, in all likelihood, when
the bomb exploded.

For a moment she resisted, but as he began to move his lips against
hers she felt herself surrender. Fighting was pointless. In reality,
the battle had been won months before. With a sigh of resignation

she hugged her arms around him, feeling the softness of his lips as he gently kissed her. They fitted so perfectly and Lexi gave herself permission to enjoy the sensations. He ran his tongue over her lips and she allowed him in, tracing his teeth with her own tongue as she drank his essence. He tasted of wine and mint, a heady combination to which her womanhood helplessly responded.

Dragging her hands from around his waist, she shoved them inside of his jacket, feeling his solid warmth as she began to caress his chest through his shirt. She felt Jae's intake of breath and, emboldened, she raised her hands higher, finding the flats of his nipples. He sucked in another breath as his tongue continued to spar with hers. She felt him groan as he pushed ever closer to her. Without losing contact he lifted her legs and secured them across his lap. With his left hand he traced the length of her limbs over the soft material of her dress.

Somewhere in the back of her mind Lexi registered this was wrong, but it was hot and heavy and it felt so damn right. Between her legs, her bud began to twitch and she knew she was lost. Their location, Cal, Fraser – everything ceased to be as she became one with Jae.

He sighed again and settled his roving hand on her waist. Their mouths remained locked as his right hand reached up and tangled in her hair pulling her head impossibly closer. Lexi complied. It was like they were trying to get inside of each other as they duelled and fought, straining to get as close as their restraints would allow. Her hands had remained on his chest and so she reached up to his nipples again, this time pinching them gently. Jae froze for a second and then slowly he pulled away.

"Shit, Lexi," he said, his face flushed, his breathing ragged. "I want you so damn much."

Lexi nodded. "I know," she replied, her voice hoarse. "I do too." She no longer denied her feelings nor added the caveat about marriage. After what she'd just entered into here there was no moral ground to be claimed. They may not be having full on sex, but they had definitely crossed the line and she, Lexi, was every bit as culpable as he.

"Dammit," he said as he brushed his dark locks away from his forehead, "I wish I'd booked a room."

Lexi took a moment to allow her breathing to return to normal. Her lips, she knew, would be bruised and her hair mussed.

"I've never wanted anyone so much in my life," he whispered. Lexi's legs remained across his lap and so he bucked into them, ensuring proof of his statement jabbed into her calves.

Lexi allowed a small smile. Her womanhood was still pulsating and she squirmed on the seat trying to ease the sensation. Taking a deep breath, she closed her eyes.

"Shit," he said again and she opened them to see him staring deeply at her. "You're struggling too?" he asked.

She nodded. "Yes."

"Bloody hell."

They continued to look at each other, eyes communicating in a way they knew their bodies could not.

"Are you going to stop denying this now?" he asked and again, she nodded.

"I can't deny it," she whispered, "not after what just happened here."

"Thank fuck," he said.

Lexi smiled. "Your language is a little colourful," she observed.

Jae returned her smile. "Sorry."

"No, don't apologise," she said. "I like it. I mean...it's hot," she mumbled. Embarrassed, she dropped her chin to her chest.

Lexi felt his erection jump beneath her calves.

"You like it?" he whispered as he reached across and lifted her chin with his finger.

Her face was aflame but bravely she nodded. She'd never been this forward with Cal.

"Fuck," he repeated and lightly she laughed in an attempt to deal with her discomfort. "Now I really wish I'd booked a room."

Jae's eyes journeyed from her face down to her exposed collarbone and from there onto the front of her dress. As his gaze reached her breasts she watched his expression change. Again, she felt his erection jump.

After a moment he raised his eyes back to hers and she could tell he was reaching his limit. His left hand, which still rested on her legs,

411

began to journey slowly upwards.

"We can't," she said urgently, "we can't, not here."

"I know, I know," he shook his head. "I just need a moment."

His hand continued its journey and Jae's gaze followed it, watching it as it reached the top of her thigh and then skimmed over her core, coming to rest, palm flat, on her belly. Lexi's every fibre quivered.

Jae closed his eyes and then rapidly he opened them again, looking around the deserted room. Their seat was secluded and mostly obscured. A large display of ornate plants gave a measure of privacy and Lexi knew Jae was weighing up how far they could go here.

"We can't," she repeated.

Again, he nodded. "I know, I know, but fuck, Lexi. So help me, I need to touch your breasts. Just once." His voiced was lowered, deep and sensual and Lexi felt herself respond.

"We can't." She too glanced around the room that had thus far remained completely deserted. In the distance the band continued to play.

"I know." Jae's eyes when he looked at her were torn, the emotion raw. Lexi watched as the inner battle raged. Slowly, he moved his hand from her belly and gradually slid it upwards. Lexi tensed.

"It's okay," he whispered. "No one can see us."

Even though she was scared, Lexi couldn't deny that this was the hottest thing she'd ever done. Moisture seeped from down below.

Jae removed his left hand and used it to drop her legs down to the floor. His right hand remained braced across the top of the seat behind her. Shifting forwards he leaned completely across her so that his jacket, as he lifted his arm and placed it around her shoulders, concealed her top half from view. With his left hand supporting her shoulders he removed his right hand from the seat and placed it gently on her belly in exactly the same manner as he'd done before. More heat escaped from her womanhood.

"Let me do this, Lexi," he implored, the gravel of his voice beyond sexy. She nodded. There was no way she could say no.

Slowly he traced a path with his right hand upwards and towards her breasts. Lexi drew in a deep breath as he allowed the flat of his palm to gently caress the valley in-between. His eyes darkened as he followed every movement of his hand. After a moment he moved to the right, allowing his palm to lightly graze her left breast and nipple. Lexi sucked in another breath. For a moment he stayed there, gently rotating his palm until her nipple stiffened. As it did so, he let out a low growl and Lexi closed her eyes. He turned his attention to her right breast and mirrored his movements, growling again when her other nipple hardened. Lexi dropped her head back, completely lost in the moment.

"Shit," Jae said as he raised his right hand to her head and gently pulled her forwards. She opened her eyes in time to see him dip his head and drop a gentle kiss on her lips. Immediately she re-closed her eyes. The kiss lasted for a second and then he pulled away, his hand once again making the journey to her breasts.

The bodice on her dress was fitted, but it was elasticated at the back to make it easier to wear. Jae placed his palm gently on her collarbone and then, looking up, he connected his eyes to hers. Silently he asked the question and Lexi nodded.

With infinite care he moved his hand lower, brushing aside the bodice as he pushed his hand beneath. Within moments he'd reached her left breast which was bare, the dress not requiring a bra. He sucked in a deep breath as his hand came into contact with her stiffened nipple. Lexi mirrored him, sucking in her own breath. It barely reached her lungs. Moving lower he lifted the swollen globe and cradled it in his hand, gently squeezing and caressing it. Every nerve stood to attention as she felt the roughness of his hand against the warmth of her breast. Again, she dropped her head back.

Within the confines of the dress Jae manoeuvred his hand to the other breast and gave it the same treatment, touching it, feeling it, playing with it almost reverently. His thumb flicked across her distended nipple and she flinched as down below, her bud throbbed harder.

"Shit," she mumbled as her head lolled back on her neck.

"My words exactly," Jae growled as he dropped his head and open mouthed began to suck on her left breast through the fabric of her dress.

"Shit," she said again and Jae sucked harder. Sensations overwhelmed her and despite their lack of full intimacy, Lexi began to melt inside. Everywhere from her toes to the top of her head tingled and impossibly, she knew she was close to losing it.

"Fuck," she said and, reaching forwards, she grasped Jae's shirt in her hands. He lifted his head. "Stop," she said, her voice small. "I can't…"

His eyes were black pools and they read every nuance on her face. "You're close, aren't you?" he whispered and helplessly, she nodded.

"Fuck," he echoed. For a moment they regarded each other, breathing uneven and then he dropped his head once more, continuing his ministrations to her breast. Feverishly she grabbed at his head.

"Stop, Jae," she whispered, "or I'll lose it."

Momentarily he raised his eyes. "That," he said, "is the plan."

Without further ado he re-commenced his sucking and Lexi drew in another rough breath. She was so close, he had to stop.

As if he'd read her mind, Jae raised his head but only long enough to connect their lips. "Lose it, Lexi," he whispered against her mouth, "I've got you."

Forcefully she kissed him, taking everything she needed as their mouths explored each other. Her womanhood began to pulsate and she knew she was nearly there. Lexi deepened the kiss, biting on his tongue and Jae reciprocated, giving her everything and more. Their mating was fierce born of a desire denied and when finally the sensations became too much, she allowed herself to let go. Her body shook from head to toe as she reached her nirvana, her cries swallowed by Jae. He held her tightly, his right arm around her body as she let the last of the sensations travel through her. Their mouths remained locked, but their kisses gentled and, after a time, they eventually pulled apart.

"Shit," Jae said one final time as he tenderly caressed her face with his palm.

Lexi remained silent. Never had she done anything so wanton and her face blazed with both passion and shame. Caught up in the heat of the moment it had felt like the only thing to do, as if she couldn't live another breath without giving herself over to this man but now, as the sensations finally died, Lexi felt the guilt of reality overwhelm her.

What she'd just done had been hot and heady and it had felt so damn right. She would be lying if she denied it was anything other than that but, with the now familiar guilt, came the metaphorical cold water.

Lexi was still a married woman and by her wanton actions tonight she'd damaged that irreversibly. Her mind wandered back to the start of the evening and how she'd felt that tonight would be some kind of judgement night. She'd been right.

Jae pulled her into his arms and with barely any strength left she allowed him to. Her gut twisted in pain and she felt her heart begin to break, shattering into tiny pieces as the nausea she'd felt earlier returned. Lexi had betrayed Cal in the worst possible way and even though he had no way of knowing, by her actions tonight, she'd just ensured that their brief but passionate marriage, was unequivocally over.

* * *

Tami

Hidden deep in the shadows, Tami smiled. From what she'd just witnessed, it was clear that for Lexi Strudwick, her marriage was done. Although Tami had always been suspicious, never had she expected to witness such comprehensive proof. Her smile broadened. Lexi didn't deserve Cal and, as far as Tami was concerned, Lexi never had.

A feeling of excitement overcame her. From here on in, it was game on. Tami knew that once Cal realised her true identity then it would all be over. For, when she finally revealed her genuine self to him, any residual feelings he might harbour for Lexi would evaporate, there was no question.

Of that she was one hundred per cent sure.

415

Chapter Thirty-Six

Cal

Monday March 9th 2015

The meeting with Tami had been in his diary for a while and Cal was glad it had finally arrived. Since deciding on his plans for Zach's land, he'd been itching to share them with the project manager. She, he knew, would find a way to make things happen.

"Boy, am I glad to see you," he said as the younger woman joined him in the portacabin on site. Although basic, the cabin housed everything he and the guys needed including hot and cold water, a bathroom and most importantly, heating.

"Brr…" Tami rubbed her hands together as she walked towards the desk where Cal sat. "Any chance of a cuppa?"

"Sure." He moved past her and filled the kettle.

"So, how come you're glad to see me?" she asked.

"Because," he began as he selected two mugs from the small kitchen cabinet, "I have an idea how to complete this project." He indicated the almost finished property outside the window.

"You do?" she asked.

Cal nodded.

"Okay," she said as she took off her coat and hung it on one of the nails in the wall, "shoot."

"Well, you know it will be handed over to Lexi?" he asked.

"Yes."

"As far as I know," he continued, "Lexi had no plans for it after that, it would just be a grand house with no life to it. So, I got to thinking." He poured milk and hot water onto the tea bags in the mugs. After stirring them both he removed the bags and dumped

416

them in the bin. "Sugar?" he asked and Tami shook her head. Picking up the two mugs, he returned to his desk. "I tried to figure out what Zach would do with it," Cal said.

"I thought it was for his retirement?" Tami asked as she lifted her mug and took a tentative sip.

"Yes, it was and he would've lived here. What I mean is, if the tables were turned and he was doing something like this for me."

"Ah, okay," she responded, "I get it now."

"Anyway, Zach and me, we went way back..." his eyes glazed for a moment as once more he remembered his friend. "I was messed up when I met him and he helped me out. So, I figured we should use the place as some kind of hostel for kids. Help them out the way he helped me."

Across from him Tami nodded. "Sounds good. I like it."

"I mean I know we'll have to do more work, but I reckon it'll be worth it."

She nodded again. "Sure. What about capital though?"

Cal shrugged. "I don't know. Do we have anything left in the budget?"

He watched as Tami reached into her briefcase and pulled out a file that she quickly scanned. "It depends. If we finish on time then we might have some left – a few grand maybe."

Cal nodded. "That could be enough. All the guys will give their time, I know they will. It might be that we have to do the extra work out of hours but the days are getting longer now so it shouldn't be too much of a problem."

"What did you have in mind?" Tami asked. "Bedrooms? Lounge area? That kind of thing?"

"We'd have to talk to the authorities," Cal said. "I'm not sure what the restrictions would be, but yeah I was thinking somewhere for them to stay. But I was also thinking it could be like an education centre. Me and the guys – we could help them learn a trade. That kind of thing."

"And Lexi's okay with this?" Tami asked.

"She is," Cal replied.

"What about Jae?"

417

"What about him?"

"Is he on board with this too?"

Cal shook his head. "I don't know, but I don't see how it's got anything to do with him. He said he'd let us do what we wanted to and then hand it over to Lexi."

"He might want to know if you needed more capital," Tami pointed out.

"I did think of that," Cal responded, "but I figured we might be able to raise extra capital ourselves."

"How so?"

"Well, once we own the property – or rather, once Lexi owns the property, then we could borrow against it."

"True," Tami agreed, "although I would caution you about taking on a debt against the property if you have no fixed income to repay it."

"I'll still have my job," Cal stated, "so I could arrange the repayments from my existing wage."

"Would you be able to afford to do that?" she asked.

Cal shrugged. "It would depend on the repayments, but with both mine and Lexi's salary, I reckon we could manage." He watched Tami as she took another sip of her tea. Picking up his mug, he mirrored her.

"What kind of children are you going to aim at?" she asked.

"Any kind. Any child that needs support."

"You'll need to get in touch with social services," Tami advised, "find out how you go about getting this place an approved centre. You might be able to offer respite for families in difficulty too."

"Yeah, I hadn't thought of that," Cal said. "I guess there's always a need for somewhere like this. I mean, imagine how different things could've been if I'd had a place like this to go."

"You had Zach though, so in a way you did have your own place like this."

"True," Cal acknowledged, "and I wouldn't have traded meeting him for the world. But it would've been good to have spent less time on the streets."

"You were on the streets?" she asked.

Cal looked up and suddenly realised what he'd said. He was

perilously close to opening up a can of worms and that was not the kind of relationship he and Tami shared.

"For a while," he said noncommittally. "So, you reckon we could do this then?"

Tami tilted her head to one side as she watched him. "I don't see why not. What do you need me to do?"

"Work your contacts?" Cal asked. "You must know people who can help us with this."

"Yeah, I have a few contacts," she replied, "but I'd advise you to call social services first and find out what you're going to need to do. As wonderful as this project is, you might find it harder to get off the ground than you think."

It was odd, Cal reflected as he watched her talk, how much he'd got used to having this woman around – and how hard it was for him to shake the feeling that he'd met her before.

"Where did you grow up?" Cal asked as, randomly, he verbalised his thoughts.

"What?" Tami queried, her tiger brown eyes regarding him questioningly.

"Oh, sorry," Cal said, "I just can't help thinking we've met before."

"Nope," she responded, "I would have remembered."

"Yeah, course." Cal shook his head. "So, where were we?"

Tami consulted the paperwork she had in her hand. "The build is going to plan and the electricians are doing the first fix this week..."

Cal let his gaze focus on her lips as he listened to her summary. She'd painted them a deep glossy red. As ever she was dressed in a sharp business suit, this one beige, and she was wearing her customary heels. He'd often wondered why she continued to wear heels on what was essentially a building site, but he'd never asked. It didn't seem appropriate. His gaze wandered lower and he looked at shapely legs that were crossed beneath the short skirt. She had a damn fine pair of pins and he knew he wasn't the only one who'd noticed. Mace had bent his ear on more than one occasion about the woman.

"Cal?"

Her voice reached him and rapidly he looked up. "Yeah, sorry," he said as he mentally shook himself, "miles away." Miles away thinking about your legs, he chastised. What the hell had he been playing at?

"So," she continued, "I think we're still running to schedule – although that might change if we need to do further works for your ideas."

"Sounds good." Cal nodded vigorously as he tried to rid himself of the mental images he'd somehow just stored of glossy red lips and long shapely legs. "Are we still okay with the suppliers?"

"Yes, I called them this morning and they have some of the bespoke furniture ready to ship."

"Great." With difficulty he forced his mind to focus. "I don't know if we might need to use them again so keep up good relations. If there are any deals we need to get them."

"Sure," Tami agreed. "I'll call them later in the week."

"Right," Cal nodded. "Anything else?"

"Er…no," Tami consulted her paperwork, "I don't think so."

"Okay, great," he said, "and you'll make some calls? To your contacts?"

"Yes, sure." She picked up her mug and drained it. Cal watched her hands, admiring their elegance.

"Do you want another?" he found himself asking as she began to rise from the chair. Suddenly, for reasons he wasn't prepared to examine, he didn't want her to leave.

"Er…" she glanced at her watch. "Sure, but we've done all the talking."

"That's okay," Cal indicated the more comfortable seating area a few paces away from his desk where the guys ate their lunch. "Call it a break. I might even be able to find a biscuit."

He watched her glossy lips break into a smile. "In that case, I'm sold."

She walked the few paces to the first of the two utilitarian green sofas and sat down. From the lower seat her shapely legs were perfectly showcased and so, resolutely, he focused on the kettle. Cal had always found the curvaceous brunette to be attractive, but today he had no idea what was wrong with him. All he knew was he was thinking about her in a way he definitely shouldn't be and the sense that he'd met her before, was stronger than it had ever been.

"So, where did you grow up?" he asked again as he placed the two mugs on the low coffee table. Turning back around he grabbed the half packet of biscuits he'd found in the cupboard and offered one to Tami.

"Thanks," she snagged a biscuit and took a small bite. "Here and there," she said after a moment.

Cal smiled. "That's avoiding the question," he said, "but it's cool. If you don't want to talk about it then no worries. I just realised that we've worked together for three months now and I don't know the first thing about you."

"I am," Tami said as she took another bite of the biscuit, "a woman of mystery." She winked at him and then smiled.

Cal laughed. "Fair enough."

"Boss?" The door to the portacabin swung open. Mace appeared accompanied by a rush of cool air.

Cal turned to the other man. "How many times?" he asked. "I'm not your boss."

"Sorry, oh, Miss Foster, I didn't know you were visitin'."

Tami turned to Mace and smiled. "And how many times have I told you to call me Tami?" she asked.

Cal watched as Mace shuffled from one foot to the other. "Yeah, sorry." Quickly he turned back to face Cal.

"There's a plumbing supply problem," he said. "Supplier says we've not ordered enough parts."

"Which supplier?" Tami asked and Mace swivelled towards her, naming the supplier as he did so.

"And what parts are we short of?" she asked as she began to check through her paperwork. Mace moved to the sofa on which she was sat and peered over her shoulder.

"There," he pointed to her papers with his grubby finger. "They've sent twenty, but I need fifty."

As Cal watched, Tami consulted a different piece of paper. "Here it is," she said, "yup, we ordered fifty. It's their mistake, Mace."

"I knew it," he said as he straightened.

"Leave it with me," Tami said, "I'll give them a call. When do you need the parts by?"

"Yesterday?" Mace responded with a smile and Tami laughed.

"I'm good, but even I'm not that good."

"Oh, I don't know, Miss Foster," Mace responded and then almost immediately reddened. Inwardly Cal cringed for his friend. Mace was a big man, but around Tami, he always went to pieces.

"Well, I'll be off," he said awkwardly as he shuffled to the door.

"Later," Cal called after him and both he and Tami watched as Mace made a swift exit.

Cal shook his head. "When are you going to put that poor guy out of his misery?"

Tami batted her eyelashes at him. "I have no idea what you mean."

"Yeah, you do," he responded. "And the only reason you figure it's safe to bat your eyelashes at me is because you know I'm married."

"Safe?" she queried, "strange choice of word."

"How come?" Cal asked.

"Well," she leaned forwards and hastily Cal redirected his gaze in order to prevent it being filled with cleavage. "Safe would suggest the alternative is danger which," she continued, "would suggest you feel you'd be in danger with me, were you not married."

Cal followed the logic. Just.

"Mace is single," Cal responded.

"He is," Tami acknowledged, "although as lovely as he is, he's not my type."

"No?" Cal asked. With difficulty he prevented himself from asking the obvious follow up question.

"No," she confirmed.

"Shame," he said.

"Hmm. Although, I'm not actually interested in finding anyone right now."

"Want me to tell Mace?" Cal asked.

Tami shook her head and her long brunette locks swished from side to side. "Nah, where would be the fun in that?"

"You," said Cal as he pointed a finger at her, "are cruel."

She dropped her head to one side. "It's not the first time I've been told that."

He smiled. "I don't doubt it. I will, however, put Mace out of his misery. He's a good bloke."

Again she inclined her head. "Sure, if you like."

"You know," Cal said after a moment, "you're one of those people who constantly talk but reveal nothing."

"It's a gift," she said with a smile.

"You'd make a good priest or priestess or whatever the hell it is," he said.

Tami laughed. "Why?"

"For confession," he said. "You'd listen, talk, reveal nothing and they, in turn, would reveal everything."

Tami picked up her mug and took a sip. "I don't know, Cal. I could say the same about you. You're not someone who reveals a lot either. I think we're both guarded in our own ways."

"Perhaps," Cal considered. He sipped at his tea too and for a moment they sat in silence.

"I grew up in the city," she said and abruptly Cal looked at her.

"Brufton?"

Tami nodded. "On the outskirts mainly."

"Yeah, me too," he responded. "Until I left home. That's when I hit the streets for a while. Ended up in a hostel right in the centre. I think that's why I love this place so much," he indicated the land outside of the window. "It's so far removed from anywhere I used to call home."

"Were you happy?" she asked. "As a kid?"

Cal took a moment to collect his thoughts. They may be having a candid conversation now, but that was no reason for him to reveal more than necessary. "Mostly," he hedged.

Tami nodded. "Yeah, same here. Mostly happy."

"That's good," Cal said.

"You ever see your parents?" she asked.

"No." Cal shook his head. He offered nothing further. Tami was getting too close.

"No, I don't see mine either."

"That's sad." Immediately Cal thought of Lexi. "I always figured

423

it was more important for a woman to maintain a relationship with her parents."

Tami shrugged. "I guess that depends on the parents. Mine weren't much cop. In the end it was just me and my brother."

"I never knew you had a brother," Cal commented.

"Why would you?" she asked. "I've never told you."

Across from her he smiled. "True. Older or younger?"

"Older," she said, "by two years."

"Nice," Cal said. "I would've liked a brother. In the end it was just me."

"Must have been tough," she observed.

"It was, but I had some good friends and then I met Zach. I fell on my feet when I met him. Then I met Lexi. Now she's all the family I need."

"And she feels the same?" Tami asked.

Cal looked at her questioningly. "Yeah, of course she does. Although she still has her parents."

"Sometimes marriages aren't always equal," Tami said, "like one party is more into it than the other. You're a good guy, Cal. I hope your marriage isn't like that."

"It's not," he defended as he tried to ignore the niggling doubts. Something had changed between him and Lexi recently and, if he was honest with himself, he was no longer sure how stable his marriage was. His heart constricted.

"That's good."

"You still see your brother?" Cal asked in an effort to change the subject. Maybe he should talk to Lexi tonight. Try to figure out if they were okay because if they weren't...

"Yeah. He lives with me. Has done ever since he got sick."

"He's sick?" Cal asked.

"Long term and no one can tell us why."

Cal shook his head. "That must be rough."

"We deal with it," Tami shrugged. "Every day we hope we'll get some answers and one day, I figure we will."

"I hope so."

424

"You know the bitch of it?" she asked.

"No?"

"He was like you, so active, full of life. He had everything going for him. He had a career in London and then bam, this hits. After the crap we've been through..." suddenly she stopped talking. "Sorry," she continued after a moment, "I get kinda mad when I think of him. It's so unfair."

Cal rose from his seat and walked around the small table to sit beside her. "I understand," he said softly. "It's like with Zach, I mean how cruel was that?"

Tami nodded. "I know. Sometimes I wonder if there really is a God. I mean, if there is, why does he keep heaping the crap on the good guys?"

Cal shrugged. "I have no idea. One minute I think the big guy is up there and then the next..."

"I hear you," responded Tami.

"Sucks," Cal agreed.

"But you and Lexi, you're sound?"

Cal turned his head and frowned at her. "Didn't we already do this?"

"We did, but..."

"But what?" he prompted.

"Nothing," Tami shook her head. "It's nothing. Forget it."

"Okay." He sat back on the sofa.

"I went to the ball," Tami said after a moment.

Cal frowned at her, wondering where that had come from. "Yeah?" he responded, "Lexi went too. She said it was a good night."

Beside him Tami nodded. "It was."

Cal inclined his head.

"I saw Lexi," she said.

He turned to face her. "Yeah?"

"Yeah," Tami confirmed.

"That's good."

Suddenly their conversation felt stilted, suffocated by an atmosphere he couldn't name and so he rose and walked back around to his side of the table.

"She looked beautiful," Tami commented. "Nice dress."

"Why are we talking about my wife again?" he asked as he settled onto the opposing sofa.

"Just making conversation," Tami said.

Cal nodded although something told him there was more to it. "Why does it feel like there's more to this?" he vocalised. Subconsciously he raised his guard.

"There isn't," she replied, but her tone did nothing to assuage his doubts. He remained unconvinced.

"Well, if you've finished your drink, I better get on." Cal indicated the desk to his right. He was keen to end what had started out as a pleasant conversation but was rapidly turning into something over which he felt he had little control.

"Sure." Tami rose and this time Cal had no difficulty not looking at her legs. The change in atmosphere had him on edge.

"See you later," Cal said as he watched her walk towards the door.

"Yeah, I'll call you when I've spoken to the suppliers. So you can update Mace," she added.

"Great."

Tami reached the door and as he followed her progress, she hesitated.

"Cal?" she said with her back to him.

"Yeah?" his voice was unnaturally gruff.

"I need to tell you something." Still she kept her back to him.

Cal closed his eyes. No you don't, he said to himself. Somehow he knew whatever she was about to say wasn't something he wanted to hear. He said nothing.

"Cal?" This time she turned to face him and wordlessly he shook his head.

"Jae was there too," she said and Cal narrowed his eyes.

"He's the boss," he responded.

This time it was Tami who shook her head. "He was with Lexi," she said quietly.

Cal shrugged in an attempt to maintain his cool. "They work together." Inside though his brain was whirring and bile was slowly

426

rising up from his gut. "They had this project to talk about."

Tami nodded and briefly closed her eyes before swallowing.

"Cal?" she said again.

"No," he said vehemently, "whatever it is, I don't want to know."

"I can't," she said, "I can't not tell you. It isn't right."

He stared at her. "No," he repeated.

Again he saw Tami swallow. "When I saw them," she said, "they weren't talking."

Cal could feel the bile reaching the back of his throat. His pulse began to race, his palms started sweating and his head felt as if it was going to split in two.

"I-said-no," he ground out forcefully, each word clearly enunciated.

"I'm sorry, Cal." Tami's eyes began to fill with tears. "They weren't talking. When I saw them, they were..." she stopped for a moment and Cal stared at her once more, willing her to keep her counsel. He didn't want to know. She rubbed her hand across the back of her eyes. "They were kissing," she said eventually. "Lexi and Jae. They were kissing."

Cal saw red. Everything around him paled into insignificance and all he could focus on was the woman before him.

"You bitch," he spat out, "you lying bitch."

Tami held her ground. "I'm not lying, Cal. Why would I?"

In his mind he saw Jae and Lexi here at this site, close together, talking. He remembered the strange atmosphere, the way she'd been, the things that had changed in their marriage. He saw it all as his anger rose and with that anger came blinding clarity. She was right. Tami was right, but pride wouldn't allow him to acknowledge it. His marriage wasn't over. Not today and not until he'd fought for it.

"Get out," he snarled at her, "get the fuck out."

Tami nodded and turned back towards the door. "I understand, Cal," she said as she prepared to leave, "but I promise you, I'm not lying."

He ground his teeth and remained silent, barely flinching as the cool air washed over him from Tami's departure. She wasn't lying, he knew she wasn't, but Cal Strudwick didn't fail and he was damned if he was going to fail at his marriage.

Decisively he grabbed his keys and followed on Tami's heels.

"Where are you going?" she called as she got into her car.

Cal ignored her. Wrenching open his own car door he started the engine and, flooring it, accelerated out of the site. In his conscious mind he had no idea of where he was going but, in his unconscious mind, Cal's fate was already decided. There was only one place where everything made sense to him and that was the place he was going. Right now.

* * *

The woman lay in repose, naked, stretched out on the faux leather couch. Cal sat in the viewing gallery alone. Glazed eyes looked out at him, but he knew she couldn't see him. The privacy glass maintained his anonymity. The place had barely changed since he'd last been here on his nineteenth birthday. Hard to believe that was only seven years ago. So much had changed.

The woman moved and rose from the couch. Slowly she began to run her hands over her body as she commenced a sensual dance, just for him. Oddly this was the first time Cal had sat in the viewing gallery. When he'd frequented the club in his youth, he'd always chosen to participate. Now though, he was happy to watch. He was running on the adrenalin that had been racing through his veins ever since Tami left. He knew he shouldn't be here, the very fact he was repulsed him, and yet it felt like the only place he could be. Cal wanted to go back to the beginning and he figured that by being here he could wipe the slate clean and start again. Pretend he'd never met Lexi.

The woman moved closer to the glass and then, after a moment, pressed up against it. Her small nipples flattened against the pane and, unable to help himself, Cal became aroused. She writhed from side to side, her palms shimmying up and down the glass as she did so and then, with a knowing smile, she walked away. Cal admired her small rear as she sauntered towards the back of the room. She was completely different in build to Lexi. More boyish, more compact. Not the type to which he was usually attracted but then she was much like Aria, and Aria had always been his favourite.

The woman collected a whip from the rack secured to the wall and Cal hardened further. Lexi had never allowed him to be adventurous and, because he loved her, he'd never pushed. He believed the love he felt was enough to overcome his base desires – desires he'd been determined to hide. The kick he felt though, as he watched the woman caress her body with the softened leather, made him remember what it felt like. What he'd been missing.

She continued dancing and Cal gently pressed his hand to his crotch. He wouldn't let it go too far – he knew better than to become a slave to this world again – but for the moment, he wanted to enjoy it. There was a sense of freedom to this and for the first time in months he forgot about Zach and the devastation his friend had left behind. He closed his eyes. In his mind he pictured Lexi, her beautiful blonde hair cascading over her bare shoulders, her smile welcoming him as he pulled her into his arms. Slowly he began to move his hand on his crotch. In his mind he kissed Lexi, tasted her the way only he could, caressed her in places only he was allowed. Pressure built inside him as he replaced the naked, gyrating woman for his beautiful wife. He threw his head back. He'd always known he'd lucked out with Lexi and, if he was being honest, he'd been afraid it wouldn't last – but that didn't diminish the sense of betrayal he felt at her hands. Abruptly he opened his eyes.

The woman lay on the couch again, her small hands caressing her breasts as she continued to look sightlessly at the viewing gallery. For a moment he wondered who she was, what her story was, why she was here. He knew he and countless other men got off on women like her, but for the first time he saw her as a person and not just an object of pleasure. A wave of repulsion washed over him. He'd come here because he thought he could cleanse himself, but all he'd done was lacerate an already bleeding wound. Nausea began to swirl in his stomach and impatiently he rose. Cal had come here looking for answers and in some respects he'd found them. He knew now that he wasn't the same person he'd been at nineteen. The thought that the woman in front of him performed like this hour after hour, sickened him and Cal hated himself for contributing to her objectification.

429

Coming here had settled that for him and he knew, without doubt, he would never set foot inside an establishment like this again.

With indecent haste he exited the viewing gallery and took the few stairs down to the main club. The scene here was the same as ever and deliberately he averted his eyes. He may still have base desires, but he finally understood it was not okay to take care of them this way and nor had it ever been.

His car was parked by the kerb and, reaching it, he gunned the engine. Adrenalin still pumped through his veins and the image of Tami, voicing words he didn't want to hear, stayed uppermost in his mind. He'd been a bastard to Tami, something she didn't deserve, but right now his focus was Lexi. They'd been to hell and back together and, even though they hadn't been married long, to him it felt like a lifetime. More importantly, he'd promised himself to her for a lifetime. As he drove home, his movements became increasingly erratic as his anger elevated. The road ahead ceased to be grey; all he could see was red as colours and objects merged into one. Somehow he made it home, pulling onto the drive with a squeal of tyres. For a moment he remained seated as he dragged in calming breaths. His vision blurred as an image of Lexi and Jae swam into view. What a fool he'd been to ignore the signs, but he'd trusted her. Trusted she believed in their marriage every bit as much as he did. With sweaty palms he grabbed the door handle and pushed himself out of the car. He'd gone to the club thinking it would help, but in reality, it had made matters worse. Now he was reminded of the side of him that had lain dormant for so long, a part of him which sickened and aroused in equal measure. A piece of him he'd given up for love – a love he thought would last forever. What a stupid, stupid fool he had been.

The front door opened before he reached it and Lexi stood there, impossibly beautiful as ever. She must've heard him arrive. For a moment he said nothing, merely clenched his hands at his sides as he looked at her. The expression on her face gave her away: guilt radiated from her every pore and Cal shook his head. Slowly. With deliberate steps he closed the distance until he stood on the threshold.

"You fucking bitch," he ground out, voice low.

He watched as Lexi grasped her throat with her hand.

"Cal," she said as she reached a tentative hand towards him, "Cal, I'm so sorry."

Again he shook his head.

"I didn't mean for it to happen. And I didn't mean for you to find out like this."

Cal snorted. "And just precisely how was I supposed to find out my wife is a two-timing slut?"

Lexi recoiled, but Cal didn't care. He was bleeding inside. His heart was in pieces and he could no longer see anything but blackness ahead.

"I was going to tell you," she said, her voice wavering.

"Huh." He nodded. "When?" The word was barked out.

Lexi looked around at the street outside. "Come in," she said stepping aside, "everyone will hear."

Cal shrugged. "I'm cool with that," he replied as he leaned nonchalantly against the doorframe. "I got no dirty secrets to hide."

He watched as she closed her eyes. "I was going to tell you."

"So you said."

"Look, it all happened so fast."

Cal laughed, the sound harsh and cruel. "Oh, Lexi," he said, "that naive innocent act won't wash with me anymore. You knew perfectly well what you were doing when you had your tongue shoved down that man's throat."

"Cal," she pleaded, "please come inside."

He remained unmoving. "Nope."

"Suit yourself." She turned away from the door and he watched her departing back, scarcely able to believe she'd walked away from him. The bitch.

"You bitch," he said again as he followed her inside. He didn't bother to close the front door. "How dare you make a fool of me and how dare you walk away from me. Who the fuck d'you think you are?"

In the small lounge she stopped and turned to face him. "I'm sorry, Cal. I don't know what else to say."

He stood in the doorway blocking her exit. "How about the truth? How about telling me how long this has been going on?"

"Don't, Cal."

He watched as she shook her head.

"Have you fucked him yet?" he asked, ignoring her plea.

"Don't, Cal," she repeated.

"Don't what?" he shook his head again. Anger raged through his veins, but oddly he remained calm. The calm before the storm. "Don't demand answers? Why not?"

For a moment she said nothing and he registered the fear in her eyes. He almost hated himself for instilling that fear, but then he remembered what she'd done.

"No, I haven't slept with him," she said at last.

"But you wanted to? Huh?"

Again she closed her eyes and he saw her hands clench at her side. "Cal," she pleaded, "please, no good will come of this."

"I disagree," he responded calmly. "You see when I find out my wife, to who I'm utterly devoted has been cheating on me, I happen to think knowing all of the details is important."

"We kissed," she said quietly. "That's all."

"At the ball?"

She nodded.

Cal felt shards of ice pierce what was left of his heart. To hear her say it, to confirm it, was harder than he could ever have imagined.

"Was that the only time?" he ploughed on.

Cal knew she was right, that no good could come of him knowing everything, but he needed to know. He needed to understand exactly what she'd done to him.

Slowly she shook her head and part of him admired her courage. She could've lied. He wouldn't have known.

"No," she confirmed.

He took a deep breath and then slowly, slowly, blew it out. "How many times?" he asked as he closed his eyes in an effort to ward off the pain.

She remained silent and so he opened his eyes. In the stark light of the darkening dusk she looked small and scared, but he couldn't allow himself to feel sympathy for her. She didn't deserve it.

"How many times?" he asked again when still she didn't respond.

"Twice," she said eventually. "Once before and then again at the ball."

"Wait," Cal said as he held up his hand. "You kissed that bastard *before* the ball? You mean I've been living with a cheating bitch for what – how long?"

He saw her swallow. "Three months," she said her voice small. "The first time was after we'd all been to see Zach's site."

"You fucking bitch," he roared as finally the anger replaced the calm. "You kissed that bastard before Zach died and you didn't think to tell me? You stayed with me, you comforted me, you made me believe you loved him as much as I did and yet all the time you'd been with another man? You fucking, fucking bitch." He began to advance towards her.

"Cal," she said as she held her hand out to him, "it wasn't like that. After that time I told him to leave me alone and he did. We kept out of each other's way and then when Zach died I knew my place was with you."

Cal laughed again. The sound was just as harsh and cold as before. "You should've known your place was with me *before* Zach died. It's called marriage, Lexi. A concept which has escaped you it would seem." He shook his head. "You bitch," he spat out the word, his voice low and menacing as he stopped just short of where she stood.

"You can call me all the names you like," she said, "and I'll take them because I know I deserve them, but you have to try to understand it wasn't as calculated as you think. I love you, Cal, and I always will."

He stared at her in disbelief. "You love me? Don't make me laugh."

"It's true," she said, her voice raised a little. "I love you and I always will. I just..." she stopped.

"Go on," he prompted, "this should be good."

Cal watched as she swallowed again.

"I'm not *in* love with you anymore," she said.

He laughed again. He couldn't help himself. "It didn't occur to you to think I might want to know that?" The pain inside him warred with anger. He had cooled some – for now.

"Well, yes, but…"

"That it might have been something you could have mentioned *before* you decided to fuck around with another man? Do you know how I found out, Lexi?" The anger began to win.

She shook her head.

"Tami told me. Tami saw you and that bastard at the ball. Can you imagine how humiliated I felt?"

"I'm so sorry, Cal," she said again, "I was going to tell you. Tonight."

"Yeah?" he asked sarcastically, "somehow I have a hard time believing you. You do realise we've only been married a year, Lexi. One fucking year." He used his finger to point as emphasis.

"I know, I know," she ran her hands through her hair and despite everything he couldn't prevent himself from thinking how beautiful she looked. "I just, I don't know. We were too young I guess."

"You might have been, Lexi, but you knew the deal from the day we met. I thought we were in this together. I gave my life to you," he growled.

"Yeah? And I didn't?" she asked, her voice rising to match his. "I didn't lie in a hospital bed sick and riddled with guilt after losing *your* baby? I didn't pick up the pieces when you were too drunk to care? No? I didn't give my life to you either?"

"You," he said as he pointed his finger menacingly at her, "have no right to throw accusations at me. I might have been messed up, but I've not played around. You don't get to take any moral high ground here and you sure as hell don't get to talk about our baby. I mean, shit, Lexi. What about the baby we were trying for? Was that a lie too?"

Suddenly another piece of the puzzle clicked into place and with that came blinding clarity. Finally he understood why she'd been so reticent to talk about trying for another baby. Why she'd not been as upset as he, each time they'd failed.

"You didn't, did you?" he asked incredulously as he moved ever closer to her. "You didn't want another baby. Un-fucking-believable."

"I did," she defended as she backed slightly away from him. "I just…when it didn't happen I started to realise maybe it was a good thing. Maybe we were too young."

"Another important fact you omitted to tell me. What else?" he asked, "what else have you been lying about?"

"Nothing, I swear." She held up her hands as he continued to walk menacingly towards her. If he'd managed to curb his anger over her infidelity then the cause was completely lost now. She'd mentioned their baby and she'd told him she'd never wanted another. The line in terms of control for him had been crossed.

"You," he spat out as he came toe to toe with her. "Who the fuck are you? I don't even know you anymore."

He grabbed at her hand and she pulled it away. As he watched, her beautiful face crumpled and tears began to cascade down her cheeks.

"I never meant for it to be like this, Cal, I'm so sorry. Please. Just try to understand."

"No. You, you had me begging for another chance." He pointed his finger into her face. "I made a mistake, I messed up, I forced you to kiss me when you didn't want to and you made me pay. You made me pay until I could barely function for guilt. And yet all the time you were sabotaging our chances and messing around with another man. Who the hell are you, Lexi, because you're bloody well not the woman I thought I married. I don't even recognise you."

She shrank against the wall behind her. "I get it, I know," she said earnestly, "I get that you're hurt and that I've betrayed you, but I need you to try to understand. I love you, Cal, and I hate that I've done this to you. To us."

"Then why," he asked as he grabbed her shoulders and secured her against the wall, "why have you done it?" His voice was vibrating with anger.

Lexi closed her eyes. "Get your hands off me," she said slowly.

Cal took his right hand off her shoulder and used it to grab her chin. Her eyes opened. "I'm your husband," he said, "and, if I want to touch you, then I bloody well will." He could feel her shaking beneath his hand, but he was too far gone to stop.

"Cal," she pleaded, her eyes wild, "let me go. This isn't how to deal with this."

"No?" he asked as he squeezed her jaw harder. To him, right now, it felt like the perfect way.

"You need to calm down," she said, her voice muffled by the restriction he was placing on her mouth. "Let me explain."

"Oh, I think I understand everything," he ground out, "I don't need you to draw me a picture."

Beneath his hand, Lexi tried to break free but Cal resisted. His conscious mind had deserted him and the anger, born of years of childhood abuse, had taken hold.

"Let me go," she shouted as she writhed around beneath him, "please."

Suddenly Cal felt a sharp pain rip through his groin and he released her. Lexi scrambled away from him as quickly as she could and belatedly he realised she'd used her knee in the only place guaranteed to fell a man. Groaning he hobbled after her, watching as she ran out of the front door. She couldn't get to her car, his was behind hers on the drive and so she continued to run. Cal grabbed his keys and with difficulty, got into his car and started it up. She wasn't going to get away from him and she wasn't going to get away with this.

He saw her turn as she heard the engine start and as he watched, her face blanched. "No!" she mouthed as he began to point the car directly towards her. "No!"

Cal continued to press his foot to the accelerator.

"No!" she yelled again, but he didn't see her or hear her. All he felt was a surge of anger that overrode any sense or control. He'd been made a fool of before, as a child. He'd been taunted by a man who he thought had loved him and he still had the scars from that lesson. Now, Lexi, the woman he'd dedicated his life to, had done the same. She'd humiliated him. She'd taken away his dignity and she'd awoken his demons.

With unseeing eyes he continued to press forwards, and, when he heard the thud he'd known would come, he kept on driving.

He kept on driving, foot pressed to the floor, and he didn't stop.

Not once.

Chapter Thirty-Seven

Lexi

Wednesday March 11th 2015

Lexi opened her eyes and looked around at the white, sterile room.

"Hey, you're awake," said a deep gravelly voice beside her and awkwardly, she turned her head. Jae reached forwards and gently traced his hand across her forehead.

"What happened?" she croaked. Her throat was dry and rapidly she swallowed in an attempt to moisten it.

"Here," Jae picked up a beaker of water and pressed it against her lips. Slowly she opened her mouth and drank the cool liquid. Everything ached.

"What happened?" she asked again.

"You had an accident," Jae said carefully. "Do you remember anything?"

She closed her eyes. Several visions swam in front of her face and then finally she grasped onto one. Cal driving his car directly towards her.

"Yes," she said after a moment, "yes, I remember. Where is he?"

"In custody," Jae replied. "One of the neighbours witnessed it. The police picked him up on the coast road about half an hour later."

Lexi nodded. "Everything hurts," she said.

Again Jae tenderly caressed her forehead. "There's no major damage, thank God," he said, "but you'll be bruised for a while."

"How long have I been out of it?" Lexi asked. She had no concept of time.

"Two days give or take. You've been in and out, but they kept you sedated for a while – for the shock."

She nodded. Right now she felt numb. There was no shock.

A light knock on the door announced the arrival of a nurse.

"Hi," said the other woman brightly, "you're awake. How are you feeling?"

"Sore," Lexi responded. "Everywhere."

The nurse smiled. "You've been very lucky – although it probably doesn't feel that way now. Only bruises thankfully."

Lexi nodded.

"I'll just check everything." The nurse moved around the bed swiftly, reading monitors and jotting notes in her folder. "You're doing really well," she said once she'd finished. "Can I get you anything?"

Lexi shook her head. No. The only thing she needed was processing time. Cal had driven his car straight at her. That wasn't something you came to terms with easily. He could have seriously injured her – or worse.

"I'll leave you to it," she heard the nurse say, "just let me know if you need anything."

"Thanks," Jae responded. Lexi closed her eyes wishing she didn't remember what had happened. Wanting to be back in the blissful peace of darkness.

"Are you okay?" Jae asked.

Lexi didn't answer.

"It'll be alright," he said after a moment, "I'll take care of you. You can move in with me for a while – or not. Whatever works for you."

She didn't respond.

"Lexi? Open your eyes. Please. Say something."

Jae's tone was increasing in urgency, yet she had nothing to say. The numbness had abated and shock had shut her down. The man she'd once loved beyond all reason had put her in hospital – again. Only this time it wasn't an accident.

"Lexi?" she felt Jae take her hand and reluctantly she opened her eyes. She was awake. She'd survived. She had to face the world. Again.

"I'm okay," she said.

"It's a lot to take in, no one is expecting you to be fine, Lexi, you need to take your time."

She inclined her head as thoughts raced. "What exactly are my injuries?"

Jae frowned at her. "Are you sure you want to talk about that? Wouldn't you rather talk about something else?"

"Jae, I'm in the hospital because my husband ran over me. What else do you expect me to talk about?" Saying the words out loud sounded alien – like they'd come from another part of her. A part disconnected from her soul.

He nodded. "It's all bruising and some damage to your ribs. Nothing serious – no thanks to that bastard."

Lexi ignored Jae's reference to Cal. He was entitled to feel that way; she just wasn't ready to deal with that. "Only bruising?" she echoed.

Jae nodded. "Mostly on your legs and torso."

"Who found me?" she asked.

"The neighbour. The one who witnessed it all. They called the ambulance."

Lexi nodded. "And how come you're here?"

"You still had your work ID badge on. The hospital called to let me know there'd been an accident."

"Have you spoken to him?" she asked. "Cal?"

Jae shook his head. "No and it's a damn good job I haven't. He'd be in the next hospital bed if I had my way."

"He'd just found out about us," Lexi stated. The scene replayed in her mind as she spoke. Her voice was monotone, all of her emotions closed. She looked at the wall ahead. Would she heal this time? Emotionally?

"I know, the police told me. They questioned me."

She nodded. The wall had yet to provide her with any answers.

"They need to talk to you too," Jae said.

Lexi nodded again. "I don't want to press charges." Oddly, that was the only fact of which she was certain. He'd driven straight at her. It could've been worse. He'd intended to harm her yet – it was Cal. Her Cal. The man who'd supported her through everything. The man to whom she owed so much. The man she'd so thoroughly betrayed. Despite what he'd done she felt no bitterness and no need to attempt moral high ground. The only emotion she could accurately identify was one of overwhelming sadness for what they'd become and the part they'd both played in that.

"You don't – what? Lexi, look at me." She could hear the disbelief in his voice. Obligingly she turned her head away from the contemplation of the wall.

"I don't want to press charges," she said again, her voice firm.

"How can you possibly know?" Jae asked incredulously. "You've only just woken up. You have so many things to think about and that's not the kind of decision you should be making now."

"It wasn't intentional, Jae."

"Lexi, my God!" he moved away from the bed and threw his hands up in the air. "He drove straight at you!"

"I know. I remember. I was there." She wondered if she would ever feel true emotion again. Right now everything within her was colourless.

"Then how can you say it was an accident?" Jae returned to the bed although he didn't sit. His voice was a little calmer.

"He was provoked. He had his reasons. I'm as much to blame as he is."

"No way. No way am I letting him get away with this."

For the first time since she'd awoken, Lexi looked at Jae properly. He looked tired; his dark hair was messed up and his five o'clock shadow was easily a day old.

"How long have you been here?"

"Since you were brought in."

"You've been here two days?" she asked. Something inside of her stirred. Memories. Feelings. Thoughts of this man.

He nodded. "Of course," he said softly, "where else would I have been?"

She smiled a half smile. She was beginning to thaw. Her emotions were returning. "You didn't have to do that."

"I did," said Jae softly. Carefully he sat beside her, taking one of her hands in his. "There was no way I was leaving you."

"He found out about us, Jae," she said again, "and he got mad."

"I know, I know," he replied. Cautiously he lifted the hand he held to his lips and gently pressed a kiss into her palm.

"I was scared. I tried to get away. He came after me."

"Yes," Jae nodded solemnly, "I know."

"I can't match the Cal I met and married to the Cal that would do this," she said aloud.

"The police mentioned something about counselling and rehabilitation," he responded. "They thought he was reacting irrationally to feeling threatened." Lexi could tell it pained Jae to offer any kind of explanation for what Cal had done and she was grateful that he tried.

"Cal felt threatened?" she asked. It hadn't occurred to her Cal would feel threatened by what had happened. Distraught maybe, but not threatened.

"Yes, very much so. He knew he was losing you."

"But doing something like this – that's not going to get me back."

"Which," Jae said with a smile, "is the beauty of your naivety. When we feel threatened and we react, we don't always stop to think of the consequences, nor do we stop to think if our actions are right. Sometimes, our gut takes over." Again she appreciated his soothing voice as he offered a rationality she had no right to expect.

"You sound like you're speaking from experience," she observed.

He dipped his head. "I've felt threatened in my time."

"The scar?" she asked.

Immediately Jae's hand flew to his right cheek. "Yeah. Kind of," he said.

Lexi frowned at him.

"Another time." He removed his hand from his cheek. "Right now, we're focusing on you."

She watched him for a moment. "Secrets are fine," she responded slowly. "But not at the detriment of a relationship. I can't have another relationship based on lies and half-truths. We had so many skeletons between us, Cal and I," she observed, "we were always going to end this way. I can't do it again."

Jae squeezed her hand as he regarded her with those dark eyes. "I understand."

There was a knock on the door and they both turned as the

nurse from before entered the room. She was accompanied by two police officers.

"Is it okay if they ask you some questions now?" the nurse asked.

"Yes, it's fine," she replied. It wasn't. She still had so much to process, but she was going to have to start somewhere. And, talking to the police seemed as good a place as any.

* * *

The questions were endless and by the time they eventually left, Lexi was exhausted. The police still had Cal in custody, but they needed to know if she wanted to press charges. When she'd firmly declined they, along with Jae, had tried to persuade her otherwise.

"I am not pressing charges," she had reiterated for the umpteenth time. "I just want to get past this. Please. Let the matter drop."

The officers had been unimpressed as had Jae but, regardless of what he'd done, Lexi didn't want to see Cal with a criminal record. Or in jail. If she hadn't provoked him then none of this would've happened. Despite feeling weak, desolate and in constant pain she'd stuck to her guns. Finally the officers had left and given Lexi their complete assurance that all charges against Cal Strudwick would be dropped.

"You're crazy," Jae said as he watched the police leave, "you have to make him pay for this."

Lexi closed her eyes. "Please, Jae. I don't want to argue about this anymore. Cal will be paying for this, and that's the part you don't understand."

Jae frowned. "I don't see how, you got them to drop all the charges."

"Because legally, it won't mean a thing to him. Even if he was charged with a diamond heist and locked up forever, it wouldn't matter to Cal. What matters to Cal is people. Me."

"I'm not sure I follow."

"Before this happened," she explained patiently, "we were having problems and you and I – well, we knew there was something between us. Cal hates losing, and after losing Zach, he was doing it tough. Now he's lost me too and he's lost the life he once had. I know it might sound crazy to you but, for Cal, that will be a greater loss to him than any number of nights in a cell. If he's going to learn anything from what's happened, that's the only way it will stick. And," she took a breath as she picked at an invisible piece of cotton on the sheet, "he wasn't in this alone, Jae. We have to take responsibility for our part in what happened. I have to take responsibility for what I did to him."

"Okay, I get that to a point," Jae concurred, "but people get cheated on all the time. I'm not saying it's right," he held up his hand as Lexi went to argue, "and God knows I fought with myself over this, but it happens. If everyone carried on like Cal, imagine what kind of world we'd live in."

"Cal isn't like other people," she stated, "he's had a tough life and losing Zach – no one can understand how much that messed him up."

"Look," Jae said after a moment, "I don't agree with your decision but, if it makes you happy, I'm prepared to live with it. Don't, however, expect me to like it."

Lexi dipped her head in acceptance. "There's one more thing you need to understand though. Whatever happened between Cal and I and whatever happens from now on, Cal was and always will be the father of my child."

"Child?" Jae regarded her quizzically.

"Yes. I lost a baby," she said, "before Cal and I were married. That's a bond we'll always have."

"Shit, Lexi," Jae said, "I had no idea."

She felt him place a comforting hand on her shoulder and she reached up to grasp it with hers.

"No," she responded, "I know you didn't. But now you do."

Chapter Thirty-Eight

Cal

Tami sat alone in the foyer of the police station. At first, Cal didn't notice her.

"Cal."

Her voice reached him and slowly he turned. He felt grubby and unkempt. Two days locked in a police cell had taken its toll.

"Hey," he walked slowly up to her, "what are you doing here?"

Tami shrugged. "I figured you could use a friend."

"I could," he said, "but I don't deserve one."

"Well, I'm here so you'll just have to deal with it," she replied. "Are you good to go?"

Cal nodded. "I think so."

"Mr Strudwick?" One of the desk constables materialised at his side. "Your personal belongings."

"Thanks." Cal took the standard issue plastic bag from the officer. "My car?" he asked.

"Impounded, sir. There's a leaflet in your bag. There'll be a release fee."

Of course there would. "Thank you," he said again. With a nod the officer departed.

"Good job I came in my car," Tami said and Cal managed a weak smile.

"You didn't have to do this."

"I know." She linked her arm through his. "Come on, let's get you home."

They walked in silence to her car and when they reached it, again, Cal noted the number plate. He felt the pull of recognition he'd experienced before but he was too emotionally gone to work it out. Tami unlocked the door and he climbed into the passenger side. In silence she started the engine and coaxed the car out of its parking space.

"You do know what I did?" Cal asked.

Tami nodded. "I heard."

"So why are you here?"

She shrugged. "We all have crap to deal with and I know it wasn't one sided. Plus, I feel responsible. If I hadn't told you about Lexi, none of this would've happened."

"I ran her over," he said, scarcely able to believe he'd actually done that. His memory of the incident was blurred, but he still knew what he'd done.

"You did," Tami confirmed. "You lost control and no, that's not something to be proud of but, in a way, I kind of understand."

"You do?"

"Let's just say I get where you were coming from."

Cal frowned.

"Have you heard how she's doing?" he asked after a moment. "Lexi?"

"Good, I think. Bruising only. I spoke to Jae and he said she was coming home."

"Bastard," Cal commented under his breath.

Tami smiled. "I agree, but he's still my boss. And yours."

"Shit," Cal said. "I can't imagine he wants me to work for him any more than I do. He could sack me. Gross misconduct or something. Shit."

Tami concentrated on the road. "You could always take some time out," she said. "Give yourself a break and," she paused, "I think you should talk to someone."

"I'm talking to you," he pointed out.

"No," she turned to face him as they halted at a junction, "not like this. Properly. Someone professional."

"A shrink?" his voice rose. "You think I need a shrink?"

The traffic lights changed and she shifted the car into gear. "To be honest, Cal, yes. I know I said I understood and to a point, I do, but it's not normal to react in the way you did. No one tries to deliberately kill their wife."

"I didn't try to kill her," Cal said mortified, "I don't know what I was thinking. I just wanted to frighten her I guess."

"It doesn't matter what your motives were," she responded, "at the end of the day you ran her down and you didn't even stop to see if she was okay."

Cal felt sick. The memories might be blurred but the feelings were not. He knew what he'd done and the guilt, shame and remorse he felt were almost too much to bear. Whilst in custody he'd seriously considered following Zach and, if it hadn't been for the police removing anything with which he could harm himself, then he very well might have done.

"The police must have mentioned this to you – counselling?"

"Yeah, I guess."

"You were damn lucky Lexi didn't want to press charges, Cal – you know that?"

He nodded miserably. "Yeah, but then I actually think I deserve to be locked up. Like you said, what I did wasn't normal."

Beside him Tami shook her head. "No, it wasn't, but it was your reaction and I for one know there's so much more to you than that. I also know you were provoked and there are deeper reasons for your reaction."

"How can you possibly know that?" he asked. "Even I don't know why I did it. How can you, who barely knows me, possibly say there are deeper reasons? You can't make it right, Tami. No matter what you say."

"I'm not trying to," she replied, "if you'd run me down I'd be charging you to hell and back. All I'm saying is I think something triggered it. Something deeper."

Cal snorted. "Nah. I got angry and lashed out. There's nothing more to it than that. I was pissed at Lexi and I was pissed at life. It's that simple."

They reached another set of traffic lights and again, Tami turned to face him. "The way I see it," she said, "is you've been given another chance here. She's let you off the hook. I know you're hurting and you hate her and Jae right now and that's understandable, but somehow you're going to have to deal with that. She's not coming back, Cal."

He swallowed as the ever-present bile rose up in his throat. He knew that, of course he did. Even if he hadn't lost her before, then he'd sure as hell lost her now. Hearing someone say it though, hearing it vocalised, it was fucking tough to take. He remained silent as he heard Tami sigh.

"Just think about it," she said after a while, "I know a guy. Matt. He's the best. He owes me."

Cal shrugged. His mind was filled with memories of Lexi, of the good times, of her laugh, her beautiful face, the moments they'd lain in bed together after making love. To know he would never see Lexi in that way again was tearing him apart. He was a broken man.

"I'm broken," he said aloud, "can he fix that?"

His question was ironic. Even if this Matt could make him forget Lexi, never would Cal be able to leave the weight of guilt behind for what he'd done.

"He's good," Tami said as she pulled up outside his house, "just think about it."

Cal nodded. Maybe. Maybe talking to someone would help because the way he saw it he had two choices. One, to fight this and make himself a better man or two, follow Zach. It was a tough choice, but he remembered how betrayed he'd felt after Zach. How he'd wished his friend had given him the chance to help. He would be a hypocrite to even contemplate the second option. He had to try to fix himself – that was the only thing he could do.

"Give him a call," he said as he placed his hand on the door and prepared to get out.

"Great," Tami said. "I'll come in with you, make sure you're alright." She gestured towards his house.

"Where's Lexi?" he asked.

"She's left, Cal. I don't know where she is, but Jae told me her stuff had been cleared. She's not here."

Cal nodded – once more he felt numb. He was returning to their marital home alone. The beautiful house they'd chosen together after moving from his flat. Now he was here alone. Alone and broken.

Accompanied by Tami he reached the front door. The place in which Lexi had been standing the last time he'd returned. The memories were too much, they overcame him and it was only with the support of the other woman that he gained the courage to cross the threshold. He couldn't stay here, not now. It wasn't his home anymore. It would never be his home again.

With his mind in turmoil and the guilt weighing heavy he slowly climbed the stairs to the bedroom. He needed to rest. He was beyond exhausted and he knew today was only the start. He had a long and tough road ahead of him. And, as he fell into a fitful slumber, it didn't even occur to him to ask Tami how she'd known where he lived.

Chapter Thirty-Nine

Cal

June 2015

"Are you okay?" the therapist asked and Cal shook his head. He was drained. Physically exhausted and emotionally empty.

"Take your time," Matt advised.

Cal closed his eyes and allowed the blissful blackness in. "That was the hardest thing I've ever had to do," he said quietly. He kept his eyes closed. He couldn't bear to see the judgement and censure on Matt's face.

"I know," Matt responded.

"It was like it all happened yesterday," Cal said. With his hands he rubbed at his eyes and then slowly, slowly opened them. He was staring at the carpet. The same patch he stared at during every session.

"Look at me," Matt said softly.

Cal shook his head.

"I can't," he responded. "What kind of monster does something like that? To their wife?" It made no more sense to him now than it had done in the aftermath of the accident.

"You lost control, Cal," Matt said. "Your anger got the better of you. It wasn't you out there, you were sick. You have to remember that."

"I can't. I mean, I thought I was angry at them for what they'd done to me and I figured you'd help me deal with that, but I finally realised it's not them I'm angry at. Not really. It's me I'm angry at. For how I reacted. For what I put Lexi through. It's all on me."

"I understand," the therapist said, "and I know you feel that way. It's normal and it's okay to feel like that. The guilt is going to weigh you down and you're going to get angry. The important thing is you've taken the first step now. By coming to see me and getting everything out there, you've taken the first step and believe me, Cal, that's a lot more than most people can do. You've been incredibly brave. Don't forget that."

Cal shrugged. "Brave? Don't make me laugh."

"Look," Matt said after a moment, "at some point you're going to have to let the past go because that's the only way you can move on. I'm not saying you should forget about it, but you need to get to a position where you can live with what you did, with what happened."

"Yeah?" Cal asked, "and how the hell am I supposed to do that?"

"With time and with support. I'll give you that support. Together we'll get you through this."

"How can you not hate me?" he asked.

Matt shook his head. "It doesn't work like that," he responded. "I've told you that before. I think Tami's right. I think you weren't in control that day and the reasons go much deeper than what Lexi did to you."

"It doesn't take a genius to work that out," he said.

Matt smiled. "No, but it takes someone with another perspective to help you see that and to help you through it. Someone who isn't connected to you or to Lexi."

"And that's you?" Cal asked.

Matt nodded. "That's me."

"You really think you can fix me?" he asked.

The therapist inclined his head. "I do."

"Honestly?"

Matt smiled. "Yes."

"Okay," Cal said after a moment. Slowly he sat back in the seat and dashed at his eyes. His breathing had almost returned to normal and now the worst was out there he had to admit it did feel as if a weight had been lifted. He was a long way to being fixed, but he understood now what Matt had said. Today he'd taken the first step.

"Let's do this then," he said and watched as Matt jotted something on his notepad.

"Let's do this," Matt concurred. "And remember," he said, "whatever happens, Cal, I've got you."

Epilogue

Lexi

Six months later ~ December 2015

She stretched luxuriously in the bed, smiling as she felt Jae's solid, naked form beside her.

"Mmmm," he said, his voice heavy with sleep, "this has got to be the best way to wake up."

She felt his warm hand slide around her middle and his flattened palm gently caressed her stomach.

"You can't possibly have the energy," she whispered as she shifted onto her side to look at him. His dark eyes opened and instantly they connected with hers.

"I could stay in this bed with you forever," he said, "and even though I'm a little older than you..."

Lexi laughed. "*Ten* years older than me."

"Semantics." Jae brushed a tendril of hair from her eyes. "I would never want for energy, that I can promise."

She squealed as he grabbed her waist with both hands and began to tickle her.

"Stop," she said, "I have to get up. I have that meeting, remember?"

"How could I forget?" he said, his deep voice resonating around the quiet room. "You've talked of little else for days."

Playfully she slapped him across the chest. "You know how important this is to me."

"I know," he leaned forwards and snagged her lips in a brief kiss, "I'm teasing you. Now, get out of bed before I'm forced to make you late."

She smiled and wriggled her naked form out from underneath the duvet. "I hope they give me the sponsorship," she said as she walked away from the bed towards the bathroom.

"No reason why they won't," Jae responded. He'd propped himself up on the pillows and was watching her.

"I'm just going to shower," she said.

A few minutes later she exited the bathroom to find Jae still sitting in exactly the same place.

"Don't you have somewhere to be?" she asked.

"Nope," he said with a smile.

Lexi picked up a cushion and threw it at him as she walked towards the wardrobe. Some of her work clothing was here and it was from these she selected a plain, black trouser suit.

"Remind me why you won't move in with me again," he said.

Lexi sighed as she began to dress. "Jae, we've been over and over this. I'm happy at Mel's."

"I'm not," he said stubbornly, "besides you spend most of your time here anyway, it seems pointless not to just move in."

"I want to wait," she responded, "you know that."

"But your divorce is due any day now."

"Yes."

"Well, then, what does a few days matter?"

"It matters to me," she said.

"You know Zach's project finally got finished?" Jae said after a moment.

"Really?" she asked.

"Yeah. That guy Mace did most of the work, but I think Cal came back on board at the end."

"Have you seen him?" she asked. Automatically her heart began to pound a little faster. She picked up her brush and walked to the mirror, trying to ignore the familiar tremors at the mention of Cal's name.

"No. There's no need. The land belongs to Zach's legacy now, I only heard it'd been finished by chance."

Lexi nodded. "That's good," she said as she ran the brush through her long, blonde locks. "I'm happy he could still give Zach his legacy."

"So, why won't you move in again?"

She sighed and turned around to face him. "We're not having this conversation."

"But Mel's place is small and cramped," he argued. Again, Lexi had heard it before.

"It works for me," she replied, "now drop it, okay?"

"Okay," he said as he inclined his head, "but you need to know I'm not giving up."

Lexi smiled at him. That was part of the reason why she loved him. "I know," she said as she walked across to the bed and dropped a kiss on his lips.

"Now, how do I look?" She did a twirl and Jae let out a low whistle. "You'll knock 'em dead."

"I hope not," she responded as she gave her slim black trouser suit another once over in the mirror, "I need their money."

"You," Jae said to her reflection, "are one of the most frustrating people I know. I've told you so many times I'll invest and give you the money you need."

"I know you have," she said, "but I don't want you to. I have to do this for myself. Surely you of all people must understand that."

"I do, but I just don't want you to get disappointed."

Lexi shrugged. "If I do, I do. It's all part of learning. If they don't invest then I'll keep trying until I find a sponsor that will."

Jae shook his head. "I hope your parents understand how much you're putting into this."

"They do," she replied as she slicked a final coat of lipstick across her lips. "I spoke to them yesterday and they said if I can secure a sponsor, they'll get more actively involved which would be amazing. I can only help to raise children's awareness of road safety so much – their parents really are the key and, if my parents come on board and lend their voice, then I'm sure other parents will more readily relate. If we do this as a family, then Bobby's Charity is going to succeed. I know it is."

"I love that you're so passionate," Jae said, "and I love that you're making this about your family."

"It just feels right," she said as she turned away from the mirror to face him. "If what happened with Cal taught me anything, it was the value of life. What he chose to do with Zach's land was something

453

really beautiful and it made me realise Bobby could live on too. If we can reach even a handful of children and prevent even one road death, then we've won."

Jae nodded. "You're an amazing woman," he said.

"No, I'm not. I'm just finally figuring out what I'm supposed to do with my life."

"Fraser misses you," he commented and Lexi smiled.

"He knows where I am," she said as she paced once more back to the bed and sat down beside Jae, "no reason why he can't take me out for lunch." She winked at Jae knowing full well he'd have an issue with her spending leisure time with Fraser.

Jae growled and she laughed. "Easy, tiger."

"Yeah, well. We both know he has the hots for you."

"That was a long time ago. I'm sure he's moved on by now."

"I'm not," Jae commented dryly.

"Don't be daft." She reached her left hand up to caress his cheek. "Even if he still has the hots for me which I highly doubt, it doesn't matter. I have you and that's all I'll ever want."

Jae enfolded her in his arms and she immediately felt the connection as every nerve began to tingle. It was always this way with them, had been since their very first time.

"I've been thinking…" His breath tickled her ear, "you talking about your parents and this project, it's made me think about doing something I've been wanting to revisit for a while."

"What's that?" she asked as she pulled away a little.

"I want to try to find my parents again," he said.

Lexi looked at him in surprise.

"You want to dredge the ocean?"

"No. No, I don't want to dredge the ocean."

"Then what?" Lexi asked. "You said their plane went down in the sea. Where else would you look for your parents?"

"I don't know," he said and frowned.

"I'm confused," she responded.

"I know. It sounds strange to me too, but the thing is, Lexi, there was something odd about what happened."

"In what way?"

"The fact nothing was ever recovered to begin with, not even the plane."

"That's not unheard of though, right? Plenty of planes have crashed and never been found."

"I know," he agreed "and that's what I told myself. The authorities did everything they could and so I had to accept it was lost."

She tilted her head at him and frowned. "But you're not convinced?"

"I don't know." He shook his head. "I can't put my finger on it, but the more I think about it now, the more I think there are things that don't add up. Their flight plan, for example, was never filed."

"And it should have been?" Lexi asked. She knew next to nothing about aviation.

"Yes. The investigators at the time figured it'd been misplaced or filed wrong and I was too overcome with grief to give it any further thought."

"But you've been thinking about it now?"

"Yes," he replied. "Ever since I met you and I saw you with your family, it made me realise I never had closure. Not proper closure. There are too many things that don't make sense and I want to find out for sure. I feel like I owe it to them."

She nodded. "I can understand that. So, what are you planning to do?"

"I'm going to open a private investigation," he said.

"You can do that?" she asked, "even after all this time?"

"I'm not sure, but I don't see why not. I want answers to my questions, Lexi."

"I hear you," she said.

Jae released her from his grasp and ran his hands through his midnight black hair. "I need to know what happened that day, what really happened."

She nodded.

"Because something's not right. I don't think," he said and then paused, "I don't think it was an accident. Not anymore. I think someone deliberately sabotaged that plane."

Lexi looked at him in shock.

"I don't think it was an accident," he repeated as he pointed to the photograph of his parents that he kept beside the bed. "I just feel in my gut there's something I don't know and I intend to do whatever's necessary to find out if their plane was sabotaged. If it was then someone killed my parents...and I need to know why."

* * *

The manila envelope hit the mat with a resounding thud. Cal exited the kitchen and walked to the door, bending to retrieve the large brown object. It was what he'd expected it to be. He threw it on the kitchen counter unopened.

"I so need coffee," Tami said as she walked into the kitchen and stretched.

Obligingly Cal handed her the cup he'd just brewed.

"Thanks," she said. "Damn, that was some night."

Cal nodded. Yeah. It'd been a night of bedroom gymnastics but, unlike Tami, he was not overwhelmed by it.

"What's that?" she asked as she spotted the envelope on the side.

"Divorce papers," Cal said.

"And you've not opened it?" she asked incredulously as she pounced on the large wad of papers.

"No," he said, "and you're not going to open it either."

She pouted at him. "I thought you and Matt were making progress."

"We are, but that doesn't mean I'm ready to see the end of my marriage written in black and white."

Tami sighed. "When are you going to let her go, Cal? You know she's moved on."

He nodded. His sessions with Matt had made him slightly less bitter towards Jae, but only slightly.

"You have to face reality," Tami tried again.

"I do," he said as he sipped from his own mug, "I face it every day."

"That's not what I meant," she said, "so quit being smart."

"Look, I turn up to work every day. I fill in all the damned paperwork I'm supposed to, I give Lexi the money for the house she

456

demands and I see Matt regularly. That, Tami, is my reality."

"What about me?" she asked.

Cal was under no illusions. He knew Tami was into their relationship way more than he was.

"And you," he said with a smile, "keep my bed warm at night."

"That's more like it," she said, "in fact, there's no reason it has to only be at night…"

Cal glanced at his watch. It was eleven am.

"It's Saturday," Tami commented as she noted his action, "we don't have anywhere to be."

He sighed. "You do understand this is nothing serious for me?"

She nodded. "Yeah. You've done nothing but tell me that since day one."

"Then why the hell are you still here?" he asked. "It's been six months. You know I'm never going to commit to you. You could find yourself someone in a much better place than me. You sure as hell deserve it."

Tami closed the distance between them and gently placed her hand on his right cheek. "I happen to be a fan of lost causes," she said softly, "and right now, I don't have any place else to be."

Cal shook his head as he reached up and clasped her hand with his own. "I don't understand you," he said. "You've stuck by me through all of this and you know I can't offer you anything, yet you're still here."

"Like I said," her brown eyes met his, "I don't have any place else to be."

Slowly he leaned forwards and dropped a kiss on her luscious lips. She tasted of coffee and he allowed himself to linger, enjoying the flavour.

Her hand travelled downwards across his taut belly and Cal sucked in a breath. He would have to be a robot not to be attracted to Tami and even if his mind wasn't always in the right place, his predictable body never let him down.

Reaching inside his boxers her hand accessed his flaccid member and slowly coaxed it to life. Cal dropped his head back on his neck and leaned against the counter as he allowed her to explore, allowed her head to graze his abdomen and her mouth to wander lower.

The manila envelope caught his eye again and he tried to close his mind to what he knew was inside. He understood he was never going to get Lexi back and he was well aware this was his life now. The thought of seeing it in black and white though – he wasn't sure he was ready for that.

Down below Tami continued to caress him and, in an effort to reach a place without feeling, he let himself be drawn in. She was an expert, she manipulated him selflessly without thought for her own satisfaction and it wasn't long before Cal felt his restraints falling away. With a groan he grabbed her by the shoulders and pulled her up to her full height. Rapidly he switched positions so that she was the one leaning against the counter and, with one swift push, he impaled her, his body responding at her answering groan.

He sank deep inside of her, letting her give him the release he needed. In many ways he hated himself for the way he was using Tami, but then she knew the score. He'd reminded her only a few moments ago that there was nothing for her here, but for some reason he couldn't comprehend, she kept coming back. No matter how many times he told her not to.

She'd loosened her robe at some point and as Cal propelled himself upwards he watched her glorious breasts bouncing around. She had a stunning body, not on a par with Lexi but stunning nonetheless and she wasn't ashamed to use it. With Lexi's naivety had come awkwardness and at times he'd wanted to push her harder in the bedroom than he knew she would go. Tami was the opposite. Tami let him do whatever he wanted to do and, selfishly, he took.

He'd spoken to Matt about Tami, about how he felt he was using her. It concerned Cal that she let him treat her that way. He never physically hurt her, it was nothing like that, but he knew how unrequited affection felt. He was still in love with Lexi and that hurt like hell.

Matt had reassured him. They were both consenting adults and, as long as Cal was upfront with Tami about what the deal was, there was nothing wrong with the way their relationship worked. Cal wasn't entirely convinced, but when she let him fuck her the way he currently was, he lost all interest in arguing about it.

He sank ever deeper inside her, acknowledging that soon he would reach that place he wished he could remain. A place with no thought or feeling. A place of true beauty.

Their bodies were damp and they slid together easily. Cal pumped harder and Tami cried out. It was always this way with them. Never tender. Just hot and hard. An itch scratched. A need taken care of. For him it was as simple as that.

He watched her for a moment. Her eyes were closed, her mouth slightly open and a wave of guilt washed over him that he couldn't give her what she wanted. He wished he could allow her his emotional self, but he couldn't and, as he sank inside Tami and surrendered to the inevitable sensations, he finally acknowledged two things.

One: the woman he was screwing was never going to match up to the woman he still loved and two: despite everything that had happened and all of the time he'd spent with Matt he was effectively right back where he'd started.

Screwing up his life.

THE END